# SKINNY DIPPING IN A DIRTY POND

## A NOVEL (MOSTLY)

## LIS ANNA-LANGSTON

Skinny Dipping in a Dirty Pond
Lis Anna-Langston
www.lisannalangston.com
@2022 Lis Anna-Langston – All Rights Reserved
Cover Design Pixel Studios
Cover Art Anthony Morais

Mapleton Press
First Edition
South Carolina
ISBN: 978-1-957730-00-4
Printed in the United States of America
Library of Congress Catalog Number: 2022903069

# Other Titles

**By Lis Anna-Langston**

Gobbledy
Maya Loop
Tupelo Honey
Tolstoy & the Checkout Girl

# Praise for Other Titles

"Hugely entertaining as well as emotionally moving." *—Kirkus Reviews*

"A delightfully entertaining novel by an author with a genuine flair for originality and the kind of narrative storytelling style that will fully engage the imaginative attention of appreciative young readers ages 8-11, *Gobbledy* by Lis Anna-Langston . . . will prove to be an immediate and enduringly popular addition to elementary school, middle school, and community library collections." *—Midwest Book Review*

"*The Wonder Years* meets *A Christmas Story* meets *E.T.* in this magical novel with dialogue that snaps, crackles, and pops, and a narrative that skips, jumps, and hops from one delightful surprise after the other. —Cathy Smith Bowers, former Poet Laureate of North Carolina, and South Carolina Authors' Hall of Fame Inductee

A loveable, engaging, original voice, Tupelo brightens this accomplished tale of dysfunction in a family where "nothing had ever been right.". —Publishers Weekly

From the delicious title (the spunky 11-year-old narrator was named after Elvis' birthplace) to every last unconventional character and careful detail, Tupelo Honey is a delight. Set in rural Mississippi, with a cast of colorful southerners, it stars one pretty dysfunctional family at the center of which is Tupelo Honey. Author Lis Anna-Langston gets into the head of her title girl completely, taking readers on a ride of a sort of haunted but beautiful mess.

It's certainly not a dull life, one full of heartbreaks big and small, but this tough sweet girl pulls it off with aplomb. It's a treat from start to end. Langston has written rich, vivid characters, and painted a vibrant mosaic of a year in one young southern girl's life. It's a hard book to put down, and one you won't want to end. I envy its future readers.
—Teresa DiFalco @2016 Parents' Choice

*Maya Loop* is Alice in Wonderland meets the Wizard of Oz, with the sweet tinge of Fortnite and Percy Jackson thrown in. I loved every page.
– Linda Sands, Award winning *Georgia Author of the Year*

"Be careful what you set your heart upon – for it will surely be yours."

James Baldwin

"Fortune is for the brave."

Pliny the Elder

*for Larry*

# PROLOGUE

*Bringing You Up to Speed*

When my uncle Thurman started boiling frogs alive in big soup pots on the kitchen stove everyone turned a blind eye. When he pulled the tail off a rabbit while it was alive, he retold the story as something funny. It *wasn't*. The problems didn't stop there. Something in my family's blood told them they were bad. Misfits woven together with a sanity of the sheerest design. As I grew older, I began to realize by natural deduction that something was wrong or that nothing had ever been right.

In my family, as far back as I can tell, there was no such thing as communication, only secrets. Big, nasty secrets that hid in the closet with the bogeyman and a layer of dust. All of the real players in the drama are dead now, or at least the ones who could tell us what everyone was trying so hard to get away from. Even so, in moments of contemplation I realize sometimes people are crushed to dust under the burden of their lives and my family was no exception.

There would be no warm, fuzzy evenings around a dinner table for me because by the time I entered this world Grand Daddy was dying. Death waited patiently for him on the second floor of our big, turn-of-the-century house. A hospital bed and morphine drip were installed so he could pass his final days in the comfort of a room wallpapered with hundreds of blue ships sailing to god knows where. He died with his clothes still in plastic, tucked in drawers.

This elusive grandfather figure fascinated me, as did the fact that we lived side by side a dead man, as if he were coming home any minute to hang up his coat and rest after a long journey into death.

Later, I said living that close to death was too much for a family like mine. It was the crack in the teapot, the leak in the dam, and finally the straw that broke the camel's back. The cancer that killed him ate away at something inside of my family until it mutated and grew into a victim, a paranoid schizophrenic, and a psychotic. A man I never knew was the thread that wove those misfits together, and when he was gone, those seams finally ripped under pressure.

But not right away. Before Grand Daddy drove that Buick up to the Pearly Gates my mom was busy trying to find herself by running off to Burning Man to be free and smoke dope.

The only thing she found was her way back home, to a chorus of "I told you so," dragging her teenage boyfriend from Georgia as if she'd hooked him on a weekend fishing trip. They were white middle-class kids who thought their revolution was unique.

"Revolution, my ass," my grandmother said. "They don't want to start a revolution. They just want to be able to smoke dope out on the front porch without anyone telling them not to."

As I was becoming a glimmer in someone's eyes my parents ran wild. Or at least they imagined themselves running wild. They were the product of a semi-revolution. Two high school dropouts hell-bent on freedom, chained to the mother of conformity, toting that hippie bible that reads just like anything else—*we like you if you're just like us.*

No one talks about my conception. My great point of origin. Were there showers of kisses, or *random-high-only-semi-good sex* that you can't remember clearly later? Were there grunts or pants or sighs? Was anyone performing that night who hadn't been chemically altered besides me? Perhaps no one knows, and if by some stroke of luck they do remember, I assure you, no one told the truth. My mother made a hobby out of feigning ignorance when asked to discuss pertinent issues. I have never met my father.

So, from thus I was conceived. Seven pounds, three ounces, on a hot summer night. I wasn't really social in those days, even though it was the beginning of disco and all. Not many expectations were placed on me just yet. My mother moved us out of the house and in with her new junkie/hippie boyfriend, who said the nicest things when he wasn't high. Then we moved again and then, again. Grand Daddy's illness surfaced. It killed him quick and from what I can tell, things began to change.

The family history hit an all-time high of hush-hush. In that room dying of lung cancer, wasting away, he begged for morphine. He said his mother came to see him every night, the same mother dead for years. He talked about how she brought him angel's wings and tiny drops she put on his tongue, making his words spin. With a smile, he recalled how she spoon-fed him hot broth while they talked about his childhood. He forgot the extreme poverty that sucked up his early years. Blood came up every time he coughed, choking him, and he didn't mention that ramshackle of a house where he grew up. His fingers were bones. He talked openly to the angel of mercy standing in the doorway.

He hallucinated, saw his death, called out, failing, fading, fighting, and ultimately losing, because I don't think he ever really thought he was going to win. He died in the middle of the night without a word to anyone.

A few years later I learned how to talk and thus deduce certain things from my environment. The first clue something was wrong with my family was that Preston Brown wasn't allowed to play at my grandmother's house when I stayed over on weekends. The second was that in my own home my mother and her new boyfriend Dave, decided that financially it would be better if they were dealing drugs.

Around that time my crazy uncle Thurman left my grandmother's house one night and reappeared the next morning, wet, with human scratch marks all over his face and arms. Caked with dried blood, and torn clothes, claiming to remember nothing from the night before except that he'd heard voices. He plodded upstairs and slept for twenty hours. When news of a murder unfolded on the radio, my family met it with the same tight-lipped resistance they greeted everything else. I was too young to understand the consequences of murder, but I wondered who those voices were, and why they always told him to kill people.

I couldn't recall a single moment when I felt affection for Uncle Thurman. I never curled up in his lap and felt safe or reached up to hold his hand before crossing the street. I learned you don't cross the street with psychotics— you cross the street to get away from them.

Psycho Uncle hung out with a bunch of dudes who thought he was a big fat ass from what I could tell, but they were nice to him for the same reason everyone was nice to him, which was that you didn't have to spend more than five seconds with him to figure out he was a few marbles short of a game. And he had weed. When you're certifiably crazy, you have to possess something that lures people in, and for Uncle Thurman weed was his saving grace.

My Uncle Stan lived downstairs and wasn't so bad. He didn't like Thurman. Stan was a good paranoid schizophrenic. He refused to take baths because he said it made his skin rot off. If someone finally laid down the law, he would plop down in the big claw-footed tub, and sit perfectly still, staring straight ahead until my grandmother sent me to tell him to get out. He lumbered out like a big old bear muttering about how baths put him in a neurotic delirium.

I loved Stan the way other little kids loved cartoon characters. Even at the age of six, I knew you weren't supposed to admit to liking Spam. Not Stan. He thudded into the kitchen wearing big boxer shorts from the Dollar General Store and ate an entire can, sitting alone at the kitchen table, lost in his own mind instead of the morning paper. He drank soda pop like someone said there was going to be a shortage. He consumed about a bazillion cans of Campbell's soup, and when we later tried to change brands on him, he politely told us that the other manufacturers put poison in their soup, and while we may be fooled, he wasn't. If you pushed the issue with him, he would also, very politely but with a tone that suggested he meant it, tell you to go to hell.

But Stan was different from the rest, and if I laughed long enough and hard enough then eventually, he'd laugh with me. Aside from the fact that occasionally he'd slice his arm open with a kitchen knife, or that he thought the people who lived next door were shooting his brain with an x-ray gun that made him hear voices, or that periodically he'd refuse to pee in the toilet for reasons that escape me now, he lived in his own world and what a world it was. Every once in a while, I'd burst in on him and catch him dry humping a pillow with all of his clothes on. He didn't care. Why would he? Everyone had the same urges, did some of the same things, but they cloaked theirs in secrecy and claimed superiority. Not Stan. As far as I knew, he was the only 40-year-old virgin high on Thorazine in the whole neighborhood. And he was great. He liked to go to the zoo and eat candy bars and fried chicken and take rides in the car every Sunday.

Aside from the fact that he was a little weird, Stan proved to be about as harmless as Bambi. The rest of my family should have been so lucky.

But I'm getting ahead of myself . . .

# CHAPTER ONE

## *The Meeting*

The summer I turned three my mother called me out to the driveway.

"Cotton, come out here. There's someone I want you to meet."

It was dark outside, but I could see a tall, handsome man who looked like he'd stepped out of the magazines I shredded to make collages. I suddenly became conscious of my scraped knees with big ugly scabs and tugged at the hem of my dress.

The handsome stranger knelt in front of me, extending his hand. "Hi. My name is Dave. What's your name?"

A lamp post blasted light against the back of his head. Shadows were everywhere. I felt my mother's eyes on the back of my neck, making my hairs tingle.

I blurted out, "My birthday is coming up."

The handsome stranger shifted, smiling. "How old are you?"

I held up my entire hand, fingers spread, then pulled my pinky finger and thumb back to touch. "Almost three."

Shadows slanted down his cheeks. "What day is your birthday?"

"Twelfth."

"Mine's coming up in June," he said, excited.

For some reason this made me like him tremendously. "What kind of cake do you like?"

"Boston cream pie with all of that creamy custard in the middle."

"Me too," I said. "My grandmother buys Boston cream cakes for me and my Uncle Stan because he doesn't have any teeth."

"Cotton." My mother cleared her throat behind me.

I turned, "What?"

"Maybe we don't need to talk about Stan right now."

The handsome stranger butted in, "What do you say we go and get something to eat?"

Early summer was still a little chilly. Suddenly I wanted my poncho. I turned, running up the knobby gravel, trying to stay upright.

Behind me I heard the stranger say, "You never told me your name."

Without looking back, I yelled, "Cotton Ann. I was named after toliet paper."

Then I ate dirt. Gravel, to be precise. The heels of my palms felt the deep gauge of sharp rocks, and my knees thundered in pain. My cheeks flushed hot. I stood up to keep running, blood trickling down my shins. I burst through the front door, horrified I had fallen and even more horrified over how I might look.

Once in the bathroom, I slammed and locked the door, looking over at the full-length mirror glued to the wall. *Oh my gosh.* Blood dripped down into my socks. Criminy. How embarrassing. Not only had someone just taken an interest in me but now, in a matter of less than a minute, I had fallen flat on my face and was bleeding to death all over my clothes. I searched frantically for a solution. Quickly I grabbed a wad of toilet paper and wet it under the bathtub faucet. I cleaned all of the blood off of my shins, and then I saw the answer. My black corduroy bell-bottoms lying dirty on the floor.

"Cotton!" my mother screamed from the other room. "What are you doing in there?"

"I'm coming," I yelled, frantically kicking off my shoes. I jerked the cords up, ramming my feet into the shoes, kicking my dress behind the toilet. I ran out front as fast as I could.

My mother stood next to the car with her hand on her hip. "What took you so long?"

I climbed into the backseat. "I had to wash my hands."

The Mexican restaurant had big velvet hats with sparkly sequins. I pointed and gushed, "Wow, that hat is bigger than me."

"It's a sombrero." Dave reached for my hand as a lady in a ruffled skirt led us to a table.

The blankets hanging on the walls were rough and scratchy. The menu had about a bajillion items on it.

"I've never been to a Mexican restaurant," I announced proudly.

"I recommend the enchilada plate." Dave closed his menu.

A man wearing cowboy boots brought chips and dip to our table. That's when Diggy showed up.

"Where have you been?" I whispered.

He cocked an ear to the side.

"Who are you talking to?" Dave asked.

"My friend Diggy," I said.

My mother rolled her eyes. "It's her imaginary friend. He's not real. She just talks to him."

"He is real." I cut my eyes at her.

Off behind a row of potted plants static crackled. Mexican music started to play. The man in boots passed by our table. My mother held up her hand and ordered a beer. I could feel blood drying on the knees of my pants. I didn't care if my mother thought Diggy was real or not. I was going to eat an enchilada.

*Whatever that was.*

Diggy was pretty jazzed about free corn chips and wagged his tail.

That night I was so excited I couldn't sleep. When I opened the door to go to the bathroom, I saw the living room light on. I walked to the doorway. My mother was on the sofa with a spoon and a lighter on the table. She had a needle in her hand.

"What are you doing?" I whispered.

She almost jumped out of her skin. "What are you doing out of bed?"

"I couldn't sleep. What are you doing?"

"I'm giving myself a shot."

"Oh." I shifted my weight to my other leg. "Why would you want a shot?" I asked, unable to believe that anyone actually wanted a shot.

Her hands trembled. "It's vitamins—you know. A vitamin shot."

"Then why don't you just swallow them?"

"Because then... I'd have to..." her words drifted off into the silent space between us. "Because then I'd have to take a lot of them. What are you doing up?"

"I had to pee. And I'm thirsty."

She reached for the syringe again. "Well go back to bed."

I hung around, watching. "Can I go to my grandmother's house tomorrow?"

"Yeah, call your uncle and get him to pick you up."

I ran off to the kitchen to get a glass of juice.

My mother watched me like a hawk. "Go to bed," she instructed.

"Alright. Hey, I had fun tonight."

She nodded but told me to go away.

The next morning, I sprang out of bed to call Stan. The phone rang twenty times before anyone picked up.

Finally, I heard my grandmother say, "Hello. Who's there?"

"It's me. Can you and Stan pick me up?"

She was quiet for just a minute. Then she said, "Hold on. Let me see if he's awake."

I packed up my hatbox and went out front to wait. My mother was asleep on the floor. Syringe, spoon, and cotton ball scattered on the coffee table. I covered her up with a blanket and walked out to the front porch.

It was Saturday morning. The public library opened in one hour.

# CHAPTER TWO

### *The Library*

My grandmother took about a million years to get out of the car. "Okay," she leaned back inside, "I'll call when we're ready to leave."

I bounced at the curb with ants in my pants. From where I was standing, I could see the security guard unlocking the front door. "Come on," I moaned, pulling at her furry poncho.

"Alright," she said to Stan. "We'll call."

"Okay," he said, his sentence cut short by the door closing.

We waited as Stan jerked the car into drive and pulled away in his old clunker covered in rust. After he turned right at the streetlight I ran for the library. It was the only place in the whole world where I had my own section. At the main door I waited for my grandmother to catch up. Together we walked over to the librarian's desk, where I hovered around her like a moon caught in the gravitational pull of a planet.

"May I help you?" The librarian stared down over the rims of her glasses.

"My granddaughter would like her own library card."

The librarian looked over the counter, down the many miles to me. "She'll need to be able to sign her name. Otherwise, she'll have to use yours."

"Bring her a card," my grandmother said. "She'll sign it."

The librarian looked doubtful because I was small for my age but seemed pretty sure we weren't going away. She brought a little brown card over and pointed to a line on the back. I climbed up into a plastic chair. I wanted my own card. I was tired of having to depend on everyone else. Ignoring the librarian and her wheezy breath, I spelled out my last name. When I was finished, before I had a chance to do anything, my grandmother put her middle finger on my card and slid it across the counter.

I was approved. I finally had my own card. Worrying and needling my grandmother incessantly paid off. I skipped over to the children's section. My grandmother followed close behind and took up residence in a little wooden chair, at a little wooden table.

Shelves of worlds waited to be discovered. I glanced around. At that time of morning there weren't many people. A quiet, warm, light filled the entire place. No one was allowed to scream or yell or make a fool of themselves because a security guard up front would come and escort the person to the door. I loved the library. It was my favorite place in all the world. It had air conditioning, silence, and was full of books, the total opposite of my house.

I filled my arms with *Ramona the Brave* and *A Wrinkle in Time*. Brightly colored worlds from the land of imagination opened before me. When I looked over, my grandmother was perched precariously on the chair, snoring. Golden light flooded her cheeks. She was beautiful even if she did wheeze.

The library was full of magic. Books were proof there were other people in the world. I wanted to be a character in a book. I wanted to be Ramona the Brave, with her freckles and short, messy hair. The shelves in the children's section were just tall enough for me, but on the other side of the divider, there was the history section, ripe with titles such as *The Ming Dynasty* or *Emperors of the Empire*. Just catching sight of the spine of a book made me want to travel the world. I climbed into a big, overstuffed chair, closed my eyes, and pretended to live three thousand years ago. I dreamed about oil lamps and cities that disappeared under piles of pumice.

I cracked an eyelid. My grandmother was still snoozing.

My eyes scanned the aisles. Diggy was in the B section, wagging his tail. He loved everything about the library except the sign out front that read *No Dogs*.

"It's okay," I explained. "You're only half dog."

I hadn't seen him all day. I snuck a glance at my grandmother, all awash in golden light. I headed down the aisle to where Diggy waited.

"She's sleeping," I whispered.

He wagged his tail.

"Hey," I sidled up closer to him. "You know how people are always disappearing in books, then sometimes they come back in the end?"

Immediate recognition. He nodded, his furry ears flopping.

"Well," I said, taking his paw, leading him over to the card catalog. "What if we could find a book on how to make people disappear. Like some kind of magic water or something that we could pour on Thurman while he was sleeping."

There was tremendous possibility in this idea. Diggy knew. He stroked his whiskers, thinking.

"Okay," I said, impatient, pulling a drawer out. "Give me a key word."

There were about a bajillion books with "disappear" in the title but no "*how to*" books.

"I think we're going to have to go into the main part of the library."

Diggy slinked back, tucking his tail.

"Come on." I grabbed his paw. I pulled him through the arch into the main section. "If she wakes up, we'll tell her we went to the bathroom."

The main card catalog was enormous. There were slips of paper and tiny pencils. With Diggy keeping a lookout I wrote down every number I could find. I had ten pieces of paper filled with numbers. The hunt began. Finally, I found a book called *Mean Co-Workers: How to Make Them Disappear.* I pulled it down from the shelf. It was pretty big. I read the first page. It assured me after thirty days the mean people would go away. The first chapter was about not letting mean people in your space anymore, not giving in to their demands. I started taking notes. Several pages into Chapter Three Diggy thumped his foot and pointed at the clock.

"Crap." My eyes went wide. It was twelve 'clock. I broke into a sweat, then into a run.

As I rounded the corner, I saw my grandmother talking to the librarian.

*Crap.*

I ran over.

"Where have you been?" she asked, brow pinched.

"In the bathroom."

Her brow twisted in with doubt.

"And then I went upstairs to listen to records."

"You're supposed to stay with me." She reached for my hand. "What's this?" she asked, pointing at the book I'd forgotten was in my hand.

I laid it on the return cart. "Oh, just something I found on the floor."

"Alright, well, get your books. My stomach is growling."

We checked my big stack of books out and went to the enclosed area in front where they had a row of pay phones. It was cool and dark with low ceilings.

My grandmother put a dime into the phone, then dialed. We waited. She shifted from one foot to the other.

"What's going on?"

She covered the mouthpiece with her hand. "It's ringing."

She hung up, concerned. Renewed, she pulled the dime from the coin return, put it in again, and said, "Maybe I dialed the wrong number."

I sat down on the ground and started reading my books. My uncle took forever to do anything.

On the third phone call Stan answered.

"Where have you been?" I heard her ask.

Looking around the edges of her poncho, I saw Diggy peeing on a fire hydrant out front.

"Okay, well, then come get us," she said.

After she hung up, I gathered all of my books so we could walk out front.

"What was he doing?" I asked.

"He said he was sleeping." The tone of her voice suggested otherwise.

It took Stan twenty minutes to drive six blocks regardless of traffic, time, or weather. I heaved my piles of books into my arms as I saw the old beater pulling to a stop at the curb.

When we got home, my grandmother went to the kitchen to make sausage and eggs.

I clambered up onto Stan's bed and asked, "What was I before I was me?"

"You was waiting to become you, I reckon."

I smelled the percolator.

Thurman's fat butt was strangely absent.

I showed Stan all of my books. Then I pulled out my prize. My very own library card.

"It has your name on it." He studied the front. "It's nice."

My grandmother poured me fresh coffee in a juice glass with milk and sugar. "Don't tell your mother I gave you coffee." She added, "I listen to her complain about everything. I won't listen to her complain about coffee."

I leaned across the table, whispering to Stan like a spy selling secrets. "Tomorrow we go to KFC."

"I know," he said. "Chicken bucket."

After eating lunch and looking through every book in my stack I went up to Grand Daddy's old room and fell asleep. It was dark outside. Locusts hummed their strange song.

I woke up sometime after the streetlights clicked on. I got up and went downstairs to Stan's room. It was empty, like my stomach. I checked his bathroom, the living room, the front porch, the back yard, looked to see if his old beater was there, and then walked back inside.

My grandmother stared at me. "Have you seen your uncle?"

I shook my head. "No. I was looking for him."

She walked down to his room. "Did he tell you he was going anywhere?"

"No."

The phone rang on the gossip bench.

She grabbed the receiver and said, "Hello?" She listened. The color drained out of her face. "Oh, God. I'll be right there." She said and hung up.

Standing in the doorway to Stan's bedroom, I asked, "Is everything all right?"

Thurman paced upstairs. Then all of a sudden, his fat butt plopped down on his bed, causing the springs to strain. The metal frame scraped the floor.

My grandmother and I looked up at the ceiling. The Bogeyman was awake.

She pointed to the phone urgently. "Call a taxi."

We always had to call a taxi if Stan was sleeping or didn't want to go anywhere, but this was the first time I'd had to call because he wasn't there. "Where are we going?" I flipped open the phone book looking for the letter *T*.

My grandmother disappeared into her room, then reemerged a second later, clutching her handbag, in a tizzy. "Oh—God." She breathed loudly.

It was shaping up to be quite an evening. I kept my mouth shut and called a taxi.

Upstairs, through the ceiling, we heard Thurman talking to himself. That meant the Voices were talking to him.

As soon as I hung up, my grandmother grabbed my hand. Together we walked through the living room, stopping only long enough for me to get my coat and a library book. Thurman stomped around above our heads. Who knew what he was doing up there?

Out front we sat down on the curb under the streetlamp. Glancing back over my grandmother's shoulder, I saw the shadow of Thurman, exaggerated and dark on the wall.

My eyes followed the dark figure along the walls upstairs. "Where's Stan?"

When she didn't answer, I turned and watched her eyes travel the distance of our street. Finally, her mouth fell open and she said, "Apparently, your uncle took off all of his clothes and ran naked down Poplar Avenue."

I felt the palm of my hand against my mouth before I heard the laughter rumbling in my stomach.

She cut me short. "It's not funny."

The thought of Stan running naked down the street was simultaneously terrifying and hysterical. Doubled over with laughter, I snorted. Down at the end of the street, headlights cut through the darkness. A bright yellow cab pulled to a stop in front of us. The inside of the taxi smelled like stale cigarette smoke and armpits. Probably my own. I'd fallen asleep without taking a shower. My stomach growled.

My grandmother leaned forward, laying her hand on the back of the seat. "West Precinct, please."

We listened to an oldies radio station and watched as the taxi driver floored it every time a light turned yellow.

Tall policemen in uniforms walked around the station. Just like in the movies I saw on TV that I wasn't supposed to watch. My grandmother took my hand as an officer led us into a room to wait. The room was really quiet. My stomach growled, then chortled.

My grandmother looked at me. "When was the last time you ate?"

I had to think about that a minute. "Yesterday."

She sighed, rolling her eyes. After digging around in her pocketbook she pulled out her change purse. "Here. We passed a vending machine on the way in here."

*Yippeeee. Junk food.*

I stood in front of a glass-front machine trying to decide between C12 and A4. It soothed my nerves. I looked around at all of the people passing by. I wondered how many of them knew my uncle had taken off all of his clothes and run naked down the street.

Finally, I chose C12, C10, and A3, and I bought myself a soda with the rest of the change.

I was chomping up a storm when Stan was led in wearing two ugly green blankets, knee socks, and dress shoes. His hair was frizzy and poofed out on his head.

The officer said to my grandmother, "Can I talk to you in the other room?"

She pointed a sharp finger at Stan. "Do not move from that chair. Understand?"

Stan nodded, his eyes dropping down to his lap.

As soon as everyone was gone, I whispered, "What happened?"

He pulled his blankets tighter. "I'll tell you later."

The door opened abruptly. My grandmother walked back in, saying, "Alright you two, Officer Jerome has offered to drive us home."

"No, thanks," Stan said, looking like he'd had enough of riding in police cars for one night.

My grandmother's finger pointed in the direction of the front door. "Get your butt in that car."

"Oh, my god," I blurted out. "You said a bad word."

"I'm going to say more of them later," she assured us, snatching up a corner of Stan's blanket.

Stan gathered himself quickly, shuffling toward the door. I followed, listening to his dress shoes clack against the linoleum. He'd done it this time. That's for sure.

Birds chirped as the sky lifted its dark blanket in the east. When I climbed out of the patrol car the clock on the dash read 5:28 AM.

We piled inside the house quietly, listening for Thurman and the Voices. Satisfied by silence, my grandmother immediately walked to her room without saying a word. I followed Stan to his bedroom.

After clicking on his bedside lamp, he turned and said, "Go on out in the hall a minute. I gotta put my pants on."

"You should have thought about putting your pants on earlier. It would have saved us a lot of trouble." I felt immensely proud of my observation, but when I turned Stan glared at me. I skulked into the hall, then found myself lured to the kitchen by the thought of liverwurst and mayonnaise.

I made the jailbird a sandwich, too.

When I came back with soda and food, he was wearing orange plaid pajamas with holes in the knees and a yellow sweatshirt that had a grouping of stains on the front that looked like the Big Dipper.

"So, what in the world got into you?" I flopped down on the edge of his bed.

He took a bite of his sandwich, lifting his eyes high enough to look at me. Mayonnaise clung to the corners of his mouth.

"Well?" I pressed, digging white bread from the roof of my mouth with my tongue.

Smoke drifted down the hall from my grandmother's room. I pointed a finger at Stan. "Oh, you're in big trouble. She only smokes when she's mad."

He blurted out desperately. "Jeever made me do it."

I shook my head. "That Jeever's some character."

"It's true," he pleaded.

I rolled my eyes. Jeever was something else. "Okay," I sighed. "What exactly did he tell you to do?"

"He said the Voices would go away if I took off my clothes and ran."

"And did they?"

"Yeah," he recollected. "Yeah, they did. At least while I was running."

I dusted crumbs off my fingers. "Can't argue that."

The lure of sleep seized me, and I wandered off in search of a good night's rest as the sun slanted through the window. I found my grandmother in bed sleeping, smelling like an ashtray. I crawled in beside her and zonked out.

Normally I had to heckle Stan for hours to get him to take me to the library, but on that particular day he'd do anything to escape the sharp glare of my grandmother. I woke at noon with him standing at the end of the bed pulling on my foot. I cracked an eyelid open. My grandmother snored next to me.

I slithered out of bed, stepping into the hall. "Yeah?"

He whispered, "You want to go to Taco Bell?"

Now was the time to negotiate. "The library."

"They ain't got no food there."

"So? It will get you out of here all day."

It only took a second for him to realize the genius of my plan. "Get your shoes," he said. "I'll meet you in the car."

Stan spent most of the day sleeping in an oversized chair in the nonfiction section. I spent most of my time reading books on how to make people disappear. Convinced that with enough mind power and some basic working knowledge of magic I could make Thurman disappear into thin air. I pressed on page after page.

I found a really good book by accident just because I was snooping around. *Magic Spells.* The title alone was enticing. I took it to the counter and checked it out while Stan was snoozing.

# CHAPTER THREE

*The Voices*

After Stan and I left the library, we drove to *KFC* and picked up a chicken bucket, then headed home. Thurman was lurking around downstairs, and my grandmother ushered us all into the kitchen for dinner.

Then the Voices joined us.

Thurman slammed his hands on the table. His chair scraped the floor like a short, quick scream. "I'm not eating this slop."

"Then don't. Get yourself something else to eat." She looked across the table at me and Stan, signaling with her eyes for us to be quiet.

"Everything around here is slop. I hate every bit of it," Thurman ranted on.

"Well, hate it all you like," she said, coolly, but the forkful of mashed potatoes trembled in her hand.

He leered, leaning over the table, his belly dipping into the carton of coleslaw. "Hate it all you like, huh? What does an old witch like you know about anything?"

She ignored him, but he didn't stop. He lit a cigarette and made a sweeping gesture with his hand, "Who lives like this?"

When no one answered, he kept on. He paced back and forth between the stove and refrigerator. "You're a bunch of sissy cowards too afraid to live any other way." He poked his finger deep into Stan's shoulder. "Coward," he jeered. "Cow-*ard.*"

My grandmother mustered another wave of strength. "We're all tired now. Eat your dinner."

"I'm not eating that slop." He slammed his hands down onto the table again. "Did you hear me? I'm not eating a bite of it, now or ever. Now or never. I don't even like you people. Just look at you," he hissed. "Cowards."

I could almost hear the Voices talking louder and louder in his head. He threw his plate on the floor and went upstairs. No one said anything.

The thing about Thurman was that you never knew what he would do. Sometimes if he woke in a bad mood, he'd get over it after a bowl of grits. Other times he stomped across the ceiling over our heads, paused in the hallway, then slammed the bathroom door. *For hours.* My grandmother put a pinch of snuff in her bottom lip. I saw her eyes drift up. Very quietly she stood and scraped the food off the floor into the dustpan. Our silence annoyed Thurman even more.

He opened the bathroom door and yelled, "Eat that slop, you pigs!"

An hour later he heaved himself down the stairs, hair slicked back, big dark circles under his eyes. My grandmother always said eyes were the windows to the soul. If that was the case then the Voices stood in his window, casting a dark shadow down his face.

Thurman walked right up and sucker-punched Stan in the back of the head. Stan screamed loud and ran before he even knew what was happening. Thurman chased him out the front door but lost him and came back inside with hideous, glowing eyes. My grandmother had the big bottle of pills in her hand.

"Why don't you take your medicine?" she asked calmly, gently.

"Why don't you take it?" he sneered.

"Because I think it will make you feel better," she said, patiently.

He leaned in so close I saw the hairs around her face blow back from his breath. "I'd feel better if you were dead," he said, so menacing, so convincing that chills ran down my spine.

She unscrewed the cap on the bottle. "I think it's a good idea."

"I don't care what you think," he said, and slapped her hand away.

Then he went back upstairs, where he chain-smoked and paced for about half an hour. I was in the kitchen getting a piece of bologna when he plodded back down the stairs. He walked right past me, and when I turned, I saw he was clutching a hunting knife in his right hand. He was headed for Stan's room. As light and fast as I could, I ran into the hall far enough to catch a view into Stan's room. It was empty.

Thurman stood about five feet in front of me looking left, then right, then back again into Stan's room. Behind me I heard steps creaking on the back porch. I turned and ran with bologna in my hands.

Stan was reaching for the doorknob when I burst out onto the back porch, knocking him into the dryer. I slammed the door behind me, yelling, "Run!"

My feet hit the ground running, and I was halfway across the backyard before I turned to see him standing on the porch, staring at me.

"What are you doing?" he asked.

Waving my bologna in the air, I yelled, "He has a knife!"

Stan's brow furrowed. "Who has a knife?"

"Thurman."

His whole body tensed visibly. "Where's Mother?"

From where I was standing, I could see directly into the sunroom. The lights were on, and no one was in there. "She's not in her room," I yelled back.

Stan hurried down the steps sideways, holding onto the side of the house so he wouldn't fall. "I bet she's on the front porch. Run around and look."

I ran fast, craning my neck to look through all of the passing windows just in case she was laying down on the sofa. The gravel crunched beneath my feet as I rounded the corner. I had to stand back several feet to be able to see all the way to the opposite end. There she was, resting on the swing, eyes closed, head tilted back.

"Thurman has a knife," I screeched loud enough to get her attention.

My grandmother's eyes popped open. "What?"

I ran to the front steps. She turned, staring straight into the house at her son, who from where I was standing looked to be in the exact same place I'd last seen him. The knife was at his side. His eyes were glassy, staring off into that distant place. That place where there was no guarantee he'd come back from. Then it happened. I saw his lips moving. The Voices were talking to him. *And he was talking back.*

Stan's footsteps crunched along the side of the house until he reached the porch. A second later, with a quiver in his voice, he called out, "Mother, are you okay?"

She didn't answer, and I looked back and forth between the two. Without uttering a word, she stood up, walked down the steps, took my hand, and guided me to the car. Stan followed with pep in his step, glancing back over his shoulder to make sure he wasn't sucker-punched again.

As we huddled around Stan's clunker of a car, I blurted out, "Who gave him a knife?"

"Not me," Stan said, getting into the car, massaging the back of his head where Thurman punched him.

Then, the three of us turned and we could see Thurman, still standing inside. A few minutes later, he disappeared from downstairs and reappeared upstairs in the window of his room. I could see him clearly, watching us, knife in hand. He was so creepy. He took the knife blade, cut into his arm, then rubbed his blood all over the window. When he was done, he flipped us the bird.

It was going to be one of those days.

"What's he doing?" Stan whispered.

"Being a freak," I snorted.

"How long do you think this will last? My radio program comes on at 9 PM." Stan looked distraught, and the corners of his eyes pinched tight. He loved his radio programs.

I felt my grandmother's hand on my shoulder. "Why don't you go play with Preston Brown."

"But what about you? Stan's a 'fraidy cat."

"We'll be fine." She steered me away from the car. "Go play now."

I didn't want to play. I wanted to sneak around upstairs and watch a movie. I wanted Thurman and his fat butt to go away. Knowing my grandmother wouldn't give in, I huffed and pouted my way to Preston's house. Mrs. Brown answered the door.

"Can Preston come play?"

"He's praying now, Cotton. You'll have to come back later," she informed me in a saintly whisper.

Double crap.

I clomped down the front steps. At my house the Voices screwed up everyone's radio programs. Down there God hogged up precious daylight. I wandered out to the street, where I could see my grandmother and Stan exactly where I'd left them.

Thurman was such a nuisance.

I marched right back down the street, my sandals clomping and scraping against the asphalt. "Preston's praying," I said. "I have to come back later when God forgives him."

No one said anything. I turned.

Thurman was in the living room, pacing, knife in hand. When he paced to the door, he was fully visible, but when he turned and walked back toward the hall, he disappeared. We couldn't lure him into the yard and then lock the doors because the front-door latch had been broken my entire life.

"Maybe we could trap him in a dumpster and ship him off to Guam," I offered, too flip to be sincere. "This is so dumb. We can't even get into our own house." I lowered myself to the concrete, feeling its knotty, gritty surface under my hands.

Thurman reappeared and stopped in the doorway.

He looked far over our heads to the Land of Crazy. Then he turned and paced back into the hall.

"This could go on for hours," I whined.

It did. When he finally put the knife down, we ventured up to the porch. The sun was setting, and my stomach was growling. Very quietly, Stan opened the window he kept unlocked for this very reason. I slid inside and tiptoed twelve feet to his dresser. I grabbed the car keys, then ran full speed back to the window.

"Grab some money," Stan whispered.

I turned. There was a twenty-dollar bill on the nightstand and some one-dollar bills. I grabbed it all in one full sweep of the hand.

I heard Thurman in the hall. My brain said to run but my body froze. Stan waved me frantically toward the window. Thurman was so close I could hear him breathing, mumbling madness. I smelled the stale scent of cigarettes and sweaty armpits. I thought about the girl in the ditch.

"Come on," Stan breathed urgently.

I could hear Thurman walking away from Stan's room, back down the hall. I imagined him walking to the edge of the universe and stepping off.

The telephone rang and scared the beejesus out of me. That was all I needed to snap out of it. I ran so fast, I practically dove through the open window.

With cash and car keys in hand, Stan drove us to Jack Pirtle's Fried Chicken. We bought chicken boxes with French fries and gravy while the Beast paced the floor back home. We ate our fried chicken dinners in the parking lot at the Brook & Banger Pharmacy because my grandmother thought the smell might lure Thurman out.

"Why don't we just move and not tell him where we live?" I offered.

My grandmother pulled meat from the bone. Stan dunked his French fries in gravy and kept his mouth shut. The thought of moving out of his room terrified him. We'd had this conversation before.

The light in Thurman's bedroom was on when we pulled to a stop at the curb. His shadow paced along the walls, but we couldn't actually see him. I ran into the house and grabbed my purse. Stan plopped down on the swing. My grandmother lowered herself onto the porch steps, where she had a complete view of the living room. I opened my purse.

Stan pointed. "Where'd you get all of that money?"

"My mom's new boyfriend gave it to me." I held my loot up, fastened together with a ponytail holder.

"Why did he give it to you?" Stan asked.

I shrugged my shoulders. "Because he's nice, I guess."

Thurman slammed a door upstairs so hard it made all of the windows rattle. My grandmother stared into the living room, eyes like laser beams.

Then, it started. The really bad part.

The Voices in his head got louder. We could hear him talking to himself upstairs, ranting, repeating the same words over and over, thundering, pounding like a drumbeat. Then we heard the loud creaking of the stairs as he descended. I ran. Once I made it to the other side of the yard, I turned around to see Stan running into the house.

My jaw dropped to the ground. "Are you crazy?" I yelled, frantically.

He didn't even acknowledge me. About thirty seconds later he came hauling booty through the front door with Grand Daddy's old bayonet in his hand. I heard Thurman's voice echoing through the house.

"Run," I urged in a loud whisper.

Stan's belly jiggled as he picked up speed, making it down the front steps before Thurman could even get to the door. Stan just kept running. Together we ran off down the ditch, next to the neighbor's hot tub. We crouched in the darkness and listened for the Beast. When the coast seemed clear we hiked up the carriage alley and down the street to hide on the other side of the house. We lowered ourselves to the ground, and from where I was sitting, I could hear Thurman's breathing, fast and raspy. He fumbled for a pack of cigarettes crammed in his pocket. The sound of cellophane crinkled. The striking of a match scorched the silence. The crackle and snap of tobacco burning singed the night. A second later he walked away from where he'd been standing, talking to himself, loud, forceful. The Voices were angry.

My grandmother stayed on the porch, but me and Stan lowered ourselves next to the basement windows. If we heard Thurman coming, we could run off through the neighbor's yard.

"Jeever goes up to that room," Stan pointed to the second floor of our neighbor's house.

Jeever was a piece of work.

"Is he up there now?" I asked.

"No. When he's there he shoots my brain with lasers."

The dirt smelled rich and moist. Purple flowers sprouted up alongside the house. Small, dainty ones with velvet-like petals.

The last thing we needed was for Jeever to show up. Stan didn't seem bothered, which was good. He clutched his bayonet to his belly and sighed aloud.

Thurman started screaming inside, "I'm going to kill you!"

Here we go, I thought, that hurricane of crazy in his head crashed against our shores.

"I hate him," Stan whispered.

Another loud scream pierced the night.

"So do I."

# CHAPTER FOUR

---

*First, NYC*

Sometime around 10 PM, my grandmother, by the grace of God, talked Thurman into Thorazine. He fell asleep after midnight. Since no one dared fall asleep during one of his spells, we waited to see if he lumbered down the stairs like a zombie. When he didn't, all three of us fell asleep immediately, huddled together in my grandmother's room.

The next morning Thurman woke at the crack of dawn. For whatever reason, he stood in the hallway slamming his door over and over.

At 8 AM when he started talking about demons, my grandmother loaded me into the car with Stan and told him to drive me home.

Rolling papers and marijuana seeds were scattered over the coffee table when I walked inside. Candles burned in pools of wax on top of the TV. Wax dripped down over the screen. Dave was in the kitchen. I walked over and stood in the doorway.

"Hey," he said. "Does your mom drink coffee?"

Happy to see him I smiled super-big. "Yeah, up in the cabinet." I walked over and stood on my tippy-toes, pointing.

He pulled it down and opened the package. The scent burst into the air.

"So, what are you doing here?" I asked, trying to figure out if he'd moved in.

"Well, I've been staying here a few days."

"Are you going to keep staying here?"

"Maybe, but first I've got to go to New York."

"For what?"

"Business."

"Oh."

"I was thinking you and your mom could go with me."

We loaded up his Oldsmobile with suitcases and drove from Memphis to New York City. Silly and drunk with happiness to be going somewhere and doing something, I entertained myself with a stack of books and a sketch pad in the backseat.

When I woke from a nap, buildings stretched down the streets for miles in all directions.

The lobby of our hotel was full of beautiful chairs the color of Rapunzel's hair. The man carrying our suitcases let me ride on the cart all the way up to our room. I stood in the elevator watching lights flash behind numbers. I'd never ridden so high before. In our bathroom we had an enormous marble bathtub as big as a swimming pool.

"Oh my gosh," I said, walking up the steps of the tub. "What is this?"

Dave stood in the doorway behind me. "It's a Jacuzzi bathtub."

I looked back over my shoulder. "A what?"

He walked over, turning the faucet on. "I'll show you."

A big bottle of bubble bath sat on the edge of the tub.

I pointed, gleefully. "Can I?"

He nodded and walked back into the other room.

I squealed and squirted a big glop into the bottom, where it smacked the rising water and began to bubble. *Bubbles.* Jets sprayed water out of the sides of the tub.

When I looked up Diggy was on the other side, staring down into the foam.

"Look at this," I whispered.

Diggy nodded.

"We can swim in here," I said, practicing my wink.

"Cotton," my mother screamed from the other room, "stop talking to yourself."

Diggy frowned; one ear flopped down in his face.

"She doesn't believe you're real," I whispered.

He rolled his eyes.

I turned around as Dave walked through the door, carrying a big leather folder. He checked the bubble status, sat down on the steps and opened the folder.

"Here," he said, "we're going to order from room service."

"What's room service?"

"It's where you order food from a kitchen downstairs, and they bring it up to your room."

My eyes scanned up and down the columns on the menu. "No way."

He nodded. "Way."

I'd never even heard of most of the stuff on the menu. "What are you having?"

"I don't know," he said. "Maybe filet mignon." The rising water level diminished my bubbles. Dave grabbed the bottle, giving it a big squeeze.

"I'll have that," I said, wondering what a mignon was.

"And a shrimp cocktail," he said.

"I'll have one of those, too." I'd seen shrimp dancing on TV while hiding upstairs at my grandmother's house.

"What do we do when we're done?" I asked.

"We stand at the window and watch all of the lights twinkle."

"Like a Christmas tree?"

"Better."

I splashed and swam and floated until my fingertips turned to prunes.

My mother appeared in the doorway. "Get out before you drown."

A tall man in a white uniform rolled our dinner in on a big cart. I'd never eaten from a cart before. Dave opened the curtains and a dark sky fanned out behind a bowl of bright sparkling lights. Just like he said. As it turned out, a mignon was a big steak. I ate steak, baked potato, shrimp cocktail, and New York cheesecake until I thought I'd burst.

Stealing glances outside the window, I asked, "Have you ever been here before?"

Dave nodded.

I noticed my mother wasn't eating. I offered her one of my shrimp.

"That's disgusting." She waved it away. "They're scavengers."

"How about cheesecake?"

She shook her head, fidgeting, then looked around the room.

My eyes drifted back to the lights. I was sure famous people must have stayed in that hotel, maybe even in this very room. My bed at the hotel was as big as my entire bedroom at home. When I whipped back the sheets on my king-sized wonder, I found candy on my pillows.

On the other side of the door, I heard Dave talking in a hushed, fast voice. Then I heard the bathroom door slam. I didn't care. I had my own bathroom, and it had a swimming pool.

Diggy climbed into bed next to me and sat down, wiggling his hairy toes.

"Can you believe this?" I swooped my arms over my head. "Judy Garland sang here at Radio City Music Hall."

Diggy nodded. *The Wizard of Oz* thrilled him. Glinda, the Good Witch, was his favorite. And Toto.

We climbed under the blankets, and before we knew it were fast asleep.

I drifted off into a subterranean slumber that left me so well rested I was delirious when I woke. Diggy was gone. Streams of light illuminated the edges of the curtains. I pushed back the blankets and scratched. *What day was it?* I climbed out of bed and walked across the room, feeling plush carpet curl under my toes. The sun was up. Everything was quiet. Tiptoeing across the room, I listened for any movement. The only sound was the hum of the air conditioning clicking on. Diggy was in the bathroom, staring down over the edge of the bathtub like it was the Grand Canyon. Life was good.

Laying my ear against the cool wood, I listened. I began to wonder if the world had stopped while I was sleeping, and time had ceased to exist and me and Diggy were the only two left on the planet. Then I heard movement. It was faint but definitely a life form. I jerked the door open to face an empty room.

I followed the sounds through the other bedroom, stopping at the bathroom door, where the shower blasted full throttle on the other side. I camped out at the door, listening to my stomach growl.

Finally, I knocked. "Hey," I yelled. Nothing. I pounded with my fist. After a second, the shower stopped. Trickles of water echoed in the chamber.

Dave yelled back, "Go get ready. You're going with me today."

"Okay," I yelled. Then the water started again.

I ran back to my room, reveling in the fact that this place was so big we could live there. I dove into my suitcase, clicking open the locks on either side. I was fully dressed and ready to run out the door when I realized I'd only brought one pair of shoes. My gnarly white tennis shoes didn't exactly match.

"Hey, kiddo. You ready?"

I spun around, startled.

Dave stared at me.

"Where's my mom?" I asked.

"I don't know," he said. "That's why you have to go with me today."

He held out his hand, and I walked over. I liked his big warm hand wrapped around mine. "Maybe she went out to get breakfast," I offered.

"Yeah, maybe she did," he sighed.

"Speaking of breakfast," I skipped along to the elevator, "I'm starving."

"Me, too."

In the taxi I turned around in the seat because I couldn't see anything. The back window was like a movie screen where everything moved in and out of focus and then farther away until rows and rows of big gray buildings lay behind us, solid, enormous, each one different. I pulled a little notepad out of my purse.

"What are you doing?" Dave asked.

"Drawing the buildings so I can show Stan."

Dave laughed. "You'll be drawing all day, kiddo."

"What are you guys doing in the city?" the taxi driver asked, glancing up into the rearview mirror.

Dave flashed a smile. "Business."

I loved that smile.

The taxi dropped us off at another hotel with a man out front who opened the door for us.

"Does he live here?" I whispered, traversing the lobby, trying to keep up.

"That's a doorman."

"Oh, yeah. Right. What about breakfast?"

He pressed the button for the elevator. "Upstairs. Johnny always has food."

As it turned out, Johnny was a big guy with bright blue eyes and a suit with no fuzz on it. Another guy, named Dale, patted Dave down just like in the movies. Then he patted me down.

"What was that for?" I asked.

"Checking you for wires, kid."

I turned to Dave. "What kind of wires?"

Dave smiled. Everyone else laughed.

"What's so funny?"

"Nothing," Dave chuckled. Then he turned to Johnny. "We haven't eaten yet."

Johnny clapped. "Someone get the kid some food."

In the other room, which was kind of like the first room but bigger, a man named Lionel, introduced himself.

"What do you do?" I asked.

"I'm Johnny's bodyguard."

"What do you do?"

"I protect him and make sure everyone has his best interest in mind."

*Oh.*

Johnny didn't just have one cart full of food. He had five. Lionel handed me a plate, and I stood on my tiptoes, checking out the options.

"Don't you just love room service," I said to Lionel.

He nodded. "Yeah, Johnny likes good food."

"What's that?"

"Quiche," he said.

"What's that?"

"Crêpes."

"What's a crêpe?" I asked.

"Umm, it's kinda like a pancake filled with fruit and cream."

"Oh. What's that?"

"It's a scone." He grabbed one. "My favorite."

After twenty questions I had a plate full of food I'd never eaten. I scored a cup of coffee with cream and sugar since my mom wasn't around.

Lionel sat next to me on a fat, cushy sofa. He smelled good, like soap and cologne, rich and fragrant like my coffee. His plate was piled even higher than mine. As I smeared butter and jam all over my scone, which really tasted like a big biscuit, I heard men talking in the other room. Occasionally laughter erupted, followed by lowered voices, then talking, then a knock on the door. Lionel and I were still chowing down when Dave walked into the room.

"How ya doing?" he asked.

"Good," I mumbled, my mouth full of quiche.

Dave piled a plate high with fruit and crêpes, then turned back to me. "I'll be in there a little longer. Okay?"

I nodded. "Take your time."

As he walked back to the other room, I caught a glimpse of someone who hadn't been there before. He had shiny black hair and dark eyes. His skin was dark like my uncle Stan. For a brief second, he turned and caught my eye. Chills ran down my spine.

I shivered.

"You cold?" Lionel asked.

"No. Someone walked over my grave."

He stared at me. "Where'd you learn that?"

"My grandmother."

"What's it mean?"

"I don't know. It's just something she says when she shivers."

"Is she alive?"

I nodded.

"Then she ain't got no grave," he said, perturbed.

I was afraid I'd made him mad.

"We don't talk about graves here no how."

I nodded.

A few seconds later, he gave me a playful punch on the arm. "Come on. You ever had a Shirley Temple?"

A phone rang in one of the bedrooms. Lionel went off to answer it. From where I was standing, I saw him pick up the receiver, then sit down on the bed with his back to me. I snuck over to the door to the main room where the meeting was being held and listened.

All of the voices in the other room were different, but one was more different than the rest. The black-haired man was Spanish. I could hear his accent through the wood. I heard him say, "I want no problems." Then someone said, "No problems." Dave said something but I couldn't hear well enough. Then Johnny's voice boomed, saying something, and everyone laughed.

"What are you doing?" Lionel's voice thundered behind me.

Horrified, I turned. Lionel stood in the doorway to the bedroom, staring right at me. "I was . . . umm . . . listening."

"Well, don't. Now get over here and have a Shirley Temple with me."

"Does it have alcohol in it?"

"No. We don't hit the sauce around here. Johnny don't allow it."

An hour later Dave opened the door. I was sprawled out on the sofa, fat as a tick, watching cartoons. Lionel walked into the front room, positioning himself next to Johnny, who was walking my way.

Johnny looked at Dave. "I didn't know you had kids."

Dave's eyes narrowed at the edges. "Why?"

"Cause it might not be safe to bring strangers in here if you know what I mean."

"I'm safe," I blurted out.

Johnny turned quick and scared me. He walked swiftly toward me, his big feet swallowing up carpet, then knelt down. "Is that so?"

"Yeah," I said. "That's so."

Johnny laughed. "You got spunk." He pulled a wad of money from his pocket and peeled off two twenty-dollar bills, handing them over.

The black-haired Spaniard was standing behind Dave, watching me. "What's your name?" he asked.

I stammered, "Cotton."

Johnny gestured to the rest of the men. "Give the cute kid some money you tightwads, and let's gets out of here."

With military precision they all lined up in front of me, digging wads of money out of their pockets or wallets. I didn't know what to do so I stood there as they filed past, smiling, saying it was nice to meet them and taking their cash. The Spaniard was the last in line. He knelt in front of me. He smelled like cinnamon toast and leather. I could see my reflection in his dark eyes.

He looked me directly in the eye. "What is your name again?"

"Cotton."

"Well, Cotton, in my country we give something that belongs to us. Do you understand?"

I nodded.

"That makes the gift special." He unlatched a small silver bracelet from his wrist. "This bracelet came from a pirate's chest near where I lived."

*Pirate's chest? Treasure. Are you joking? Gimme Gimme.* My heart beat so fast, I thought it would pound out of my chest.

"Give me your arm," he said.

I held my wrist out. I heard Johnny breathing behind me. It was so quiet my ears started ringing. He clasped the bracelet on my wrist. It was big and dangled. He unclasped it and wrapped it twice around and then secured it. It fit perfectly.

"What do you say?" Dave asked.

"Thank you," I blurted, breathless. "Thank you."

"In my country we say *gracias.*"

"*Gracias,*" I said, with equal gusto.

The Spaniard stood up.

"What's your name?" I asked.

The black-haired man laughed. "Everyone knows my name."

I looked back over my shoulder at Johnny, who snorted and said, "Everybody knows that sonofa..."

The Spaniard laughed. "Watch your mouth, Johnny. She's a kid."

Then we all left. Everyone took separate elevators or the stairs. No one said a word in the hallway.

Standing at the curb while Dave flagged a taxi, I stared down at my wrist. The bracelet looked like silver hair braided together.

Dave said, "Be careful with that bracelet. It's white gold."

"Gold is white?"

"Yeah." He reached down and pulled my wrist in for a closer look. "Yeah, looks like a real score for you." He returned his attention to the street to wave his hand furiously until a taxi stopped.

I couldn't wait to tell Diggy.

The taxi jiffed us back across town. I was in wonder and awe of riding in the backseat with buildings whizzing past and more people than I'd ever seen in my life.

We hiked the huge expanse of the lobby to the elevators.

"What are we doing?" I asked.

"We're going to get your mom."

*Oh, that's not very interesting.* "Do you know where she is?"

"I'm hoping she's upstairs." Dave ushered me into the elevator.

When the doors slid open on our floor, I stepped out first and saw a man coming out of a room. Dave saw him too and pulled me back in the elevator. He jammed his finger into the "close door" button.

My heart started beating faster. "What are we doing?"

The doors closed in front of us, and I heard the breath pushed out of Dave's lungs.

I looked up as I felt the elevator descend. "Was that man in our room?"

Dave nodded. "Yeah, that was definitely our room."

"Maybe it was room service," I ventured.

"I kind of doubt it." He pulled me out onto a new floor as the doors opened.

Dave's eyes darted up and down the hall.

I was scared. "What does this mean?"

Still thinking, he said, "It means you're going to have to wait here."

"Right here? In the *hall?*"

"Yeah." He lowered himself onto one knee, turning us eye to eye. "Listen, I'm going to go back upstairs," he said, pulling his watch off and handing it to me. "If I'm not back in five minutes, I want you to go downstairs and ask for help."

My heart beat really fast. "But what do I do?"

"Just wait right here. If the big hand touches the three before I get back, go get help. Don't talk to anyone up here. If anything happens, then run. Got it?"

Big tears swelled in my eyes. "*What?*"

Dave rubbed his hands on my shoulders, "You're okay. We're okay. I just need to go upstairs and check out the room. Okay?"

"Okay." I looked down at the watch, my hands shaking.

Dave stood and pushed the elevator button. "Stay right here." When the doors opened he stepped inside, turned, and just as they were closing gave me a quick wink.

It made me want to cry. *What if he didn't come back? What if someone bad was up there? What if something happened to my mother? Where would I go? Who would take care of me?*

Just then the elevator chimed, and the doors opened again. Two strangers stepped out. I realized I'd been holding my breath. They stepped around me, walking toward their room. I watched, but they didn't look like criminals, and pretty soon I turned back to the elevator. My right eye started to twitch.

In my panic I turned and saw Diggy walking down the hall toward me.

"Thank god you're here," I whispered.

He nodded, ears flopping.

I looked around to make sure no one else was in the hall. "Something's happened," I said urgently. "Have you seen my mother?"

Diggy shook his head.

"Yeah, that's what I thought."

The elevator dinged behind me. The doors opened as I turned, and I saw Dave walking toward me.

"Who are you talking to?" he asked.

"Diggy."

"Oh. Get in."

I rushed into the elevator and wrapped my arms around Dave's leg so he wouldn't leave me again. Diggy stood in the hall staring at us. The doors closed.

On the ride up I noticed Dave had a gun stuffed down the front of his pants.

"Is that real?"

His eyes watched the numbers light up. He looked down at his waist, then over at me. "Yeah. It's real."

That worried me. Suddenly I wanted to run and hide. I was so confused. What had happened? As we walked to our room, I held out my hand for Dave. The feeling of his big warm hand made me feel better.

Inside our hotel room I passed by the doorway to Dave's room and saw my mother lying limply across the bed, one arm dangling over the side. I could see a gnarled purple highway of veins running from her wrist to her elbow.

Dave stepped in front of me, pulling the door closed. "She's sleeping. Let's go get something to eat."

I knew she wasn't sleeping but didn't say anything. I'd seen it on the late, late movie. People always said it was bad.

We rode to dinner in silence. I stared out the window, watching storefronts and buildings pass. I wanted to move to New York, to live in the big city, to never go home again. The taxi dropped us off at a restaurant, and Dave paid a man at the door extra money to get us a seat. As we set off across the dining area, I saw dark, glistening eyes at a corner table.

I tugged at Dave's suit jacket. "The Spaniard," I said, under my breath.

Dave looked around. "What Spaniard?" Then he saw him and waved. Leaning in close to me, he whispered, "He's from Colombia."

"Where's that?"

"A long way from Spain." Dave steered me toward our table.

"I may need some new tennis shoes."

"Really?"

"Yeah." I hoisted a foot in the air. "Mine are old."

"Alright." Dave stepped away from the table for the waiter to clean it. "We'll go shopping."

"How about we start with that Box-O-Magic I saw in the window at the hotel gift shop?"

"How about we start with some new shoes?" He said, giving me that *'I'm a sucker for buying presents'* look.

"Only if I can have dessert first."

"Deal."

We shook on it.

Across the restaurant the Spaniard held up his hand to get Dave's attention. "Mi Amigo," he yelled. "May life be good to you."

Everyone in the restaurant turned to stare at us.

Dave's cheeks flushed pink. He hurried me into my seat. "Come on," he said, "Let's finish eating before the elves call it quits for the night."

# CHAPTER FIVE

## *Dirty Laundry*

A week after returning from New York, Dave rented a house. My mom and I had been living in a small two-room apartment for as long as I could remember, so a house was huge. She was scarce for a few days after we moved the boxes in and then disappeared entirely to her bedroom. Diggy and I were thrilled. We had an entire house to explore. There was a basement, an attic, a carport, and lots of empty closets. I found a jar of pennies under the sink in the basement. I put my money from New York in the jar, and Diggy and I were rich. Under the exposed light bulb hanging from a cord, Diggy and I talked about our treasure.

"Look, we have treasure." I held up my wrist, showing off my bracelet. "Pirate's treasure."

Dave helped me with food when he was around, but when he was gone, I had to fend for myself. Me and Diggy stole bananas, yogurt, peanut butter, and bread from the kitchen and took it back to my room for a picnic.

I sent Diggy to snoop around outside my mother's door. He came back when I'd finished my peanut butter sandwich. "Did you find anything?"

He shook his head.

I dragged a box of my toys out into the middle of the room and started rummaging. Dave came home later that day when the sun was setting with a trunk full of paper bags. Being nosey, I walked out into the garage.

"Hey," he said. "How's it been going?"

"Good," I said.

"Help me get all of this stuff inside." He handed me a bag. "I went to the store and bought you some presents."

*Presents?* The word alone motivated me. With lightning speed, I dragged brown paper bags bigger than me into the kitchen while Dave brought in the heavy stuff. I thought my mother would come out to see what was going on, but her door stayed closed.

Dave reached into a bag, pulled something out, and ceremoniously hid it behind his back.

He knelt down in front of me. "Okay, close your eyes."

I did.

"Now put out your hands."

I did.

The weight of several items filled my hands. I opened my eyes. There was a stack of flashcards and books.

"Do you know what these are?"

I nodded. "Yeah, they're flashcards."

Dave pulled several cards from the box, holding one up like a game-show host.

"What's this word?"

"Balloon."

"And this one?"

"Rabbit."

"And this one?"

"I know how to read, Dave."

"What about spelling?"

I nodded.

"Oh," he said, chunking the flashcards back in the bag. Then he reached for a plastic bag and pulled out a little faux fur coat. "Well, then I guess you'll just need to put this on so we can go to the movies."

My eyes widened so far, I felt my scalp tighten. "Is that mine?"

"Yep," he said, "and so is this." He pulled a fuzzy pink purse out of the bag, holding it up. "Now, go get ready. Since you've already learned how to read, we're going to the movies."

I snatched my coat and purse and tore through the house.

Diggy was sitting on my bed inspecting the fur between his toes.

"Hey," I belted, breathlessly. "Look what I got."

His eyes lit up as he reached for the purse. He rubbed it against his cheek.

"And we're going to the movies," I winked.

Diggy stood up, smoothing his fur.

Down the hall I heard the door to my mother's bedroom open. We ran to my door, which was still open, and craned our ears as far out as we could. The muffled sound of voices filled the hall, but I couldn't make out any real words. I didn't care. I was going to the movies.

I thought *Star Wars* would be about Civil War stuff that bored me to tears.

It wasn't. I couldn't decide if I wanted to be Han Solo, Obi Wan, or Princess Leia.

Diggy wanted to be Chewbacca.

That night Dave made dinner while I ran around the living room with a cardboard tube as my light saber, defending rebel forces behind the couch, practicing to be a Jedi by standing for long periods of time balanced on one foot. Then I ran off down the driveway because the Imperials were in hot pursuit. I came back when I was hungry.

Dave and I watched another movie on the flat box he called a VCR. It was fantastic. Movies in the living room. Mashed potatoes, Salisbury steak, carrots, and a perfect little apple cobbler in its own section of the tray.

After dinner, Dave made me a hot chocolate.

"Here," he said. "Take this to your room and drink it. I have to go out."

I felt my brow furrow.

"Don't worry." He ruffled my hair. "I'll be back. I just need to take care of some business."

My face scrunched up.

Dave knelt in front of me, reasoning, "It's way past your bedtime."

I forced my bottom lip out as far as it would go.

"Cotton . . ."

I stomped my foot.

"Okay. We'll watch more movies tomorrow, *and* we'll have French toast for breakfast."

I stumbled in my resolve. "What's French toast?"

"You'll have to wait and see." He steered me off in the direction of my room.

"Promise me you won't leave the house."

"I promise."

Diggy and I huddled in the middle of my bed, slurping hot chocolate. The house was perfectly quiet. We listened. Not a sound. It started to give me the creeps.

"What if she's dead?" I leaned forward, whispering.

Diggy didn't say anything, but he had that worried look.

"Let's go see if she's okay."

Slowly and silently, we crept over to the door, then tiptoed down the hall. Dave had turned off the lights and only moonlight from the living room illuminated our path. At the bedroom door, I stopped. My heart started beating faster. I studied the shadows of grooves carved into the big metal doorknob. Diggy started scratching.

"Shhh—," I said.

Finally, taking a deep breath, I reached out, grabbed the doorknob, and turned it slow as molasses. It glided open. Moonlight filled the room. In the middle of the bed, piled under a lump of blankets, was my mother. I couldn't hear her breathing. With a clear determination I walked over to the bed, peering up. As my hand moved through the blue light to touch her, she woke up, pushing herself away from me.

"What are you doing in here?" Her voice choked in her throat, gravelly, loud enough to scare me.

"I wanted to—"

"Get out of here." She coughed, covering her mouth. "I'm sick."

"But Dave is—"

"Get out. Don't come back in here. Do you understand?"

Her voice rose so high it frightened me. Her eyes were wide, funny looking.

"Get out," she yelled at me.

I backed away.

"Don't come in here. Do you understand?"

"No," I said, feeling my voice quiver.

"Don't come back in here." She coughed.

Diggy ran.

I ran, too, slamming the door on my way out.

I leapt up onto my bed so fast I turned just in time to see my own door slamming shut. Diggy's fur was all bristled up.

"I don't think she likes us," I whispered.

We listened for a long time but never heard anything. Eventually, I pulled my Box-o-Magic book out and started reading. It had a bag of magic dust. Late that night I heard Dave's car in the garage. I opened my eyes long enough to sees the outlines of boxes against clear white moonlight. When I woke again, Dave was standing over my bed holding a new stuffed rabbit.

"Hey," he whispered. "How's it going?"

"Okay," I said, trying to let my eyes adjust to the light in the hall.

"Come on. You're going with me."

"Where?"

"To your grandmother's house for a few days."

"I'm hungry."

"I know," he said, giving me a hand up. "Let's go to the Pancake Hut."

There weren't many people eating pancakes at six o'clock in the morning. We sat in a corner booth. I loved syrup. I wanted to put it on everything. After we ordered, I asked, "Why do I have to go to my grandmother's house now?"

"I'll tell you later." He poured himself a cup of coffee.

I was beginning to learn that *I'll tell you later* meant *I don't want to talk about it right now.*

No one was awake when we parked at the curb in front of my grandmother's house. Dave helped me out of the car and carried my hatbox. There were smashed malt liquor bottles on the front porch. Signs Thurman had another one of his *spells*.

Dave walked around the glass shards. A worried look furrowed his brow. "When does everyone usually wake up around here?"

I shrugged my shoulders. "Depends on when they went to bed."

"Okay." He knelt down in front of me. "Will you be okay?"

"Yeah, I think I'll practice being a Jedi Knight."

He laughed. "Alright. Watch out for the Imperials."

Darth Vader didn't have anything on Thurman.

I crept quietly up the stairs, pressing my hands against the walls to pull myself over the creaky steps. Everything was quiet. All of the ashtrays and soup bowls that Thurman kept in the hall were full of cigarette butts. The air smelled stale.

I snooped around in the bathroom for a minute. It smelled like urine and aftershave. Then I went back downstairs and fell asleep in my clothes on the sofa. I woke later to the smell of coffee brewing. Since no one in the house owned a clock, I walked to the gossip bench and called Time and Temperature.

*The time is eleven fifty-two AM. The temperature is sixty-two degrees.*

I sat on the bench for a minute, listening, looking around. We had no plastic wall clock or cuckoo or grandfather or even a cheap plastic thing that was a free gift. I caught a reflection of myself in the shiny metal address book that sat next to the phone. My hair was wild and crazy, circling my head. I hoisted myself down and walked into the kitchen.

My grandmother was standing at the sink. She turned when she heard me walk in.

"How did you sleep?"

"Good," I said, looking down, realizing my clothes were really wrinkled.

"What do you want for breakfast?"

Smoothing my clothes with both hands, I thought for a minute, then said, "I want to go to the zoo."

Her eyes drifted up to the ceiling, then back down to me. "I think it might be good for us to get out."

That's when I knew Thurman had been bad.

Mattress springs creaked in Stan's room, and I ran off down the hall. When I found him, he was sitting upright, all disheveled, on the edge of his bed, staring off into that great divide of nothingness.

"Are you even hungry?" my grandmother yelled from the kitchen.

Rolling back on the heels of my new plaid tennis shoes, I thought for a minute.

Stan scratched, shifted a little, scratched some more.

I rocked back and forth, then said, "No. Just the zoo."

Stan spoke up, "I want some sausage patties if I gotta drive." Then he looked at me, "Now go on. I gotta get dressed."

I skittered around the room as he tried to shoo me out. "There's nothing to do out there," I whined.

"Go on. I'm busy getting dressed." He pushed me toward the door. "A man deserves his privacy."

The door closed behind me. "Dang it," I said.

"Cotton, what have I told you about swearing?"

I skulked off to the phone again. I thought the Time and Temperature man was a real man who sat in a room all day picking up the phone whenever it rang to tell people the time. I figured he must have a big clock on his desk.

He picked up.

I blurted out, "Hello. My name is Cotton . . ."

But before I had a chance to finish, he said patiently, "The time is eleven fifty-seven AM."

I slammed the receiver back into the cradle. "Come on. It's almost noon, dang it."

"Cotton, watch your mouth," my grandmother huffed.

"How am I supposed to watch it when it's positioned under my nose where I can't see it?"

"Don't be a smarty pants."

"They say 'damnation' in the Bible," I argued.

"Then say that if you have to."

"Damnation," I muttered, stomping back into Stan's room, where I found him sitting on the edge of the bed, wearing a large flannel shirt and big work pants. The work pants were yellow, making him look like he was being swallowed alive by a man-eating banana.

He looked up at me, then a second later smiled. "Damnation," he said.

We tittered like sorority girls.

"I heard that."

I circled Stan like a shark, then grabbed his big arm, pulling. "Come on. We're going to the zoo today."

The next weekend Stan drove me home. All of the sheets and linens and clothes were in garbage bags in the driveway.

"What's that?" I asked, pointing.

"Stuff we're getting rid of," Dave said.

That night after my mom and Dave smoked a joint, I sneaked through the kitchen door to snoop around outside in the trash bags. Everything was in perfect condition. I couldn't figure out why we were throwing it all away.

Dave scared the crap out of me when he stepped out of the shadows.

"Stay out of the bags, Cotton. They're contaminated."

"What's that?"

"Your mom was really sick, and we have to get rid of it."

"I tried to go in an see her."

"I know."

"Doesn't she want to see me?"

He laid a hand on my shoulder, steering me toward the door. "She's sick, Cotton."

"What made her sick?"

Dave slowed, thoughtfully staring squinty eyed at a night full of stars. Finally, he swallowed like his mouth was really dry and said, "She's got a really bad habit. That's what made her sick."

"Like leaving dirty clothes on the floor?"

He considered this a moment, then frowned. "Like leaving dirty needles on the floor."

That was all he had to say. I understood.

"Come on," he said. "I bought a box of cupcakes." Then, as an afterthought he added, "And a guard dog."

# CHAPTER SIX

*A Dope Growing Machine*

The subscription to *High Times* magically appeared in the mailbox. I saw it first. My grandmother saw it second. Her brow furrowed when she flipped it over to read the name on the back. Thurman plodded down the stairs, t-shirt yellow around the collar and in the armpits.

He snatched the magazine out of my grandmother's hand. "That's mine."

Her eyes stared straight through him. "The mailman just saw that."

"So?"

"So, now he knows what kind of people live here."

Thurman walked off. "Screw him."

He spent the rest of the afternoon up in his room poring over the sacred text. I personally had never seen him read anything, so it fascinated me. Whenever my little head appeared at the top of the stairs, he raised up on one elbow and said, "Get out of here. I'm busy."

"I didn't even know you could read," I yelled, perched on the edge of the stairs, ready to run.

"Go away you little pest. Doesn't your mother teach you any manners?" He slammed the door in my face.

After a few seconds I shrugged my shoulders, wondering how to spend my afternoon since my game of Taunt the Psychopath had been cut short.

My nostrils caught a whiff of the percolator. Lured by the prospect of coffee with cream and sugar I walked back downstairs. As I entered the kitchen, I heard my grandmother talking on the phone. I crept along the cabinets quietly until just outside the door and heard her clearly.

"Well, I just don't know," she sighed. "She was sick for almost two months."

My ears pricked up. My mother had been sick for months.

"Hepatitis doesn't just go away. She can get sick again. This time she had that boyfriend of hers watch Cotton, but the boyfriends come and go."

My brow furrowed. There were other boyfriends, but Dave was there to stay.

"Connie was a difficult child and now she's a difficult adult. Heaven knows what goes on in that head of hers. And now Thurman— do you know what he did?" She paused for effect, took a breath and whispered, "He ordered a *marijuana* magazine."

The garbled sounds of a woman's voice on the other end murmured. My grandmother listened, then said, "Uh huh. That's right. Now we've got pictures of marijuana in the house. I know he learned it from Connie. Where else could he have learned it? She constantly talks about how good dope is."

Stan farted in his bedroom and made me giggle.

My grandmother paused, then said, "I have to go. I hear Cotton in the kitchen. She's probably hungry." She hung up the phone, then called out, "Cotton?"

"Yeah?" I stepped into the hall.

"What have I told you about eavesdropping?"

"That it's rude."

"That's right. So why are you still doing it?"

"Because it's fun."

Stan snorted.

My grandmother stood up in a huff. "Are you hungry?"

I nodded. Seized by guilt, I blurted out into the pockets of her housedress as she passed, "I'm sorry."

Her hand touched my head. "Go find something to do and I'll make lunch. You are the nosiest child I've ever seen."

I went to Stan's room. He was reading a book about World War II. I climbed up on his bed, getting as close as I could, then whispered, "What's hepatitis?"

He shook his head. "I don't know."

"Do you have a dictionary?"

"Over there," he pointed.

I climbed down and walked over to a stack of books taller than me. Most of the titles had worn off of the spines. Some spines had fallen apart completely. My finger trailed down the stack. Finally, crouched down at the bottom, I said, "Nope. No dictionary."

"Try over there," he pointed to another stack of books.

I started to wonder why he didn't know what hepatitis was with that many books around. "Do you read all of these?" I asked.

"Not really."

"Then why do you have them?"

"They were Daddy's."

"Oh."

Halfway down the second pile I found a dictionary. I flipped to H, running my finger down the columns. I found a word that looked to be the right spelling. I read the definition, then said, "It says it's an inflammation of the liver. What's inflammation?"

"Swelling," he said.

"So, her liver swelled up?"

"I reckon."

"Why would that make her sick?"

"Dunno." He shrugged his shoulders. "Maybe it will explode if it gets too big."

That didn't sound so good. I heard bacon frying.

"Cotton," My grandmother called from the kitchen. "Lunch is ready."

Stan rolled off the bed with a hungry look in his eyes. I walked to the gossip bench and called Time and Temperature. I loved the Time and Temperature Man.

He picked up.

"Hello," I said, excited to have the chance to talk to someone that talks to people all day. He never called in sick, never missed a day and was really dedicated.

"The time is two forty-two PM."

I slammed the receiver back in the cradle. "Dang it."

"Cotton," my grandmother yelled from the kitchen, "who are you talking to?"

"The Time and Temperature Man."

"Watch your mouth and get in here and eat."

I skulked in and sat down at the table.

Stan was eating Thorazine and green beans for lunch. A smile crept across his face.

My grandmother scooped a pile of mashed potatoes onto my plate. I glanced up at the ceiling. "Thurman is up there looking at pictures of marijuana."

My grandmother clenched her jaw. "That's not for us to discuss."

Exactly nine days later, the mail lady knocked on the front door. I hadn't ordered anything COD, so I answered, eager to find out what was waiting to be discovered.

"I have a package for Thurman Moore."

I reached for it when I heard my grandmother walking across the living room behind me.

"I'll take that," she said.

The box was huge, and it weighed more than me. My grandmother and I dragged it into the living room. The two of us stared down at the brown box.

Stan appeared in the doorway cramming Vienna sausages into his mouth. "*Wha's* that?" he mumbled.

The corners of my grandmother's mouth turned down. "I don't know."

Thurman tumbled in stinking drunk last night. None of us wanted to make that long, unknowing journey upstairs to wake the Beast. We all stared at each other.

My grandmother said, "Quick. Go get a knife."

We kept a cache of big knives hidden behind the refrigerator in case we needed them for cooking but didn't leave them out in the open anymore because Thurman was bad. I stooped down and turned so I could see the stairs just in case Thurman sneaked up on me. I stuck my hand in the dark nether regions where dead bugs and dust lingered until I felt the handle of a chopping knife. Mission accomplished.

I ran back to the scene. Stan stared down at the box like he expected it to move. My grandmother had a look of suspicion unlike anything I'd ever seen. You could practically hear a drum roll as she sawed into the packing tape.

A collective breath exhaled as she pulled back the flaps and we glimpsed what was inside. I had no idea what he'd bought. It was a lot of tubes and a plastic tub and some rocks.

"What is it?"

Stan leaned over, looking closer at the box. "What's it do?"

"I don't know." My grandmother reached for an instruction booklet covered in plastic. After ripping it open, she pulled the booklet out and opened it. Her eyes scanned page after page until her mouth dropped open in horror.

"What?"

The booklet fell from her hand as she reached out to steady herself.

"What?" Stan asked.

When she didn't answer I grabbed the booklet off the floor, flipping through page after page of diagrams and instructions that meant nothing to me until I turned to one of the last sections, where a full-color photo shined back at me.

"Oh my gosh," I clamped my hand to my mouth.

My grandmother gave me a knowing look.

"What?" Stan asked, irritated. "What is it for?"

"You grow marijuana with it," I said, hardly able to believe it myself.

"What? How?" He reached for the box.

My grandmother slapped his hand away. "Don't ask how. We shouldn't even have something like this in the house. Oh no," she slapped her forehead, "we're on a list now."

"Send it back," I said, empathically. "I mean it. Send it back."

"It's Saturday." She looked around the room for a clue that would tell her what to do. "The post office is closed."

Boards creaked over our heads. All of a sudden, my grandmother stood straight up, pointing down at the box. "Stan, put this in the car immediately. Cotton, go with him. I'll get the car keys."

I threw the booklet on top, and Stan heaved the box into his arms. Out the door we went. Stan's butt jiggled and swayed as he ran for the trunk, clutching the heavy box with his pelvis tilted forward, to brace the weight. I ran behind him and glanced up at the windows in Thurman's room to make sure we weren't being watched. My grandmother practically jumped down the front steps after us. I'd never seen her move so fast. She jammed the key in the trunk lock. Stan unloaded his cargo, hitching up his pants. Then we jumped in the car and slammed the doors shut.

All of us stared at the upstairs windows. Still nothing.

"Go," my grandmother said.

Stan fired up the engine, threw the car in reverse and we were outta there.

Once we turned onto the main road, Stan glanced into the rearview mirror, "Where are we going?"

"I don't know," my grandmother confessed.

I was pretty happy to be out of the house. We drove around aimlessly for an hour while we all contemplated the purchase. Finally, my grandmother pointed to a dumpster adjacent to an empty lot. Stan stopped the car next to it and left the engine running. All three of us got out.

"Here. Help me rip the label off." She clawed and tore at the sticker with our address. I dug with my fingernails, getting a good piece. I ripped it off, handing it over. She shredded the rest.

Stan heaved that enormous dope-growing kit over the side. We jumped back in the car. Silence bore into the empty spaces between us.

Stan articulated what everyone in the car was thinking. "I hope he don't find out we threw away his pot-growing machine."

"What pot-growing machine?" my grandmother said. "Let's get out of here before someone arrests us."

# CHAPTER SEVEN

*Trash to Treasure*

Since television would supposedly rot my brain, I was never allowed to watch anything except *Fantasy Island* and *The Love Boat*. Both of those still rotted my brain but they came on at midnight. By then my grandmother was too tired to argue. I was allowed to watch movies. We had copies of *Casablanca* and *King Creole*. I memorized the lines to most of *King Creole* and all of the songs. Nearly all of the scenes in *Star Wars* could be successfully imitated by me except for the ones with R2D2. I ran around cracking my homemade whip until I got in trouble for conquering the couch. When I wasn't trying to find something better to do, I was begging for the new 007. *Bond. James* Bond.

However, on Saturday afternoon just after fall break, in a wild fit of boredom, I snuck upstairs, pulled the 13-inch portable TV into the farthest corner of the room, covered it with my blue blankie, and fired that baby up. My grandmother had been napping for a while and the likelihood of being caught was slim unless Stan turned his focus from his radio program to my absence. Thurman was out drinking malt liquor and wouldn't be back for hours, if he came back at all.

Before my eyes a blue speck fanned out until it covered the entire screen. There it was. *Abbott and Costello Go to Mars.* My favorite. Cramped up in the dark corner, reveling in the blue glow, I lost track of time, my brain slowly rotting, eyes glued to the screen. Downstairs, the garbled words of public radio seeped up through the floor. Not a stitch of movement could be detected. Still, during commercials, I turned the sound down low just in case. I stayed really, really, close to the TV, worried Abbott and Costello would be the reason I might not get into college.

Outside, clouds masked sunshine, illuminating a dull gray. It smelled like rain. Even with no sound, a commercial caught my eyes. Old bottles turned into painted vases, old soup cans into decorative pencil holders. First, they'd show the old, rusted gnarly can and then, *voila*, a brand-new planter filled with African violets. The *voila* got my attention. *Presto* fascinated me. There I was, glued to the front of the set, brain cells diminishing by the nanosecond, stricken with a case of the *gotta-have-it*. The name flashed up in front of my eyes. *Trash to Treasures.*

At the end of the commercial, after making me salivate over items I could create if I, too, had this kit, an 800 number flashed up onto the screen. *1-800 . . . oh gosh, where's a pen? A pen, a pencil, eyeliner . . . anything. I must have this kit and there's no guarantee that I'll ever get to watch TV long enough to get this number again. In my entire life. A pen...a pen . . . Gees, doesn't anyone write in this family—*

Clambering around in Grand Daddy's old wardrobe I found a pocketknife, a pair of pajamas, a pack of handkerchiefs, but nothing to write with. Out in the hall I frantically repeated the numbers over and over like a Buddhist chant until finally in the back of a drawer in the bathroom, behind six pairs of false teeth, I found a tube of old red lipstick. With great haste I wrote the number down on a long piece of toilet paper.

That's when I heard Stan at the bottom of the stairs. The first step creaked.

"Cotton?"

The TV set was still lit up in the other room with the volume turned off. My eyes flashed into the hall to see if the blue light flickered against the wall. I couldn't see anything.

"Cotton?"

*Crap.* "Yeah?"

Stan stopped four stairs up. I heard his labored breathing. "What are you doing up there?"

"Why?"

"Cause you're making an awful lot of noise and Mother sent me to check on you."

*Double crap.* "Yeah, that's cause I'm—ummm, playing hide-n-seek with myself."

There was a pause. Lightning cracked outside. The stairs creaked under his shifting weight. "Yeah, alright," he said. "Let me know who wins."

"I will, dummy."

He thought about it a moment, then said, "Oh." I heard him turn around and make that long hike down those four stairs.

Garbled words of my grandmother carried up the stairs. Stan said something that sounded like "Nothing," then the muffled radio program assumed its dominance. *Whew.* I dabbed my forehead with some tissue. Seconds later Stan started digging through the refrigerator. He yelled up the stairs, "Storm's coming! Said so on the radio."

"Good." Rain meant everyone in the house would fall asleep indefinitely and I could go back to Mars.

Huddled up in my corner, I planned it out. When the movie ended, I'd sidle quietly out to the hall, drag the thirty-pound rotary phone back into the room, cover myself with the blankie to muffle sound, and call to order my kit. Trash to Treasure. The possibilities were endless.

I turned back to the screen just in time to see all of the starving children of the world staring back at me. Out on dusty plains, with no water, tormented by flies. And me, hunkered upstairs, rotting my brain, coveting the one thing that would turn all of my trash into a treasure. The guilt was tremendous. Outside, rain began to fall in torrents.

"Did you know there are children starving in the world?" I blurted out at dinnertime.

My grandmother's suspicions were immediately aroused. She looked over at me.

"That's the most curious thing I've ever heard. Where did you learn that?"

"I don't know." I shrugged off her stare. "In school. I can't remember."

"Really?" she asked, a blend of sophistication and intrigue mingling in her tone.

"Yeah, they're going to be eaten by flies."

Stan focused on the rising foam of cola fizzing on ice. Without looking over at me, he said, "Flies don't eat people."

A spoonful of grits and gravy hung in the air as my grandmother noticeably contemplated all of this. "Well, where do these children live?"

This was beginning to sound like a setup. I knew she was sitting there in her large pink and blue housedress waiting for me to say

"Africa" because that was the country they said on the commercial, but I wasn't budging. "I don't know," I said. "Anywhere, I guess."

"You sure don't know a lot for someone who knew *so much* a minute ago."

"It was three minutes ago, and I saw it on a commercial."

"Humph." She thumped the grits and gravy into a bowl with an eyebrow arched so high it touched her headband. "I thought so."

Sidetracked with guilt earlier I had to wait until everyone fell asleep to order my kit. I planned to save someone from starving to death while I was at it.

Stan couldn't understand it. "You wanna do what?"

"Sponsor a child."

"Why?"

"Because they don't have any food."

After thinking about this for a long time he finally said absolutely nothing and went back to prying Spam from the can with a butter knife.

It was clear I was going to have to busy myself until everyone in the house went to sleep. No easy task. No one ever put on pajamas to wind down for bed in my house. As far as I could tell, no one even thought about it. We just fell asleep wherever we were and woke whenever we weren't tired anymore, usually wearing the same clothes from the day before. Tonight, though, Stan listened to the radio *forever.* I skulked around the house half a dozen times, spying on him from every room until my grandmother caught me.

"What are you doing out there, Cotton?"

The sound of her voice was very unexpected.

"Nothing," was the only thing I could come up with on the spot.

"*That's a first,*" she said from the dark confines of the leopard-print room where she slept.

"I'm bored," I blurted out, as if that would make everyone go to sleep faster.

I expected her to say, "So what?" but instead she told me to go upstairs and watch *Fantasy Island* until I fell asleep.

"Really?"

"Really," she said.

On the way upstairs I stopped off in Stan's room, "Whatcha doing?"

Looking up from his world history book, he shifted around and said, "Nothing."

"Are you going to bed?"

"Yeah."

"When?"

"Sometime."

*Well, that's specific.* "Can you go to bed now?"

"Nope. Not sleepy."

For some reason I thought I'd stand around willing him to yawn until all of my questioning aroused my grandmother.

"Leave your uncle alone."

"But—"

"But nothing." An exasperated sigh filled up the hall. "I'm old. Let me get some sleep."

Fine. One down. One to go. I thundered up the stairs. The television was back in its respective place, giving me a sly grin. Without hesitation, I turned it on, adjusted the knob until I found the island where fantasies come true and scampered over to drag the phone into the room.

I left the door open so I could see down into the stairwell in case someone turned the kitchen light on.

"Specialty Kits," a woman's voice chimed.

"Hi," I said, barely above a whisper.

"Hi," she whispered back.

"I'd like to order the Trash to Treasures kit."

"I can barely hear you," she said.

Clearing my throat and sitting up straight I deepened my voice. "I'd like to order the Trash to Treasures kit."

"Certainly," she chirped. "Let's start with your information."

When I was three years old, I was required to memorize my grandmother's address, phone number, and all other pertinent information in case I was kidnapped to be sold into slave labor camps or lost in a horrible disaster or in case my mother was arrested.

"And how would you like to pay today?"

"COD," I said, clearly, precisely, confidently.

"Certainly."

When you're six years old, six to eight weeks is a small portion of eternity. The next weekend I paced restlessly, waiting for the postman. By the third weekend I had become the poster child for obsessive compulsive.

Peering through the front door, I turned and yelled over my shoulder, "Has anyone seen the mailman?"

"It was a mail lady yesterday," Stan yelled from the kitchen.

My eyes rolled back into my head, "Okay, has anyone seen the *mail lady?*"

"Don't reckon."

My shoulders jerked and my feet ticked, tapped and shifted in frustration. My left eye started twitching. A low squeal moved through my lungs. By lunchtime I was impossible. The mail lady dropped envelopes into the box but no COD. Tomorrow was Sunday, which meant no mail, and I was sure I'd explode. There was hope. The kit could arrive on Monday, and I'd be called from class to leave school early to seize my treasure.

That was something, regardless of how far-fetched.

No such luck. At the end of the school day on Monday I thought I was going to spontaneously explode. A wild fit of anticipation seized me, and I huffed loudly, right in the middle of math.

After the last bell I was called to my teacher's desk. "Cotton, are you alright?"

"Never better," I said, too flip to be taken seriously.

"Hmmmm." She tapped her pen against her porcelain cherry red apple. "You seem to be having trouble concentrating."

I sighed, too depressed to respond.

"Is everything all right at home?"

She wasn't going to let me go without a fight, so I gave in. I nodded with such insincerity I actually felt guilty. She let me go. Dave was waiting out front in the car. I burst into tears, and he bought me an ice cream cone.

Exactly five weeks and seven days from the date of purchase the mail lady knocked on the door holding an enormous package. My grandmother was in the hall sitting on the gossip bench, talking to her friend from way back when she had a job.

I heard her cryptically announce, "Let me call you back. Someone's at the door."

When she walked into the living room, I was on my knees, pressed deep into the back of the couch, staring outside, trembling with excitement.

Her eyebrow raised in a question mark. "Do you know anything about this?"

The mail lady announced through the screen door, "I have a COD package for Sara Moore."

That really got her attention. Especially the amount. I wasn't sure she'd cough up the money, so I played dumb.

"That's so interesting." My grandmother reached for her eyeglasses and pocketbook at the same time. "I wonder what I could have possibly ordered that I don't remember buying in the first place that costs so much."

The mail lady shrugged, waiting for the money to be counted into the palm of her hand.

By then, Stan's curiosity was aroused. "What's going on?" He shuffled in, scratching his big belly that didn't fit under his shrunken t-shirt.

Granny gave me the eye. "It seems little Miss 1-800 over here has been ordering merchandise COD again."

Stan turned to me, "So, what's in the box?"

Deciding to give up the charade early on, I said, "It might be my new Trash to Treasures kit."

With the money counted out and the mail lady gone, my grandmother held the box for ransom. "And what kind of kit would that be?"

"You make stuff with it."

That eyebrow shot up again. "Really?"

"Swear." I crossed my heart.

After sawing through the packing tape with a butter knife, I pulled back the cardboard flaps to reveal an impressive array of colored tissue paper, sheets of gold and silver, ribbons in green, yellow, apple red, ocean blue and every other color imaginable, big buttons, little buttons, square buttons, glitter of every color, pink shiny tinsel, bottles of paint and brushes, glue, and plastic scissors.

My grandmother studied the contents, quietly unraveling a rainbow-colored bundle of yarn. She hoisted herself off the sofa, tossing the yarn back in the box.

"This just might be the thing to keep a mischievous little girl like you out of trouble." Then, she went off to her room to balance her checkbook.

I quickly enlisted the services of Stan since he'd been unemployed his entire life. It became his job, his *mission*, to find every battered, old, empty, useless, rusted, discarded, worthless thing in the house that could be transformed into treasure. It was my job to unpack the box and spread the contents across the kitchen table.

Stan found glass jars under the porch collecting rainwater and dead bugs. From where I was standing, I could see him out there, as slow as Christmas, searching with unflinching dillydallying. Because I needed trash before the end of the century I set off to the basement, sneaking down each step carefully, to find a rusted coffee can full of old keys. I kept up the search, looking in every corner and every box but for a house I perceived as being so full of junk, we sure didn't have enough of it.

When Stan returned empty-handed from his mission to the upstairs closet, I knew we had to resort to drastic measures.

"Do you think we should go through the trash?"

"Trash man came yesterday." Stan hitched up his pants, exhausted.

"Well, then, what are we going to do?" This wasn't supposed to be a long, drawn-out process where I create new treasures over a series of weeks. I wanted treasure now.

"We got them old pickle jars in the icebox." Stan pointed. "You could put them pickles in a bowl and wash out the jars."

Digging through the refrigerator did not make the light bulb click on in my head. Stan announcing his decision to have Ovaltine and milk caused the heavens to open up and angels to sing. Lumbering over to the cabinet, he opened the big double doors, and sparkles dropped from the sky. Row after row of canned peas and hominy cried out to me. Tiny jars filled with pimentos begged to become paperclip holders. Large cans of whole tomatoes I'd never seen anyone eat longed to be glitzy planters for paper flowers I was about to make with my eager little hands. Cans of boiled new potatoes yearned to see the light of day. Peaches did flips in heavy syrup, crying out to be released.

Stan was oblivious. He unscrewed the jar of Ovaltine and dumped a considerable amount into a plastic tumbler. I generously opened the refrigerator again, pulling out the gallon of milk, passing it over. He was right. The pickles were a sad sight. Four bread and-butter slices floated aimlessly in a cloudy green liquid that poured easily down the drain. Stan slurped his beverage, regaining energy expended walking the length of the backyard.

I returned to the fridge. Old grape jelly looked in need of a proper burial. A can of what might have been baked beans was now green and furry. Gosh, I thought to myself, this thing needs to be cleaned *bad*.

I dragged the trash can over to Stan, gave him a big plastic spoon, and put him in charge of dumping. I was in charge of washing and drying. Stan glopped all of the furry, gross old stuff into the trash as I removed the labels from all potential treasure. Each piece of trash lay upside down on a stack of paper towels, waiting to be transformed. I sat down to have a bowl of strawberry ice cream and read the manual. Stan announced he was going to take a nap. A prime opportunity dawned. I opened all of the cans in the pantry and put the food in bowls, stacking them precariously on shelves in the refrigerator.

Someone had to open the cans eventually. Might as well be me. It was the perfect plan. We'd have to live off of peaches and green beans and send Stan out for fried chicken. We'd spend less time cooking and more time making treasure.

I'd never longed for an electric can opener so bad in all my life.

With everyone in the house asleep, I commenced to painting first. Blue can. Green can. Red can with orange swirls. Yellow can with feathered green fringe. White can with big black polka dots. Then came ribbons and buttons in the shape of a smile, and *voila*. After only forty minutes I had a bona fide toothbrush holder and a small jelly jar converted to a decorative vase with dried flowers sprouting out of the top like pigtails.

Since Stan had no teeth and my grandmother only had false teeth, the toothbrush holder was mine. The pencil holder, which I was currently working on, with yellow ticking and pink feathers from a bird of paradise's butt, was to go on the gossip bench.

And the vase—well, it was very special.

"What do I do with it?" Stan asked, rubbing his eyes, yawning.

"You put it on your bedside table, dummy."

Holding it up to the light, he looked confused. "For what?"

"To look at. It's decorative," I explained, recalling the exact word they used in the manual. "You obviously don't know treasure," I said, matter of fact.

It was getting late, and I was hungry, so I finished the flowerpots and pasta holders and soap dishes while eating a liverwurst sandwich. Then my second wind kicked in and I kept going. Twilight closed in. I heard my grandmother stirring in the other room. Pretty soon she was standing in the doorway, sleepy-eyed, trying to get used to the light. Feeling her way over to the percolator she started a pot of coffee. Within moments a rich aroma filled the air. Taking a break I leaned back in my chair, waiting for my juice glass full of caffeine and sugar. The elixir of awake.

It took a minute but finally my grandmother scanned the table with her eyes. "You've been busy," she said.

I nodded, very pleased with myself.

Carefully choosing a piece of treasure, she held it up to the light, squinting, "What's this?"

"Pasta container."

"Hmmm... and this?"

"Flowerpot."

"And this?"

"Candle holder."

"Interesting... and this?"

"Decorative sugar bowl."

"Hmmm," she said.

We sipped our fresh hot coffee in silence, admiring my cache of priceless creations.

She chose another item. "What's this?"

"Decorative holder for your false teeth."

"Oh." She raised an eyebrow of interest. "I should have guessed that, shouldn't I?"

I nodded, beaming.

Stan walked into the kitchen but had a funny look on his face and left.

"What's this?" she asked.

"Utensil holder."

"That will come in handy."

I couldn't tell if she was joking. We didn't have any utensils. Stan cooked everything with a fork. It wasn't until she stood up to open the refrigerator door that it occurred to me, I'd opened an awful lot of cans. My palms started sweating. Instead of going for the fridge she veered off to the cupboard to get the Ovaltine, which, thankfully, I'd left untouched. My eyes were glued to her every move. By the time she put the Ovaltine on the table, my armpits were damp.

Then she opened the refrigerator in one swift movement. Clutching the door handle she stared inside, then reached for the gallon of milk. She pulled the milk out and closed the door. *Whew.* After putting the gallon on the table, she turned and opened the fridge again.

*Crap.*

Her eyes travelled over shelves of food stacked in bowls and plates. Coffee mugs full of baked beans, tumblers stuffed with sliced carrots, plastic baggies sitting upright globbed full of corned beef hash, a Bundt cake pan full of peaches floating in syrup, and exactly six glasses of English peas.

It hadn't seemed like much when Stan and I opened cans faster than I could clean them.

"That is very interesting." My grandmother closed the door and walked back to the cupboard. She opened the double doors, this time really looking. The cupboard was bare.

For several minutes her eyes followed along the dusty shelves lined with old, sticky paper peeling up around the edges. Rogue cans of mushrooms and cake pans full of pennies my grandmother collected stood next to industrial-sized cans of pinto beans and tomato sauce too big to lift so I'd left them in the bottom and taken everything else except dust and mouse turds.

Stan hid in his room waiting to see if the shiz was going to hit the fan. *Traitor.*

I was sure I was in serious trouble.

Then she took the white bread, mayo, and liverwurst from the refrigerator. When she sat down at the table to make a sandwich, she said, "When I was a young woman it was during the Depression. Do you know what that is?"

"Back when everyone was depressed because they had no money," I said.

She laughed. It had been a long time since I'd seen her laugh, and it felt good. "Something like that," she said. "There weren't any jobs or money, and we had barely enough to live on."

I drank my coffee, paid attention, and kept my mouth shut, hoping my armpits would dry out. Stan wandered over to the doorway, snarfing down a candy bar. Neither one of us could predict the outcome of my brilliant idea.

"We didn't have any extra money," she continued, "so at night I'd walk over to the rich neighborhoods and go through the trash. People who had money threw out all kinds of good things. I'd find pieces of furniture, glassware, and piles of clothes. God, they threw away some of the most beautiful clothes. I'd find so much that I couldn't carry it all so I asked my brother if I could use his wagon."

I stole a piece of liverwurst from her plate. "Why didn't you just drive the car."

"I've never driven a car in my life," she said.

Come to think of it, I'd never seen her drive anywhere.

"Anyway," she went on, "I'd walk across town pulling that wagon and fill it up with clothes. Then, I'd take them home and cut the bodice from one and the skirt from another and I'd spend all night making dresses for myself."

I liked the story but wasn't sure if the moral was that bad little girls get in big trouble. "Why didn't you just wear the dresses as they were?" I asked.

"Because then I'd be wearing some old dress I found in the trash. By taking them apart I made my own dresses, and I could wear them with pride."

I'd never heard the story before, and I thought my grandmother was the coolest person in the world for wanting to be beautiful when everyone else was depressed.

She stood up and said, "Put your coat on."

Curiosity was killing me. "Do you like my treasures?"

"I like them very much." She guided me to the door. "Now, put your coat on. We're going to get some fried chicken to go with those six cans of English peas you just opened."

# CHAPTER EIGHT

## *Jeever*

Rumor had it Stan was pretty weird before his all-inclusive vacation to the state mental institution in Bolivar, Tennessee. Cooperation was not his finest quality. He refused to wear a watch, went to bed when he wanted, ate when he pleased, had no master plan and never taped up little notes to remind himself of all the important things he had to do. To top it off, he hated to clean. In fact, I'd never, in all my years of being alive, seen him clean anything.

Every Sunday at 5 PM we all clambered into the rusted Oldsmobile to drive to Dr. Jeever's house. Dr. Jeever was the name of the man who sent *the voices* to torment Stan. Jeever lived in the Chickasaw Gardens district. Every Sunday we'd drive past the same house, where Stan would point and say, emphatically, "That's where he lives. In there. *He's in there.*"

Most of the time the ordeal ended, and we drove away none the wiser. But sometimes a coldness flickered in Stan's eyes so foreign and eerie it made me sit back against the seat, quiet, hoping Jeever didn't send any voices while we were out front. Then, with a forceful jerk, Stan would throw the car in park and open the door to get out, chilling me to the bone.

"I'm gonna go and get him for what he does to me," Stan said, one foot on the pavement, the other ready to follow.

By the looks of it, he meant it.

My grandmother was on him quick, "I don't think that's such a good idea." She reached for his arm.

Stan pulled away but she got a hold of his sleeve.

His eyes glazed over, pulling on the door handle, "I can't take it anymore, Mother."

"I know," she whispered, like it was a secret.

"I can't take it anymore." He shot me a look in the rearview mirror. "I can't take it anymore. I can't take the voices anymore."

"I know," she said.

*We all knew.*

"It torments my brain . . . *torments . . . torments . . . torments . . . ,*" he chanted, door handle clutched firmly in his hand. With the other hand he started to pound on the steering wheel. *Torments, torments, torments.* He picked up pace, adding pressure.

*Torments. Torments. Torments.*

My grandmother held tight. "Why don't we go get some ice cream at the Polar Bear and stop thinking about this?"

Stan squeezed the door handle again. "Dr. Jeever," he wailed, like a cat when you step on its tail. He clutched his head, trying to contain his throbbing brain, and lurched forward in the seat, banging against the steering wheel. *"He torments me, and you let him do it, Mother . . . oh, jesus god help me . . . make him stop . . . make him stop tormenting me."* In the middle of his merciful plea, he pounded on the steering wheel with the heal of his palms. A slow, deep chant of eternal damnation whimpered, soft and steady, in his throat.

I picked lint off of my purple velvet jumper and tried to think of a joke, but my mind went blank. I bit my lip, praying he didn't jump out of the car and run across the lawn and kill some poor, unsuspecting, person who happened to be living in Dr. Jeever's house. I was so used to it by then that all I really wanted to do was leave.

"No," he thundered, the muscles in his neck twitching.

"Listen," my grandmother offered softly. "Let's get some ice cream, and I'll talk to Jeever for you."

Stan fell quiet, staring straight ahead. If I moved just enough to the left, I could see him in the rearview mirror. I could tell he was thinking about making a run for it.

"Oh, god," he wailed. *"Oh, Mother, he torments me to death day and night, day and night, day and night. It hurts so bad."*

"I know." She patted his hand, steady and firm. "We'll get him to stop, won't we, Cotton?"

*Huh?*

"He won't." Stan slumped back in his seat. "He'll torment me forever."

Well, so much for positive thinking.

Jeever must have been a piece of work, and I'm not talking about the poor yutz that actually lived in the house. No one in my family actually knew who lived inside. Finally, Stan decided not to kick the front door in and make Jeever pay for all of those collect calls in his head. He started the car and drove back across town, where he locked himself in his room, clutching his skull, pleading with Jeever to leave him alone.

My grandmother went in the kitchen to start the percolator.

"Does anyone actually live there?" I asked.

"I don't know." She pulled the lid off of the coffee can, filling the air with its scent.

I pulled up a chair. "Does *anyone* know who lives there?"

She dropped a scoop of fresh grinds into the metal basket. "I don't personally know who lives there, and I suspect no one else in this house does either."

"So why that house?"

"I don't know," she grunted, pulling a fresh five-pound bag of sugar from a shelf.

"Is it possible that someone named Jeever might live there?"

Now she looked at me. "Why?"

"I don't know." I dangled my shoes from my toes, wondering about the place where a man like Jeever must live. A man who spends his days tormenting the likes of Stan. "Because don't you think it's strange that we drive across town every week and we don't even know who lives there? We never get out of the car or talk to anyone. We just sit out front. I mean, who is Jeever anyway? Was there a Jeever at the hospital?"

I could tell she was thinking about her answer. Without saying anything, she walked to the sink and washed two coffee cups. When the cups were clean, she turned. "There's no record of a Jeever. I checked. But it could have been an orderly, maybe even another patient or someone he had contact with. I don't know." She shook her head. "There was no Jeever before I took him to that stupid hospital. I shouldn't have taken him. There was nothing wrong with him. He was just quiet, different, but he wasn't going to hurt anyone." Her voice trailed off into the *blurp blurp* sounds of the percolator. The smell of coffee filled the room.

"Why doesn't one of us just walk up to the house, knock on the door and ask if Jeever lives there?"

"No."

"No? Why not?"

Setting a cup down in front of me, she opened her mouth to say something, then closed it, took the milk out of the refrigerator, and said, "Because if there is a Jeever, then I don't ever want to meet him, and if he doesn't live there then I don't want to know. I just want to let it be what it is. I think Stan needs Jeever to stay right there so he can keep an eye on him."

There was a pause. A second later Stan walked into the room and asked for his Thorazine. Unlike crazy Thurman, who rampaged even if you shot him with tranquilizer darts, Stan usually slept on his medication.

I drank my creamy milk and coffee but still managed to fall asleep. When I woke up in the dark room, my grandmother was sleeping next to me. I could smell her hair. In the eerie silence I heard her breath mingle with the sounds of streetlights buzzing outside. The sky was black. I could smell the dew. Dawn was approaching.

Stan's door was open, and a soft light tumbled into the hall. Sliding carefully down over the edge, I climbed out of bed and shuffled toward the light, rubbing my sleepy eyes.

Stan laid across his bed, staring down at a red high school banner that said ROSELL HIGH in big white letters. A spam-and-mustard sandwich sat on his mattress, precariously close to the edge.

"What's that?" I asked, pointing to the banner.

"From my school," he said, reaching for his sandwich.

I couldn't imagine Stan anywhere outside of this house for more than an hour.

"Well, what do you do with it?"

"Hang it on the wall," he said.

The idea of Stan carrying a lunchbox was very curious to me. "Did you like school?"

"I reckon," he said, mashing Spam in between bread slices.

"You reckon?"

"I guess." He shrugged.

"What did you do?" I asked, sliding closer, nosey.

"Sat at my desk. Answered a lot of questions, mostly."

"I just started first grade," I blurted out, excited and afraid.

"I know," he answered. "Mother told me."

For some reason Jeever was bothering him more than usual, and he asked me to leave him alone. I shuffled back down the hall as the sun came up and went back to sleep. Hours later I woke to a commotion. From the middle of the bed I could hear my grandmother out in the hallway, hissing at Stan in a low whisper.

"You have really gone and done it this time," she said. Disappointment dripped from every word.

I peered around the corner and saw Stan's head hanging low, his eyes tracing the scuff marks on his tennis shoes. "Dr. Jeever told me to do it."

"Well then you'd better get Jeever's ass over here to help you get out of this mess." She jammed her finger into his chest.

My grandmother pointed at the baseball bat in the corner of the living room and said, "What in the hell would make you smash the neighbor's car window out?"

What seemed like a good idea turned out to be another one of Jeever's famous tricks. Stan stuck to his story. "He told me to."

"Oh, *Jeever this and Jeever that.* I've had enough of both of you." She threw her hands up in the air.

I still couldn't tell what time it was or how long I'd been asleep or what other good antics I'd missed. Stan was wearing the ugliest brown flannel shirt I'd ever seen. When he turned and caught me spying, I ducked back into the room, suddenly feeling sorry for him. He looked so confused.

My grandmother wasn't in the mood for understanding. Showing no mercy, she pushed big ole Stan into the living room, where she grabbed her pocketbook and pulled out her checkbook. Then a whole new argument ensued. Apparently Jeever had told Stan the neighbor was shooting him in the head with x-ray beams. That's why his head hurt all the time. Since the neighbor caused all this misery, Jeever instructed Stan to pick up the baseball bat no one ever used and walk across the street and smash the neighbor's car window out. Stan listened to Jeever. That was the hard part of being a good paranoid schizophrenic. The trust.

Thurman lumbered into the hall, scratching his butt. "What in the hell is wrong with you people?"

My grandmother pointed an angry finger, "Go back upstairs. Your brother has done a very bad thing."

Still perched on the end of the bed, peeking through the doorway, I wanted to remind everyone that Thurman did bad things all of the time and we ignored them.

"What did this moron do?" Thurman sneered, eyeing Stan from head to toe.

"Apparently Dr. Jeever told Stan to go and bust out the neighbors' car window. Now go on back upstairs."

"Oh, now you've done it," Thurman said, more amused than ever. "That Jeever's done gone and gotten you into a heap of trouble."

Stan just stood there, silent, still staring at his old tennis shoes.

Thurman laughed. "God, you're such a dipshit. When are you going to learn to stop listening to that butthole? All he does is get you in trouble."

Stan finally looked up. We all stared at him, horrified to admit the truth. Thurman was *right*. Jeever always got Stan in trouble.

When my grandmother came back from writing a check for the neighbors' window, she threw the newspaper covered in plastic onto the floor and went to her room, where she dipped snuff and smoked cigarettes for the rest of the day. Because I was bored and Thurman was the only one actually in a good mood, I walked over and grabbed the paper, prepared to be unavailable for the remainder of the afternoon.

After making myself a bowl of cream of wheat that clung desperately to the bottom of the pan in a thick layer of goo, I slid the paper from its plastic tube. Unfolding it across the table I was stricken by the headline. For a long time I stared at the front page, wondering if it was a joke. *A terrible joke.* A cold, clammy feeling moved up my spine, causing a shiver. When I finished reading the article from top to bottom, I realized it was fact, not fiction. Without putting butter or sugar on my lumpy hot cereal, I climbed down from the chair and dragged the front page behind me.

Stan sat on his bed, staring deep into the same book of world history he'd been reading for the past three years. I spread the page out over the bed and watched as his eyes scanned the picture and then the article. Several minutes passed, then he asked, "Is this true?"

I nodded, shrugging my shoulders at the same time. "I don't know. It says it is. I read the whole thing."

He stood up. Rocking back and forth on his heels. "It can't be," he said, finally.

"Turn on the radio."

He nodded, walking over to turn it on. The announcer was in mid-sentence describing the details of the death. Stan and I looked at each other. It was true. The radio announcer played "Imagine." Stan lowered himself onto his bed, tears running down his cheeks.

John Lennon was dead.

Above us only sky.

# CHAPTER NINE

### *The Tiller*

Right after Halloween, crazy Uncle Thurman decided to take up horticulture.

Seemingly out of nowhere, a shiny, brand-new red tiller appeared in the backyard. From the balcony of the upstairs kitchen, I stared down into the yard, suspiciously, wondering what kind of spectacle this was going to turn into. The thought of Thurman digging in the backyard made me nervous.

My grandmother was downstairs frying eggs. Stan signed for the new contraption. The warranty was next to his bowl of grits.

Sipping my creamy, sugary coffee, I found myself musing aloud, "Well, at least someone had the good sense not to buy him a chainsaw." *Heaven help us.* "Thurman is dangerous enough without learning how to operate potentially life-threatening equipment."

"Thank you, Cotton," my grandmother intoned. "That will be enough."

Another woman had been raped at the laundromat. I'd heard it on the radio, and even the bright blue sunny sky couldn't alter my current mood. My suspicions had been raised along with all of the hairs on my neck. Thurman had been sleeping for more than twenty-four hours already. He'd done something. I just knew it. I could feel it in my gut. That fat bastard had walked right out in the middle of the night and done god knows what. Then he'd come home and ordered a piece of equipment to dig graves. *It gave me the shivers.*

The bright-red tiller glimmered in the sunlight like a criminal's smile. The scent of biscuits baking wafted up through the late morning air. I had no idea what the outcome would be. *Disastrous* got my vote. I was sure he wanted to dig up the backyard for a reason, and not a good one.

I snuck upstairs to spy on the Beast.

Thurman' door was closed, and upon closer inspection there seemed to be nothing human moving inside. Lucky for us.

My grandmother had a spatula in her hand as I pittered back into the kitchen, deep in thought.

She cracked another egg into a pool of grease. "Go tell Stan breakfast is ready."

At the top of my lungs, I yelled, "Stan, come eat."

That gnarly, twisted frown was on her face when she turned around, "Cotton, how many times have I told you not to yell like that?"

"More than a million."

"If you're going to be a smartass, then you can go outside."

Stan plodded in wearing his uniform of t-shirt and boxer shorts, both too big in case they shrank. He'd recently devised a new hobby that primarily consisted of wearing his clothes so long they had to be replaced instead of washed. He sat down and started eating in his wordless way.

"Hey, what's that thing out back?" I asked.

Even she didn't believe the words coming out of her mouth. "Thurman wants to plant a garden."

"A garden?" I couldn't help but laugh. "That jackass couldn't plant a kiss on a horse's butt. What's he going to plant? It's November."

"Cotton, it's not nice to make fun of people. *Or to swear.*"

"I'm not making fun of him. I'm serious." She had me on the swearing.

Stan looked up, herding all of his food together with half of a biscuit, that grin stretched across his face.

"Both of you behave. Stan, wipe that smile off of your face. There are plants that grow in winter."

"Oh, you can't be serious. Did he actually say that? 'I want to plant a garden.'"

Stan thought it was pretty funny, too. "Thurman thinks he can grow something."

"Grow a big, hairy turd right out of his butt." I spit out the words in a howl of laughter.

"Alright." My grandmother's hand came down on the table. "Eat your breakfast, and leave your uncle alone," she said firmly. While she never really disciplined me in any way, I occasionally gave in to her authoritarian tone just to make her feel like she was doing her job.

Today was not going to be one of those days.

Stan smiled again, which triggered my giggle box. I couldn't help it. This I had to see. But not right away. Thurman's green thumb wasn't in full bloom yet. He stayed in his room all day listening to Lionel Richie on the record player. *Yeah, he's three times a lady alright.*

Stan and I stood in the backyard, staring at the big metal contraption.

"Needs gas." Stan scratched his armpit, then smelled his fingers.

"How do you know?" I asked, looking around for clues.

Pointing down, he stated the obvious. "It's got a motor."

*Oh, so it has. Sort of like the lawn mower.* I admired the lawn mower. Its miserable existence was mostly spent out in the dark confines of the garage, but the lawn mower did what no mortal had done—it had attacked Thurman repeatedly and lived to tell. Each time funnier than the last. Needless to say, Thurman hated the big, clanking, thundering nemesis.

I looked across the yard to the garage door. My heart tingled with nostalgia for the lawn mower.

The first incident was middle of last summer. Thurman tossed his windbreaker on the ground, then proceeded to attempt to start the lawn mower. In the process, he pulled a muscle in his shoulder, ripped off part of a fingernail, and got a sunburn to top it off. Thurman wasn't going to let up. From what I could tell, neither was the lawn mower. I watched from the back window of the flower-cutting room, squeezed in between the wall and broken refrigerator no one wanted to throw away.

Sweating and swearing was pretty much all Thurman did out there. He probably had trouble pouring a glass of water, let alone trying to fix a lawn mower. It was a struggle between two opposing forces, and the outcome was a mystery.

It was better than TV. Thurman took the hammer to the lawn mower, although I can't imagine why, and accomplished absolutely nothing. *Big surprise.* Then he kicked it. Then he let out a stream of cuss words that fixed absolutely nothing.

That spectacle needed refreshments. After pouring an ice-cold glass of soda, I returned to my post and continued to keep score. For some reason, the mower decided to start, and the grinding roar caught me off guard. But no one could have been more surprised than Thurman, who, in his simultaneous moment of severe irritation and startled conquest, decided he'd won the battle and jerked that hunk of metal in the direction of the overgrown backyard.

But that wasn't really the end. At least not from where I was standing. In his haste and stupidity, Thurman hadn't bothered to look where he was going and rode right over his windbreaker. I swear I heard that mower laugh above its own roar as it spit the shredded pieces out the back in an act of utter defiance.

For that act of treachery and assault, it spent three weeks in solitary confinement in the back of the garage.

The next time was quick and to the point. Within minutes of being dragged out of the garage, it chewed off a piece of Thurman's hand. Just the fleshy part on the side, but it gnarled off some muscle tissue as well. The blood was incredible and gruesome, running down Thurman's arm as he rushed inside to get his mommy, cussing the bad, bad lawn mower.

For that disaster, we were all hustled into the bowels of the city hospital again, where my grandmother's pharmaceutical-stealing hospital-worker friend found a first-year resident who bandaged Thurman back together (off the record) for two hundred dollars cash.

Thurman was administered first aid, sitting on a crate in the old, abandoned wing of the hospital, while my grandmother and I waited around the corner in the hall. Stan was outside in a parking space, driving the getaway car.

The third time created a brand of hysteria in me the likes of which I'd never known. Weeks and weeks and weeks had passed. The backyard was hideous. Stan hated the lawn mower, flat-out refusing to have anything to do with it.

Thurman dragged that loathsome contraption out again, paranoid, irritable, and then tried to start it. It started right up.

Strange.

Thurman didn't think so. This was war.

Not to me. I was very suspicious. I had visited the lawn mower several times during the weeks of isolation and had seen no signs of surrender. But there Thurman was, outside, mowing away, sweating, swatting, flies, plodding along in his glowing white new tennis shoes with a bandage still wrapped around his hand.

I stayed at the window, watching for a little while, but mowing the lawn isn't really that interesting, and I wandered off.

Until…

Lord have mercy on my soul. I could have married that lawn mower. For reasons we couldn't explain, in ways I can't explain, somehow Thurman burned the entire palm of his hand so bad that a blister formed, swelling with fluid until it rose up four inches.

It was never very clear what had happened out there, but one thing was certain.

We had the greatest lawn mower in the world.

Thurman came in swearing. Slamming doors, dropping ice, swearing some more. When I found him standing at the sink, cold water gushing down over his hand, he screamed, "Mother, could you freaking help me?"

"What happened?" I walked into the kitchen, alarmed.

"I'm burned. Can't you see that?"

If only that lawn mower could have devoured him like a snake devours its prey. Or spit him out in tiny pieces the way it coughed up that windbreaker.

Passing through on my way out to congratulate the winner, I said, "Ooh, Thurman said a bad word."

My grandmother shot me a look.

"Shut up you little cretin," Thurman growled.

"Why? Are you gonna cry?" I mocked him, running off.

I didn't stick around for a reply, but I was pretty sure that made him mad.

We didn't go back to the hospital that time. Thurman got the first-aid kit (treatment administered by my grandmother) and stolen pain killers.

He was out like a light. Snoring, with his hand hanging over the edge of his bed, like a corpse falling out of a coffin, for days.

I figured it was okay. At least in his condition he couldn't kill anyone.

Now we had a newer, shinier piece of equipment, sure to please.

The tiller waited in the backyard for him like a faithful hound.

What an interesting day it was when Thurman finally announced what he was planning on planting out in the backyard.

My grandmother's blood pressure hit the roof.

Weed.

It was the end of the world. Thurman could not be talked out of it.

Weed.

It was the beginning of all things bad.

Weed, glorious weed. *This I had to see.*

# CHAPTER TEN

*Mexico City*

Dave was convinced banks were going to collapse, that money would become obsolete, that only people who possessed gold, gemstones, hash, and marijuana would ever survive. It was weird but it worked for him. Anyway, that's how we ended up in Mexico.

The worst part of any vacation was that I had to spend it with my mother. We packed up the car and drove for an eternity through Texas.

In the backseat, playing with my stuffed animals, I asked, "Where are we?"

Dave glanced up into the rearview mirror. "Texas."

I took a nap. When I woke up in the backseat wondering how many days had passed, I asked again, "Where are we?"

Dave replied, "Texas."

I passed out, drooling on my rabbit and woke with my stomach growling. "Where are we?"

"Texas," Dave said, slumped over the steering wheel like an old bull put out to pasture.

"I'm hungry," I said.

"Well, you'll just have to wait. It's three AM," my mother snapped from the front seat.

Dave bought me dinner at a truck stop.

Dave and my mother took turns driving and sleeping until we rolled into El Paso. It seemed so lonely. The border was quiet. Dust blew across the highway, pushing tumbleweed.

Dave slowed the car down, and the familiar rumble of highway diminished. It was dark and late, virtually no other cars on the road. I sat up in the backseat, clutching my blanket, and I could see a few cars ahead of us stopped at what looked like tollbooths. Men with rifles and uniforms guarded the booths. Something told me we weren't going to just toss a few dimes in and go. Outside, the air was warm and quiet on that long stretch of terrain, and whether real or imaginary, the sense of crossing over into an unknown place shimmied up over my skin until I felt cold and clammy.

A man with a rifle asked a lot of questions, checked the papers for the guard dog, Inca, in the backseat with me, and shone a bright flashlight into my eyes no less than half-a-dozen times. As Dave pulled away, I saw him glance up in the rearview mirror only once, but I turned around backwards in the seat, watching the border of the only country I'd ever known fade into a flat, inky darkness.

"Who was that?" I asked.

"Border patrol," Dave said.

I whispered the name aloud as dusty plains swallowed up our headlights. We sped through the night. In the dark silence I peeled an orange from the snack bag I'd filled up at the last truck stop and fell asleep with the dog snoring next to my head.

Drifting into the lull of the road, I remembered a man back at the border pointing, smiling, saying, "Bueno. Bueno. Si?"

I didn't know what it meant, but I liked the sound of it.

"Bueno," I whispered to the dog, who pricked up an ear and licked my face.

The most embarrassing part of the trip began when we got to Mexico City. It was there my mother and Dave begin to speak what I affectionately called "Stupid Foreigner Spanish." I woke up from my golden sleep to find the dog perched at the car window, tail fur swishing back and forth over my face. Outside the car, Dave attempted the most inane conversation with a Mexican man I've ever heard. "We're trying to findo el hotelo."

The Mexican man stared at him.

"Driving." Dave pantomimed holding a steering wheel. "Um...do you speaka English?"

"No hablo ingles." The man shook his head, trying to get away.

Doing his best impersonation of Marcel Marceau, looking out across the great divine space of Mexico City for our hotel, Dave said, "We're looking."

It was so embarrassing, *and* I had to pee. I wanted to tap on the glass and yell to Dave, *"Bathroomo retardo."*

Dave was still outside the car pursuing his dream of becoming a street mime when the Mexican man just nodded at him and walked away. I wondered how to say "freak" in Spanish.

Stopping the next woman he passed, Dave desperately blurted out, "Do you speak English?"

She shook her head, moving back into the flow of pedestrians. Buses belched exhaust and cars bleeped like steel insects on the street. From what I gathered in my hungry, sleepy, perch in the backseat, apparently no one in our car had given any thought to the fact that everything in Mexico was probably written in *Spanish*. I wanted to get out of the car and slap Dave, but I was too short. Besides, I had to pee.

Though my years on Earth were still in single digits, I understood that Dave spoke the worst Spanish anyone had ever heard. Comprenda? Un minuto while I checka mia translation bookletta. Mexicans must have one hell of a sense of humor. I bet they made jokes about how living too close to the border lowered their IQ.

It was almost noon, from what I could tell. The sun blazed over the top of the car. Dave looked like he was hallucinating, slowly coming apart at the seams. I hadn't seen him shower in days. In a huff, my mother got out of the car and slammed the door. Me and the dog turned our attention. Wearing a dance leotard and a wraparound skirt that looked ridiculous but, hey, what the hell, in her big cork platform shoes she clomped over to the first man she saw and asked, "Hotel Zocalo?"

*Okay*, it could have been a declarative statement.

The Mexican man impatiently looked to the stoplight, waiting to cross.

"Zo-cal-o," she repeated, definitely declarative.

In seconds, the man's face lit up like a carnival. "Hotel Zocalo?" He beamed.

"Yes. Yes." My mother bobbed her head up and down. "Si. Si."

"¿Dónde está la Zocalo?" he asked, watching her reaction.

She nodded too fast to stop. I could tell she had no idea what he was saying. I didn't care. Maybe he'd feel sorry for us and lead us to our hotel, where we could shower, eat, and stop making fools of ourselves.

He pointed. Then he counted streets on his fingers. *Uno. Dos. Tres.* Then this way he motioned with his right hand, then straight ahead, he motioned with his left, then go this way.

Dave stared at the man like he was from Mars. I was sure Dave would faint any second.

"Si. Si." The man said good-naturedly, then walked off, commending himself on his good deed.

All I knew was that for two people who had no idea what the other was saying, he guided us straight to the hotel. Hand gestures really do work. Universal language in action.

Before he filled out a single piece of check-in paperwork, Dave bought an English-to-Spanish dictionary from the gift shop in the lobby while I stood next to him doing the pee-pee dance. I had never seen Dave so unprepared and uncool. Granted, I wasn't that old. There was still time for him to really make a fool of himself. Eyes squinted, searching column after column of English words, he flipped page after page until he finally looked directly into the face of a passing porter and inquired, "De baño?"

"Si." The porter pointed down the hall.

"That way," Dave said to me.

I broke into a full-throttle run. My patent leather shoes clacked frantically against the tile. The universal gender signs of woman with dress and man with no dress were glued to doors directly opposite each other. I chose the one with a dress, ran into a stall, hoisted my own skirt, and peed half my weight. When no one came to get me, I dawdled a little, checking out the differences between where I came from and Mexico. Not much that I could see. Pretty standard stuff. Toilet, stalls, mirrors, and sinks. There were soaps wrapped in paper. Each one honeysuckle or rose, so I helped myself to a few, stashing my loot in my pink fuzzy purse.

Back in the lobby, a very distinguished member of the hotel, wearing an impeccable navy pinstriped suit, explained to Dave he had to park in the underground parking garage because there was twenty-four-hour security. His English was excellent, clear, almost British, and his nails were perfectly manicured. I was so sleepy I saw three of everything, including him.

Fifteen minutes later Inca trotted through the lobby at Dave's side. I waited by the elevators with my mother, who'd left her sense of humor in Arkansas.

Dave had the dog leash in one hand and a suitcase in the other. Behind him, a small Mexican man in a bellboy suit rolled the rest of our luggage on a cart. Dave's eyes were stretched so thin at the edges I wondered if he was going to collapse.

The bellboy jammed his finger into the call button for the elevator, keeping a strict eye on Inca, who hitched up his hind leg and peed on the potted plants positioned between the doors. Dave rolled his eyes. The bellboy pointed, clicking his tongue against the roof of his mouth. Suddenly the green arrow flashed and dinged. A wave of relief passed as the doors opened like a great big yawn. We all filed in behind the big luggage cart. Everyone except Inca. The bellboy pressed the "hold" button and smiled politely.

"Come on." Dave pulled the leash.

Inca reared his head back, tracing his eyes up and around the edges of the metal door.

"Come on," Dave repeated, slower, more like a growl.

"Come on, Inca." I clapped my hands together, trying to get him to play along.

"Oh, lord have mercy" Dave exhaled, stepping out of the elevator. "You are the worst guard dog in the world."

Inca wagged his tail, happy to be acknowledged. Dave grabbed his collar, pulling him towards the opening. Digging his toenails deep into the tile, Inca threw all of his weight back on his hind legs.

"Get in the elevator," Dave groaned.

Prisoner to exhausted anger, Dave marched around to the back of the dog and began to push. Inca mysteriously turned his body into a block of immovable stone. Determined to get the big block of stubborn fur into the elevator, Dave wedged himself behind the dog and began pushing. Inca didn't slide an inch. Red-faced and annoyed, Dave kept pushing, hands digging into flesh and fur. I glanced out at the lobby and realized we'd begun to draw attention to ourselves.

Lines of extreme agitation popped out on Dave's forehead as the rest of us watched him push against a force that simply would not move. Just as the curse words began, Inca stood up, completely unperturbed, and walked away. Dave lost his balance and fell to his knees like he was praying to an elevator full of people wondering why he couldn't get that stupid dog to obey. Inca did not walk into the elevator but instead walked into the middle of the lobby, hitched up his tail, and shit on the floor.

Right in front of everyone.

I thought Dave was going to explode. This time the Bellboy rolled his eyes and let go of the "hold" button. There was no way he was cleaning up dog poo. The last thing I saw was Dave grabbing the dog by the collar, yelling, "We'll take the stairs."

*I bet you will.*

Fourteen floors up, the bellboy opened the door to our room, handing the key to my mother. Hungry, disoriented, and riddled with nerves, I collapsed on a queen-sized bed. My mother pulled out a bottle of Valium and swallowed three.

I lifted my head. "Can I have one?"

She eyed me, then said, "Yeah, you can have one, but you have to swallow it dry. Don't drink the water out of the faucet."

I worked up a mouthful of spit and took my Valium like a good girl.

The last thing I remember was my head falling back into the pillow. I woke much later to the black haze of night held back by a skinny stream of bathroom light. Rising up on my arms, I saw everyone was gone except for Inca, who was miraculously in one piece, perched close to my head, licking his feet. Someone had thrown a blanket over me, and I loved the cool feeling of a freshly washed pillowcase against my cheek. Luggage was stacked up on the dresser, and a carry-on spewed its contents across the other bed.

Standing up to stretch, the twinkle of lights cascaded over Mexico City in all directions. It was very different from the dark woods of Mississippi. I counted sheep in Spanish to celebrate this new world and fell asleep with the smell of wet dog fur hovering around my nose. I only knew how to count to three: *uno, dos, tres.*

The next morning, I awoke to the sound of Dave's electric razor buzzing in the bathroom. For someone who barely spoke a lick of Spanish he would not be deterred. Before we left for breakfast, he took Inca down for a walk. Fourteen floors down and fourteen floors up. When he returned, his armpits were damp with dark stains marring his perfect cashmere sweater. Sweat gleamed on his forehead, trapped in his brow.

Inca was very pleased, wagging his tail, ready to go back to sleep.

"Where did you guys go last night?"

My mother looked over. "Why? Did you talk to anyone?"

"No."

"Then don't worry about it."

For the first time in my life I had tortillas for breakfast. Under the canopy of an outdoor café I ate tomatoes, onions, warm tortillas, eggs, ham, beans. The coffee was rich and black, and it wafted through the open windows until I could smell nothing else. I begged openly for a cup with thick cream and sugar. My mother told me no. When she went to the bathroom, Dave gave me the rest of his. It was delicious.

A big pile of steaming dog poo greeted us when we got back to our hotel room. The veins on Dave's forehead exploded. The smell was noxious. Inca had dropped a load in the middle of the floor and passed out on the bed. Dave tried to pry a window open. It wouldn't budge. Inca lifted his head, wagging his tail. For some reason that really irked Dave. Pointing his finger at the dog, he yelled, "How many times have I walked you up and down those stairs because you're too afraid to go in the elevator? You *butthole.*"

Inca didn't seem to mind.

Dave used an entire roll of toilet paper to clean up the pile. Afterward, he turned the fan in the bathroom on, sprayed air freshener kept on hand to dismantle marijuana smoke, and we left again even though we didn't have anywhere to go. For an hour we sat in the hotel lounge while Dave drank tequila and lime, occasionally swearing under his breath at the dog. When sufficient time for the room to air out had passed, we trekked back to the elevators.

The first thing I noticed when we opened the door was that Inca had dragged his plastic dog dish into the middle of the floor and shredded it into a thousand pieces. The second thing I noticed was that it still smelled like poo. Minty poo.

"Just open the door and get some air in here." My mother flopped down on the edge of the bed.

Dave turned. "We could be robbed," he said through clenched teeth.

"I thought we brought the dog to protect us."

Everyone looked over at Inca sitting proudly in an overstuffed chair.

Over the course of the next few days hundred-dollar bills become my babysitter. Dave handed them out like candy to off-duty housekeepers who wanted to make a little cash. As it turned out, all of them wanted to make a little cash. A twenty-four-hour babysitting posse followed me everywhere, smiling, pointing, giving me full glasses of soda whenever I asked. None of them spoke English. Translation: I ran wild.

My favorite sitter was Maria, a lovely Mexican woman who let me do anything as long as I stayed right by her side. I watched television, ate cookies, drank glasses of soda filled to the brim with sweet carbonated, icy fizz. She helped me make a tray out of a cardboard box to eat my dinner on. When I spilled a new soda smack dab in the middle of my bed, she took my hand, and descended with me into the bowels of the hotel for clean linens.

Down in the basement everyone knew Maria. She was a celebrity there. Holding her hand tight I followed her as she wound through a steamy, warm laundry room, where she grabbed a stack of fresh linens, pillowcases, and blankets. She never yelled at me or jerked me up by my hair or slapped me for spilling a soda. She spoke to me in smiles. In the elevator, on the way up to the room, I decided I loved her.

The elevator music was in Spanish. I was beginning to love not knowing what everyone was saying. I was beginning to love not having to analyze every word coming out of the mouths of strangers. I was able to move freely through the labyrinth of my own mind without interruption. The *ding* was universal. The smile was universal. The doors opened. I imagined that when I was old enough to vote and drive, I would move back to Mexico City. I would live in that country filled with millions of people. Someone would teach me the language. I would never have to go back to Mississippi again.

Maria took my hand, leading me back down the hall to our room. Once inside she stripped the bed sheets, laying a towel over the wet soda spot. In my excitement I jumped up on the other bed, telling her in great detail how I would stay here and live with her, and she would smile at me every day. I told her that I would call my grandmother collect and that she would send us money. I told her, nearly breathless, how we could go to the market and shop and hold hands. She laughed and smiled, holding her arms out to dance with me on the bed. I jumped straight into the air, holding tight to her hands, and we both let out whoops of laughter. While she spread the clean sheets on my bed, I told her we could drink coffee in the afternoons and listen to records on my portable record player. She smiled so warm and bright and true that in my ecstatic delight I passed out in my clothes, and when I woke in the middle of the night Maria was gone. Dave was across from me, snoring. I laid my hand against the sheet, feeling the towel underneath.

The next morning, I set about worrying the crap out of Dave to have her baby sit me again. "Pleeeeeeeeeeeeeeeeeeeeease," I whined all of the way through shaving. Then I offered to help him walk Inca so I could drive him crazy fourteen floors down and fourteen floors up. "Pleeeeeeeeeeeeeeeeeease," I howled in the stairwell, listening to my voice fill up the empty space.

Finally, in the lobby, Dave said, "Hold on. I'll see if she's working."

Thrilled to the brim, I clung to Inca's collar, holding him tight. Dave walked to the desk and spoke to the clerk on duty. A second later, he nodded and walked back over to me.

Dave leaned down close and said, "Not today, Cotton. She's off work."

My spirits plummeted. Then rebounded. "I could go to her house."

Dave laughed, snatching the leash of our ornery dog. "We don't know where she lives."

"We could ask the manager."

"No. Your mother will never let you go."

That night Dave and my mother took Inca and the car to "take care of business." My new sitter was nice, but she wasn't Maria. After a plate of burritos and an hour of TV, I fell asleep.

Maria wasn't at work the next day either. That evening Dave packed up the car. I dragged my feet through the lobby, eyes scanning every person and object for a sign of her. Fourteen floors' worth of exercise had tested Dave's patience. He had that look. I decided not to push my luck. Me and Inca climbed into the backseat. The *ding* of the car door reminded me of the elevator, which reminded me of my friend.

In complete silence we drove out of the city, down a dark grove of trees, past a lake with great feathers of moonlight splashed across its surface. The sound of breathing filled the space in the car. My mother was acting quiet, weird. After an hour or so, we left the concrete behind for a gravel road and after that a dirt road that had big ruts. Because I didn't know where we were going and because no one was going to tell me, I looked in all directions for some idea. Up ahead lights danced like fireflies. The closer we got, the more I could make out the shape of a house in the woods. All of the lights were on. As we pulled to a stop Dave turned the headlights off. Directly in front of us the dark outline of a man stood at the screen door holding a gun.

Dave got out of the car. "Wait here."

*No problem.*

Dave walked across the dusty patch of yard to stand at the base of the steps. He said something to the man at the screen door. Then, as if drawn together like magnets, they met in the middle of the porch, shaking hands. It was Pablo. He looked different out there, in the middle of nowhere, away from the sparkle of New York. Wearing a simple pair of pants and a brown shirt, he looked like a farmer.

The two of them returned to our car. Dave opened the back door, holding Inca so I could get out.

Pablo leaned down close and said, "I am waiting to see you again."

I took his hand, stepping out. He made me feel like a princess. Then he mussed up my hair.

Pablo and Dave sat at a wooden table on the porch for a long time, drinking coffee, talking, as men and women from the house took out our entire backseat and replaced the inside with bricks of hash. My mother sat off at the end of the porch, clinging to Inca's collar, gnawing on her fingernails. I watched the men and women, memorizing the shapes of their faces and the colors in their shirts. They had work boots or went barefoot. They had dark skin and shiny hair, and if they moved too far from the light, they looked like shadows. They worked quietly, efficiently, not uttering a single word. Pablo and Dave talked in English, sometimes broken up but clear, keeping their voices lowered.

When our backseat was replaced, Pablo stood up, inspecting the car. "Good," Pablo said.

Dave nodded.

We loaded back into the Hashmobile and drove off. *Goodbye, Maria. Goodbye, Pablo. Goodbye Mexico City.*

Hello, Texas. We drove for days. Back in our old house, we all fell asleep for the better part of the weekend. When we went to visit people, I told them what I'd seen and smelled and tasted. I told everyone about holes in the craggy mountains where women made crosses out of hay and twigs and ribbon that Dave had driven us out to see. I smacked my lips, recalling thick, creamy chocolate in cups with cinnamon on top, the taste of onions, tomatoes, and garlic.

I blabbered incessantly to anyone who would stand still.

Everyone stared at me with a blank expression, and only Stan said, "Yeah, I know what you mean. I like Taco Bell myself."

# CHAPTER ELEVEN

## *Stolen Sears Truck*

We didn't have a house phone. Dave didn't believe in phones. He said it was too easy for people to listen in. He never bothered to explain who might be listening in, and he made me solemnly swear not to tell anyone at school about our personal business. I agreed because I didn't really talk to people at school anyway. Preston Brown was my only friend, and I figured God told him all about my family a long time ago. Preston prayed too much not to get dirt from the Almighty.

Dave sported a tiny black box-like gizmo concealed in his pocket. When the beeper started making noise, Dave got into the Hashmobile and drove to the nearest convenience store. Newfangled late-night stores figured greatly in our lives. Back and forth we drove. No phone to tap, or crazy ringing when you're in the bath, just the constant motion of getting in and out of the car.

The beeper went off at 10:30 PM, when decent people were sleeping. I was in my room with Diggy, pretending to be asleep, when Dave opened my door. Light flooded in from the hall.

"Come on, kiddo. Put your coat on. We gotta go out." Going out was way better than going to sleep.

We drove thirty minutes to a Speedy Stop Spot that closed at midnight. Dave leaned against the phone in his dark sports jacket and trousers, looking cool. My mother sat in the front seat sipping wine from a plastic tumbler.

Dave shook his head, listening, said a few words I couldn't hear. He had that look. I knew it by now. The look that told me we weren't going home right away.

After a few seconds, he hung up and got back into the car. My mom said nothing.

Putting the car in reverse, Dave said, "We have to go into town."

*Hmmm. This could be anything,* I thought. Slinking down in the backseat, I wondered if I was going to be dropped off at my grandmother's house. Sometimes I was just left there with no explanation.

"What's going on?" my mother asked.

Dave pulled onto the highway, accelerating like a bat out of hell.

"Tommy's girlfriend called. He's done something."

"What?"

"She won't say, but she's hysterical and pissed."

"He probably hit her."

Dave shook his head, "No, I asked. He's been pretty mild since she nailed him with that clock radio while he was shaving."

My mother looked wholly unconvinced. This could be bad. From what I gathered, Tommy was, had been, and always would be a bona fide screw-up. I personally had never met him, but occasionally Dave would talk about a job Tommy had done for him.

Dave watched me in the rearview mirror. "You okay back there?"

"Yeah, I've got my bunny."

"Good. Why don't you and that rabbit take a nap."

*Take a nap? Are you kidding?* Take a nap and sleep through whatever that moron has done? *No way. If this is as good as I think it's going to be, I should be back here selling tickets.* I settled in for a long night.

Tommy's girlfriend, Louise, was sitting out front on the steps, chain-smoking, when we pulled into the driveway. Before we even got out of the car, she stomped across the yard in a pair of shorts cut so high it would have made a pope cry, waving a cigarette, swearing like a sailor.

Dave moved fast. Cool and smooth, he wrapped his arm around her waist and leaned in to whisper in her ear like the perfect date, attempting to steer her toward the front door. Louise was having none of that crap.

In the backseat, with the windows rolled up, all I could hear was "Blah, blah, blah—puff, puff, exhale—that fricking . . . blah, blah, blah."

Dave turned on the charm. My mother got out of the car and stood by like a vulture.

"Come on, let's go for a drink somewhere," Dave suggested, pulling Louise closer.

Normally, women didn't resist Dave's even-tempered invitations, but Louise was a force of nature tonight.

"No way. I'm waitin' right here for that low-down sack of shit."

"Shhhh," Dave offered, knowing the entire neighborhood was about to be involved if Louise didn't shut up. "Where is he?"

"How should I know." She waved her long, slender arms in the air, indicating she didn't care if the whole neighborhood showed up. *In fact, invite the city. Call the mayor. Get everyone down here. Turn on the Lynyrd Skynyrd. Fire up the barbecue. We're gonna have a frikkin' party.*

Dave turned so Louise faced him. She grinded up against him, which elicited a dirty look from my mother.

Dave spoke calmly, evenly, while she blew smoke in his face. "Come on. I'll get you a hotel room."

Dave had a rule to never bring crazies home, so we always knew the location of the nearest hotel.

"Nice try, sugar, but I'm going to wait here, and stomp his balls when he gets back. If that spineless piece of shit ever decides to come back."

Dave's patience wore thin. His smiled stretched tight at the corners. Situations like this came with the territory. Hysterical boy/girlfriends could bring down entire empires. Hysterical people with telephones were every drug dealer's worst nightmare. An occupational hazard that had to be dealt with. I'd been paying attention to life in our house. Eavesdropping mostly but keeping notes all the same.

Louise leaned into him like a wily teenage girl on the prowl.

"Do you have anything I can take? My nerves are shot."

Dave removed a prescription bottle from his jacket pocket and popped two Valium in her mouth.

My mom walked across the grass, clearing her throat. "Louise, tell us what's wrong."

*She needs to lay off the cigarettes and the beer,* I thought to myself.

Louise swallowed the pills, washing them down with a swig of warm beer. She took a deep breath, looked at my mother, then back at Dave. Without answering, she glanced over at the car and squinted her eyes, pausing long enough to light another cigarette.

Shielding her eyes from the porch light, she asked, "Is Cotton in there?"

Dave nodded his head.

Louise took a few steps toward the car, staring at me. "Oh, I'm sorry, honey. Did I wake you up?"

"No. It's okay," I yelled back.

Louise motioned for me to get out of the car. Dave watched her every move. After I slammed the door shut, clutching my bunny, she walked over, took my hand, and started walking toward the garage door, saying, "Come on. I've got something to show you. You won't believe this shit."

And you wouldn't have. I'd never seen anything like it. The garage was filled from floor to ceiling, wall to wall, with boxes. *And* the kitchen. *And* the living room. *And* the hall. *And* the bathroom. All of the available space in her house was filled with boxes. New boxes. New boxes that had "television" and "microwave" and "stereo" printed on all sides.

Tommy was in big trouble. Apparently, he'd walked up to the loading dock of a department store and driven away with a semi-truck full of merchandise. Then, because he didn't have a house of his own, he'd unloaded everything at Louise's place. TVs, microwaves, hi-fi stereos, and VCRs filled up empty space like cardboard invaders.

She was justifiably irked,

Dave slipped his hands into his pockets, which meant wheels were spinning in his head.

Louise blabbed on and on like her mouth was connected to a runaway train. Blah, blah, blah, blah. "And if this isn't out of here by tomorrow, then I'm calling the cops."

*Cops.*

The magic word.

"Okay. Be reasonable, Louise," Dave started.

"I am being reasonable," she interrupted waving her cigarette in the air like a nicotine ballerina.

I personally had never found Louise to be reasonable.

Dave surveyed the scene. Mountains of electronics. So many boxes stacked floor to ceiling I couldn't count them.

Finally, Dave asked, "Where's your phone?"

"On the table, next to my bed."

Dave disappeared into a sea of stolen merchandise.

Louise lit another cigarette from the one she'd been smoking and turned to my mother.

"You want a beer?"

"Yes," my mother sighed, resigned to the fact that none of us were going to get any sleep.

Louise took my hand and squeezed softly. "Come on, honey, I got some of them popsicles you like."

Dave always looked cool entering a room. Mostly, because he walked in like he owned it. That's the trick to being cool. Somewhere in your mind you have to believe you own the world. Sniffing cocaine helps to facilitate these types of delusions. Little tidbits about life from my environment.

Louise hoisted herself on top of a box. It was after two AM.

Her Valium would kick in soon. "So?" she asked, sipping her beer.

Dave walked into the kitchen and returned, popping the top on a beer. "I'll have all of this out of here before your neighbors start waking up."

"Good." She hopped down and tried to stand on wobbly, clean-shaven legs. "It's making me claustrophobic."

During times like that I realized why cops hate criminals. It's because criminals are smart (at least the good ones are), and they're forced to respond and act under a tremendous amount of pressure, which sharpens their wits, making them that much more dangerous.

Forty-five minutes later, eight guys showed up with moving trucks and quietly and efficiently backed each one up to the garage. Dave gave instructions. The trucks filled up quickly.

Box after box disappeared from the living room, the bedroom, and the kitchen until there was nothing left except for furniture and a couple hundred bucks Dave left on the table for Louise and her trouble.

A drunken, sedated Louise had passed out in the bedroom a long time ago. She slept through all of it. Dave closed the front door behind us.

Jimmy, Tony, Stevie, Johnny, Billy, Ritchie, Eddie, and Rick stacked every piece in two trucks and drove away just as quietly as they'd come.

The next day, reports of the stolen truck were all over the news. You'd have thought it was the crime of the century. Dumb old Tommy was famous. We had a brand-new microwave. I talked Dave into giving Stan a stereo so he could listen to his radio programs in style.

# CHAPTER TWELVE

## *Beauty Pageants*

When I turned seven, my mother took up a new hobby. I was called into the living room. Bong smoke drifted through the air like the rings of Saturn. It was extremely suspicious.

"Cotton, you're going to be in beauty pageants," my mother announced.

"Huh?"

"Beauty pageants."

"I don't want to do that."

"How do you know you don't want to do it when you've never even tried it?"

*Oh, I don't know. I've got this feeling.*

First came ballet lessons for grace.

"A *what*?"

"A leotard, Cotton. What colors do you want?"

Dave dropped us off at the mall and went to do something infinitely more interesting.

"It's like a giant pair of panties I stretch over my whole body," I said, terrified of the cotton crotch.

"It's what you wear to be a ballerina."

"I thought I was going to be in pageants."

"You are."

I began to map an escape route. I could run.

A saleslady approached. She smiled big and wide.

"Cotton, what do you want?" my mother asked loudly.

"I don't care," I said, completely uninterested.

Big mistake. I ended up with two bags of clothes that made me look like a garden gnome dipped in Pepto-Bismol. I screamed every time my mother tried to make me put them on.

I was promptly enrolled in etiquette and poise lessons. A crusty old lady sat very erect in a chair and stared at me, mentally daring me to misbehave. Her hair was pulled so tight a drill sergeant could have bounced a quarter off of it.

"Yes. Yes. She does have those wild eyes." She sighed to my mother. Then she asked, "Can she sing?"

"Of course."

The two of them spent an hour talking about me like I wasn't in the room.

"Hmmm," Crusty said. "Does she always wear her hair like that?"

Suddenly, everything on my body had to be curled, painted, plucked, scrubbed, or combed. Curling irons, pink hair rollers, eyelash curlers, eyeliner, lip gloss, cuticle cream, pore refiner, powder, and the dreaded pantyhose. The items appeared, stacked precariously on the back of the toilet and edge of the sink. It got worse. I had to get up at the crack of dawn on weekends and miss Saturday morning cartoons.

Then I had to sit in the car with my mother for an hour while we drove to another city where the pageant took place. On the dreaded day of the first pageant, it was dark, and the sun didn't rise. Instead, a gray sky opened up and began to rain. Finally, we turned into the parking lot of what looked like an auditorium. Ten cars clustered together in the mostly empty parking lot. Dreariness made my stomach growl.

The car came to a complete stop, and I reached for the door handle.

"Stop." The sudden sound of my mother's voice made me jump.

Rain pummeled the windshield. I had to sit there for fifteen minutes while she fixed her makeup in the rearview mirror and smoked a joint.

A deep groan rolled my eyes into the back of my head.

"Get over it," she said.

When other cars started pulling into the parking lot, she stubbed her joint out in the ashtray, sprayed a ton of OnJaLee perfume all over her clothes, grabbed her purse and stopped. Thunder boomed. She turned around in the seat, rummaged in the floorboard, then produced a plastic grocery bag. "Here put this over your head so your hair doesn't get wet."

That is how I went to my first beauty pageant.

With a plastic Piggly Wiggly bag on my head.

The only real shred of hope I'd held onto throughout the entire travesty was the potential for glamour. I'd seen a lot of black and white movies and regarded myself as something of an expert on the subject of glamour.

Glamour does not begin with a grocery bag. Joan Crawford does not walk to the top of the staircase with a Piggly Wiggly sack on her head.

I arrived in the front lobby of the auditorium completely water-logged with perfectly dry hair. The building smelled like a basement.

Three women sat at a table.

The one in the middle asked, "Name?"

My mother was really stoned. It took her a minute to figure out what in the world the women were talking about. "Oh," she said finally, glancing around like a room full of people were watching. "Cotton Alexander."

Middle woman referred to a clipboard then flipped through a box and pulled out a large envelope, handing it over. "Down the hall," she instructed.

Not exactly the welcoming committee.

The only other hope I'd been clinging to was the thought that I'd get my own private dressing room. In the movies women always had their own dressing rooms where they kissed, collapsed in sorrow, yelled at the stage mangers and drank too much.

The second big disappointment of the day came when my mother opened the door at the end of the hall. Not only was it *not* my own personal dressing room, it was a big room with no glitz whatsoever.

A mere conference room full of tables and metal chairs. Boring to the point of tears. Two little girls sat on top of a table across the room. They were twins. The creepy doll like twins gave me shivers. To my utter horror I also realized anyone who came into the room would be able to see my mother who was slowing down considerably given her current state. Stoned, my mother moved about as fast as a drunk snail. Her squinty red eyes glazed over.

Just to annoy her, I said, "I'm hungry," really loud.

The sound of my voice echoed. The twins glanced over. My own mother glared at me. She couldn't figure out if I was really loud or she was really stoned. After a few seconds she couldn't even remember what she was thinking about and dug through her purse for change. "Here," she said, handing over a fistful of coins. "I'm sure there's a vending machine in this place somewhere. Don't get chocolate on your face."

The chance for exploration was my salvation. Hallelujah. Being nosy was my best talent. Down the hall and to the right was indeed a welcome sight. A bright soda and vending machine side by side. My favorite part about vending machines was trying to decide. It wasn't like a shelf where you could take a bag of chips off, study them and put them back. No. A vending machine required absolute certainty. There was no going back from C3. Vending machines were the ultimate commitment.

D4? Maybe. E9? Possibly. C5 was a major consideration. I studied my reflection in the glass as I contemplated my definitive food choices. My hair was curled and fluffy, my pants had no grass stains, my face was freckly and well-scrubbed.

Hmmmm, I thought. Granola bars held a certain appeal but—

"Hurry up," my mother yelled down the hall.

I saw my reflection jump. "What?" I yelled back.

"Get your butt back here. Now."

My mother was too stoned to argue about a Moon Pie and Pepsi for breakfast.

As soon as I returned to the room she came after me with an eyelash curler. "I swear to god if you scream like that again, we're going to the car," she growled.

I screamed louder. We weren't going to the car. I could scream all day and she'd still make me sit there while she curled my eyelashes.

"Stop." I squirmed. "That hurts."

"No one said it wouldn't. Listen." She squeezed my cheeks hard. "You're going to start making some money around here."

My cheeks burned hot. I couldn't see the other people in the room, but I knew they were looking. I shut up and ate my Moon Pie.

Before I finished my Pepsi someone opened the door and said, "It's show time, ladies."

Then everything else happened really fast. Go out, twirl, walk to the end, twirl. I had to belch so bad. Smile. Very slowly and quietly I let the carbonation seep out through my smiling lips. It made me feel better to think beauty and belching went together.

Then I had to go back out and do the same thing in a different outfit. My mother hustled me around backstage, pulling new dresses over my head. *Over and over.* Just when I thought it couldn't get any dumber, it did. My first beauty pageant was a total disaster. When I heard the judges call my name, my heart started pounding.

I'd won Second Place.

With utter dread I walked onto the stage where a woman handed me a trophy. I saw the look in my mother's eye. That was just the type of fuel she needed to fully terrorize me. The woman handed me an envelope with cash. All of the embarrassment was suddenly worth it. Now I had money to buy items for a fort I was planning in the backyard. Sticks, tarp, canteen, sleeping bag, camping lantern. I was in heaven. I drifted down the stairs next to the stage in bliss clutching my envelope and trophy, smiling and waving like Greta Garbo.

Before I'd even made it to the last step my mother snatched the envelope out of my hand.

"Hey," I said, trying to snatch it back. "That's mine."

"It's mine," she said, jerking me up by my arm.

I wasn't giving in without a fight. "I was the one who had to do all of the work."

She stopped, pinching my cheek hard. "You'll smile like a sweet little girl and shut up. Got it?"

*Yeah, I got it.* The joint had worn off.

The next morning, she made me wear a cotton crotch and stand in the living room while she determined what my talent would be.

Still pretty miffed about the money, I asked through clenched teeth, "How much money was in the envelope?"

"None of your business."

I grabbed my Blondie album off of the sofa. "Then I want this to be my talent."

"You can't sing 'Heart of Glass' in the talent competition," she snorted.

"Why not? Debbie Harry sings it and she's *famous.*"

"Whatever," my mother huffed, digging in the ashtray. "Where's the rest of my joint?"

I begged to go to my grandmother's house. My mother was going to an Italian restaurant with Dave, so she caved. My grandmother and I spent all day at the zoo. I could stare at the wild animals all I wanted without curling my eyelashes or plucking my eyebrows. Most important, I did not have to wear the dreaded cotton crotch.

At the entrance to the monkey house I begged my grandmother to help me.

"Make the tweezers stop," I wailed.

She held the door open for me. "That mother of yours doesn't have a job."

"So? That doesn't give her the right to terrorize me. Please, please help me get out of it. Just talk to her."

"I already did."

That got my attention. "Huh?"

"You heard me."

"Well, what did you say?"

"I told her I think you're adorable and precocious and it might be good for you."

I glared at her. "Are you sure you wouldn't feel more comfortable in the Snake House?"

She breezed right past me into the loud chatter of chimpanzees. "No, I'll be fine in the Monkey house, thank you."

I sat next to my grand*traitor* in the big concrete room that smelled like a monkey's butt and watched the gorilla, waiting for an epiphany. After a while a group of school kids came in and gawked at the gorilla until he charged across his cage, slamming into the glass. Everyone ran hysterically from the building. The sudden jolt of adrenaline brought forth an idea.

I had a plan.

The next day, I was sent back to my mother's house with messy, wild hair.

"Hold still," my mother growled with a comb in her mouth and a brush in her hand.

I ignored her, implementing my plan.

"Cotton," she said.

After several seconds she pulled out the most hideous green and gold thing I'd ever seen.

"It's your disco costume." She jiggled it back and forth.

I walked out of the room pretending not to hear. That was my plan. Feign deafness at all costs.

I started doing bad things to draw attention. Like spitting on the floor in restaurants.

My mother jerked me up by my arm. "Stop that! Now!"

Nagging deafness descended. I drooled.

"Did you hear me?" The back of her hand came down fast on my face. I felt my lip cut on my tooth.

Silence. My new best friend. Blood trickled down my chin. People stared. She grabbed me and the pizza box and dragged us both to the car.

Trying to regain some sense of control in my life, I planned entire days around old black and white movies. I loved how everyone drank martinis, smoked, and collapsed onto the chaise. I had to have something to do while I was pretending to be deaf. My fort had been temporarily put on hold due to lack of funds.

"Cotton, come try this dress on."

I ignored her, eyes glued to the television set I wasn't supposed to be watching.

"It's a sailor suit," she declared, spinning around in her chair. She pinched me roughly on the shoulder, then pointed at the navy-blue suit.

"I don't want to be in the military," I said, nonplussed.

It wilted in her hand. I wanted no part of it. I was sent to my room for the rest of the day, which was fine because it meant no hot rollers.

In school, I decided to expand my plan to include teachers.

"Do you know the answer to the question?" Ms. Bishop asked.

"Yes."

"Then why didn't you raise your hand?"

"Huh?"

"Are you okay?"

"*What?*"

My teacher leaned in, so close I could smell cinnamon candy on her breath. "Can you hear me?"

I shook my head, confused.

A parent/teacher conference was called.

Ms. Bishop looked from my mother to me and back again. "Well, it's very disconcerting. Her scholastic performance is dropping because she claims that she can't hear."

My mother glared at me.

Ms. Bishop furrowed her brow. "Cotton, can you hear me?"

My eyes drifted over to the window. I sat silent. Leaves fluttered in the breeze. I began to drool.

An appointment to see an ear doctor was scheduled after my photo shoot the following week. It didn't get me out of the pageant that weekend, but it did help me get even. After the director herded us into a big conference room where everything was curled and plucked, we all walked on stage, smiled, walked to the end, turned, smiled, and walked off. *Thrillsville.* I disappeared before the talent competition and reappeared later, claiming not to have heard the announcement. That meant I didn't place in the contest. That meant no money. *That* meant revenge.

My mother would not be deterred. Crusty Lady taught me to twirl a baton. I took out a few glass angels learning the basics. I had to practice in my cotton crotch with a book of Shakespeare balanced on my head. I decided my baton was much more interesting and practical when used as a sword. I challenged a concrete gargoyle and had to spend the next hour beating the dent out of my baton with a tack hammer I found in the garage.

On Friday I was sent back to my grandmother's house because I was worrying the shit out of my mother. Her words, not mine.

My friend, Preston Brown called to see if I could go camping with him and his cousin next week.

"No," I said, kicking at my baton, "I'm busy."

"Doing what?"

"I have to be in a beauty pageant."

"Really?"

"Yeah."

"I'm sorry. My aunt Dolores used to be in beauty pageants," Preston said half-heartedly.

On Sunday night I returned to hell. My mother made me exfoliate before dinner. "Preston told me stories about his aunt Dolores," I said.

"Dolores is a drunk who sleeps around," my mother snapped.

"How do you know?"

"Because we went to high school together."

"*Humph,*" I said. "*She used to be in beauty pageants.*"

Her eyes shot right through me as she pulled her hand back.

I leaned forward, precisely uttering each word. "I have a photo shoot tomorrow. Go ahead. *Hit me*"

Her hand dropped to the table. Mentally, I dared her to hit me. *Go ahead*, I rehearsed in my head. *You can explain it to the judges tomorrow.*

She sent me to bed in pink curlers rolled so tight it pinched my brain. When the alarm went off, I pretended not to hear. Then I pretended not to hear her standing in my doorway, wearing a hippie tie-dye housedress.

"Get up and take a bath. Don't get your hair wet."

I pretended to be asleep.

She slammed my door. "Now."

I showed up at the table ready for breakfast. She gave me a piece of sprouted wheat bread and told me to tough it.

"Where's Dave?" I asked. I hadn't seen him hanging around for a few days.

She started the car. "He's in jail."

"What?" Still dark outside, I could see the moon. Frost glistened on the windshield. "Where's our dog?"

"He's in jail, too. A different kind. One for dogs. We'll go get him this afternoon."

"I'm supposed to go smile and look pretty after you just told me that?"

"Yep." She backed out of the driveway. "It's a skill you'll thank me for later." She jammed the car into gear. "Besides, you shouldn't have asked if you didn't want to know."

"I wanted to know. I just don't want him to be in jail."

"Well, he is," she stated emphatically and didn't speak again until we got to the portrait studio.

The photographer rushed toward me. "You look adorable. Look at your beautiful curls."

"Sorry, we're so early," my mother sighed. "I have to bring her in before she gets dirty."

The photographer escorted me to the back, where a changing room doubled as a props closet. He handed me a pair of white tights and I rolled my eyes.

He knelt down in front of me. "What's wrong?"

"I hate these things."

"Hmmm, so do I." He tossed the tights over his shoulder. "Okay, hold on."

He disappeared into a back room and seconds later returned with a bright pink feather boa. I'd never seen anything like it. My hands reached for the feathers. It matched my pink fuzzy purse. Women in black and white movies always wore feathers.

"Okay," he said, "but you have to behave. No talking back. And when I say 'smile,' I mean smile. I want to see teeth. Got it."

My smile was so big it could have wrapped around the planet. "Deal."

My mother rolled her eyes when she saw me wrapped up in the boa, but I didn't care. I was Bette Davis. I was Mae West. I was Marilyn Monroe.

It started raining on the way to the dog pound. "What about Dave?" I asked.

"What about him?"

"Are we going to get him?"

She turned into the parking lot. "No, we are not."

"So, where does he go?"

"To hell for all I care," she muttered, climbing out of the car. "Don't touch the gear shift or the steering wheel. I'll be back in a minute."

A few minutes later she emerged from the crappy gray building with our dog trotting along. He had a rope leash around his neck and seemed happy to see someone he knew.

That afternoon the sound of the sewing machine mysteriously stopped, the hot rollers cooled, and the miniature satin evening gown hung, strangely unfinished, in the hall. The entire house was silent except for the dog coughing in the back room. I took eyeliner and painted a warrior face across my cheeks and forehead. I cut the cotton crotch from all of my leotards. I put on my disco costume and a pair of cut off shorts and went to build a fort.

# CHAPTER THIRTEEN

## *Taxidermy*

I laughed so hard I thought I'd pee my pants.

"You'd think you'd be happy for him." My grandmother continued.

"Happy?" I almost exploded. "Happy? You're kidding?"

"He needs a hobby. This will be good for him."

I guess when you think about it, people who have a passion for killing probably should take up taxidermy. Visions of crazy old Thurman salivating while stuffing sand up a fish's behind ran through my head, until finally I just sat down in the middle of the hall and surrendered to a wild fit of hysteria. Stan stood in the doorway to his bedroom, smiling at me.

"He's going to scour the neighborhood late at night to find dead things so he can bring them back and hang them on the walls," I howled.

"Maybe he'll be good at it," Stan offered.

My howl turned into a roar. Tears ran down my cheeks. My grandmother clicked her false teeth at us and went to her room.

But then, you never knew. Maybe Thurman had found his calling. Since his hydroponics dope-growing scheme had failed, he was going to need a career or at least something to keep him busy.

Off he went to the Morton School of Taxidermy. Three times a week he plodded through the living room carrying a folder stuffed with papers and textbooks with cigarette ashes in the creases. Boy, were they in for a surprise. Thurman wasn't the type to win approval by taking teachers apples unless they had razorblades in them. Strangely enough though, he did seem to try. That was weird in itself. When school let out, he plodded back through the living room, brow furrowed, complaining of starvation. I could hear him in the kitchen making liverwurst sandwiches. Then he disappeared upstairs for the night.

I snooped around after his fourth class and found him upstairs, chain-smoking, staring blankly at a page of text. Very quickly I backed down the stairs. He had sharp tools now, reason enough for me to avoid him.

Mostly it kept him occupied, so no one said anything. Except Stan. "Don't you think he's a little weird for wanting to put sawdust in dead things?"

"Don't you think he's weird anyway?" I shot back.

"Well, I guess he's bad but bad don't really got nothing to do with stuffing things."

"He's as mean as a snake if you ask me. I'm just glad he's gone for three hours a night, three nights a week."

"Yeah, me too."

So, in the end, that's what it came down to. We'd have encouraged him to be a camp counselor if it meant he'd leave the house more often.

One night while Thurman was in class, we drove to get fried chicken. Stan and I snickered incessantly, pointing out things Thurman could stuff in class.

My grandmother was not amused. "You two are rude. Thurman is participating in something that he enjoys. He's advancing himself, bettering himself. What are you two doing?" She paused, giving us time to answer the question, then said, "That's what I thought. The only thing you two do is laugh at him."

Stan glued his eyes to the road and shut up. I couldn't. Thurman was such an idiot. I knew he was up to something, and it wasn't a career change.

Still, he didn't prove me wrong right away. Proof of his work suddenly appeared on the living room wall above the old piano. Creepy stuffed dead fish stared with glass eyes. While my grandmother was napping, I dragged a Victorian chair over and climbed up.

At first touch, the scales felt funny, not real. The entire fish was hard as a rock. I knocked against its midsection, but it hurt my knuckles. Very carefully I looked for signs of incision, signs its guts had been ripped out, but it was mounted tight on a plaque.

Stan had a hammer next to his bed in case Thurman attacked him again. I could use that to see if the fish would crack open. The ceiling creaked. Thurman would notice. Maybe he checked his victims after hanging them on the wall. Maybe I should just get down.

Then it happened. Six weeks into the taxidermy semester I was running around in the front yard like a wild animal when I noticed how hot I felt. A warm fever washed over my body, and my stomach felt itchy and sweaty. When I pulled my shirt up to investigate, I was horrified to find spots. Big red spots all over my stomach. When I looked up again Diggy was standing there.

I pointed to my stomach. "Do you have spots?"

Diggy looked down at his fur-covered belly, then shook his head.

I ran into the house to show my grandmother. "I got spots," I blurted out.

"You got what?" she asked

"Spots."

"Let me see."

I jerked my shirt over my head.

Her hand muffled a gasp.

"Oh, Cotton, you've got chicken pox." My grandmother walked into the hall and grabbed the phone book.

"How does she know?" I whispered to Diggy.

She hustled me into the car. "Come on. Stan's driving us to the doctor."

Stan drove us to the doctor's office, where Dr. Jack told us what my grandmother already knew.

"She's got spots?" he asked.

My grandmother nodded.

Doctor Jack looked at me over the rim of his glasses. "Well, let's see."

I pulled up my shirt.

He gave my grandmother a knowing look. "Chicken pox."

This sounded serious.

"Does that mean I can stay up late and eat junk food?"

Diggy thumped his foot.

My grandmother sighed. "It means you won't be going back to school for a few weeks."

The first night got progressively worse. I went home feeling crappy and fell asleep in my grandmother's bed. Sometime in the middle of the night, I felt really hot and woke her up. She went to the kitchen and came back with a glass of ice water and cold washcloths for my forehead. I felt feverish, dizzy. I couldn't keep my eyes open, but I couldn't sleep. My skin was hot and itchy. My grandmother turned on the air conditioner so I'd stop saying I was going to die.

"You're not going to die, sugar. You just don't feel well."

When the sun started to rise, I drifted off to sleep but faded back in and insisted my grandmother make me a pallet directly in front of the air conditioner. I curled up like a small animal and faded off again.

I faded back into the smells of dinnertime and the sound of Thurman breathing.

He yelled into the other room, "Mother, what's wrong with the brat?"

"She doesn't feel well, Thurman. Leave her alone."

"Well, I can see that, but why is she sleeping on the floor like an old dog?"

"Because she's hot. Now come in here and eat."

"Humph," he said. "She don't look so good." He nudged me with his toe.

"She's not. Now leave her alone," my grandmother yelled back.

He snarled, flicked his ashes on the floor and left.

A few days into my delirium, I managed to make it out of the small room to go to the bathroom on my own. New dead things had appeared on the living room walls. Eerie eyes glared at me. More fish, a few small birds, and what might have been a squirrel in life but was indiscernible in death. That's when I knew I had to get better. If I died, he was going to stuff me. I knew it. He was probably upstairs right now thinking about how much fun it was going to be to break my bones and fill me with sand so I'd sit in some creepy position. *I just knew it.*

I fell asleep and woke up two days later.

Thurman stood over me, holding a plate of pot roast and a two-liter of soda. "You hungry?"

"No," I croaked.

"Yeah, you don't look so hungry. If you die, try not to stink up the place. Okay?" And then he was gone.

Late that night Stan sneaked into my room, lowering himself to the floor next to my pallet in a series of grunts and thuds. In the dark, he whispered, "The neighbor's cat disappeared."

"How do you know?"

"I heard Mother talking on the phone."

I tried to raise up on my elbows, "Is it on the wall?"

He shook his head. "Not yet, but I snuck upstairs last night when Thurman went out to buy cigarettes."

"Did you find anything?"

"He's been rolling joints up there."

"If I die don't let him stuff me."

Ever the existentialist, Stan nodded seriously. "I won't"

Over the next few days, I checked the walls. The cat didn't appear. I was relieved, although still delirious.

Stan appeared in the doorway, fidgeting with a hem coming loose on his flannel shirt. "The taxidermy school called to ask why Thurman hadn't been in class. I heard Mother talking on the phone. They wanted to know if he would please return the materials he'd borrowed."

"What materials?"

"Tools to cut things open."

"Great. That's just what we need." I moved around, picking at pink flaky crust on my arms.

Stan lowered his voice even more. "Someone's pet rabbit disappeared."

"Oh, gosh." I rolled my eyes. *I knew it.*

That night I couldn't sleep. Beams of light flashed across the ceiling. I climbed up onto a chair next to the window. In the dark, moonless night Thurman plodded back and forth across the backyard. A box in one hand and a flashlight in the other he moved his workshop of slaughter to the garage. I could see him through the dusty windows. I watched him walking around, moving equipment. At that hour his light was the only one on the block still glowing.

Stan shuffled around in the kitchen. I gathered up my blanket and walked quietly down the hall. He was digging around in the freezer as I walked in. He turned, startled.

"Thurman is outside," I said.

"I know. Do you know if we have any peach ice cream?"

I walked over to the freezer and wedged my arm back behind the piles of frozen pork chops. "I hid some back here."

A loud clanging noise rang out from the backyard. We both turned.

"God knows what he's doing out there," I grabbed what felt like the ice cream container and pulled.

"I don't think we should sleep until he returns those things he borrowed from the school."

"It won't matter. He'll just use his bare hands."

Stan's eyes went wide. "You think so?"

"I know so," I said, handing the carton over. "We're out of peach. It's mint chocolate chip all the way."

From where I was standing, I could see the dark outline of the tiller still sitting unused in the backyard.

My only hope was that eventually he'd give in to laziness like he did with everything else.

After a few seconds, I nudged Stan. "Look."

He leaned over, looking out the window. "Ain't that something. It's snowing."

# CHAPTER FOURTEEN

## *I Gave Santa a Beer*

Santa had always been a little shady. I mean, he came and went without a sound, supposedly thumping on the roof in a sleigh driven by cheerful reindeer. Staying up past my bedtime was fairly easy, but once Diggy fell asleep the hours dragged on. The house was so quiet. I lay in bed trying to remember fractions to keep myself awake. When I was about to drift into a sugar-plum slumber I jerked myself awake, dedicated to the cause. *The Santa Cause.* I'd spent half the day making cookies just in case he had the munchies. I wasn't about to fall asleep before the hour of reckoning.

At sixteen minutes past midnight I heard the door to my mother and Dave's bedroom open. The smell of marijuana drifted down the hall. I gave it a few minutes, then sneaked over to my window to spy. Off in the silent distance, our front door closed quietly. Fairly certain Dave was up to something, I followed him out to the driveway.

The air was so cold and still, little puffs of breath hovered in front of my face. The sight did not amuse me.

"Jesus, Cotton." Dave accidentally slammed his head against the trunk. "What are you doing out of bed."

I tapped my bunny slipper against the gravel, "I was going to ask you the same thing."

Smart little kids give adults the creeps, and I could see it in his bloodshot eyes.

"I'm helping Santa," he offered.

For a single, solitary second, I fell for it. "Santa's here? Where?"

Dave used my momentary burst of excitement to regroup as I stepped back, craning my neck to look up at the moonlit roof. My kneecaps were frozen. I couldn't feel my nose, but I was going to find that big, fat jolly guy who for two years in a row hadn't left me what I'd asked for.

Dusting his hands off, Dave stepped away from the trunk, reveling in the distraction of a well-told lie.

"Hoist me up so I can get a better look." I kicked up a slipper. "Let's see if he's over by the chimney."

"Hold on, cowgirl. I didn't say he was here. I said that I was helping him."

*Santa's Helper.* "What are you helping him with? You're too tall to be an elf."

"I'm unloading all of the presents he left for you."

*Sucker.* "He left me presents. Where?"

"Um, well, he handed them to me, and I put them in the car."

"The car? I thought he was supposed to come down the chimney?"

"Sure," he said, a little unsure. "He is— it's just—except that— sometimes—well, I left the fire burning when I went to bed, and I guess the flames must have been too hot and he—well, um—he singed his beard and the fur on his boots. I'm sorry. It was an accident."

"You caught Santa on fire?" I gasped. My bunnies were frozen. "Where is he?"

"Uh—I ummm— I gave him some ice packs and aloe vera."

"What about my cookies?"

"Yeah, and I gave him the cookies too. And a beer."

"He's *driving* a sleigh."

"I was kidding about the beer. Anyway, didn't you hear the reindeer hooves on the roof?"

"No."

"Well, it was impressive. I'll tell you."

"Why are my presents in the car?"

I was sure Dave had been counting on the fact that the conversation would end earlier. He looked up into the clearest sky of stars and, with a straight face, said, "Santa put them in the trunk so no one would steal them."

"Uh-huh." My teeth chattered so loud I could barely talk. "No one knows where we live."

Dave gave the biggest punch-drunk smile I'd ever seen and said, "Santa does. He knows everything. Let's go make hot chocolate."

"Why didn't you wake me up when Santa got here?"

"There was a lot going on."

Yeah, I bet there was. The truth was probably stranger than the ridiculous lie he'd just told. My Santa probably worked for the drug cartel and used his cover-up of delivering presents to transport big bags of weed. Who knew what he carried in that secret sleigh compartment, much less the huge velvet bag full of presents. *Wink. Wink.*

My Santa had connections.

A coyote howled. My cold fingers needed a cup of hot cocoa with gobs of marshmallow spilling over the side. A burst of warm air rushed out to meet me before I'd even stepped inside. The house was completely silent. Over near the fireplace, the Christmas tree glowed in its colored light. Shimmering icicles twinkled. My stocking hung over the mantel, so fat it looked like a tick. The air smelled of pine and firewood.

Without a word, Dave ushered me into the kitchen and put on a double boiler to warm the milk. I sat down in the much-too-big-for-me dining room chair, with my legs stretched out in front of me, wondering how I could have ever been so gullible. My present list was taped to the refrigerator. Santa hadn't even bothered to check off the items he'd left for me. When I looked down again, my bunnies stared up with their glassy eyes. It was Christmas according to the clock. I glanced over again at my list taped big and broad to the front of the refrigerator. *Magician's Cape* was written in big, block letters across the top. I'd underlined the words in red crayon. Three times.

For the past few years, the trend had been to give me dolls from all over the world. Dutch girl. Spanish girl. French girl. *Yawn.*

I looked down into my cup of cocoa and asked, "Did Santa leave me a magic cape and wand?"

Dave looked stricken. "Ummm—I believe Santa consulted with your mom this year."

*Crap.*

# CHAPTER FIFTEEN

## *The Dollhouse*

On Christmas morning I woke, groggy from lack of sleep. It was frigid in my room. Outside my window gray sky fanned out over the front yard. When I was coherent enough, I made my way down the hall to find—

*Huh?*

I looked everywhere for my magic cape and wand. There was a Swiss girl and a China girl and that… *thing.* It loomed over the other presents, with its creepy, freshly painted, empty rooms.

"Cotton, don't you like it?" My mother glared me into submission.

I stared. I scratched. "What else did I get?"

Inca jumped up on the sofa and wagged his tail.

She did not get the reaction she wanted. I did not want a dollhouse. It was not on the list. The next day my mother drove to an after-Christmas sale and bought her own dollhouse. Tiny ceramic cookware, fingernail sized tile, and miniature claw-footed bathtubs filled it to the brim. Mine sat in the corner. She bought a new marble table for hers, blankets for the tiny beds. I couldn't have cared less. The only thing I'd gotten for Christmas that I'd actually asked for was a box of Hardy Boys books. When she was done, she started in on mine again.

I watched my empty house fill with furniture I had not ordered. I begged for Magic Rocks. "Pleeeeease."

"No."

"A new chemistry set?" *New parents? Anything but that stupid dollhouse.*

"No."

"Well, then what am I supposed to do with it?"

"You play with it."

"How?"

"You move the people around in the house. Like this." She dragged the little rubber man over to the table to sit down for dinner.

"That's not very interesting."

"Oh, Cotton, use your imagination." She threw the rubber man on the cobbled bathroom floor.

I wasn't making my point very well, so I slept in the hall to protest. At 5 AM I woke to the sound of the bedroom door opening, then I heard my mother say, "You are so ungrateful."

"Is it time for cartoons?" I cracked open an eyelid.

She stood over me, glaring. "No, get in bed."

I wasn't going without a fight. "I don't want to sleep with the evil, evil dollhouse."

"Do you know how much money we spent on that thing? The house alone cost Dave a thousand dollars."

"So. It's *evil*."

"Stop saying that."

"Well, it is. It's a haunted dollhouse."

"It is not."

"It is."

"I'm not going to argue with you. It stays." She slammed the bedroom door.

*Okay*, but my rubber people weren't dull. They threw china, slammed doors, had affairs, ran away with pirates, returned from voyages overseas, collapsed in piles of sorrow, drank too much, developed acute paranoia, formulated theories on why their house seemed so small and why therapy wasn't helping them with the sensation that they were always being watched, and although not realistic, never once sat down to dinner. I took my old Barbies and let them stay upstairs without paying rent. The butler, Sam, developed a drinking problem. The oldest daughter, Sadie, slipped into a deep depression and disappeared for days in my sock drawer.

"Hank," Sadie would say, "you've simply got to help me. I've been wearing the same clothes my entire life." She clawed at the front of her dress. "It's like it's glued to me or something."

She constantly auditioned for parts on soap operas. She'd practice all day in the kitchen driving the hired help closer to the bottle. Angeline was the cook. No one knew anything about her except— "Cotton," my mother screamed.

"What?"

"Who are you talking to in there?"

"I'm not talking to anyone. It's the rubber people."

"Well, stop. It's creepy."

Sadie turned to Hank as he refilled the ice bucket. "Darling, don't you think it's strange that none of us remember anything before we came to live in this house. It's like we didn't exist," she whispered.

Sadie was a sharp one.

Hank looked over, his eyes swimming in stolen bourbon. "Honey," he'd say, "let's just forget about it."

"Only because you can't remember either," she slapped back.

Then she took a lover. I didn't have any more rubber people, so Sam had to double.

"Cotton, it's time for bed."

The next week Sam stole the plastic Mercedes and ran away with a Barbie six inches taller than him because he couldn't take the stress. Barbie thought he was rich because he always wore a tuxedo.

In the meantime, Dave had begun trafficking loads of narcotics out of our basement. Men who didn't speak carried boxes out to trucks in the middle of the night. These people had no names, no identity, no past, no future. Sort of like the rubber people.

"Hank," Sadie slurred, "Hank, why don't we have a front yard, honey? I feel so confined. Honey, I feel like someone's watching us."

Sadie was going to have to go on medication. Little pellets of artificial sweetener I'd stolen from the kitchen cabinet appeared on her bedside table. Hank left every day saying that he was going to the office, but he really spent his entire day on the windowsill.

"What a fake," Sadie exhaled.

"Cotton, it's time to do your homework," Dave yelled from the other room.

"But Sadie's waiting on a call from a TV producer."

"Don't worry about that."

Sam came back after a week. Barbie dumped him and kept the Mercedes. Penniless and rubber, he returned, smelling like exhaust and cigarettes. Angeline poured him a stiff one.

Later that night a bright light flashed in Hank's eyes. He bolted upright. "What was that?"

Sadie looked around in a daze and said, "Aliens."

I turned off my flashlight and went to bed amused.

"Cotton?"

"Yes?"

"Stop talking to yourself," my mother yelled at the top of her lungs.

The next day my mother curiously disappeared.

"She has a headache," Dave said. "She's resting."

"Where?"

"In a comfortable place."

"Like a chair?"

"Yes, like a chair."

Then he bought me a Happy Meal.

With my mother gone the antics of the dollhouse were less interesting, so I went to discover lost civilizations out in the woods behind our house. I looked for Mars in the night sky and tried to imagine the world three thousand years ago. I lay very still, under the stars, and traveled on caravans through ancient worlds.

The next morning, we had runny, undercooked, hardboiled eggs for breakfast.

Dave stared down at his plate.

"There's a diner down on the highway," I said, trying to be helpful.

"Yeah." He stood up.

Then he threw our plates in the trash. *The glass plates.*

After breakfast Dave took me to the mall and bought me Magic Rocks. When I got home, I went into my room and saw Hank lying face down on the tiled floor. When the coast was clear I sneaked across the hall and put him in my mother's empty dollhouse. There were no porcelain cats, no felt-covered birds in tiny cages, no squatters, no renters, no hired help, no nothing. Just a big, empty, perfect house full of perfect furniture that looked good if you were on the outside. Hank hated it. There wasn't a drop of booze anywhere.

Dave went outside to smoke a joint. I heard the glass door slide shut. I went into the kitchen to finish my homework. Dave came back in, bleary-eyed, looking like someone hit him in the head with a rock.

"You okay?" he asked.

"Yeah."

Really, I was kind of bored, so I was happy when Sadie had a relapse, and the butler drained the bank account.

On Tuesday Dave left me alone in the house. He made me promise not to turn on the stove or tell my grandmother I was ever by myself. I read a Hardy Boys mystery, ate leftover Italian, then padded down the hall and stared at the empty dollhouse in my mother's room. Something about its perfection made it tainted, jaded, unfit.

"I'll drink to that," Sadie said, just before running off to Mexico.

Late that evening Dave guided my mother through the door. Her eyes were heavy, with dark circles underneath.

"Someday," she told me over breakfast the next morning, "you'll get married and have a house too, and you'll be happy you learned something."

"But you're not married," I pointed out.

She stared down into her grape juice.

Dave hustled me out of the kitchen and took me to my French lesson.

"I don't want the dollhouse anymore," I announced in the car.

"Cotton, now isn't the time to start changing things around. Just play with the dollhouse the way your mother wants."

"But I don't want it."

"It's just a silly toy," he sighed.

I started crying. "No, it's something else."

The dollhouse loomed dark over my thoughts, placed on the floor in between the dresser and window. Four stories tall, filled to the brim, secrets stashed in every drawer. Late at night, when everyone else was sleeping, it whispered and creaked like it was alive.

I slept in the hall again. This time my mother ignored me.

For days I sat in my desk at school, plotting. How does a seven-year-old make an entire house disappear? We had a hammer in the kitchen junk drawer, but I knew my mother would blow a gasket over demolition. I slept on it, obsessed, considered my options, begged for aliens to come and take it away, slept on it again, paced the hall in my footed pajamas, obsessed, and then at the end of the week a light bulb clicked on so bright in my head it nearly burst. That night while everyone was sleeping, I took the rubber people out to the side of the house and buried them.

"Cotton, where's the family I bought for the house?"

Not bothering to glance up from the Hardy Boys mystery, I said, "They're not a family and I don't know."

"Well, they were here a few days ago."

"Yes, they were." I picked at the dirt under my fingernails.

"And you don't know what happened to them?"

"Nope, maybe the dog ate them."

Later that night I eavesdropped outside my mother and Dave's bedroom door.

"Don't you think the whole thing is a little creepy and a little odd?" my mother asked.

The Christmas tree was upside down in the trash. It was snowing. Ronald Reagan was on the TV again.

Dave shook his head hopelessly and let it go.

I went back to my room and thought about the rubber people. If Sadie had been there, she would have said, "Hank, honey, hasn't anyone noticed that the backside of the house doesn't have a wall? Don't you think that's strange? I mean, people could be watching us."

Angeline would hear the whole thing as she dusted the furniture with a cotton ball. Sam would have been wondering why there were so many lamps in the house and no electricity.

And Hank would have stopped making gin martinis long enough to say, "Honey, I think you're making a big deal out of nothing. I mean, we have three sides. So what if the back is missing. It's always been that way."

# CHAPTER SIXTEEN

*Digging up Money*

Since my family had no formal means of communication, I had to rely on my suspicions to formulate an exact idea of what we were doing. Naturally my suspicions were aroused when I was summoned from my explorations in the backyard, where I had just outfitted Inca with a travel pack to carry our supplies.

My mother stood on the front porch holding a hairbrush and my Buster Brown shoes. "Come on. Brush your hair and put your shoes on. We're going to the health department."

My brow furrowed.

I'd seen the darkened corridors of the public health department in science fiction movies I wasn't allowed to watch. People woke up there at the end of the world and ran down empty hallways screaming hysterically, *Is there anyone alive?*

"But me and Inca are going to find a lost city."

She advanced on me with the hairbrush, which often doubled as a weapon. I took off running. She didn't even bother to chase me.

When Dave found me, I was huddled in the back of the doghouse sharing my peanut butter sandwich from the supply pack with the dog. Dave looked funny, all crouched down at the opening, sunlight blaring across the yard behind him.

"Come on," he said. "It's not a big deal."

"Am I going to be quarantined?"

"Where do you learn these things?" He dusted hay off of his shoes.

It took me a minute to remember. "The late, late movie."

"Figures," he said, shifting his weight back onto his heels. "Come on. It won't take long and then we can go for ravioli."

I was on the verge of climbing out when it occurred to me to ask why I was being bribed with Italian food.

"Well," Dave started with a weak beginning. "I think we'll be going out of the country soon. And well, you'll need a checkup."

"Then why can't I see Dr. Jack and Mr. Ducky?"

Good question. One he was obviously not prepared for. "Ummm, because it's different when you leave the country."

"Because of the fruit flies?"

"No. More like because you need—um, certain immunizations."

"*Shots?* You want me to come out of here for shots? No way, buddy." I retreated deeper into the doghouse.

My mother yelled across the yard, "Tell her to get out of that doghouse right now."

Panic flashed in his eyes. "I'll buy you whatever you want."

Opportunities like that were golden. "The complete Hardy Boys set," I announced from my bargaining position.

"Okay." He agreed so fast I wanted to get it in writing.

"The complete set. Not just a few of them."

"Okay, the complete set," he nodded, extending his hand to shake.

There wasn't a soul in the front corridor of the health department when we arrived. I imagined it was because only hours before, a very contagious man, eyeballs liquefying, stumbled in from the street pleading for mercy as he fatally contaminated every person he came in contact with. The epidemic spread throughout the entire building. The last few people gasped for help and died while my mom and Dave smoked a bowl in the parking lot.

"Keep up," my mother yelled back at me as if I should be excited about needles and alcohol rubs.

We walked miles to the end of the hall and entered through the last door on the left. There were two survivors. The first survivor instructed us to follow her.

"Now I'm just going to poke your skin with this. It won't hurt." The doctor held up a device that looked like a fork missing its teeth.

That didn't hurt, but the rest did. I howled like a caged mountain lion just to liven the place up a bit.

The next day Dave picked me up at school with a box full of Hardy Boys books in the backseat.

"I think that's all of them," he said, flashing a smile. "I counted."

The moment of triumph made me feel warm and fuzzy inside.

The next suspicion was Spanish classes at night school. I was okay with the new development because it meant I spent one more night a week at my grandmother's house. Plus, if we did leave the country I wouldn't die of embarrassment every time someone opened their mouth.

I poked around in Stan's room after Dave dropped me off. Stan came back from Taco Bell and caught me. "Is it Friday already?" He flopped down on his bed, unpacking the paper sack.

"Mom and Dave are taking Spanish classes."

Stan looked around the room like he was trying to remember what Spanish was when I realized he was looking for his soda. "Hmmm." He sucked soda through the straw.

"I think we're going to South America."

He remained quiet, focused on his bean burrito. I begged a taco off of him and went upstairs. Thurman was up in his room listening to Barry White, smoking a joint.

"What are you doing here, you little cretin?"

"Wondering why you're so ugly." I turned around to leave.

My grandmother was out back cleaning pots and pans with bleach.

I went looking for Diggy and found him in the driveway.

Stan walked out onto the front porch in an orange hunting vest and boxer shorts.

Holding a book high in the air, he pointed to a map, asking, "You're going here?"

I squinted. His index finger was pressed to South America. "Yeah, I think. No one's told me yet for sure. But somewhere around there."

"How far do you think that is?"

"I don't know." I glanced over at Diggy, who was quiet. "It's farther than Mexico and it took us a million years to get there."

I'd never seen Stan's brow so knitted with confusion. "Why do you want to go so far away?"

"I think it has something to do with his career," I said.

*Weed Cartel Career.*

Stan scurried off, clutching his book.

Thurman was in the kitchen throwing sticks of butter on the floor. "Who ate all of the pimento loaf?"

"Not me," I said, pushing past him to get a soda.

Stan passed by the doorway looking guilty, trying to get to his room before anyone noticed.

Thurman eyed me. "What are you doing here, you little turd? You're only supposed to hang around here mooching on the weekends."

"My mom and Dave are learning Spanish."

"HA." He slapped his fat, jiggly thigh. "That'll be the day." Walking over to the door, he yelled out down the hall. "Someone go to the freaking store and buy some more pimento loaf. Jesus Frick. What's wrong with you people?"

I was about to tell him to kiss off when my grandmother appeared, wiping her hands on a dish cloth. "Come on, Stan. Let's go to the store."

Stan dutifully pushed himself up from the bed and grabbed his car keys from the floor. "Let me take a leak."

"I'll meet you in the car." My grandmother headed for the front door.

I followed her across the room, watching her heave her sixty-ton pocketbook onto her shoulder before walking out onto the porch. The screen door slammed behind her.

"Are you coming, Cotton?" she asked, without turning around.

"No."

Diggy was out back waiting for me, half person, half dog, looking for magic rocks in the driveway. I took a seat in front of him, steering myself into a patch of shade that cast a half-moon shadow in front of us. "We're going to South America," I blurted out with no introduction.

Diggy looked up at me, a gray rock resting in the palm of his furry hand.

"Do you want to come?"

Diggy nodded, wagging his tail.

"Do you think it will be any fun?"

"Loads," Thurman boomed behind me, scaring the crap out of us.

I felt the color drain from my face down to my toes where they suddenly throbbed. "Go away," I said, trying to ignore all two hundred and fifty pounds of him.

"Screw you," he sneered, walking in front of me, blowing smoke in my face. Then, he raised his big ham hock leg in the air and let it thunder down onto the gravel, digging his heel deep into the ground. "Did I get him," he laughed manically. "Where's your stupid friend *now?*"

I spat back. "Go away."

His foot came down several inches from my hand, grinding, kicking up gravel. "How about now? Did I get the little imaginary beast that time?" *Ha ha ha* he howled, choking on cigarette smoke.

I'd had enough. "Has anyone ever told you how absolutely frikkin ugly you are?" I was fully prepared to race across the back yard if necessary.

Lowering himself closer to my face, picking his teeth with his tongue, he breathed, "Ugly like you."

"No, really, you're more ugly," I said, matter of fact. Big hunks of gravel dug deep into my palms.

"Am not," he bit back, digging his other foot down into the gravel, kicking up dust.

"God, you're such an idiot." I pushed myself up from the ground, walking away, praying he didn't chase me. For several seconds I held my breath, listening to make sure he wasn't going to pounce from behind.

He yelled after me. "You need to get some Jesus."

That made me snort. "What a dipshit you are. You just said that like Jesus is a soft drink."

Puffing hard on his last bit of cigarette, he pulled one of his flip-flop shoes off, throwing it at my head, where he missed. It sailed over my left shoulder, landing in the holly berry bush. "You need to get with Jesus," he yelled again.

*Now I'd heard it all.*

At ten-fifteen that night Dave knocked on the front door. The springs on the sofa creaked when my grandmother got up. She walked over, opening the door. I was hiding under the bed with dead moths and dust bunnies.

"She's hiding," I heard my grandmother say, closing the door.

"Cotton," Dave called out, walking down the dark hall.

"She might be upstairs."

When I crept out from my hiding place and saw that everyone had gone out into the backyard with a flashlight to look for me, I walked over and sat on the sofa, pretending to be imaginary.

"She's in here, Mother," I heard Stan yell out the back door.

Everyone came into the living room. I was still invisible. Dave gave me that look. I was pretty sure he could see me. I needed tips from Diggy on how to be imaginary.

"Didn't you hear me calling for you?" Dave asked, propping his hand on his hip.

"No," I answered, averting my eyes, immediately sorry for lying in the first place.

He frowned and reached for my hand. "Come on. Your mother is waiting in the car."

*I know. That's why I was hiding under the bed.*

My mother, true to form, was irked. "Why does it take you twenty minutes to walk fifteen yards?"

"I'm constipated," I said, climbing into the backseat.

That was the end of that conversation.

The next morning, Dave got up early to drive me to school. After practicing my sniffle under a blanket for half an hour, I rubbed my eyes to make them look red and itchy. I successfully convinced Dave that I was too sick to go to school. Since my mother would be hanging around the house all day, me and Diggy camped out in the closet with a pile of pillows and blankets and a flashlight to read 007 comic books. The rest of the day was pretty uneventful, and I passed out on my bed in the warm thick glow of sunset streaming across my body.

The sound of twigs snapping underfoot woke me up in the middle of the night. The warm glow had given way to a cold chill. I sat up in the middle of my bed rubbing my arms. That's when I saw it. Light from a flashlight cut a deep line through the darkness, hovering, trembling. Very quietly I slid out of bed and crept on tiptoes to the window. About twenty yards out, Dave walked to the back of the yard, carrying a shovel and the new flashlight he'd bought at Sears.

Since he didn't believe in banks, he'd devised a system. All along the edge of the woods behind our house he buried cash, sealed in plastic baggies, stuffed in old army ammunition cans. It was weird, but it worked for him. It had been a long time since I'd seen him out there. I was sure South America was close. Breath clouds puffed on the window. My nostrils flared. Dave's shadow wound through the moonlight in a clear stillness that gave me the shivers. Digging up money meant an extended vacation.

# CHAPTER SEVENTEEN

### *Bogota*

By the time the plane landed in Colombia I was exhausted. I fell asleep in the taxi on the way from the airport. I woke up in a room that looked like a regular house. I was sure my mother must have sold me.

I bolted out of the room, into a long hall, looked both ways, and ran. Just as I reached the stairs, running for freedom, a door opened behind me and I heard Dave say, "Hey, where are you going?"

I screeched to a halt, spinning around, one pigtail flopped over in front of my face. "What?"

Dave stepped into the hall, looking uncommonly refreshed. "I said, 'Where are you going'?"

"Uhh— I don't know. Where are we?"

He walked patiently toward me. "This is where we're staying for a few weeks."

My eyes flashed wildly around the walls. "It looks like a house," I said, trying to discern if the real Dave had been kidnapped by aliens.

"It's an inn," he said, quietly, kneeling down in front of me. "Are you hungry?"

"It looks like a house," I said, stubbornly.

"Well, it is a house." He lifted me into his arms. "But it's an inn, too."

I felt too out of sorts for words. "Are you sure?"

"Yeah, come on. We'll go downstairs and get something to eat while your mom's sleeping."

Magic words. *Your mom's sleeping.* He carried me three floors down, to the front door, and then let me slide down his leg. We walked into a huge dining room, where big women the color of cinnamon spoke to Dave in Spanish. They smiled and gestured, then brought us big bowls of food and clear bottles full of orange-colored soda pop.

Dave pulled a drumstick from a whole roasted chicken. "So, what do you think?"

I pointed to the soda pop. "What's that?"

"I don't know." He lifted the mouth of the bottle to his nose. "Smells fizzy."

"Can I have mine?" I asked, eager to start my vacation with items on the forbidden food list. Soda first.

"Sure." Dave leaned back, letting his eyes trail over the hand-carved woodwork along the walls.

My nostrils sucked up the scent. Even though it was orange it smelled like cream soda. *Mmmm... heavenly.* I turned the bottle up, taking a big swig before coming up for air.

"Easy there, Tiger," Dave said, cutting bread from a cast iron skillet.

An enormous burp exploded from my stomach, and even though I tried to swallow it back down, it erupted from my lips, rattling my insides.

Dave laughed. "Do not tell your mother that I gave you soda pop for breakfast, and especially don't tell her I let you burp in public."

"Deal." I slapped the table, feeling a smile stretch so far across my face it touched the ceiling.

The women bustled back in with big ceramic bowls full of berries and cream. I decided right then and there that South America was delicious.

After breakfast or lunch or whatever it was, Dave and I waddled up the stairs together for a nap. We stopped in front of my door. Dave pointed two doors down, across the hall, next to a marble table with flowers on it. "That's my room. Come get me if you need anything." Then he pointed all of the way to the end, back near the stairs. "That's the bathroom. Okay?"

"Okay." I wobbled into my room, my belly sloshing with soda and berries.

After I'd closed my door, Dave yelled from the hall, "Lock your door."

"Okay." I reached up, turning the big metal key in the door.

Then I passed out, drunk on fizz.

When I woke up, Diggy was standing next to the bed.

"Where are we?" he asked.

I sat up in bed and looked around in the moonlight. A draft fluttered through the old windows.

"South America." I pulled the blanket up to my neck.

"What's that?"

"Well, there's North America and South America in the Western Hemisphere," I repeated, just like my teacher told me.

"Oh," he said. "Are there any more of those sodas?"

*Good question.*

Time to snoop around.

Thank goodness my door didn't creak when opened. Moonlight streamed down the hall from the big window at the end. Everything was a chilly silence. Diggy took my hand and we crept softly toward the stairs. At the first landing, we stopped, listening for sounds.

Diggy whispered, "What's an inn?"

"Remember when Mary and Joseph went out on that mule, and they stopped off at the inn and were turned away and the little baby Jesus had to be born in a shed?"

Diggy nodded.

"Well, it's kinda the same thing." I ventured forward to the steps leading down to the next landing.

At the first floor, I stopped, listening. I remembered the women had come and gone through a door in the dining room, so I retraced my steps. Diggy and I both held our breath as I pushed the door gingerly with the tip of my finger. It swung open easily. We stepped inside.

The kitchen was dark. Without turning on the light we wandered around. Long metal tables stretched the length of the room. At the very end, over in the corner, I spotted the biggest refrigerator I'd ever seen. It was as big as a bathroom. The handle looked big, metal, and heavy. I laid my palm against it for several seconds before I slowly pulled it toward me. There was a loud click, then the latch released and a stream of light spilled down onto the floor. I stood very still, listening to my heart thundering in my chest, wondering if anyone had heard us. The low whir of the refrigerator and the *tick tick tick* of a clock over the stove were the only sounds.

Washed in a creamy glow of yellow light, I pulled the door completely open, stunned to see shelf after shelf filled with rows of soda. The orange glow of bottles called to me. I was elated. With this many bottles no one would ever notice one or two missing. A symphony of delight was orchestrated on top of my taste buds. My eager little hands grasped the cold bottle, pulling it to me.

Diggy asked, "What's that?"

I told him, "The forbidden fruit."

He believed me.

I gave him a soda.

Very, very quietly, I pushed the door closed.

Now that I had my treasure and my eyes adjusted to the light, I noticed the contents of the room. Everything looked like a prop from an episode of *I Love Lucy*. The stove, the bread box, the meat grinder. It was as if 1950 happened there, but not 1960, or 1970 and definitely not 1980. The chrome table legs were speckled with flecks of rust. Finding a bottle opener was easy because there was one as big as my head screwed to the end of the cutting table. *Pop. Fizz. Phifffff.* Bubbles tickled my nose. One whiff sent my taste buds reeling. Cream soda with a splash of orange tantalized my senses. I turned the bottle up for a taste. Lip-smacking good. I hunkered down, next to the table, my butt resting against the floor. I told myself to savor the flavor, make each liquid moment count, but it was so yummy I gulped the entire thing, then rolled back on my bottom and belched. *Gosh, that was good.*

In my sugar-coated delirium I stood up, hid the bottle in the corner with all the other empty bottles, and walked to the door to listen. Gas bubbles popped and sloshed in my stomach as I crept up the stairs to my room, careful to avoid creaky steps. Spooky, dark hallways greeted me at every landing. I imagined the silence in Spanish.

I pushed open the door to my room just enough to slip inside, then I promptly closed it, turning to run to my bed. Instead, I ran smack into Dave's leg and almost scared myself to death.

"Where have you been?" he asked, standing in the middle of my room, barefoot, in his robe.

The wind whipped itself out of my lungs. I stared at him in shock, stammering to find a word.

His fingers drummed along the bedpost. "Well?"

I didn't know why I couldn't talk. I just couldn't think of any words. Finally, I croaked, then sputtered, then said stupidly, "I thought you were asleep."

"Yeah, I bet you did," he said, more sarcastic than before.

But instead of yelling at me, he knelt down, resting back on his heels and said, "Cotton, you have to tell me where you were."

I wondered if my breath smelled like cream soda. Without expelling much air, I muttered, "I was—ummm. I was down snooping around. I promise I wasn't being bad."

"Where were you snooping?"

"Downstairs. Everything is old down there. Diggy went with me."

"Okay," he said, taking my hand. "Do not leave this inn without me. Got it?"

I nodded, ready to comply with any wish that kept me out of trouble.

"Let me hear you say it."

"Okay. I won't leave the inn without you."

"It's very important." He led me over to my bed. "This is not like being at home. This is a *very* big city, and it's not a safe one."

He hoisted me up on top of the quilts, making me so paranoid that I blurted out, "I stole a soda."

"Fine," he said, unperturbed, tucking me in. "Go to sleep. Do not leave this building without me. And don't give me any more heart attacks."

I grabbed my stuffed rabbit, nodding furiously, thankful to have thwarted punishment. As he closed my door on the way out, I sank back into the fluffy softness of the feather bed, letting my gurgling stomach lull me to sleep.

The next morning, I awoke to the sound of rain falling on the roof. There was no clock in my room. I couldn't remember what day it was. I listened. Everything was quiet. I threw my legs over the edge of the bed ready to snoop around.

Since my mother usually got stoned before bed there was fat chance she'd wake up. Dave might hear me but walking down to the first floor and back wasn't breaking any rules. I tiptoed to the door. The floor was cold, and the metal doorknob clicked when I turned it. I peered into the hall. Complete silence. Just the way I liked it.

The only thing hanging out in the hall was the Oriental rug. Its threadbare softness cushioned the stealthy tiptoeing I did as I made my way down to the staircase. Raindrops thundered onto the roof. Light and nimble, I made my way down fast, fizz already tickling my tongue, sweet cream soda calling me.

Once I got to the second-floor landing, I broke into a full run. A room-service tray by the stairs held the remnants of someone's breakfast. The temptation to stop and see if there was any coffee in the pot was strong but I rushed ahead, willing myself to become invisible. Feeling bolder now, I charged down the hall, thumping and creaking, running full throttle to the kitchen door. The taste of carbonated soda drove my entire existence. My hands slapped the swinging door hard, and I skidded to a stop right in the middle of the kitchen. That's when I got the surprise of my life. The entire room bustled with activity.

Huge soup pots, bigger than a sink, steamed and rumbled on top of the stove. The fragrant, humid air smelled of garlic, onions, and bread. Cooks in white aprons chopped tomatoes and peppers. A radio blared in the corner, positioned on bags of rice taller than me. My heart skipped a beat. I thought this joint was empty. My senses were electric; each one frantically tried to determine the trouble I'd gotten myself into. Just when I was about to turn and run, a really tall cook spotted me. He spoke rapid Spanish, waving his lethal butcher knife in the air. I blinked. Twice. I couldn't understand a single word. It didn't matter, because even if I could, I was about to pee my pants.

By now my presence had attracted a crowd. Three other cooks and two women in bright purple dresses stared at me. My heartbeat rose to a terrible thud in my ears; sweat formed on my upper lip. I considered turning to run but was afraid they'd run after me.

*Oh, sweet heaven, how am I supposed to explain this in Spanish?*

One of the women smiled at me. I could see a pineapple in her hand. For a split second I felt better. People with pineapples must be kind. Then she said something in Spanish. I didn't understand. I was so overwhelmed that I blurted out, "May I have a soda?"

She cocked her head to one side. "Show me," she said, plain as day.

I pointed to the refrigerator, sure I was about to die of embarrassment.

She pointed at me, then the refrigerator and repeated, "Show me."

I toughed up, sucked in my breath, walked over, and heaved that big handle back to reveal the glorious orange contents. I took out a soda, holding it up for everyone to see. A chorus of "Si. Si," rang out in the room. Everyone turned back to their work, even the woman with the pineapple.

Suddenly I felt very self-conscious and made a beeline out of there, running three floors straight up, tiptoeing quickly to my room. Like the coyote from Road Runner, I closed my door lightly, ran across the room to my bed, leapt under the blankets, and went to twist the top from my treasure. The carbonated jewel glistened. I twisted again.

*Dang it. Twist. Twist.* I looked down and remembered. *The bottle opener.*

A door opened down the hall. The dreaded footsteps. Without wasting a second, I threw the blankets over me, sliding my bottle under my pillow. My head thumped into the feather pillow. A second later, my door opened, creaking. Through my squinty eyes I saw Dave peering into my room. I could see one eye, part of his nose, and the tuft of hair that always stood up on his head in the morning.

I tried to be still and quiet and normal. The glass bottle was cool against the palm of my hand. Dave's one eye scanned the room. Playing opossum was working. Without a suspicion in the world, he closed the door and walked back down the hall.

I whipped the blankets off, jumping to the floor, prize in hand, trying to think of a plan. I could sneak back down to the kitchen, but Dave was awake and somewhere on the other side of my door. The cooks might not let me back into the kitchen. They might call the Federales. I paced, trying to figure out how to gnaw the top off with my teeth. That's when I saw it. Joy of all joys. At the end of my dresser, on the corner, a bottle opener was screwed into the wood. I actually sailed through the air. I held the bottle tight, careful not to tilt it too much. Without much strain the top popped off. I guzzled half the bottle in four seconds, stopped to breathe, listening to the slow churn in my stomach. *Wurgle wurgle glop.* Carbonated air ascended the back of my throat, where I pressed one enormous *beeeeeeelch* into the sleeve of my shirt. Several less impressive belches followed.

I held the bottle high, admiring the contents.

The orange cream smell made me delirious.

A knock on my door almost gave me a heart attack. Lost in soda pop paradise I hadn't even heard footsteps. Without knowing what else to do I stuffed the bottle behind the curtain and ran like hell for my bed. Out of the corner of my eye I saw the door opening. I rolled into the sheets just in time to see my mother standing there.

"What are you doing?"

"Nothing."

She stepped into my room, glancing over to where I'd indulged.

"What were you doing out of bed?"

"Playing."

"With what?"

"Diggy."

That really annoyed her. She walked closer to the window, eyeing me. "I don't believe you."

First, she looked under the dresser, finding the top to the soda I'd been forced to leave behind. She turned it over in her hand as her eyes trailed across the floor to the curtains. Grabbing the bottle, she snarled, "What is this?"

*Creamy, delicious contraband.* "I don't know."

"You don't know," she sneered, stepping closer. "You're not supposed to have soda. It rots your teeth."

"Someone must have left it in here."

"Yeah, someone like you." She slammed my door on her way out.

I sat in the middle of the bed, my face pinched into a scowl so tight I could barely breathe. Fifteen minutes into plotting my next heist, Dave knocked, then walked into my room. I sat in the middle of my bed obsessing over orange colored soda.

He leaned against the dresser. "I think we're going to have to go down to the airport."

"Are we leaving?"

"No," he said, reluctant to speak the truth. "Ummm, well, there's a problem with our luggage."

This was not a big deal to me. I didn't actually need anything in my suitcase. "Is it stolen?"

"They haven't actually used the word 'stolen' yet. They're calling it *missing.*"

"It's stolen." I launched myself to the floor. "So, what do we do?"

"I have an appointment with Airport Administration," he reached for my hand. "You'll go with me."

We left, walking down the quiet stairwell together. Out front, as traffic whizzed by, I noticed my mother wasn't joining us.

Dave noticed me looking around. "It's just you and me kiddo."

That thrilled me. The taxi drove us to a store where they sold gemstones. Big, round dazzling rubies and emeralds winked at me from black velvet trays. Dave looked at diamonds with a little round thing he called a "jeweler's eye". I picked out everything I fell in love with in the store. Dave bought me a smooth lavender amethyst that I put in my pocket. The jeweler packaged the stones in a flat leather pouch that wrapped around Dave's waist, under his clothes, next to the wallet strapped to his stomach. A taxi was waiting outside to take us to the airport.

After the taxi dropped us off, Dave unfolded a piece of paper with instructions. We walked through twisting dark corridors, around and down hallways that looked completely abandoned, and at the very end, there was a small, windowless concrete room. A woman looked up from her desk, smiling. Then she asked us a lot of questions in English. What was in our suitcases? How many? Did they have locks? Were we carrying contraband? When did we last see our luggage? Was it plaid or checkered or plain? Would we miss it if it never came back?

After we answered all of the questions, we had to go back into the hall. As we wound our way back through a maze that resembled the public health department, I asked, "What's going on?"

"It's stolen," Dave said.

All of my valuable possessions like my stuffed rabbit and Hardy Boys books were in a hatbox I dragged on and off the plane with me, but Dave had lost everything. Everything but his wallet, of course.

Next stop. Drugstore. Have wallet, will replace. Toothpaste. Toothbrushes. Razors. Soap. Shaving cream. Deodorant. Since neither of us read Spanish very well, we opened each box, inspecting the contents to determine what it was. Then off we went to the clothing store. T-shirts. Jeans. Underwear. Socks. It was like charades for survival.

The whole time Dave had emeralds, diamonds, sapphires and rubies strapped to his waist.

With bags full of loot, we caught a taxi that drove us to the nearest restaurant. Dave left our four bags of stuff at the coat check. The man who walked us to our seat wore a perfect, crisp black suit. He smelled like onions and garlic. I ordered cheese enchiladas and a shrimp cocktail.

"So, do you think we'll ever see our luggage again?" I dipped the butt of my shrimp in sauce.

"Nope," he said, taking a long pull on his beer.

"Why do you think they stole it?"

"Because it's full of expensive stuff. *My expensive stuff.*"

"Oh." I paused, looking around at the bright paintings up and down the walls. Women carried large baskets full of food on mountain roads. "Is the airport going to give us money for it?"

"The airline pays us back."

"Are you sad?"

Dave looked around distracted, then said, "No, not about that."

Back at the inn I followed Dave into his room to get my packages of stuff. That's when I saw my mother laying on the bed, arms sprawled over the edge, needle and spoon on the bedside table. Muscles in my stomach tensed. I was learning what that meant. I knew it made her sleepy and sick and Dave had to carry her to the bathroom. I knew it left marks on her arm so that she had to wear long sleeves in the middle of the summer. I knew I wasn't supposed to see it, and I really wasn't supposed to tell anyone at school. I'd seen it in movies before.

Dave took my hand, the bags of stuff, and guided me to the door. My mother groaned and rolled over. Dave ignored her, laying his hand on my shoulder, steering me out. In my room he divided up the goods. I was excited to have my own things that I didn't have to share with anyone.

Dave put his stuff back in the bags. "Are you going to be okay?"

I nodded. When he left, I carefully unwrapped each new item. The fresh, minty bar of green soap, the toothbrush with its plastic case, the trial-size bottles of cherry-scented lotion, mouthwash, and a tube of toothpaste with a cartoon bird on the front. I lined them all up in front of me and stared at each one. I opened another package and sniffed.

Diggy climbed up on the bed next to me. He thumped his foot and smiled.

"Hey, I was just opening my stuff." I tore open a pack of gum.

Diggy wagged his tail.

"I thought being in South America would be different than being at home, but it's not."

Diggy was quiet, twirling the fur on his ears.

"I thought maybe we could have fun and it would be great."

"It's still great," he said. "We don't need them to be great."

I thought about it for a while. Outside the window, a fresh bright moon rose over the city, casting light in a cool glow through the branches of the trees. Cars honked their horns on the boulevard several blocks away. Diggy thumped his foot against the bedpost. "Yeah, you're right." I managed a smile.

He hopped down from the bed and pointed at the door. "Soda," he whispered.

*Whew. What a good idea.* Three sodas later, I was propped up against my dresser, hiding the empty bottles in my drawer, belching, rumbling, and snickering with my best imaginary friend. Silence unfolded all around us. Another belch exploded from my chest like an old volcano. Diggy thumped his foot like he had fleas.

A door down the hall closed. Slammed, actually. My light was out, but I wasn't in bed. I made a run for it, quiet and quick, and cleared the footboard in no time, yanking the covers up to my neck. My breath stuck in my nostrils.

*Thump thump thump* went the footsteps in the hall. *Boom boom boom* went my blood in my ears. Diggy was still over in the corner scratching. *Thump thump thump.*

*Wham*, went the door, then *wham* again, then *thump thump thump* and a lot of swearing.

*Shit*, Dave muttered only a few feet from my door.

*Gosh*, I thought to myself, *it was just a few sodas. You don't have to stand out in the hall and swear.*

*"Dang it,"* he said. Then, *thump thump thump, slam, thump thump thump.* The sound of his footsteps disappeared down the long, dark staircase.

I caught a glimpse of Diggy in the corner, inspecting the last empty bottle on the floor. "What do you think that was about?" I whispered.

He shrugged. Then he looked out the window.

I leapt from my bed, not afraid of being caught, and ran to the window. On my tiptoes, with my nose pressed to the glass, I could see my mother and Dave standing at the curb, hailing a taxi. My breath fogged up the window. I wiped it with my sleeve. A taxi pulled to a stop. Dave opened the door.

I glanced at Diggy. "Do you think they'll come back?"

He shrugged.

Finally, I backed away from the window and whispered, "Let's go see if they make cookies in Spanish."

The next morning, I slept until I heard one of the housekeepers open my door. She poked her head in, checking on me. I was so tired my face felt glued to the bed. She spoke to me in Spanish, smiling, then walked in, carrying a breakfast tray loaded with yummy piles of food. I pushed myself up in bed, helping her guide the tray down onto my legs, extended out in front of me. I thanked her and she smiled again.

Scrambled eggs with onions and tomatoes, hot fresh bread, jam, butter, fruit, and a pot of the blackest coffee I'd ever seen, with a creamer shaped like a cow. I poured my coffee, stirred in cream and sugar, smeared butter and jam on my bread, grabbed my book from the nightstand, and leaned back into a blissful breakfast in bed. *My gosh. I wish my mother and Dave disappeared more often.*

Diggy showed up around noon, asking if anyone had come back.

I shook my head. "Not that I know of."

He looked worried.

I pointed to the empty soda bottles next to the bed.

He smiled. Soda made everything better.

The housekeeper, who I'd learned was named Sophia, returned with a lunch tray, and then later, when shadows slanted across my floor signaling the onset of evening, she returned with a dinner tray. She touched me softly on the head, pointing to my door. I didn't understand. She made her fingers walk like people. I still didn't understand but noticed the two big sodas glimmering in the lamplight.

Then she said, "They come later."

That caught me off guard. "You know English?"

She pulled her thumb and index finger very close together and said, "Little."

For some reason that made me laugh, and she laughed with me.

Then she left.

I sat in the middle of my bed, staring down at the shrimp on my plate. Part of me hoped my mother and Dave never came back so that I could go live somewhere else. And, of course, part of me wondered why I'd just been left there. I wasn't hungry and played with my food until I fell asleep in my clothes, with the light on.

Much later, I was startled awake. Dave's shadow loomed over me, blocking the light. "Hey, kiddo," he said.

I stared up at him. "Where have you been?"

"Doing business."

"What time is it?"

"Around four in the morning." He reached for my hand, pulling me up.

My eyes squinted and tensed in the light.

"I need you to get your stuff together," he said.

"You just left me here." I pulled away, flopping down onto the bed, glass clinking against silverware on my dinner tray. "I wasn't bad, and you guys left me here anyway."

"Oh, gosh," he exhaled, "it's not like that. I'm sorry you couldn't go but it's too dangerous. I don't know these people down here, at least, not like I know the ones back home. It's one thing for me to get hurt. It's another thing to do something stupid that hurts you."

"I was scared today. That hurt."

"I know." He sat down on the edge of my bed. "Look." He lifted his shirt, unzipping the wallet strapped to his waist. "I'll give you some money so you can buy yourself whatever you want."

He handed me three one-hundred-dollar bills, a ten, two fives, and six ones.

"That's all I have on me." He stood up, his shirt falling back in place. "Now I need you to get your stuff packed."

He left the room. I crammed the cash in my pocket. Then I climbed down, stacked all of my empty soda bottles in the corner, packed my hat box, loaded my new items back in the bag from the store, stuffed most of my dinner in a bowl wrapped in a napkin, gathered it all together, and waited in the hall.

About five minutes later Dave appeared in the hall with eight leather suitcases I'd never seen. He carried them, two by two, downstairs into a waiting taxi. Then he grabbed all of his new items, still in the shopping bags, and we walked down the stairs together.

"What did you buy?" I asked, curious.

"Nothing."

"Then, what's in the suitcases?"

"Money."

*Oh.*

The taxi rumbled through the cool blue night to a big hotel across town. A bleary-eyed bellboy loaded all of our new suitcases onto a luggage rack and rolled us up to a room Dave had already checked into. My mother was asleep on the bed.

"Do you want to sleep in one of my new t-shirts?" Dave asked.

"Sure."

He ripped a pack open with his teeth, tossing me one. I put it on. Nice and soft and new.

The next day Dave shipped all of his suitcases and gemstones to a "business partner" back in Mississippi. He packed them up nicely in big brown boxes. The three of us went shopping for clothes. My mother hadn't said a word in days. It didn't matter anymore. I could buy myself whatever I wanted.

# CHAPTER EIGHTEEN

### *Don't Drink the Water*

Everyone at the hotel said, "Don't drink the water. El agua es no bueno." *The water is no good.* Huge bottled-water dispensers were everywhere. Shop owners wagged their fingers. *Do not drink the water.* Waiters at fancy restaurants brought bottles of fresh water to the table. *Do not drink the water.* Old women weaving blankets in the back rooms of the market popped open bottles of water. *Do not drink the water.*

Gringo.

Dave drank the water. By his estimation they were all sissies. Water is made to drink. Period. For two days he wasn't able to move more than six feet from the toilet. Brutal. The sound of him, alone, in that porcelain chamber with all of those splattering, moaning sounds actually made me feel sorry for him.

My mother was irked. We were supposed to go horseback riding. Our name had come up on the list. An Indian named Juan had been by two days in a row.

"Go now?" he asked in English that sounded like Dave's Spanish.

My mother pointed across the room at the very pale, wilted water-drinker slumped in the corner chair.

Juan shook his head. "Water no good. No drink."

My mother slammed the door, throwing an angry finger in Dave's direction. "Everyone in the entire freaking country knows not to drink the water. *Except you.*" She didn't call him a butthole. The sarcasm alone could have killed him.

Dave shifted in his seat, butt cheeks clamped together. It looked exhausting. A deep, horrific groan moved up his chest but was barely a sigh by the time it escaped. My mother glared at him. I mean, really glared—like evil eye, voodoo glare. Dave was too sick to lift his eyelids high enough to notice.

I went back to reading the Hardy Boys mystery everyone had told me was dumb to bring on vacation. Everyone said there would be no time to read it. Good thing I hadn't listened. I was finished with the first book, well into the second.

We ordered room service. That was fine with me considering the options, which narrowed down to going out in public with my mother. *No thanks.* The kitchen staff put the manager on the phone. He recited the entire menu in English. Dave wasn't hungry. During the past twenty-four hours he'd formed a theory that if nothing went in, then nothing could come out. Not exactly the truth. My recent addiction to soda had become a welcome distraction. I ordered three with my dinner because no one was in the mood to argue. No one noticed anyway. My mother watched lions kill water buffalo out on the Serengeti in Spanish. Every so often she looked back over her shoulder, glaring at the bathroom door.

*Spppppllat. Spppppppppttt. Plufffffffff. Spppllat.* Dave had been locked in there for the last forty minutes. It was gruesome.

A very tall man wearing a white uniform rolled our food up on a cart. His hair was so black it glistened in the hall light. While my mother dug through her purse to find money, the attendant asked why we had come so far to stay in our hotel room. My mother jammed her finger in the direction of the bathroom door.

"Ah," he said. "Water no good. No drink."

"You hear that?" she yelled at the closed door. "Everyone in the entire freaking country knows not to drink the water."

*Take that.*

Two bites before I finished my shrimp Vera Cruz, Dave emerged looking haggard and droopy. Empty soda bottles lined my cart.

"To hell with it," he championed, guzzling down the rest of my mother's beer.

This act of defiance sent him back to the john, where he actually made gasping sounds for an hour. Afterwards he moved the chair directly next to the bathroom because he was afraid he couldn't run fast enough. I had chocolate cake for dinner with whipped cream and blackberries and fell asleep in my clothes.

The next morning was more of the same. Glaring. Ham and eggs. Door slamming. Hot coffee. *Screw you.* Breakfast on a cart. Strawberries. *Everyone knows not to drink the water. Moron.*

Nothing new happened. We were still chained to the toilet. On the fourth day, my mother said to Dave, "You've spent so much time in the toilet that you actually look like crap yourself."

That pretty much covered day four.

Day five. Dave wouldn't even wash his hands with tap water. He was terrified of anything that came out of a faucet.

Day six. A pale, shaky Dave answered the door when room service knocked. The woman attendant clucked her tongue against the roof of her mouth. *Tisk. Tisk. Tisk.* When she patted Dave, motherly, on the cheek, she almost knocked him over. That's when I knew it was bad. Even the locals started to feel sorry for him. His hand reached out to steady himself. Overall, he'd stopped sleeping. The room service attendant wrote down the name and address of a doctor and handed it over.

"Here," she said, "give this to taxi man." She pointed to the piece of paper. "Go here."

Dave nodded, his brain sloshing around in his head, liquefying, preparing to seep out his ears. The overhead fan in the bathroom was on twenty-four hours a day. It still smelled like an outhouse. At cleaning time when the maids rolled their cart down the hall, Dave sheepishly stepped out, asking for six extra rolls of toilet paper. *Seis rolls.* They all knew by the way his butt cheeks were pinched together it wasn't a sinus problem.

The next morning. Day seven. At the crack of dawn, I was corralled into a waiting taxi where we zoomed across the dark city of Bogotá. The driver kept glancing up into his rearview mirror, shaking his head. Dave shifted, gingerly crossing and uncrossing his legs in the cramped backseat. His face was pale and gray, with ghastly dark circles that swallowed up his eyes. The air smelled of exhaust. The only sound to be heard was that of the motor rumbling like a giant cage under the hood.

Our savior's name was Diego. We knew because he wrote his name on the back of a business card whose edges had gone soft. He gestured to the taxi, then to the front door of the doctor's office. "I come here for us soon one hour for today."

*Gotcha.* Good enough for me.

Dave nodded, beaten into submission by diarrhea *cha cha cha.* Silent, single file, we marched through the iron gate to the front door. No one in the doctor's office spoke English. C'est la vie. Even with the language barrier, the nurses knew that look. Pasty. Puny. Droopy. Diarrhea is not a game.

One of them wagged a playful finger. "Bottom on fire," she snickered.

Dave was privately escorted back to an examination room to expose the last shred of dignity he had left. Forced to explain to a perfect stranger, making notes on a clipboard, why he'd traveled four thousand miles to make friends with a commode. There was no pride in that. *Cha cha cha.*

Diego did, in fact, return for us. The edges of Dave's mouth curved up in a hopeful, thankful smile. With a little bottle full of tiny purple pills tucked safely in his pocket, he had a whole new outlook on life. My mother still wasn't speaking to him, which, in my opinion, couldn't be that bad. Back at the hotel, we all learned that not only would the pills plug up his butt as promised, but they also eased the pain and knocked him out. For the first time in eight days, I heard snoring. It was kind of nice. I had custard for dinner to celebrate. And three more sodas. The room service woman pointed at Dave sleeping and snorted.

The next morning Juan knocked on the door. A freshly showered Dave opened the door and announced we'd all be ready to go horseback riding the next day.

Juan just stared at him, then shook his head. "It is always tomorrow with you."

*Tomorrow,* I wailed. The entire vacation was *tomorrow.* I missed valuable Stan time to sit in a hotel room in a country where I barely understood anyone. Tomorrow sucked. I was bored to the very core of my existence. I said this aloud just to stir up a heap of trouble.

My mother looked up from *Star Trek* in Spanish long enough to snarl, "Yeah, well, we're not stuck in this room because I'm a dipshit."

No, we're not. *That's a first.*

It wouldn't matter. My mother was too mean to succumb to parasites, South American or otherwise.

To avoid mutiny, Dave said, "Hey, I know. Let's call Diego and go out to dinner."

Diego. Our new best friend. He possessed a car.

The taxi screeched to a halt in front of us. I was not convinced Diego had a driver's license. He leaned over, rolling down the passenger's side window.

Loud music assaulted us as he screamed, "Get in! Go now!" It sounded very urgent. We jumped in, locking the doors, quick. We sped off into a darkness that did not translate.

The taxi dashed through the streets to the main part of downtown. With the help of the Spanish/English dictionary and a pile of cash that spoke for itself, Dave rented Diego and his vehicle for $385.00. American money. *Cash.*

At a stoplight I glanced over and saw a boy, maybe nine years old, dancing on the corner for money. *Why would he be doing that?* His pants were too short, shoes at least three sizes too big. Buttons were missing from his coat, so were some of his teeth. His hair looked like it was trimmed with a rusty steak knife, yet he smiled bigger than any human being I'd ever seen. Tap dancing seemed to be his specialty. He smiled so big he barely had room for his eyes. I smiled back. It felt good. I hadn't seen anyone smile in a week except the housekeepers. Dave rolled down the window, handing the boy a twenty-dollar bill. Now he smiled bigger. Dave gestured for him to take the money. The boy looked dizzy with thanks and grabbed the money. As the taxi drove away, I saw the boy run wildly down the street, clutching the money to his chest. I had no idea, but from the looks of it, twenty dollars was worth a lot in that place.

Dave rolled up the window, celebrating his recent escape from the commode. Housekeeping was going to have to find someone else to make fun of.

My mother rolled her eyes. "Show-off."

At first, the evening began innocently enough. That immediately made me suspicious, but I let my guard down anyway. Diego drove us around Bogotá, pointing, saying, "See this?"

We nodded. Then he told a story in a mish-mosh of English, Spanish, pantomiming, gestures, laughs, squeaks, while his hands circled his head wildly. We kept nodding.

Driving out into the country, he kept saying, "My family at home live on country land. Like farm, you know?"

It was obvious he loved his mother very much by the way he clutched his hand to his heart every time he spoke her name. My mother was bunched up against the opposite door not speaking to anyone.

Diego wanted to take us to see clam diggers. I thought he was taking us to see a pair of pants cropped a few inches above my ankles. Instead, he drove us out of the city. When we crested a hill directly below us, there were all of these women standing waist deep in the grayest mud I'd ever seen, with huge, brown, scratchy-looking sacks slung over their shoulders.

"What are they doing?" I asked, craning my neck to see.

"Digging clams," Diego laughed. "Clam diggers."

That was not funny to me. I stared down at the women. Caked mud clung to their arms and faces, matting dark strands of hair to their necks and foreheads. It was depressing. I thought we were going shopping. As we pulled away, I vowed never to eat pasta with clam sauce again. I would never be responsible for someone standing waist-deep in mud. I turned in the seat to watch the women fade to dots as we drove away. When the taxi crested the next hill, the clam diggers disappeared.

We toured villages made of cardboard houses with sheets of plastic for roofs. It was so depressing. To liven things up, Diego dug around under his dash and pulled out a bag with three neatly rolled joints inside. Dave and my mother exchanged looks.

Before Diego fired one up, Dave leaned forward, throwing his arms over the seat. Moving in really close to Diego's face, he said, "If I smoke this joint with you are we suddenly going to meet up with the Federales so that I have to buy my way out of prison?"

I was stunned. Truly.

Diego didn't even flinch. In fact, he looked very serious. His head shook back and forth, "No. Swear by true."

The tone in Dave's voice was so menacing and new. I'd never heard this *cause if you're messing with me then I'll come hunt you down and scalp you* voice.

Dave said, "Swear by true. I hope so. We're getting off to a really good start." *Oh. My. Gosh.*

Diego shook his honest head. "No, senor. You have plan wrong. I share with American friend."

*$385.00 buys fast friends.*

"Why?" Dave exhaled like wind across a glassy lake.

"So, maybe you share with Diego."

"Yeah." Dave eased back in his seat. "Maybe I will."

For the rest of the evening I had the privilege of riding around in an automobile with three very stoned, very annoying human beings. The only time my mother actually touched Dave was when she was stoned. Just when I thought it was going to stop, Dave rolled another joint, sharing the hash he'd carried through customs in his cowboy boot.

The lobby of the hotel was empty when we finally stumbled in at 4 AM. I was vexed. After what felt like forever, my mother locked herself in the bathroom, and Dave walked down the hall for soda. I grabbed the phone and frantically pressed zero for the operator. A voice came on.

"Please, please help me. I've got to make a collect call."

"¿Le cómo puedo ayudar yo?"

*Huh?*

"I need to call my grandmother right away."

"¿Habla usted Espanola? ¿Qué número de teléfono, por favor?"

"A collect call. I need to make a collect call." I heard my mother snorting the famous Colombian cocaine in the bathroom. Diego had proved to be a total pain in the butt.

"Una llamada a cobro revertido?"

"Crap."

"¿Qué?"

"Por favor. Telefono right away."

The key turned in the lock of the door. A soda can smacked the floor, then Dave started swearing.

"Help me," I whispered. "I've got to get out of this place."

"Gracias para llamar. Yo no hablo inglés. Tenga un buenos días."

The line went dead. I hung up the phone. My mother and Dave entered the room simultaneously, stoned out of their gourds. They looked at each other and laughed. Then they started doing *Saturday Night Live* skits they had memorized. It was bad enough I had to be there but now I had to fall asleep to my mother doing Roseanne Rosannadanna for the bajillionth time.

The next morning, I woke to the sound of Juan pounding on the door. He entered our room, holding his leather against his chest. "Go now?" he asked.

"Yep," Dave said, proudly.

Juan looked at me still laying in bed. "She go too?"

"She go too," Dave repeated, cheerfully.

"Good." Juan plopped his hat on his head. "I wait for you now."

Of course, my mother and Dave were starved. They begged Juan to stop off at a café, but he refused. He was my hero. Make 'em starve. "Schedule." He pointed at an old clipboard that looked like a cat chewed on the corners. He took us to a big forest with flowers all around. While Dave was off buying food and bottles of water from a street vendor, I was led to a bed of flowers to meet the sweetest pony I'd ever seen.

Juan petted the pony's head. "His name is Rodrigo."

I touched his soft, furry nose.

"Small people ride small horse." He hoisted me up in the air.

Halfway through the day, high on junk food, I saw a boy on the path selling cigarettes. He was small like me, maybe nine years old, but instead of dark black hair and golden red skin he was perfectly pale, with blond hair and blue eyes. It was the first time during the trip I'd seen anyone who even slightly resembled me. I smiled, so lost in the feeling of camaraderie that I didn't notice I was staring at him in a dreamy stupor. But he did.

I nearly fell off my pony when the boy yelled across the way, "Senorita!"

*Oh gosh.*

He pointed at me, a stream of Spanish rushing from his mouth.

*Huh?*

I dug my heels into the flanks of my pony. He started trotting. It didn't matter, though, because the boy was hot on my trail. I nearly fell off, straining to look over my shoulder. He was following me. Yelling in Spanish, he changed his route, following the path behind me. Juan looked over at me. *He knows,* I thought. *Of course, he knows. He speaks Spanish.*

"What is he saying?" I asked Juan, teetering on the edge of a nervous breakdown. Terrified to draw attention to myself.

Juan looked at me patiently, then said, "He thinks you're beautiful."

Quickly I looked around, trying to find my mother, who, *thank goodness,* had veered off onto another path without Dave. Dave was in front of me, unwrapping packages of junk food, trying to balance on the back of a horse. I was going to get into so much trouble if anyone found out. I was not supposed to talk to strangers. *Ever.* I was certainly not supposed to have them follow me. The boy called out behind me. I nudged my pony again, breaking into a full trot. I started sweating. I had somehow attracted attention to myself. Boys were bad. Except Preston Brown, who never had time to ask to see my panties because his mom kept him praying all day.

I kept up the same pace, but when I looked behind me again, there he was, following along, still yelling out a lot of *va va vavoom* in Spanish. Juan started laughing.

"What's so funny?" I demanded.

Juan shrugged. "He says you angel."

Glancing over I saw my mother was coming back down the trail. The boy was catcalling behind me. I was going to faint for sure.

Juan rode up close to me. "Let him love you. He is just a poor boy who will remember you forever."

"What is he saying?"

Juan listened for a minute, glancing over his shoulder at the boy. "He says he has no nice clothes to offer. Only pots of black coffee and kisses. He says he will give you moonlight and flowers he steals."

*No. No. No.* The blood stopped running to my brain. I was dizzy. I was always getting in trouble. I didn't want any trouble. I wanted to ride my pony.

The boy whooped loudly.

My mother trotted next to me. She looked over at Juan, then at the boy. "Why is that boy following us?" she asked.

Juan said, "He's making money. Selling cigarettes."

My mother hated cigarettes. It was okay. My mother hated everything.

The boy followed me another two miles and stopped occasionally to sell cigarettes.

Dave caught up with me, enjoying the leisurely stroll. He said, "Juan says he'll take us to the temples high in the mountains."

I nodded, distracted by my lovesick stalker persistently following. Over my shoulder I heard Juan snort.

Dave tensed self-consciously, "Did I miss something?"

"No," I snapped, giving Juan the eye.

"No, Senor," Juan said. "I am having laugh of boy."

"Yeah," Dave agreed, glancing back at the serenading cigarette seller. "He's been following us for miles. I was thinking about buying all of his cigarettes just to get him to go away."

"It will do no difference, Senor. The boy is in love."

Juan was *not* my new best friend.

"With who?" Dave asked, clueless.

"With the flowers, the sky." Juan said, kinda dreamy.

Juan *was* my new best friend.

"Oh," Dave said. Too much poetry for him.

When I slid down off my pony at the entrance to the stables, the boy walked directly up to me. I saw the colors in his eyes were green like gemstones Dave bought when we were at the inn. I saw a reflection of myself in his eyes. Then, very slowly, very sweetly, he lifted my hands to his face, kissing them. I was flabbergasted. *Oh my gosh.* After a few seconds, he lifted his head, smiled, gave me a pack of cigarettes, and walked off.

My mother glared at me. "He probably saw your panties when you were getting off that pony. Be more careful."

She hadn't seen the pack of cigarettes yet, so I hid it in the folds of my shirt.

"And go wash your hands," she snapped. "This place is filthy."

Back at the hotel I hid my secret love smokes while my mother and Dave huddled around the phone calling Diego. Half an hour later, he was at our door. Sharing. That's what Dave called it. *Sharing.* How nice. Diego wasn't staying, just dropping off a joint.

Dave patted Diego on the shoulder, saying, "Thanks for sharing your stash."

For some reason this flipped my switch.

*Why can't we go anywhere without everyone getting stoned?*

Everyone was either stoned before we got there, stoned while we were there, or stoned when we left. I locked myself in the bathroom with my rabbit and my book. I hadn't eaten in hours. Who cared? Everyone was stoned. I wanted to shred the shower curtain with my teeth. Instead, I unlocked the door, turned off the light, piled towels in the bathtub, pulled the curtain shut and went to sleep. It was actually kind of nice. The porcelain was cool and quiet. The towels were thick and comfortable. I dozed off.

I thundered back to reality with a pounding on the hotel door. Sure it must be the police, I bolted upright, ready to run. In my haste to find somewhere to run I jerked open the door just in time to see room service rolling a cart into our room. I let go of my anger momentarily because it was difficult to be that angry and that hungry at the same time. The stoners looked like poo. The polite Southern way to say it. I could tell we weren't going to get an early start.

I woofed down a ham and cheese omelet. My mother fired up another joint. *Are you kidding?* I was so perturbed I blurted out, "If you drank beer at this hour, you'd be alcoholics."

"Good thing it's none of your business," she snorted, taking a long toke.

It was the all-time stupidest thing I'd ever witnessed. I had a feeling it was about to go on and on.

It did.

It turned out that Diego's secret stash was the size of Rhode Island. I was totally screwed. Six days into the pot-smoking marathon I stopped speaking to them. They didn't notice. They were stoned. On the seventh day, Bloody Marys rolled in on the food cart. This new development added to the spectacle. We lived with towels rolled up at the bottom of the door to keep the smoke in. I watched twelve episodes of *The Twilight Zone* in Spanish. Each one made more sense than my vacation.

I waited for Dave and my mother to pass out and called my grandmother collect. I memorized her number from the English/Spanish translation book that lay around unused.

I whispered, "Telefono, por favor," then the number. It worked. The phone rang and rang and rang. A fit of agitation seized me. I suddenly remembered I was usually the only one who answered the phone. Pick up the phone, *por favor.*

No one answered.

When my plan didn't work, I dragged my suitcase from under my bed and felt around for the pack of cigarettes. I found them stuffed in a pant leg. Before taking them out I looked over at the pot smokers passed out on the other bed, snoring. Carefully and quietly, I took the pack out, holding it in my hand, looking out across the city. I didn't understand what it meant to have a pack of cigarettes, but I wanted to know where the boy lived so I could walk to his house on days like this. His mom would make us cakes and pinch his cheeks and talk to me in Spanish. I would say *"Telefono, por favor"* and impress her.

Dave grunted, throwing one of his legs over the edge of the bed. I watched him closely, ready to hide the smokes. He didn't wake up. I went back to wondering about the boy's name. I held the cellophane wrapper to my nose. The rich smell of tobacco filled my nostrils. I thought about the pack for a long time, then returned it to my suitcase. It was my secret. He was my secret. I slid my suitcase back under my bed.

Diego called at four. The sound of the phone ringing shattered the world of the stoners. Both of them jerked awake, hair matted to foreheads, dark circles shadowing frowns. The ringing was so loud it sounded like the emergency signal for disaster alerts.

I looked up from my Hardy Boys and smiled.

Dave grabbed the phone, breathless from trauma. "Hello?" Seconds later, he nodded, rubbing his face, saying, "Sure. Sure. Si. Si. We'd love to."

"What's going on?" I asked, hopeful.

"Diego's coming over." Dave rubbed the back of his neck. "I gotta get a shower."

"I'm bored," I wailed.

"Then do something," my mother snapped, reaching for the half-smoked joint in the ashtray.

That day Diego drove us high into the mountains to visit the temples. The huge stone buildings were so mythic. The air was thin. My mother almost fainted and had to sit on the steps leading to the entrance. Dave and I walked on without her. Everything always happened too fast for me in my life, and I wanted that moment to linger longer than most of the trip. I wanted the still beauty of the place to claim me. I wanted to sit alone in the quiet chambers and think about the cigarette boy.

I was still mad at Dave and gave him the silent treatment until I met a mule along the way. His big ears twitched and flickered, and he grunted and snorted, rubbing his nose and face against my shoulder. That made me laugh. It was the first time I'd laughed in a month. Once we were inside the temple, the cool, fragrant air comforted me. Dave watched old women with brightly knitted shawls tied over their shoulders. The lines around his eyes were deeper. He looked tired. There hadn't been a lot of love shared during this trip.

Looking out across stone benches I realized I didn't want to go home. I wanted to stay in that place and eat tamales and talk to Stan on the phone every day. I didn't want to go back. Neither did Dave. I could see it in his eyes. It was the first time in three weeks he wasn't stoned. In a wild burst of confessional delirium, I told him about the boy and the cigarettes. I told him they were hidden in my suitcase.

Then I said, "I don't want to go home."

Dave sat quietly for a long time. I shifted on the stone bench, then shifted again, aware of its cold, hard surface. The angle of the light changed, dimmed.

Finally, he said, "Don't tell your mother about the cigarettes. She'll just take them away from you."

Two days later we flew back to America and never saw our luggage or Diego again.

# CHAPTER NINETEEN

*Chicken Pox & Other Disasters*

On Sunday morning I woke to the sound of a bus idling at the curb in front of our house. Since we were the last house on a dead-end street such odd occurrences aroused my suspicions. I'd fallen asleep on the couch after playing checkers with Stan all night and only had to lift my head slightly to see through the curtains.

My grandmother breezed through the room, wearing a wig and lipstick, carrying her pocketbook. I rolled over, listening to the sound of the engine outside.

When she saw my eyes open, she stopped. "I'm going out," she said. "Get Stan to help you make breakfast."

"Where are you going?" I turned back to the window. Waiting at the curb was a big white bus with bright blue letters painted on the side. The moving Tabernacle of Faith.

Someone in our house had summoned Jesus.

"I'm going to church," she stated emphatically. "They're going to pick me up and drop me off. You can go next week if you want."

I slumped back down in my blanket. I'd been getting enough of the snake in my Bible class at school. She breezed past again on the way to the door.

I waited until the bus pulled away from the curb before I ran to wake Stan up. When I rounded the corner to his room, he was sitting up in bed, staring out the window at the big puffs of exhaust trailing behind the Tabernacle.

"Did you see that?" I pointed.

He nodded.

"What do you suppose she's doing?"

"I don't know," he said.

Between the two of us we were absolutely clueless, so I looked up the Tabernacle of Faith in the phone book. I found the listing and dragged the phone book into the kitchen where Stan was making coffee.

I pointed to the address. "It's on Chestnut Street."

"That's kind of far," he said, as he scooped coffee into the pot.

Something scraped the floor upstairs. Our eyes shot to the ceiling.

The weight of Thurman's demons bore down hard lately. Spell after spell came week after week. It had never been that bad. My grandmother gave him four times as much Thorazine. The medicine made his eyelids droop, but nothing made the Voices shut up. They lived in the house now. He talked to them all day long. They heckled him incessantly and he started taping pictures of witch doctors to the bathroom mirror. Day after day the entire upstairs smelled like a reefer pit. He paced and talked to the Voices until he couldn't take it anymore then went to buy malt liquor.

When the movement upstairs stopped, we determined the Beast wasn't awake yet.

Stan went back to making coffee. With his brow knotted together in a perplexed way that was a novelty on Stan's face, he asked, "Why do you suppose Mother went to church?"

I jerked my thumb toward the ceiling. "I bet it has something to do with *you know who* up there."

"But how did she find them? Maybe God called her in a dream. I seen that on TV."

"I don't think so."

"Then what?" Stan reached for a can of corned beef hash. A light bulb dinged on in his brain. "Your friend knows a lot about the Lord. Go ask him."

"Preston's at church."

Thurman barreled down the stairs into the kitchen like a cold wind in June. Stan and I turned, startled.

"What are you two freaks doing?" he snarled.

"None of your beeswax," I shot back.

He wagged a finger at us. "Losers. I heard you talking about God. Ha." He started laughing and kept up his snorting guffaw all the way to the front door. "You two losers need to get with Jesus." Then he slammed the door and left.

"Thank god," Stan said, finally taking a breath.

I poured myself a cup of coffee, but our relief was short-lived. The front door slammed again. *Thud. Thud. Thud.* Thurman plodded back through the living room. Stan and I exchanged glances.

"I thought he was gone," Stan whispered.

Thurman barreled into the kitchen, slapping a fat hand against the refrigerator.

"Call your mother," he ordered.

"Mother's at church," Stan said, matter of fact.

"Your mother is my mother, you moron." Thurman pointed at me. "I'm talking to you. Call your mother."

"What? We don't have a phone," I said, suddenly annoyed by the turn in conversation.

"Yeah, so call her boyfriend on that beeper thing and put in this number."

I opened the five-pound bag of sugar and grabbed a spoon to finish making my coffee. Maybe if I ignored him, he'd go away.

His fat hand slapped against the refrigerator. "Get to it, you little cretin."

I poured milk into my cup, intentionally ignoring him. I finished, stirring my creamy, dreamy concoction and asked, "Why do you want to talk to my mother? You don't even like her."

"No one likes her," he growled. "Now get to it." His fat arm pointed to the gossip bench.

A chill shimmied down my spine. The tone of his voice changed.

"Alright." I stomped into the hall. "You're so annoying."

"Takes one to know one," he said, following me to the phone.

He positioned himself over my shoulder, so I turned to conceal the number as I dialed. After I called the number, I waited. Then the electronic voice instructed me to enter the telephone number. I did. When I heard the beep beep that signaled the end of the call, I slammed the phone back in the receiver and walked off. "There," I said. "Don't bother me again."

He laughed in a deep, menacing way, and swatted at my head with his hand. I felt the wind against the back of my neck and his fingers brush my hair. I picked up my pace a little, trying to get to the kitchen and thus closer to the back door.

Stan leaned across the table. "What do you think he's doing?"

I whispered back. "I don't know. He's so creepy."

Cigarette smoke wafted in from the hall. The sound of Thurman's footsteps paced back and forth. I could hear Stan breathing. Suddenly the phone rang. Thurman grabbed it on the first ring. I shuffled quietly to the sink to eavesdrop.

"Yeah," Thurman snarled, puffing his cigarette. "No, Cotton don't want nothing. I called."

There was a pause.

I heard a garbled voice talking on the other end.

Then Thurman said, "Yeah, I need a favor. I need some of that stuff you guys got."

Thurman took a long drag on his cigarette, then said, "Okay. Fine. How much?"

Stan waved frantically from the other side of the room to get my attention. I looked over. He held up his hands and mouthed the words, *what's going on?*

My lips twisted into a frown. Frankly, I didn't know what was going on, but I didn't like it.

Thurman's voice interrupted my thought. "Hey, man, come on."

Another pause.

"Yeah, I got cash," Thurman said confidently. He listened for a second. "Yeah, I know where that is. I'll meet you there."

Then he hung up the phone, lit another cigarette and left.

Stan's eyes were huge. "What was that all about?"

"I don't know," I said, dismayed, "but I'm sure it has something to do with weed."

When his car jerked away from the curb, I went upstairs to snoop around. Marijuana seeds littered the floor. Dirty clothes were strewn all over the place. The pillow on his bed had a huge greasy stain where he laid his big, fat greasy head every night. I lifted the pillow gingerly with my thumb and forefinger. Underneath, on the mattress, was a pack of rolling papers and a small paperback book entitled *Do It Yourself Spells*. The words "human sacrifice" immediately sprang to mind.

We still had a garage full of taxidermy tools, so I picked up the book, thumbing through the pages, looking for clues. It described itself as "a practical guide for practitioners of Voodoo." All of the pages were untouched except one. The "Spell for Power Over People" was dog-eared at the top.

*Great*, I thought, closing the book. I looked out the window to make sure I didn't see him driving down the street. Then I snooped around some more to see if I could find anything to support my conclusion. I looked for dried chicken feet, jars of ground-up bat eyeballs, anything that could serve as an indication of how far along he might be in his quest for hocus pocus. I found socks under the bed so old and dirty they were stiff. I found dead flies, old tennis shoes, but no dried lizard tails.

Out front the Tabernacle bus ground to a halt. After a few minutes I took the voodoo book and went downstairs. When I rounded the corner to the kitchen my grandmother was sitting alone, with the lights out, smoking a Kool cigarette. In front of her a juice glass full of malt liquor sat on the table. The only light in the room slanted through metal blinds casting half light, half shadow.

She turned to look at me, her face dark with shadows. "Where's your uncle?"

"Which one?"

She took a sip of malt liquor. "Thurman."

"He left." I stepped forward, handing her the book.

"What's this?"

"I found it upstairs."

Her eyes squinted, then focused on the title. After several minutes of staring she said, "Thank you," and put it in her pocket.

I didn't know what else to say so I went to Stan's room and sat on the floor, listening to him snore through his midday nap.

That night Dave drove over to pick me up. My grandmother was in the kitchen when I heard the horn honk out front. I picked up my hatbox and walked in to tell her goodbye. She seemed so strange and otherworldly, staring off across the room to windows that looked out over the backyard. A full moon lit up the night.

"I'll be back next weekend," I said.

Neither of us moved.

Finally, I sucked in a breath and told her the truth. "I have a book of magic. I can make him disappear."

For the first time all afternoon she looked up at me and smiled so thin and bare that a burst of air could have blown it off of her face. Quietly, she said, "The Lord will help him, Cotton." She patted my hand softly.

*Honk. Honk.*

I ran out into the dark and climbed into the car. I turned around in my seat as we drove off.

"Do you see anyone following us?" Dave asked.

"No, I was just looking to see if my mother was here."

"It's just me and you, kiddo."

My eyes tightened at the edges. "Did you talk to Thurman today?"

Dave gripped the steering wheel tighter. "Why?"

"No reason," I said, trying to be more smooth than I felt.

"Then why are you asking?"

"Why are you asking me why I'm asking?"

"Oh, Cotton," he sighed. "It was just business."

"What kind of *business*?"

His eyes glistened and flashed as we passed under streetlights. "What's with the twenty questions?"

"I don't know," I answered gruffly. I was irritated and itched like crazy. I dug my fingers into the loose fabric of my shirt and scratched.

That night I took a shower and slathered myself in oatmeal lotion. I put on my softest pajamas and laid in bed trying to remember what God said on the first day.

On the first day God said let there be light, and there was, and it was good because that switch in the bathroom finally worked. I scratched.

The next morning, I woke up feeling hot and crappy. "I don't feel good," I whined to my mother.

Since she didn't want to deal with me, she put me in the car and drove me back to my grandmother's house. In my pajamas.

Stan was sitting out on the front porch. "Cotton, why are you scratching like that?

You got them chicken pox again?"

"No," I shuffled around, rubbing up against the railing. "You only get those once."

"Well, what's wrong then?" Stan cracked a smile.

"I don't know." *Scratch scratch.* "I think I got a rash. Don't tell anyone. Okay?"

"Yeah."

Then he walked right into the kitchen and told on me. "Mother, Cotton's scratching like she's got fleas."

"Maybe she has a mosquito bite," I heard her say.

"Naw, I don't think so. She made me promise not to tell anyone. That Preston Brown's probably given her chicken pox."

*Dang it, Stan. You've got to be the only forty-year-old in the world that cannot keep a secret.*

"Cotton? Where are you, child?" my grandmother called out, walking room to room.

"She's hiding," I heard the Traitor say.

She finally found me in the living room, braced up against the high-back chair, scratching like a cow. "Come here."

"I'd rather not," I offered politely, backing away.

"Well, I'd rather not hear about what you'd rather not do. Now come here."

"Can I go play with Preston?"

"He's at school. Now come here."

"She's got them big red spots all over her, Mother."

"Shut up, Stan," I growled.

"Stop telling your uncle to shut up and *come here*."

The she tried to catch me. "Now, what's got you out here scratching like the devil?"

"This," I jerked my shirt up to reveal my bare, flat, very pale, speckled chest.

"Oh, my gosh," she gasped, hand flying up to her mouth. "You're going to the doctor."

*That's exactly what I was trying to avoid.* "Stan, why'd you have to tell on me?"

"Stop harassing your uncle and go get in the car," she ordered from the hall, grabbing her pocketbook off the gossip bench.

"But I don't wanna."

"I don't care what you wanna or don't wanna. You're going to see Dr. Jack."

Doctor Jack was my pediatrician. Stan thought he was weird. He talked a lot about Mr. Ducky. Tons of toys littered the waiting room floor, but I was never allowed to play with them.

"Cotton, don't touch that," My grandmother jerked me up with amazing speed. "God knows where they've been."

I'm still afraid to touch things because *God knows where they've been.* I have this fantasy of one day walking up to God, who is popping open a Pabst Blue Ribbon. I hold up a funny little blue rubber chicken and ask, "Do you know where this has been?" He squints, takes a swig of beer and says, "I have no idea. Go ask your grandma."

"Sit still, child."

"I'm itching like crazy."

Doctor Jack appeared in the doorway to the waiting room. "I hear someone's got an itchy."

I called Preston when we got home. "I got shingles."

"Like on a roof?"

"Sort of. Except they're not on a roof, they're on me."

"Do they look like shingles?"

"No."

"Oh." Long silence. Then, "What do they do?"

"They make me itch."

I woke in the middle of the night. On my way to the bathroom, I passed through the dark rooms. Out back I saw firelight flickering against the windows. I called the Time and Temperature Man. It was 3:13 AM and the rest of the world was sleeping. I tiptoed over to a window. My grandmother seemed so ancient and otherworldly out in the dark, ripping out pages of voodoo spells. She stood there burning and praying in the middle of that dirt plot Thurman tilled up for the pot garden he never planted. I didn't know what to say. I was just happy to see her get rid of the book of spells.

The next morning, I woke to the sound of religious fanatics screaming at us from the TV. I flaked pink, crusty ointment off of my skin with my thumbnail. As I walked down the hall to Stan's room my grandmother started begging for forgiveness. She pulled a can of tomato soup off the shelf in the kitchen. "Help me Jesus."

For no reason she squeezed out the faintest little gasp while plugging in the percolator. *Praise the Lord.* She reached for the carton of eggs. *Praise the Lord.* She poured juice into a glass. *Save me Jesus.*

A minister dropped by for a house call that afternoon. He sat on the Victorian sofa for hours, talking about God with an ease and familiarity that suggested Our Father could have been napping in the other room. Stan and I gawked from across the room where my grandmother insisted we sit and pray. I itched like crazy.

Biblical passages appeared all week, scribbled on anything—the backs of phone books, bank receipts, notebooks, old KFC napkins. And they also disappeared. Thurman grew more and more agitated. When the minister showed up again on Friday, Thurman promptly locked his fat, unforgiven soul upstairs in his bedroom. He paced back and forth overhead like a caged animal. Thurman wasn't interested in developing a healthy relationship with God. To make matters worse, God didn't seem all that interested in him either.

The minister's eyes drifted up to the ceiling. A heavy thudding of footsteps interrupted the prayer session. Secretly, I watched from the hallway, fascinated. He knew we had the devil living upstairs. Tiny beads of sweat formed on his brow. My grandmother touched him lightly on the hand to make eye contact. Upstairs, the Beast flopped down on his bed, springs squeaking. *Praise the Lord.*

The minister nodded aimlessly, eyes drifting back up to the ceiling. Something heavy landed on the floor overhead. Probably, Thurman's taxidermy kit or some poor animal that didn't get away. The Beast was up there. Soon, we'd all be washed away in a river of blood. *Praise Jesus. Our Father who art in heaven, hallowed be thy name.*

Stan turned his stereo up. He couldn't stand the constant praying. *Praise the Lord.* The minister shifted on the sofa, and I saw his eyes rest on the door. He wanted to leave but he would stay because he was doing God's work and God doesn't let you leave early.

"Can I get you something to eat?" My grandmother begged him with her eyes.

"Huh?" The minister jerked back to reality, patting his stomach. "I ate just before coming over."

*Never face the Beast on an empty stomach.* Afternoon light faded. An eerie calm settled over everything. I waited. The minister helped my grandmother down on her knees to pray. *Dear Father, look upon us with forgiveness. Know that in our hearts we dwell without sin.*

Yeah, right. I hoped sound travelled up. The minister glanced through the bay window out into the ditch, and I saw a shiver tingle down his spine. He knew.

*We all knew.*

I felt feverish most of Saturday and tried to ignore Jesus and the Voices, who'd become prominent figures in our lives. But on Sunday, Thurman woke up early talking to himself. It made me shiver.

My grandmother brought me a clean pair of pants and shirt. "Put this on. You have to go with me today."

"No," I whined.

"Yes," she said. "This is not a discussion."

Stan drove us over.

I went to Sunday School, and my grandmother went to the main service. I was so mad. She just dumped me off in a room full of people I didn't even know and expected me to jump for joy. The lesson of the day was to write down sayings our family lived by. Then we sat in a circle and politely read them aloud. The Voices constantly cut into my TV time, but now Jesus was quite the nuisance. I was supposed to sit in a room full of strangers and pretend I wanted to be there instead of at home watching old black and white movies about romance and space invaders.

*Fine.*

I wrote my sayings. I read them aloud. The problem was that no one else thought they were very funny.

Stan was sleeping when my grandmother and I walked out to the car. He woke up when she got in and slammed the door.

Stan bolted upright. "*Wha?*"

My grandmother politely tucked her pocketbook on her lap and glared at me. "We're ready to go home now."

"Oh," Stan said, fumbling for his keys.

At home my grandmother went to her room and smoked cigarettes with the door closed.

Stan gave me the eye. "What happened?"

I handed him my list of family sayings. His eyes scanned the page. "It says 'Words my family lives by—Pass the joint.'" It took him a minute but then he covered his mouth with his hand. "Did you show this to anyone?"

"Yeah. It was my assignment. So what?"

"You're in trouble," he cooed.

"Yeah, well, you're funny looking," I said. "What did God create on the second day?"

"Jesus, I reckon. Why are you still scratching?"

"Cause I got the devil in me."

That night was a warm one. Night-blooming jasmine and honeysuckle wafted down the carriage alley into my nostrils, suffocating my senses. A few blocks away I heard the animals at the zoo kicking up quite a racket. Monkeys chattered loudly back and forth to each other in a wild hullabaloo. Fireflies hovered over the grass like an ethereal connect-the-dots.

And upstairs at our house the Bogeyman paced the floor, arguing with the Voices all night long.

# CHAPTER TWENTY

### *The Bad Uncle Comes to Visit*

After we got back from South America, I talked Preston Brown into starting a fitness routine with me. All of those Colombian sodas had given me fat thighs. Every pair of jeans I owned were tight. I ripped a workout schedule from a magazine, and we started right away. We were pitiful. Even on our best days we could only jog down to the wooded area where the snakes lived and back. We plodded breathlessly down the street and collapsed into a pile of thick heaving blubber on his front porch. On the third day Preston Brown said, "Why don't we relax today."

Fine with me.

Thurman's car was not parked out front, which meant I could go inside, make a pot pie and sneak around upstairs watching exercise programs to learn new techniques. I ran up the front steps and into the house, where Devo blared from Stan's radio. I went to the kitchen and started making lunch.

About fifteen minutes later Thurman came home. Everyone in the house heard him because he slammed the front door so hard it broke all of the glass panes. Suddenly the music stopped. I heard the sound of shoes crunching broken glass and hid in the pantry. From my hiding place I heard something fall, then something break. Footsteps thundered across the floor. I sank deeper into the pantry and listened to my heart beat faster and faster.

For some reason, even though insane stuff happened all of the time, I got really freaked out. The pantry wasn't such a good hiding place if

Thurman was hungry. At the bottom of the stairs there were built-in storage boxes that no one ever paid attention to. I forced myself to open the pantry door enough to listen. I thought I heard Thurman's footsteps in the living room, so I made a run for it.

I opened the top of one of the boxes, hoping the hinges didn't creak, and climbed inside.

It was so dark and quiet. The only sound was my heart racing and my breathing.

Stan screamed.

My heart thumped so loud in my chest I thought I was going to have a heart attack.

Maybe this was it.

Maybe this was the one time I should've run.

The sound of someone falling into a wall made my skin crawl.

Stan screamed, "You get away from me."

I knew he must have his bayonet because Thurman laughed and said, "You think you're going to kill me with that rusty old thing?"

I heard my grandmother talking.

A spider crawled up my ankle. I felt its little skinny legs touching my skin and freaked out. I popped the top of the box open and frantically jumped out, brushing my hands down my legs and over my clothes. I shook my hair. Someone walked down the hall. Without thinking, I ran out the back door. I crept along the side of the house out to the street, where I could see inside perfectly. I heard a car and turned just in time to see Preston Brown's dad backing their car out of the driveway. Preston saw me and waved. I waved back.

I turned and saw Thurman running across the living room at Stan, who stood there, gripping his bayonet as tight as he could.

Thurman was going down.

Well, maybe not. But at least he was going to the emergency room.

True to form, Stan clutched that old relic, which sliced right into the side of his big fat brother. The room was quiet for a moment.

Then Thurman screamed, "I'm bleeding."

*Served him right.*

I heard another car and looked up our street. It was Dave. *Crap.* It was Sunday. I'd forgotten. I was so tired of Thurman that I didn't even go inside to get my stuff. I took one look at the broken front door and got in the car. All I'd wanted to do was lay around and eat a pot pie.

A few blocks away from my grandmother's house, Dave turned to me in the car and said, "How's it going, kiddo?"

I didn't even know what to say. "Okay."

"Hey, what were you doing out front?"

I had to think about my answer. Finally, I said, "I was waiting on you."

"Oh, good timing."

That night when Dave drove to the payphone, I begged a quarter and called Stan.

The phone rang fifteen times before anyone picked up. "Hello?"

"Hello?" Stan said, sounding like he wasn't sure.

Dave motioned toward the store and said, "I'm going to get something to drink. Do you want anything?"

"Yes."

"What?" Stan asked.

"It's me. Cotton."

Dave nodded his head and walked into the store.

"Where are you?" Stan asked.

"Out front," I whispered.

"Really?"

"No. Listen, what happened today after I left?"

"Mother made him go to the emergency room and get stitches."

"Did you go?"

"No. I went down into the basement."

"For what?"

I could tell Stan was looking up and down the hall to make sure no one was watching. Then he spoke softly. "I kept seeing him go down there. I thought he might be doing something bad, so I went down and snooped around."

"Did you find anything?"

"Yeah, he's keeping marijuana in the air ducts."

"What?"

"In big plastic bags. There's four of them. But one of them isn't full."

Dave walked out of the store carrying two brown paper bags full of stuff.

"What's he doing with it?" I asked.

"Judging by the way the house smells, he's upstairs smoking it."

Dave handed me a root beer.

Stan was quiet a second and then said, "Mother was worried. Where did you go?"

"Dave came to pick me up. Listen, I'll talk to you this weekend. Okay?"

"Okay," Stan said and hung up.

Two days later I walked home from the bus stop to find Thurman's big fat butt lounging on our sofa. Thurman didn't even acknowledge me when I walked in. My mother was at the kitchen table smoking what was left of a joint.

"What's he doing here?" I demanded.

Tiny strands of smoke curled around her face. "Your grandmother thought it would be a good idea if he recuperated around people his own age, get out, make some friends, get laid."

"What?"

She stood up, reaching for a box of chocolate cupcakes. "Yep. He's our guest."

"Are you crazy? This is where we *live*."

"Shhhh." she hissed. "Don't be so freaking loud. He'll be fine. He only pulls that crap at Mother's house because she lets him get away with it."

"He pulls that crap because he's crazy," I said, throwing my backpack on the floor. "Hasn't anyone noticed that he's nuts?"

Her eyes narrowed. "Well, Miss Smart Mouth, your grandmother is paying me good money to let him lay in there and watch TV, so cram it."

I was so mad I thought I'd explode. My mother grabbed her box of cupcakes and stomped off to her bedroom.

I skulked through the living room and headed outside. As I passed behind the sofa Thurman looked up and sneered, "You need to show some respect to your elders."

"Screw you," I yelled, changing direction, walking down the hall to my room. I stopped and looked over my shoulder to make sure he wasn't following. I locked my door and dug around in my closet until I found the Disappearing Dust from my Magic Kit. I stuffed it down my front pocket and sat on my bed. When I got bored, I climbed through my window to go outside and play.

The shovel Dave used to straighten gravel in the driveway was propped against the house. I grabbed it just in case Thurman came running out.

Diggy was standing by the doghouse picking at the fur between his toes.

"Gosh," I slammed the shovel into the dirt. "Why does that moron have to come live here?"

Diggy shrugged his shoulders. I sat down on the ground in a huff.

I looked up just in time to see Dave's car turn into the driveway. My beacon of hope. My salvation. Surely, Dave would not be enticed to put up with the devil for a measly wad of cash.

Diggy and I ran over to his car as he pulled to a stop. "Did you know Thurman is in *our* house?"

Dave got out of the car and slammed the door. He looked distracted. "Yeah, just for a few days until he gets better."

"He doesn't get better," I insisted.

"He might. It's just a flesh wound." Dave looked up at the sky, thinking. I watched his eyes drift from treetop to treetop.

"No. He can't stay here," I went on, "he's dangerous."

Now, he looked me in the eye. "What did you say?"

"He's dangerous."

"That's what I thought you said. Listen, I've got a meeting. I have to change clothes."

Then he walked off to the front door. Diggy and I exchanged a look. Dave's gun was stuffed down the back of his pants. Today had shaped up to be quite a day.

"Come on." I grabbed Diggy's paw. "Let's get out of here."

We spent the rest of the afternoon hiking through the woods around our house. I told Diggy about the cigarette boy as we climbed over rocks and tree logs.

That night after my mother and Dave went to sleep, me and Diggy sat up in the middle of my bed and scoured the magic books I'd bought. I reviewed the notes I'd copied from books in the library. With my handy flashlight we went through every page to find a spell to make Disappearing Dust work.

Thurman paced out in the living room, chain-smoking. I sent Diggy to spy on him.

Finally, I found something. The directions in the book said it was used to invoke a spell.

Invoke?

Thank goodness I kept a pocket dictionary in my bedside table. I wedged the flashlight under my chin and flipped through the pages. *D . . . E . . . F . . . Honesty, honor, hopeful . . . Improper, indentation, invoke . . .*

*Invoke means "to call upon." Got it.*

Thurman slammed a door. Diggy ran and jumped back in bed with me. A few seconds later I heard Dave and my mother whispering in their room.

The *psssssst* of a malt liquor bottle being opened hissed down the hall.

*Great.*

Thurman mumbled around the kitchen, clanging pans. It was bad enough that I had to deal with his crap on the weekends and all summer long, but now he'd taken over our house. *Slam. Clank. Clank. Whop.* The Voices were obviously dialed in tonight.

I heard more whispering in the bedroom. Diggy looked at me. I rolled my eyes.

The smell of canned beef stew wafted through the air.

I pulled the packet of Disappearing Dust out of my pocket. On the front it read *Guaranteed to activate any spell.*

Dave whispered in the bedroom.

Thurman was in the kitchen digging through the refrigerator, clanking jars.

Very quietly I crept over to my door and pushed the back of a chair under the doorknob just in case. I'd learned that in an Abbott & Costello movie. Sometime later on I passed out in my clothes on my bed.

The next morning my mother pounded on my door. "Get up. You missed your bus." She jiggled the doorknob ferociously.

I rolled my eyes.

"What the frick is wrong with you?" She yelled from the other side. "Open the door. You don't pay rent around here. You can't just go around locking doors."

I climbed out of bed and pulled the chair away.

She had that pinched look. "Why are you still here?"

I wasn't really sure, so I said, "Thurman kept me up all night."

She rolled her eyes. "Whatever. I'm going out. You can stay here or get Thurman to drive you." Then she stomped off to the bathroom and slammed the door.

The last thing I wanted was to be seen pulling up in front of my school with my uncle Thurman. "I'll stay home," I yelled down the hall.

Thurman was an unbelievable turd.

"You're a redheaded stepchild," he sneered as I walked to the kitchen to get a bowl of cereal.

I jerked the refrigerator door open. "I might be a stepchild but you're ugly. There's no cure for ugly."

"Screw you," he said.

His tone dropped low enough to send shivers down my spine. I made a mental note to be less confrontational and ignore him entirely.

"Your mother wasn't married when you were born. That makes you a bastard," he happily pointed out as I walked down the hall with my bowl.

"Takes one to know one," I yelled back over my shoulder.

As I passed Dave's bedroom I looked over and saw him sitting on the edge of the bed staring blankly into the hall. I stepped inside quickly, pulling the door closed.

I whispered urgently, "Did you hear him?"

Dave nodded. "Yeah, I did."

I shoveled a mouthful of granola in my mouth. "We have to get him out of here," I mumbled through my chewing.

Dave sighed. "I know. Somehow I don't think he's the kind of person you can just kick out."

I swallowed. "Are you joking? He's the biggest nut job I've ever met. That's for sure."

Dave stood up, sliding his arms into a sports jacket.

"What are you doing?"

"I've got a meeting," Dave said, filling his pockets with his keys, money clip, driver's license.

"*What?* You're leaving me alone with him?"

Dave looked at me for the first time all morning. "That's probably not such a good idea, huh?"

I nodded profusely. "Probably not."

"You were supposed to be at school today," he said, distracted. "Well, get dressed and bring some books to read. We're going to be in the car a lot."

I put my bowl of cereal on the dresser and ran. I pulled on my purple velvet pants, grabbed my book bag, stuffed my magic book and a brain teaser book into my bag, and I was outta there.

Dave leaned against the Oldsmobile as I burst through the front door. A shudder quivered across Dave's skin as he glanced at the dark windows of our house.

"Did you see him?"

"No. I think he's in the bathroom."

I dove into the front seat of the car.

"Is he always creepy like that?"

"Actually, he's been kind of friendly these past two days."

I pulled at the back of Dave's sports jacket. After a second, he climbed into the car and started the engine. I turned around in the seat, watching our house disappear in the distance. The Bogeyman had wedged his way into our abode.

Dave drove us to a diner with a big shiny counter and red stools. I was famished. Every ordeal with Thurman left me more hungry than before. I ordered pancakes with extra syrup, scrambled eggs, hash browns and a cup of coffee filled to the brim with cream and sugar. Lip-smacking good. After the waitress took our order Dave excused himself to go to the payphone and make a call. As soon as he was out of sight, I put more sugar in my coffee. Five minutes later he walked back to our table, took exactly two gulps of orange juice, tapped his fingers a minute, then went back to the phone. The third time he walked back to the table and then back to the phone, I got up and went out front to buy a newspaper. Dark storm clouds rolled across the sky, blotting out the sun. I put my money in the machine, pulled it open and got my paper. At the table I read the funny papers as I snarfed down bite after bite of pancakes drenched in maple syrup.

Dave finally sat down after half an hour and ate his western omelet.

I hoped Thurman wasn't at our house boiling chipmunks alive on the stove. To divert my attention from that thought I looked at Dave and asked, "Are you okay?"

"Yeah. Why?"

"Because you're acting a little weird," I pointed out.

"Yeah, today is a little weird," he raised his hand in the air for his check. "Come on. We gotta go."

At the cash register I talked him into buying me a piece of chocolate cake for the road. Behind me I heard the rain come down. I turned to watch drops splatter and roll down the glass window. I clutched my styrofoam container and my newspaper to my chest as I ran to the car. Sprinkles splashed against my eyelids and cheeks. Dave unlocked the car door and we jumped in. He stared up at the sky, frowning.

"What's wrong?"

He put the key in the ignition. "I'm going to need to buy an umbrella."

Rain pounded against the windshield. I finished reading my funny papers. The gray skies, rhythmic beating of the rain, a big breakfast, and my lack of sleep the night before all conspired to give me a nagging case of the yawns. I tried to fight it. I opened my eyes really wide and stared at the highway, but eventually the landscape blurred out of focus. I closed my eyes for a minute. When I came to, I opened my eyes just in time to see Dave running across the Dollar Discount parking lot holding an umbrella.

He got in the car and looked at me. "Hey sleepyhead."

"Do we have a blanket?"

"They have one in the store. Do you want one?"

I nodded, somewhat delirious. I watched him run back across the rain-soaked divide with his umbrella. Ten seconds later I passed out. When I woke up again, I had a new, soft, green blanket. Rain beat in a steady rhythm on the roof of the car. I sat up and looked around. We were parked in a hotel parking lot. Dave wasn't in the car. A yawn the size of Texas seized me, and I snuggled back down in my new blankie and went to sleep.

When I woke again Dave was driving.

"How ya doin?" he asked.

"Good. Sleepy."

"Are you hungry?"

"No. Where are we going?"

"I've got a few more meetings."

I forced myself upright. Dave had the weirdest meetings. "I thought people had meetings in office buildings?"

"Some people do," he said thoughtfully. He winked and added, "Some people are more creative."

Scenery whizzed past us. We sped down a two-lane highway in the country. Wooded groves and rolling hills stretched out from the road. I didn't recognize anything. Mile after mile passed. Dave stared straight ahead, the corners of his mouth tight. I could tell he was thinking about something.

After forty-five minutes I noticed we hadn't passed a single house. The rain slowed to a sprinkle.

Dave glanced up into the rearview mirror, then over at me. "Do you have any gum?"

"In my bag."

I dug through pens and Chapstick to find three pieces of Big Bubble Peppermint Burst. My favorite. I handed over a piece.

We kept driving.

After another hour of no houses or cars Dave turned off onto a dirt road. Our car bumped and jostled over potholes, back into a wooded area. The rain picked up again. Dave drove through a clearing and into the trees, where no one from the road would ever be able to spot our car. He cut the engine off and left the keys in the ignition. It was so still and empty and quiet that my ears rang with silence. Dave's eyes searched the wooded area.

"What are we doing here?"

He opened his car door to get out. "Keeping a low profile. Stay right here."

As he stepped out, I saw him take his gun out. That spooked me. I pulled my blanket tight, wondering why I hadn't seen Diggy all morning.

Twigs snapped under Dave's feet as he walked out into the maze of trees. Raindrops slid down the windshield obscuring my view. I reached over and locked my door. From where I was, I could see Dave as he walked through a grouping of trees. After that, I couldn't see him anymore.

Jeepers. Maybe I should have let Thurman drive me to school. I had the urge to roll my window down really quick and yell, "Dave," but I was afraid he'd get mad. Footsteps crunched and twigs snapped behind the car. I whipped my head around.

Three dark-haired men walked toward our car. The one in the middle was Pablo. If I'd known we were going to meet Pablo I'd have worn my bracelet. And put on some clean clothes. The two men approached the car. In deeply accented voices they asked me to get out.

Pablo walked over and knelt in front of me. "Do you remember me?"

I nodded.

"How have you been?"

"Good. You?"

He shook his head. "Not so good."

Oh. I looked up and saw Dave walking back to the car. The two men searched him.

"Is there anything I can do," I asked Pablo.

He touched my cheek sweetly and said, "You can tell the U.S. government to shove it up their ass."

*Sure thing.*

Dave opened the car door and grabbed his umbrella. When he stood upright again, he said, "Cotton, why don't you wait in the car."

As I turned to get back in the car Pablo asked, "Do you still have the bracelet I gave you?"

I nodded.

"That makes me happy."

I climbed back into the front seat to wait. Dave and Pablo stood under the umbrella in the middle of the woods and talked forever. The clock on the dashboard showed five minutes, then ten, thirty, forty, fifty-six minutes passed. My hair was damp and smelled funny. I rolled down the window. Because I am nosey and prone to eavesdropping, I sat very close to the window and listened. Dave said something about the heat. It wasn't really hot outside. I kept listening.

Raindrops rolled down the umbrella, disappearing into Dave's jacket. "I'm gonna have to lay low," he said.

Pablo's face twisted into a pinched frown. He exhaled long and deep. He didn't look happy. Come to think of it, neither one of them looked happy. For a second, they turned their backs to the car and the sound of rain drowned out their words.

Then Pablo asked, 'Can I trust you, Amigo?"

Dave nodded, then said, "Yes."

"Then we have no worries."

Dave did not look convinced. Pablo leaned in and whispered something I couldn't hear. I craned my ears. Dave nodded his head. They shook hands. Then Pablo put his arm around Dave's shoulder and walked him back to the driver's side, where Dave closed his umbrella, tossed it in the backseat and climbed inside.

Pablo tapped on my window. I looked over. "How is your day?" he asked.

"Okay," I said. "I had coffee for breakfast."

He raised an eyebrow. "Do you know that the best coffee in the world comes from my country?"

"Really?"

"Yes," he said. "I am going back to my country, back to Colombia. I want to give you a gift."

I rolled my window down all of the way. The last time he gave me a gift, it had diamonds.

"My friend has it," Pablo said. One of the men stepped forward laying a box in his hand. Pablo turned back to me, handing it over. "My mother gave this to me. Keep it with you always."

I looked at the box and smiled. "Thank you."

"Gracias," he said.

Pablo leaned forward so he could see Dave through the window. "Remember what we talk about, Amigo."

Dave nodded. Then we backed out.

I opened the box. Inside was a puff of tissue paper. Underneath was a ceramic donkey with packs on his back full of green rocks.

"What are these?" I asked, pointing to the stones.

Dave inspected it a minute as we bumped down the muddy road. "It looks like jade."

"What's that?"

"It's a stone," he said. "The Chinese believe it will bring you good luck."

# CHAPTER TWENTY-ONE

## *Always the Same*

The front window of our house was busted when we got home. A porcelain bowl lay smashed on the brick walk.

Dave glanced over at me warily. "What do you think that's about?"

I studied the broken pieces on the ground. "I don't know. It could be anything, but if it's the Voices then I don't want anything to do with it."

"The what?"

"The *Voices*. No one's ever told you about the Voices?"

Dave shoved the car in park and shook his head.

"I can't believe my mother never told you about the Voices. He hears voices and they tell him things. It goes on for hours, sometimes days. He's dangerous."

"Has this happened before?"

I stared at him, dumbfounded. "Yeah. All the time." I stuffed my donkey with green stones into the glove compartment for safekeeping.

"What do you normally do?"

I thought about the best way to say it. "Well, I normally hide until he passes out from exhaustion."

Dave's eyes widened. "Are you joking?"

Inca came trotting around from the other side of the house.

"What's he doing loose?" Dave said, getting out of the car.

I remained perfectly still in my seat. I wasn't getting out unless I had to. In fact, I wasn't getting out unless an alien spaceship dropped out of the sky onto the car. And started shooting at me. With poison darts.

Dave walked across the front yard as Inca ran around him in circles. A loud banging erupted inside the house. Dave slowed down, leaning over to peer through the broken window.

"I wouldn't go in there," I yelled from the car.

He waved his hand to acknowledge he'd heard me but kept walking toward the house anyway. Suddenly, the front door flew open, and my mother came running out.

Blood ran down her chin as she screamed, "That idiot hit me."

*Duh.*

Dave reached out for her arm. "Are you okay?"

She touched her hand to her lip, then looked at the blood on her fingers. "No, I'm not okay. I'm bleeding."

Dave didn't see what happened next, but I did. Thurman thundered out of the house, his big fat belly jiggling under a stained t-shirt, and rammed his fist into the side of Dave's head. Dave never even knew what hit him as his head bent horribly to the side, mouth twisted in pain. His body toppled, losing balance. His arms reached desperately around for something to hold onto as the top part of his body careened to the ground. My mother ran at Thurman, clawing at his hair. He hitched his big fat belly up and charged again. She managed to get a handful of his hair. His enormous ham hock of an arm reared back, and with one hard blow she was on the ground.

Seeing my mother twisted sideways on the ground, not moving, terrified me. I started sweating from every pore in my body. What if he killed everyone and then got in the car to drive away? What if he found me? My breath caught in my throat. I wanted to jump out and run but I was sure he'd find me and drag me back to his treacherous pile. I slumped further and further down into the seat, hoping to disappear. I could hear his raspy breath fifteen feet away. It sounded artificial, like it was inside a can.

He grabbed Dave by the hair, slamming his fist into his face. Blood spewed out of Dave's mouth onto the stones of our front walk. Inca started barking, lunging at Thurman. Thurman turned with a hideous troll look on his face. Dogs were not Thurman's best friend. Thurman let go of Dave and snarled at the dog.

Inca hunkered back on his hind legs and bared all of his teeth.

That's when I remembered. The Magic Dust. I'd taken it out of my pocket and put it in my purse. *Where was my purse?* My eyes scanned the seat and floorboard. Nothing. I wanted to lean forward but was sure Thurman would see my head. My purse? I felt along the space in between the seat and door. My purse must be underneath me. Quickly I felt around for its fuzzy softness. After a few seconds, I glanced up and over long enough to see Thurman lunge at the dog. Inca tucked his tail and ran.

Out of the corner of my eye I saw Dave move slightly. I saw that his eyes were open. My heart beat fast as I pulled my purse up to unzip the top. I reached in and felt around for the plastic bag.

Inca barked like crazy, charging over and over at Thurman, who kept grabbing for his head and tail. I saw Dave's hand slowly reach around toward his back. I had Magic Dust in hand just as Thurman chased Inca closer to the car.

*He saw me.*

My blood ran cold.

His eyes narrowed. His fat legs thundered to the open door of the car. Up close I saw his face had bloodied scratch marks.

He leaned down into the car and said, "Looky what we have here."

Too scared to even think, I dumped the Magic Dust into the palm of my hand and blew. *Hard.* With my eyes closed.

I heard Thurman's head hit the ceiling of the car, then the crunch of gravel as he backed up. "What the fu—," he said.

I opened my eyes just in time to see Dave standing behind Thurman, gun raised.

Thurman rubbed his eyes with angry fists as Dave clocked him hard in the back of the head. For a second, Thurman wobbled, still upright, but Dave hit him again. The Bogeyman toppled to the ground.

Shivers ran wild down my arms and legs. I jumped out of the car and ran toward Dave, who was trying to get Inca in the car.

When he saw me, he yelled, "Cotton, get back in the car."

I just stared at him. Blood trickled out of his nose.

"Now," he yelled. "I mean it."

All of the trauma suddenly washed over me. Snot clogged in my nose. I managed to stammer, "I thought he was going to kill you."

Dave took my hand and led me back to the car. "So did I."

He helped me back in and then scooped my mother up in his arms. I leaned over the front seat to see what he was doing. "Is she alive?"

"She's breathing," he said, carrying her around to the backseat. "We have to get out of here. He'll wake up."

Dave heaved my mother into the backseat, slamming the door. Drops of blood from his nose splashed down onto her forehead.

"Start the car," he instructed.

I clambered over, turning the key in the ignition. The sound of the car starting cracked open the hideous silence. Tears streamed uncontrollably down my cheeks. Inca jumped up onto the seat next to me. Dave was outside, walking in circles.

"What are you doing?" I whispered urgently.

"Looking for my money clip. It must have fallen out of my pocket."

"Over there," I pointed. "Next to the broken bowl."

Dave spotted the money on the ground, grabbed it, wiped his nose on his sleeve and walked to the car. Thurman's body was slumped up against the car. In one deft movement Dave wedged his foot against Thurman's head and pushed him out of the way.

It was the coolest thing I'd ever seen Dave do.

As we drove away, I turned and saw the fat lump of Thurman laying in our front yard, frozen on the dirt, legs buckled off to one side. His mouth was open. A trickle of blood ran down his chin. I had never seen Thurman lying on the ground before.

Dave looked over at me. "What was that you blew in his face?"

"Disappearing Dust from my magic kit."

His busted lip curled into a smile. "*Nice.*"

Everyone rode along in silence until we got to a rest area off of the highway. We just sat in the car staring at the buildings.

"What are we going to do?" I asked.

Dave inspected his bloodied lip in the rearview mirror and said, "I don't know. I'll be right back."

I watched as he walked into the rest room. Minutes later he emerged with the blood cleaned off his face. He walked to the soda machine, brought three sodas, two candy bars and a bag of chips. From behind he looked okay except his shirt was really dirty.

I turned around in my seat, briefly, to look at my mother. She was breathing but hadn't moved an inch. "Hey," I whispered to her. "Can you hear me?" Dave opened the car door and stepped inside. He handed me a soda.

"What are we going to do?" I asked.

He unwrapped his candy bar, taking a bite. After chewing thoughtfully for a minute, he said, "Well, for starters, we're not going home right now."

That seemed kind of obvious.

Dave stopped at the first motel off the highway. He parked in front of the office and walked inside. I looked across the parking lot at the sign. The Admiral Inn.

My mother had to be carried upstairs. Dave heaved and grunted, handing me two keys. "Here, open my door," he said. "The other key is your room next door."

My own room. What could be better? I opened the door and walked inside.

Dave stepped in behind me. "I'm going to go and check on your mother and lay down for a minute. If you need anything then come get me. Don't wander off. Okay?"

I nodded. After he was gone, I ran around my room looking for all of my bottles of lotion, shampoo, plastic cups, ice bucket, note pads, pencils and postcards. When I turned around Diggy was sitting on the big king-sized bed.

"We got our own room," I whispered.

He smiled so big his whiskers twitched.

I turned on the TV and planned on watching so much TV that my brain oozed out my ears.

Late that night, someone knocked on my door. I'd fallen asleep watching *Pippi Longstocking* on cable. I shuffled over and asked, "Who is it?"

"Dave."

I unlocked the door. Streetlamps illuminated the edges of his jacket. He was holding a stack of styrofoam containers. "Step aside," he said. "I brought dinner."

Onion rings, burgers, fried cheese sticks and French fries filled the containers. I was so hungry.

Dave sat down on the bed next to me, grabbing a burger. "After we eat you have to ride over with me and see if that maniac is still out front."

I was about to sink my teeth into an onion ring. "What if he's dead?"

"Yeah, that's what I'm trying to avoid. Dead bodies in the front yard aren't so great in my line of business."

"Where's my mother?"

"She took a bunch of pain pills and passed out. Your uncle hit her pretty hard."

"He's not a nice person."

"No, *he isn't.*"

There were no other cars on the road driving over, which made it kind of spooky. Since we didn't live on a main street or have any neighbors Dave parked far away. The kitchen and living room lights were on inside our house. I rolled my window down to listen. Wind blew through the trees, rustling leaves.

"What are we going to do?" I whispered.

Dave exhaled, craning his neck to see in the dark. "I don't know, but I've got to get him out of there."

"I could create a distraction."

A stern look fixed itself on his face. "I hope you're joking."

"Kind of," I said. Then after a second, "Not really."

He continued to stare at me, shaking his head. "No, I don't ever want you to create a distraction." He watched me a moment more, then his eyes drifted over to our house. "What do you think he's doing in there?"

"Suffocating small animals so he can stuff them with sand."

Dave's left eyebrow arched high. "Are you being serious?"

"Kind of."

"Why would your mother ever let someone like that come to our house?"

I nodded my head, filling my cheeks with air. "Yeah, that's the big mystery."

Moonlight slanted across Dave's face, illuminating his busted lip. "What do you think he'll do?"

I shrugged my shoulders. "Honestly. I don't know. Normally my grandmother gives him a lot of pills and he passes out."

His brow furrowed and his jaw dropped, "Are you serious?"

"You keep asking me if I'm serious. That's beginning to make me nervous. Hasn't anyone ever told you about Thurman?"

"I know he's a little weird. What else should I know?"

I couldn't believe my mother had never told him about that maniac. I took a deep breath and told him everything I could think of. When I was done, he just sat there staring at me. It was a little warm outside and the temperature in the car had heated up. Sweat dawdled on my upper lip.

Finally, Dave tapped his fingers on the steering wheel and said, "So your mother thought it might be a good idea if he just came and stayed with us a while?"

"She said my grandmother gave her money."

"Holy lord," he said, shaking his head.

"Thurman is dangerous."

Dave touched his lip. "I'm learning that."

Suddenly, down the street, a light clicked on in our living room. Dave sat up straight, craning his neck.

The Beast was in there.

A second later our front door opened. Thurman swaggered into the yard and peed. We were parked too far away for him to see us in the dark, but I saw him. The outline of his face shone against the moonlight. He zipped up his pants, spit, and walked back into our house.

"Thank goodness it's too dark to see his tallywacker."

Dave spewed a little burst of laughter. "You can say that again."

Thurman had never lived alone. He'd never actually had his own house or apartment. "What if he likes living by himself and won't leave?"

"Then he needs to get his own house."

Shadows of Thurman passed across the curtained windows. Something deep down in my soul told me the police couldn't help us. Something told me we were going to have to work all of this out by ourselves in a way that cut out the middleman.

"Okay, listen," he said. "We've got to get out of here, but it's so quiet he'll hear the car start. I don't want him to know I'm watching him. I'm going to put the car in neutral and push. Okay?"

I nodded.

He pointed at the brake. "We're stopped on a little rise so the car should roll back. When you hear me whistle, put on the brake. Got it?"

"Yeah. What are we going to do if he doesn't leave?"

Dave paused a minute, jaw clenched, fingers resting on the door handle. "Then I'm just going to have to find some way to make him disappear."

*Disappear?* I'd wanted Thurman to disappear forever. I'd scoured every page of my magic book trying to find a secret spell to make it happen. It was my secret. I hadn't actually told anyone except Diggy. I wondered if Dave meant disappear the same way I meant disappear.

He put the car in neutral and got out to push. I shimmied over on the seat to press on the brake, but my legs weren't long enough to reach the pedals. I had to lay down on the seat in order to touch my foot to the brake. I couldn't see, but the window was rolled down. Twigs snapped and cracked under the tires. We didn't really have any neighbors so the only person who might see us was Thurman. The car rolled backwards, picking up speed. A flicker of panic startled me when

I began to wonder if too much time had passed. A quick breath caught in my throat. My foot felt around for the pedal.

A second later I heard the soft whistle outside the window. I used all of my weight to press against the brake. The car slowed down, then rolled to a stop. I heard Dave running. It occurred to me he might be running because Thurman was chasing so I sat up quick and looked around. The car started rolling again.

Dave's face was at the window. He ran alongside. "Put it in park."

I pressed down on the brake again and reached up to put it in gear.

"Good job," Dave breathed, getting in. "Now, let's get out of here before that lunatic sees us."

Morning birds chirped as we walked along the metal railing to our rooms. Dave opened the door to my room and checked under the bed and in the bathroom before telling me goodnight. "Don't open this door for anyone but me. Got it?"

I yawned and nodded at the same time.

# CHAPTER TWENTY-TWO

## *The Motel*

I loved having my own room. I felt so grown up. I turned on the TV, kicked off my old brown shoes and tossed myself back in bed. A Bugs Bunny Marathon was on. I watched until my eyes felt droopy. Light slanted around the edges of the curtains. Diggy was at the bathroom mirror, combing his fur back with his big paw. The golden-brown color of his eyes sparkled in the artificial light. I inhaled deeply, stretching out, admiring my own personal home.

Hours later I woke to the sound of knocking on my door.

"Housekeeping," the voice yelled. "Do you want your room cleaned?"

I'd forgotten to put out the Do Not Disturb sign. "No, thanks," I yelled back.

When I heard the cart roll away, I jumped out of bed. I ran over and laid my cheek against the door that joined my room to Dave's room. When I didn't hear anything, I pulled it open and stepped through. Once my eyes adjusted to the dark, I saw the room was empty.

I walked back into my room and closed the door. My stomach rumbled. I unwrapped a plastic cup, drank some tap water, grabbed my pink fuzzy purse and went in search of food.

The sun was bright outside. I shielded my eyes and looked around in all directions. There was a barbeque joint across the street, but I was afraid to cross the six-lane highway by myself. Leaning back against my door I counted the change in my purse. *Every motel has a vending machine,* I thought, as I headed in the direction of the swimming pool.

I rounded the corner and saw Diggy dipping his furry foot into the deep end.

"Hey," I yelled. "I got money for the machine."

He thumped his foot, his lips curled on the sides of his face, stretching his whiskers into a funny grin. He ran over to me, thumping and pointing.

"I know. I know," I said. "Moon pies and corn chips."

The cool dim light in the concrete alcove was nice. The ice machine rumbled like my stomach, then dropped a fresh pile of ice down into the bin.

Diggy pointed at the corn chips, salivating.

"Alright, alright. Hold your tail. I don't know what I want yet."

A4, B11, A10, C13, D7. So many choices. I heard the door to a room open behind me. I looked back over my shoulder and saw a man in Bermuda shorts and a blue button down walk out to the pool.

I whispered to Diggy. "What if he asks why I'm not in school?"

Diggy shrugged.

"You're a lot of help. Okay, if he asks why I'm not in school I'll tell him we're here from New York on business. Um, no. Um, vacation. Oh, I know. I'll say we're here visiting my uncle, who just graduated from school." The image of Stan holding up a diploma from the University of Jeever made me smile.

Bermuda Shorts glanced my way, then went back in his room.

After much deliberation I chose a bag of cheese puffs, a peanut butter crunch bar, two lemon lime sodas, a bag of barbeque potato chips, a yellow moon pie and a granola bar because it's healthy. The machine pushed each purchase toward the glass until it spiraled off and fell to the bottom, where I stuck my hand in and retrieved the goods.

I hiked back to my room, prepared to snarf down all of my food while rotting my brain on cartoons. Listening for Dave to return, Diggy and I spread our food out on the bed and ate everything but the wrappers. After we'd watched *The Brady Bunch, Gilligan's Island, I Dream of Jeannie* and two episodes of *My Three Sons*, I decided to heave my fat thighs off the bed and get some fresh air. I figured I could roll my pants up and splash off some calories.

When I was close enough to smell the chlorine, I looked up and saw Bermuda Shorts sitting in a chair poolside. I dragged a chaise lounge under an umbrella to sit in the shade. Then I rolled up my pants and waded down the steps of the shallow end.

"Hey," Bermuda Shorts said.

"Hey."

Minutes later a pizza delivery man walked across the courtyard.

Bermuda Shorts stood up and said, "That's for me."

It smelled heavenly. I lifted my nose high enough to catch a whiff. Hot, melted, cheesy tomato sauce made my taste buds dance a jig.

Bermuda Shorts wiped his fingers on a napkin. "Do you want a piece?"

The smell was intoxicating but I snapped back to reality. "I'm not supposed to accept food from strangers."

"It's not just any food. It's double cheese, pepperoni, onions and extra sauce."

My mouth started salivating. I swallowed. Double cheese. Extra sauce. "No," I forced myself to say. "That's okay."

"It's really good." He sunk his teeth into another bite.

I wanted to throw myself on top of the box and inhale the yummy, cheesy pile of pizza perfection. Bermuda Shorts walked over and sat on the edge of the pool next to me. I splashed my feet in the cool water.

"Hi," he said, extending his hand. "My name is Lawrence Benner. My friends call me Larry."

Happy to have something to do other than obsess about food, I shook hands.

"Nice to meet you. I'm Cotton."

He gestured to the box. "So there. I'm not a stranger anymore."

"No, thanks." *My thighs are fat,* I thought to myself. *But then, he is right. I mean, now I know who he is. No, I shouldn't.* I shook my head.

"Come on," he laughed. "You've been ogling my pizza for at least ten minutes."

"*Was not.*"

"You were."

"Okay, maybe just a little bit."

"Come on, Cotton. You saw that man deliver it. It's a perfectly good pizza."

The smell of its perfect goodness made me waver. No one had been back to get me all day. As much as I liked plinking change into the vending machine, I didn't exactly relish the thought of cheese puffs and root beer for dinner.

"Okay," I gave in, scooping up the biggest slice. "Just one." The first bite flooded my taste buds with dreamy tomato, garlic, Italian herbs.

Larry asked, "So where do you live?"

"Off Cross Road."

"That's nice. Where's your dad?"

"I don't have a dad." I took three little bites, grabbing whole pieces of pepperoni.

"Oh, then who's the guy I saw you with?"

"That's Dave. He's my best friend."

"Do you know where he is?"

"Yeah. I mean, he's working. He'll be back later."

"I see," Lawrence Benner said, handing me another piece of pizza.

Three pieces later I lay under a pink-orange sunset, dangling my feet in the water, too full to move. The phone in Lawrence Benner's room rang. He stood up, dusting off his hands. I decided to get up and take a shower with my mini bottles of shampoo.

"See you around," he said.

I nodded.

Halfway to my room I remembered I'd left my key on the dresser inside. I walked down to the front desk. A bald guy wearing a blue satin shirt sat behind the counter listening to disco music.

"I locked myself out of my room," I said.

"Yeah? What number?"

"227."

He turned, inspecting keys hooked on a pegboard.

"Hey, have you seen my parents?"

He turned back around with a key in his hand. "Aren't they supposed to be with you?"

"Yeah. Never mind."

I followed the concrete path to the stairs and saw Lawrence Benner talking to a man by the pool. I waved but he didn't see me. I went up to my room and called Stan. The phone rang twenty-four times before I hung up. From the window I could see the Drive Inn movie screen perfectly. I sat at my table and watched big faces kiss with no sound. Then I ran back over and called Stan. That time he answered. After thirty rings.

"Hey," I tried to sound sophisticated in my own personal room.

"Cotton?"

"Yeah, dummy. It's me. What are you doing?"

"Eating soup."

"Oh. That sounds good. Hey, listen, have you seen Thurman?"

Seconds passed. Mentally I counted to ten.

Finally, he took a deep breath, smacked his lips and said, "Yeah."

"Really? When?"

"Earlier today."

Thank goodness. The Bogeyman had left our house. "Are you serious?"

"Yeah, I think it was today."

Uh-oh. Stan's memory wasn't the best.

"Why?"

"Because he attacked Dave and we all had to leave."

"No one makes us leave when he attacks me."

I couldn't tell if he was perturbed or just pointing out the facts. Eventually, I decided he must be stating facts. "Anyway, then Thurman wouldn't leave our house and he tried to beat everyone up."

"That sounds like him. Mother gave him some medicine."

"Good."

"I gotta go now and eat my soup and look at my map of Russia."

*Sure thing.*

I hung up. The movie people ran wildly across a field. Then a giant dinosaur bird swooped down from the sky and snatched one of them off the ground.

I took my shower and went to bed. I zonked out quick. Sometime in the middle of the night I woke to the sound of breathing. My eyes popped open to see Dave sitting at the end of my bed. I sat up.

"Where have you been?" I asked, rubbing my eyes. "We can go home now because Stan said Thurman came home."

Dave shook his head. "No, I've got to get us out of here." He turned, leaning closer to me. "Did you talk to anyone here at the motel?"

"No."

"Are you sure?"

"Yeah, except for the man by the pool."

His hand slapped his forehead. "Did you tell him anything?"

"Why?"

"Did you tell him *anything?*"

"No, he just gave me a piece of pizza."

Dave stood up. "Okay, come on. We've got to get out of here."

"Why? I didn't do anything bad."

"I know. We're under surveillance."

"What does that mean?"

"It means the FBI bought you a pizza tonight."

I yawned, trying to make sense of it all. "But he wasn't wearing a uniform."

"The good ones don't. Come on. Put your shoes on. I'm not letting you stay with your grandmother as long as that maniac on the loose, but I've got to get you somewhere safe."

"I need some clothes," I said, swinging my legs over the edge of the bed.

"I know. I packed all of your stuff. It's in the trunk. I parked five blocks away and snuck up to your room. Let's get out before someone notices I'm here."

"What's going to happen to you?" I asked, squeezing my feet into my Buster Brown shoes.

"Nothing if I'm careful. I've just gotta lay low for a while."

I glanced over and saw his hands were dirty. I had the feeling he'd been digging up money in the back yard again.

# CHAPTER TWENTY-THREE

*California*

My mother took the money she'd gotten from Thurman taking over our house, and we went to stay with her friend Joanna in San Diego. Everything had gone to hell on the home front, so my mother was quick to get out of Dodge. When we arrived, I found an apartment full of potted plants and unemployed surfers. An evil cat hid behind said plants and launched himself at the ankles of unsuspecting passersby. Since I was lowest on the food chain, I became his primary target.

Everything in California was bright and sunny except my mood. Surfers stopped by after the waves were tame to say, "Man. Whoa. Duuuude." The furniture, carpet, and walls were beige and white. Three days into the vacation I was so tired of eating fresh sprouts I wanted to scream. But no one really screamed in California. They talked to a therapist or took a yoga class or drank a green protein drink. Joanna expressed her angst by throwing very sophisticated wine parties. No one ate Spam.

To keep me quiet, my mother took me to Universal Studios, where I proceeded to elevate "surly" to an art form. The shark looked fake. The corn dogs sucked. And that last ride wasn't worth the fifteen minutes of my life it took to climb to the top. In the amusement park bathroom, I uncontrollably burst into tears. Eight years old and my entire life was falling apart.

The lights in the bathroom were bright, and they buzzed. Noise from the amusement park disappeared. It was just me and the porcelain sharing a moment together. Under the buzz of the florescent lights my tears sounded sunken, hollow, feverish. I cried to different pitches, sucking back snot, trying to get control of myself. My eyes dropped to my patent leather Buster Brown shoes, staining my socks black around the edges. I tried to stop the salty waterworks from staining my purple pantsuit, but it was no use.

*Please let me stop.*

I couldn't stop.

I couldn't stop anything. I couldn't stop Dave from leaving or being stuck here or this sinking feeling that sucked me so deep inside myself, I could barely breathe. For a moment I pulled my emotions up into my throat, croaking, globs of snot stuffing up my nose. I looked around. The floors were so clean it was criminal. The very idea that a public bathroom was more orderly than my life made me cry even harder.

I jerked a big wad of toilet paper from the roll. The horrifying sound of tears choked in my throat. After a few minutes my head fell into my hands, and I gave up. I stopped trying to hide behind *be a big girl* or *chin up* or *everything will be okay.* I cried the purest, heaviest tears I'd ever cried in my life. With my pants hanging down around my ankles I sat there and wept until my mother came looking for me.

"Cotton," she screamed, banging the door against the wall, scaring the crap out of me. "What the frick are you doing? I've been waiting out here for half an hour."

*Lucky you,* I thought. I've been in here *crying* for half an hour.

The jig was up. I had to come out of the stall. Trying to dry my tears, I fanned my face with the backs of my hands. I didn't want her using my own pain to torment me. I took two deep breaths, pulled my pants up and hurled myself out before I burst into tears again.

With a hand perched on the hip of the designer jeans Dave just bought her, she demanded, "Why is your face so red?"

Since I was too short to see my reflection in the mirror, I grabbed the first lie to come along. "I think I'm having an allergic reaction."

"Oh," she said.

I stepped to the side of the sink, stood on my tiptoes, and washed my hands. "Can we go home?"

"No," she said, irritated. "Hurry up."

The door slammed shut behind her.

I flipped her the bird.

For the rest of the day, I was the only one at the amusement park who was not amused.

For weeks we went to malls and ate vegetarian food. Dave ate steak. I hadn't seen a proper slab of meat in weeks. I got the message. No more meat. No more Dave. There's a new dietary sheriff in town. That moment of keen awareness arrived right about the time my mother began getting friendly with an Eskimo named Mike. Mike lived in LA. I couldn't figure out for the life of me why an Eskimo would live in a place with no snow, no sled dogs, and no igloo. I asked him if he lived in an apartment made of ice with a hole in the middle for fishing. He laughed. "No. I live in apartment off Ventura Boulevard."

*Well, there you have it.*

Not only was my mother a big fat cheater but Eskimos lived by the beach. The entire episode was carried out in such a shameless display of flirting and kissing and *wink wink nod nod* I thought I'd barf. I scowled from every corner of the room, wedged in between a potted plant and something made of bamboo. *Thank you,* I wanted to scream from the top of my lungs, *but we won't be having anymore wink wink, Mr. Eskimo. We have a boyfriend at home.* But I didn't scream. I ate my crab puff and shut up. Due to circumstances beyond my control, I turned into a total pain in the butt.

One morning after a lot of *kiss kiss wink wink*, the Big Fat Cheater and I drove to a bakery in Joanna's car.

"Well, at least we get to go home tomorrow," I said, wiping my brow in a *whew* kind of way.

Hands firmly gripped the steering wheel. Her frizzy hair swirled on top of her head. She was too quiet. It made me nervous.

"Gosh, it sure will be great to get home and sleep in my own bed," I blabbered on.

Silence. Not even a *humph*, or *grunt*, or a *snort*. At a stoplight, cars whizzed by in front of us.

I couldn't stop myself. "I am so happy we're leaving tomorrow. I miss Inca. I bet Dave will be at the airport waiting on us."

The light changed to green. My mother gave the car too much gas, and it lurched forward. I'd never heard so much silence from her in all my life.

Determined to push the ticket, I said, "So, if you don't mind, after we get back to Joanna's I'll just go and pack."

She made a right-hand turn and glanced over at the side-view mirror, attempting to avoid my gaze. "Don't bother," she said. "we're not leaving."

I'd suspected that but it didn't stop me from blurting out, "What? Are you joking?"

"I am not joking." She jerked the car into a parking space and slammed it into park.

"We are supposed to leave tomorrow," I wailed, feeling trapped inside the car, holding onto the dashboard for dear life because the carpet had been yanked out from under me.

"Well, *supposed to* and *are leaving* are two totally different things."

"I want to go home," I interrupted, defiantly. "I don't want to stay here. I want to go home." Muscles tensed in my neck. I could hear my teeth grinding.

"Too bad," she said, getting out of the car. Standing outside, she yelled, "Are you coming?"

I shook my head so furiously I started to see stars.

"Fine." She shrugged, walking away.

I hated her. I was suddenly seized with so many conflicting feelings I couldn't sort them out. I wanted to spit, scream, shred the upholstery, jump up and down. All of these were so bunched up in my head they started pushing tears against my eyelids, which were already pinched shut. *I will not cry.* Insistent tears popped out, big and round and mean. *I will not cry.* Salty drops descended down my cheeks. The back of my hand flew up, swiping dreaded tears. *I will not cry. I* hated that place. I didn't want to cry. I wanted to open my eyes and run wild in my grandmother's backyard with Stan eating potted meat and mayonnaise sandwiches. I was so angry I wanted to rip the carpet from the floorboard with my teeth.

I looked across the street. Through the plate glass window of the bakery, I saw my mother. She stared into a display case, pointing. I dug deep in my nose, wiping boogers under the seat. I spat on my hands, then wiped them all over the steering wheel. Some of the slimy boogers tried to wrap themselves around my fingers so I jammed them back under, rubbing violently against the scratchy carpet. *I will not cry.* My tears were so heavy. I fell under their weight and collapsed in a pile of sorrow.

Cars swooshed by, stopping occasionally to idle on the other side of the door. The rumble of engines stirred up a sick feeling in my chest. I wanted to go home. I didn't want to stay and play footsie with the Eskimo. My tears ran hot and fast, in a race with my breath. My chest was so clogged air just circled around in my mouth, trapped. In a fit of panic, I hurled myself upright, staring at my mother again.

There she was, cool as a cucumber, kneeling in front of the display case, still choosing pastries for the next big make-out session. My heart thundered. *I must get a plan.* If I could actually pull myself together then I could devise a plan. *I've got to pull myself together. How was I supposed to get out of here? I could get my grandmother to send money or call Dave again. Yeah, that's it. I'd beep Dave and when he called back, I'd beg him to please help me get home.* I looked up in time to see my mother crossing the street. *Cheater.*

I nearly knocked myself out trying to wipe tears from my face. *I had to get a plan.* I was in potted-plant hell.

My mother slammed the door, leaning around to put the pastry box in the backseat. I wanted to stomp on it and watch cream ooze all over the seats. I wanted to be old enough to say things like, *you can shove that pastry up your butt.*

"I hope you're done with your little episode." She started the car.

"I want to go home," I demanded.

"Tough titty."

"That's not fair!" I screamed. "You stay here. I'm going back." The shrill hysteria in my voice frightened me, and I recoiled to the farthest side of my seat, clutching the door handle.

I felt the back of her hand hit my face. Blood trickled into my mouth. My tongue ran quickly over my teeth, making sure they were all there. I felt her eyes on me. I stared straight ahead.

"Don't tell me what's fair," she hissed in my direction. "I make the rules around here." As punctuation she jammed her finger into my cheek, hard. "Got it?"

I swallowed a mouthful of blood and spit.

"Got it?"

"Have you had sex with the Eskimo?"

Something sinister crept into her eyes. "That's none of your business." Throwing the car into gear she pulled out onto the street. "And screw you for asking."

"Thanks," I snarled, in the meanest voice I could muster.

We did not speak to each other for the rest of the day.

I made sixteen collect calls to my grandmother's house. No one answered. Stan must have fallen into the commode and drowned. Finally, on the seventeenth time, I was saved. I heard the operator's voice say the magic words, "I've got a collect call from Cotton."

Wind returned to my lungs; exhalation flooded my brain. The heavens opened up. I danced a jig next to the phone. The angels were about to sing when to my utter horror I heard Thurman snarl, "Tell that little rat turd to go away." He slammed the big rotary phone back on the hook. The line was still open.

The operator sighed. "I'm afraid he's refused the charges. Is there anything else I can help you with?"

*Yeah, can you give me a ride?*

I paged Dave three times in a row and hovered near the phone for half an hour, but he didn't call back. Joanna prepared for another dinner party. After the cat attacked me, I locked myself in the bathroom and pretended to take a bath in order to bide my time and come up with a plan. After half an hour of sulking, the best I could come up with was *nice first, ruthless second.* Sitting on the toilet seat so long I rose up like a stooped old man. I checked my armpits, dabbed some Fracas on them. Out in the living room I heard a knock.

Okay. Deep breath. I jerked the bathroom door open and hurled myself into the hall.

People arrived. I plastered on my biggest smile. Look at me, *I'm an angel,* my words and deeds proclaimed. My mother looked very guarded. She folded her arms across her chest and didn't take her eyes off of me. I was too full of *please* and *thank you* to notice.

There was another knock at the door. I danced gaily around the potted plants, ready to charm the dickens out of anyone. I threw open the door, thrilled to be attending such a fabulous party. It was the Eskimo with no igloo. I greeted him warmly. This immediately aroused all kinds of suspicions. Everyone in the entire room turned to stare at me. They acted like I'd dropped my pants and peed on the floor.

"*What?*" I said, exasperated. "I'm just trying to be nice."

"Nice is not your strong point," my mother said, slipping her arm around the Eskimo, leading him over to the couch. *The seat of sin.*

"It's not yours, either," I said, wearing the biggest grin of my life. *Bleah. Yuck. Ick.*

For the next hour I made a concerted attempt to be polite and gracious even though my mother, the big fat cheater, was sucking face with the Eskimo. Out of the corner of my eye I saw her toss her head back and laugh at one of his stupid jokes. She was wearing the emerald necklace Dave bought her. I wanted to choke her with it.

No, I wanted to walk over, rip it off her neck, and slap her with it. Twice. No, three times.

At some point my Nice-O-Meter reached maximum capacity, and though I fought it, I had to turn to plan B: ruthless.

"Cotton," someone said to me. "Are you enjoying yourself?"

"Can I have a glass of wine?" I ventured, sure no one would hand it over but willing to try, nonetheless.

"That's so cute," the person cooed.

"I'm not trying to be cute, lady. I was thinking about practicing to be an alcoholic since my mother is a big, fat cheater."

The entire room went silent.

It was impressive.

In the calmest, deepest voice I'd ever heard, my mother said, "Get your ass back to that bedroom. Now."

"Gladly," I stomped off down the hall, swerving to avoid being attacked by the cat.

For what seemed like a very long time, I sat on the edge of the bed, willing myself not to cry. Without warning, it happened. First, an overwhelming feeling of despair crashed down around me, followed by the feeling that I was about to lose everything important in my life. Tears flooded down my face in a waterfall of sickening grief I never knew existed.

With no other sensible thing to do, I just sat there and counted tears as they fell to my legs. *One two three four five six . . . fourteen fifteen sixteen . . .* When I got to thirty-two, I stopped counting. Not a single soul from that crap party came to check on me. No one cared. They were out in the living room talking, laughing, eating berry tarts and rum-soaked cakes. No one cared enough to come back and ask me if I wanted to go live in an orphanage.

Well, I cared.

That was the most empowering thought I could come up with. I looked down at my shoes dangling over the edge of the bed.

*I could leave. I could walk away.*

All I needed was a plan.

Marijuana smoke drifted down the hall, seeping under the door like an insidious ghost. *Good.* That would keep them occupied long enough for me to make a getaway.

First, I needed to sneak back down to the bathroom and pee and get my bottle of Fracas.

When I got back to the bedroom I shoved a pillow under the blankets, packed my rabbit, pink purse, plaid bell-bottoms, and my purple sweater in my hatbox, took twenty dollars from a purse on the floor, brushed my hair, checked my courage, turned off the lights, climbed out the window and ran like hell.

Four blocks into my escape, I realized I'd forgotten to close the window. Standing on the sidewalk, I wavered over returning. I could blow my cover. All of the indecision made me lose my nerve. I turned to the right but suddenly couldn't remember how to get back to the main street. Everything was so clean and spacious. Pavement rolled away in all directions, illuminating the shadows. Tears caught in my throat.

Then Diggy appeared.

"Hey," I said.

"Hey," he nodded, kicking up imaginary dust.

"I'm really confused," I said, still pushing back tears like a mob of teenage girls at a Beatles concert. "I ran away back there but I don't—"

"That's okay," he said. "I've got a plan."

Just in case you were wondering, if you go to a bus station and tell them you're lost, they will let you ride for free. Especially if a police officer pulls over in a patrol car and asks you why you're standing under a streetlamp talking to yourself.

The shrieking *whooooop whooooop* of his siren exploded into the night. I jerked around in his direction, scared to death.

"Hey," he said. "What are you doing out here all by yourself?"

Diggy whispered in my ear, "Tell him you're trying to get home."

"I'm trying to get home," I said.

That satisfied the officer tremendously. "Great. Get in. I'll take you."

A ride was good. Diggy and I ran around to the passenger's side and clambered in. The officer smiled at me, put his car in drive and zoomed off.

Cruising down the empty streets, he asked, "So, where do you live?"

*That's where it got a little complicated.*

His brow furrowed. "How did you get all of the way to California?"

Diggy whispered in my ear, "Tell him you got lost at Disneyland."

"I got lost at Disneyland," I insisted.

The officer didn't look convinced. He picked up his walkie-talkie thing. Static cracked inside the patrol car. A voice came on, then said, "Go ahead."

"I've got a child in my custody that says she's lost. Can you check Missing Persons for me?" Then to me, he asked, "What's your name?"

*Please Lord, don't let me be on that list.* "Cotton Alexander."

He repeated my name. I sat for an eternity with palms sweating, heart palpitating. Finally, the same voice came back on. "Negative."

It took a lot of convincing, a big story about how my grandmother was old and forgetful, and a lot of Diggy whispering in my ear to convince the officer to take me to the bus station. Eventually he pulled a U-turn in the middle of the street, and we zoomed off in the opposite direction, headed for salvation. On the way over, he picked his walkie talkie up again. Static crackled. The voice came on.

"I need you to check this out for me," he said.

Then he asked for my phone number. With my fingers crossed tight under my hatbox I told him my grandmother's telephone number. He recited it back to the voice. We waited. Lights flickered and blinked on the console. Special superfly gizmos only for the Federales filled up the dashboard.

Static crackled again. "Affirmative. The person who answered verified her identity and confirmed that is her residence." The voice stopped, hovering in nowhere land.

The officer thanked the voice and clipped the walkie-talkie back on the black box.

The two hours I waited at the bus station, sitting next to Officer Darnell, shaved ten years off of my life. My fingers were crossed so tight and shoved so far under my thighs they were blue. *Please don't let them find me gone and report it.* Every time his police radio crackled with static I was prepared to run. I counted on my mother to drink more alcohol, smoke more marijuana and not notice me missing until at least tomorrow.

All and all, Officer Darnell was pretty nice. He bought me a hot chocolate and a sticky, gooey thing I would have never been allowed to eat under different circumstances. As we watched lines of people file past, he told me a story about how he'd trained his dog, Skippy, to stand on his back legs and dance. Officer Darnell scored big points with Diggy.

My nerves were on high alert. Every ten seconds my eyes checked the front entrance. I repeated in my mind, *please, do not let her show up here dragging that Eskimo and force me back to that pit of sin and despair.* The big clock over the concession stand ticked. Every new second became a new minute that became a new hour. Finally, I heard my boarding call.

Officer Darnell stood up. "That's us."

People took forever to board the bus. A nice man wearing a beanie offered to put my hatbox on the luggage rack, but I was afraid someone might steal it, so I shook my head, pretending not to speak English.

Officer Darnell talked to the bus driver, who glanced up in his mirror at me. A very old woman, with deep creases in her face, sat down next to me. She smelled like mothballs and gave me cinnamon candy that stuck to my teeth. Ten minutes after we pulled away from the station all of the adrenaline drained from my bloodstream, and I fell asleep.

I woke up and noticed, through squinted eyes, that someone had covered me with a blanket. I was safe. I was warm. I was moving. Outside Flagstaff the older lady woke me up and we changed buses together. She held my hand. I could feel the fan of bones under her skin. It was nice. She told me her name was Josephine. On the next bus she gave me lemon drops and half of a hot dog. Together we shared a can of ginger ale. With my stomach full of carbonated bliss, I dozed off again.

The *thump thump thump* of tires on the highway rumbled me into slumber.

When I drifted back in, who knows where, Diggy was standing in the aisle, saying, "See. I told you I had a plan."

The entire trip took two days. During that time I relied on the generosity of Josephine and twelve bus drivers, all of whom made sure I had popcorn, pie, cookies, and hamburgers, along with someone to help me change buses. I rode through Arizona, New Mexico, Texas, and Arkansas before I finally got home.

Josephine was on her way to South Carolina. "You be good now." She waved goodbye to me from the window seat. My heart was breaking. Gosh she was nice to me.

"Do you want me to get some money from my grandmother to pay you back?" I asked, looking for any reason to get back on the bus and talk to her again.

"Don't worry," she said. "The Lord always pays back kindness."

It was 6 AM at the bus terminal. Stan sported faded brown pants, a gray flannel jacket and a t-shirt that had seen better days. He looked like a big, rumpled scarecrow, standing perfectly still next to my grandmother, who was wearing a green flowered housedress and hiking boots. Neither one of them had brushed their hair.

I'd never been so happy to see poorly dressed people in all of my life. In my attempt not to appear foolish, but as the savvy world traveler I'd become, I walked calmly down the steps of the bus carrying my hatbox. Stan nodded at me.

"Hey," I said, casually.

My grandmother looked at me for a long time, then she said, "Are you alright? Nothing bad happened to you, did it?"

I shook my head. "I didn't want to stay there anymore."

She was quiet again. Then she reached out, taking my hand, saying, "I understand."

And that was that.

In the predawn darkness we drove back to the stillness of our house. Stan pulled to a stop at the curb. I looked out at the big, dark windows, unsure as to whether or not I was dreaming.

"Come on," my grandmother said, opening the car door. "I'll go make us some grits."

*Man, that was music to my ears.*

Grits with butter and sugar, sausage, and coffee. No one talked about vegetarian food, wine, or Eskimos. After breakfast, I went to my grandmother's room to take a nap. Soon after, she joined me, slowly lowering herself to the bed. I lay very still, under a stack of blankets, allowing myself to feel how much I loved her. Next to me, her breath came low and steady. I breathed a sigh of relief. I was finally home.

Hours later, the rotary phone started ringing off the hook. I heard Stan walk into the hall. "Yeah," he said. There was a pause. Then, "Naw." His shoes scraped the floor. "Naw," he said, "she's sleeping." Then he hung up. After a second, he yelled down the hall. "Mother? Mother?"

She stirred, rolling over, "Ummm-hmmm. Yeah? What is it?"

"Connie keeps callin'."

"Well, let her call," she said, rolling back over. "Maybe she'll learn to be a nicer person. God knows, I don't know why she has to be such a bitch all of the time."

# CHAPTER TWENTY-FOUR

*End of Summer*

After that, no one said much about my mother, and she didn't come back from California until the end of the summer. Tanned to a dark golden brown, wearing frosted eye shadow she picked me up on a fateful day in August. I'd spent the rest of my summer digging through closets and making my own chicken pot pies in the late afternoon when everyone was sleeping. I read my library books, stretched out on my back, in the cool, dim rooms where classical music drifted in from Stan's radio. I didn't want to go home with her, but I hadn't seen Dave in a long time.

My mother dragged our luggage into the house, heaving and swearing. It was dark and empty. Dirty dishes, crusted with ketchup, were piled in the sink. An old box of graham crackers lay knocked over on the counter. Everything was still and quiet and cold. I went to my room and locked the door. I sat on my bed, staring out the window into the back yard, looking out beyond my jungle gym, to a place in the woods where I envisioned some kind of future for myself. *Maybe.* Dave didn't come home that night. I waited until my mother smoked a joint and passed out before I unlocked my door, then crept down the hall. There was nothing to eat in the refrigerator. I didn't care. I wasn't hungry anymore.

The next morning, I woke up with Diggy standing next to my bed.

"Hey," I said, sleepily.

He pointed to the hall.

I climbed out of bed, half asleep, lumbering for the door. In the hall I stopped and looked around. When my eyes finally focused, I saw Dave standing in the living room, flipping through a stack of mail.

"Hey," he whispered. "Long time no see."

"Yeah," I said, scratching my arm.

"How was California?"

"It sucked."

He laughed so loud it startled me.

"I'm serious," I insisted.

"I know you are."

I looked around. "What time is it?"

Dave glanced at his watch. "Pancake time."

It took me a second, then I understood. Pancakes. Syrup. Creamy, dreamy coffee at the Pancake Hut. "Hold on," I whispered urgently. "I'll be right back."

I dashed into my room, tripping over my own feet, and lunged for my suitcase. I tugged the zipper open and started pulling out clothes. Dirty. Dirty. Kind of clean. Dirty. Finally, I ran to my drawers. All of my clothes smelled funny because they'd been sitting in the dark confines of my dresser for months. I pulled out a t-shirt. It smelled like old wood. I pulled out another one. Same thing. It would just have to do.

Dave stood in the driveway waiting on me. He opened the car door, ushering me inside. It was delightful. Just like old times. I rolled my window down, feeling the warm breeze in my hair.

"So, what have you been doing all summer?"

"Well," he thought for a minute. "Working, I guess. What about you?"

"I stayed at my grandmother's house for most of the summer."

"I thought you went to California."

"I did. But I didn't like it very much, so I left."

His right eyebrow arched high. "Really. How did you get back?"

"I went to the bus station and had a policeman tell them that I'd lost my grandmother at Disneyland."

He just stared at me. "Are you serious?"

"Yeah. Didn't my mom tell you?"

He shrugged. "Your mother isn't exactly talking to me these days."

*Oh.*

"Well, it worked."

He cruised along on the highway, glancing over. "Weren't you scared?"

I stalled a few seconds, debating on whether I should tell the truth. Finally, I sighed, "Yeah. It spooked me. I got lost and wondered if maybe I should just turn around and go back."

"You want some good advice?"

I nodded.

"Don't ever go back."

"Where?"

"Anywhere. So, what happened?"

I had to think a minute. "Oh, Diggy showed up."

"Good ole Diggy."

I couldn't tell if Dave was being sarcastic.

"Yeah. He's a good friend. My best friend, really. And you. You're my best friend."

Dave didn't say anything but pulled his lips tight and sighed. "Well, I had no idea you'd been here all summer. I would have called. What was your mother doing out there?"

The moment of truth. "Hanging out with an Eskimo who doesn't have an igloo."

Dave turned to me, his foot letting up on the gas. "That's just a stereotype. Eskimos don't necessarily live in igloos."

"You can say that again."

The exit for the Pancake Hut came up on our right. Dave veered into the turn lane. He didn't say another word until we were in the restaurant. I kept trying to figure out if that was a good thing.

I ordered a pile of food. French toast. Ham and cheese omelet. Hash browns. After I'd poured six packets of sugar and half of the milk from the creamer into my coffee, I sucked in a breath and asked Dave if I could go live with him.

"I don't think your mom will ever let you do that, Cotton."

"Why not?"

"Cause I don't think she likes me very much anymore."

"So?"

The waitress brought a basket of biscuits and butter to the table.

"She's your mother."

"I don't care." I had an incredible urge to tell him about the Eskimo kissy-face spectacle.

He laid his hand gently on the table. Maybe he thought I'd calm down or forget about it, but he was wrong.

"I don't care," I said, with more conviction than the first time. He sighed, sipping his coffee. "I don't think it's an issue of caring."

"You can say that again."

By that time, I was so disgusted with where the conversation was going, I didn't even want to eat my French toast. "Then I want to live on my own."

Dave couldn't help but laugh. "Where did such a little bitsy thing like you get so much gumption?"

"I don't know," I said, annoyed with how lightly he seemed to take the rest of my life.

"Well, you've got guts, kid, and brains," he said, squeezing my hand, "and that puts you ahead of the game."

"I'm not talking about a game. I'm talking about living with you."

"Well, it ain't over 'til it's over. At least we've got each other for now."

"But it is over, *isn't it?*"

Dave looked out across the rows of booths for a long time, then lifted his cup. "Between your mom and me?"

I nodded, forcing tears back to wherever they came from.

"Yeah," he said quietly, shaking his head, "Yeah, it's over."

"And you don't even care," I sulked.

In the bright light, I watched his expression change. The waitress stopped next to our table, holding an enormous tray. Carefully, she stooped over, setting our plates down in front of us.

"That's not true, Cotton," he whispered across the table. "How can you say that?"

Tears I'd held back for so long now came easy and fast. "Because I love you. I don't want you to go away. I don't—" The sucking, hiccupping sounds coming from somewhere deep inside of me cut the words short.

The waitress cocked her head to one side, looking at me. "You alright, baby?"

I nodded, snot running down from my nose. You could tell she didn't believe me but went to check on another table because some annoying guy kept waving his hand in the aisle.

Dave pulled a silk handkerchief out of his pocket and dabbed gently at my cheeks.

"Oh, Cotton," he sighed. "This is just such a mess."

"Can't you stay?" I pleaded. "Please. I mean, just for a while."

Shaking his head in an apologetic way, he lowered his eyes, saying, "Oh, little Cotton, I'd do anything if I could."

But he couldn't, and even though I wanted him to stay more than anything, I knew what was done was done. I ate my French toast and put the rest of my food in a take-out box. I could at least drench my sorrow in maple syrup.

I didn't say anything on the ride home, figuring it was best to anticipate the end in silence.

The next morning, I woke to the sound of screaming. As the day progressed events unfolded, and it became increasingly obvious that something had gone terribly awry. "Don't you talk to me like that, you—"

"Connie. Stop," Dave said firmly.

The sound of slapping echoed down the hall.

My mother screamed at him. "Don't touch me. I mean it. Don't you touch me."

He must have touched her. From where I was eavesdropping, it sounded like she slapped him clear across the room. I walked across my room and laid my ear against the door.

"I don't have to take this," he said, presumably on his way out of the room.

Then I heard someone running. Footsteps slammed into the hardwood floor. A second later, something fell against the wall. More slapping. A lot of screaming, shuffling, thudding and door-slamming.

"I can't believe you hit me in the back of the head," Dave screamed.

I locked my door and dragged my record player out of the closet. Occasionally, when my Blondie record ended, I'd go out to check on the score, but it was hard to tell.

I was standing in the middle of the hall trying to figure out what was going on when my mother saw me.

"Go outside," she yelled.

"But—"

"Get out of here."

I stomped to the back door.

I knew the shit had hit the fan. Apparently, the Eskimo without an igloo caused quite a ruckus in our house. On the way down the hall, I saw a piece of scalp with hair attached to it laying on the floor. I leaned closer to inspect, eyeing the tiny white particles of skin clinging to the strands. It was horrible. Someone slammed a door, loud, then there was slamming and slapping, and I ran. I didn't need to hear anything else. A piece of scalp was worth a thousand words.

In the backyard I played with Inca until Dave appeared on the back porch. I had no idea how long he'd been standing there. Since there wasn't much to do except kick at the dirt, we just stood in uncomfortable silence wondering about our futures. I knew we'd reached that point. Eight years old and I finally understood the word *inevitable.*

He turned and I saw the bloodied gap on his head where his hair was missing.

The day was clear, sunny—one of those days where normal people sit in the backyard eating lunch, laughing, playing cards, grilling out. Dave and I wouldn't be so lucky.

Kicking up some dirt near the doghouse, I said, "Guess this is it, huh?"

He nodded, tightlipped.

Taking out his wallet, he handed me three one hundred–dollar bills. "Go buy yourself something nice, Cotton."

Then he closed the door and was gone. That was it.

"I can't believe you're leaving me," I screamed, but it was too late. The door to the car slammed shut. I went running for the front yard and made it just in time to see taillights turning onto the street. I ran out across the grass but was no match for the speed of the Oldsmobile.

Since we didn't have a car, my mother rode an old bike she found out in the barn to a neighbor's house to call Louise. She came back with her sweaty armpits and emptied every drawer with cash in it into a duffel bag. When she caught me spying on her from the hall, she said, "Go pack your stuff."

It was over. I knew it. I stuffed my three hundred dollars into my pink fuzzy purse and crammed all of my clothes and toys into every suitcase I could find. About an hour later a car horn honked out front. I ran to the window, thinking Dave had come back. It was Louise. She clomped onto the front porch, smoking a cigarette. She jammed her bony finger into the doorbell. I opened the door.

"Hey," she said. "Is your mother here?"

"Yeah. She's in the bedroom."

Louise walked down the hall, where I heard her say to my mother, "Ain't this some shizz? Men ain't nothing but trouble. Come on, sugar. We gotta hurry. I gotta date tonight."

# CHAPTER TWENTY-FIVE



*Flashback*

ot knowing what else to do, my mother packed us up and moved to a different town in Mississippi. Food from the local church and homeless shelter pantry appeared in our cupboards. Cans of navy beans, sauerkraut, hominy, and other mismatched items donated for poor people filled the shelves. Poor people like us with antique furniture, fur coats, and exquisite sets of bone china no fork ever touched. Poor people like us who owned a closet full of designer jeans and bottles of French perfume and hordes of cashmere sweaters that kept us warm when we had nowhere to go. We were casualties of the drug trade. Single mother with no high school diploma, no job skills other than being able to pack a bong, no technical training, and certainly no customer service skills. There we were all dressed up with nowhere to go.

My mother was a pretty little princess dangled from the arm of fate who was a mean pimp. She was going to have to get a job. If I thought she was mean before, man, things got worse. There's no pot of gold when the rainbow got caught cheating. As soon as she settled in, she found a new guy, except he was a little damaged by the Vietnam War. His name was Carson. He was weird. He might as well have been an alien.

One night I found Carson crawling around in our front yard wearing face paint. I liked the paint because it reminded me of Halloween, so I walked closer to check on him. His eyes were dull and lifeless. I couldn't tell if he could see me. I waved my hand in front of his face. Nothing. A twig snapped. His head jerked around in my direction. Now I looked down the barrel of a very big gun. I'd never had a gun pointed at my face. He didn't move. His eyes focused on something behind me. I turned very slowly to see what it was. There was nothing there. Just a dark wooded area.

I tried to make sense of the situation by calling out his name. Still nothing. Finally, I threw a rock at the living room window. You should have seen my mother and her stoner friends when they came outside and saw me staring down the barrel of that military issue handgun.

I heard someone whisper urgently, "Cotton. Cotton, we need you to slowly back away."

The black grease on Carson's face caught the light. I wondered why he couldn't see me.

There was a lot of activity at the front door of the house. A voice whispered, "Oh my god get her out of there."

I wanted to back away slowly, but an invisible string holding the moment together held onto me pretty tight. Grease made the whites of his eyes stand out. I could see all of the way through to the other side of his soul. He wasn't there anymore.

He was back in the jungle he hated so much. Back in the darkness.

"Cotton," our neighbor Sera said, "we can't come out to get you. You're going to have to back up real slow. Alright? Back up. Just back straight up."

I did. Carson followed me with the barrel of his gun but not with his eyes. At some point I backed close enough to the group and Sera grabbed me and ran. I was sideways, my arms bumping against her legs, watching her flip flops slap the heels of her feet in a furious madness. It was all madness. That's all it had ever been.

Sera sat me down at her kitchen table, flipping on all of the lights. Tilting my head up, she asked, "Are you okay? Did he hurt you?"

I shook my head, blinking.

She stood up and checked me for scratches on my arms and face, muttering, "That psycho. I can't believe this."

"Can't believe what?"

Sera checked behind my ears and down my neck. "He could have killed you."

"Why?"

"Because he was having a flashback."

Standing up, she grabbed a hand towel and wet it at the sink. "What's that?"

Wringing out the towel, she turned, pressing it to my forehead. "It's like he goes back to the jungle and relives it. He can't help it. He thinks he's back in those jungles in Vietnam being hunted."

"Why?"

"I don't know. He got lost out there. When he came back to the camp all of his buddies had been murdered. It screwed him up real bad. He gets stuck there."

The cold pressure on my forehead felt good. "Why does he want to go back to that moment of his life? That moment sucks."

Sera stopped, staring straight at me, thinking about her answer. "Because I don't think he ever really left it. I don't think he'll ever be normal again."

Looking down at my Calvin Klein jeans, I kind of understood. I wasn't exactly normal either. I wanted to have a nervous breakdown so I could go live somewhere else.

The next weekend Stan picked me up. My grandmother bought me some ribbons and felt at the fabric store, and I started making clothes for the leprechauns on Saint Patrick's Day. Maybe the little people could help me get my luck back.

When I finished with the green hats and scarves and tunics I'd carefully sewed by hand, I showed my grandmother. She helped me put together little pouches of food the little people might need. Since I couldn't wait for St. Patrick's Day, I put the stuff on top of the speakers in the living room. My grandmother gave me little chocolate candies to complete the offering. We admired my work, then she put her arm around me and said, "Gosh, Cotton, how I love you."

It was music to my ears.

The next morning my offering was gone. In its place was two twenty-dollar bills and a four-leaf clover made out of green construction paper.

I could live with that. It was better than nothing.

# CHAPTER TWENTY-SIX

*Mississippi*

School was perfect for me. It was the one place in the entire world my mother was not allowed. With that in mind I buried myself in a myriad of school activities, clubs, class productions, and extra credit because I'd do practically anything that gave me an excuse not to go home. My teachers helped me plan schedules, choose my classes, and narrow my focus to subjects I really liked. In the blue glow of the portable TV, I watched cooking shows on Saturday morning to learn how to make my own meals. I went to the library every weekend looking for books on fashion, news, or how to arrange flowers in a vase. I searched through a host of other magazines to find things that would potentially come in handy. I sat in dark movie theaters with Stan smacking popcorn in my ear and watched movies, trying to learn how real people related to one another. I learned comedic timing and love. Funny as it sounds, it worked.

While I tried to figure out what to do with my life, my mother descended into an isolated pot stupor the likes of which would have confounded Freud. None of it made sense to me. Weeks passed before I saw her sometimes. I heard her at night, though. Sometimes she'd get up, real late, and leave. I never asked where she went. She never offered to tell me.

When I did see her, it was usually because I'd done something wrong. I'd wake up with her hitting me in the middle of the night as she screamed, "You left your clothes on the floor again!" Then she'd throw her dirty t-shirt at me and leave. One night, by accident, I left a pan of water boiling on the stove until all of the water evaporated and caught the kitchen on fire. I was completely horrified when I got out of bed the next morning to find the kitchen charred and black. I grabbed my book bag and a peanut butter sandwich I'd left on my dresser the day before and ran to the bus stop. *Fast.*

Big sweat stains seeped through the thin fabric of my shirt during my first three classes of the day. I was convinced my mother was going to pull me out of class and scream at me in front of everyone. When the final bell of the day rang, I pretended to have extra work in the theater. While other kids were picked up promptly by mothers who loved them, I was always left to wait. My mother picked me up whenever she felt like it.

I was digging through a prop box, trying to find a glove to match the one in my hand, when I heard a loud, obnoxious horn honking outside. The muffler had gone kaput on my mother's car months before. It roared and rumbled like an earthquake every time you turned it on. My blood pumped ice into my fingertips. Little prickles moved down my forearms. I tried to take a deep breath. Little short bursts of air stuck in my throat. Beyond the walls of my protection, she gunned the engine. I should just make a run for it and go hide. I could get a job and learn a foreign language on CD and cook Beef Burgundy on the weekends. I could buy a bed and decorate with sprigs of lavender.

*HONK HONK HONNNNNK.*

A sigh pushed its way out of my mouth with a resounding huff. Fine. Whatever. Better to face the music and get it over with.

*HONK HONK HONK.*

"I'm coming." I hoisted myself up off of the dusty wooden floor.

The Oldsmobile my mother bought for four hundred dollars heaved at the curb like a ninety-eight-year-old chain smoker. It lurched forward a few inches. Not noticing me, she laid on the horn again.

"I'm right here," I said, getting into the car. Resigned to my fate I slammed the door, prepared to duck and dodge and ultimately get slapped to kingdom come. The worst thing she could do was hit me and that wasn't such a big deal anymore.

The silence was intimidating. She didn't say a word as she jerked the steering wheel and slammed her foot on the gas pedal. We rode in silence. No "hello" or "what's wrong with you" or anything. When she didn't scream at me during the entire ride home, I became extremely suspicious. Every time she turned her head to make a turn or look in the rearview mirror, I wanted to duck. At home, I was afraid she was going to drag me by my hair into the kitchen and make me scrub it with my nose hairs. It didn't happen.

*Nothing happened.*

When she fired up her evening joint, I made a tomato-and-cheese sandwich for dinner and ran to my bedroom. White bread stuck to the roof of my mouth as I huddled in the middle of my bed, listening. The sound of doors opening and closing came and went but otherwise there was silence. I fell asleep in a pile of worry.

The next day was more of the same. And the next. And the day after that. By the end of the week the black, charred walls of the kitchen held a secret I couldn't unravel. The biggest mystery of my life loomed dark. I spent hours running scenarios through my mind, trying to come up with a way to bring up the subject. I thought about just saying, "What in the hell happened to the kitchen?" but I was sure she'd glare at me and say, "I thought you knew." Besides, what if it made her mad? Really mad. It was one thing to be forced to acknowledge something. It was a whole other thing to have to talk about it.

Three weeks passed. Then one day I got off of the bus and walked home to find the walls scrubbed to a dingy gray. Still, not a word. I made macaroni and cheese and went to my room. I unwrapped a square of cornbread I'd saved from lunch and listened. Nothing. Sometime in the middle of the night I heard the distinctive growl of the car engine rumbling through the night. Lots of doors slammed, then her and her drunk date staggered through the night.

That weekend when I finally returned to my grandmother's house, I told Preston Brown the whole story.

"But she didn't yell at me," I concluded.

Preston was thoughtful. "Are you sure you did it?"

"Yeah. Why?"

"Because she probably can't remember if she did it or not."

*Nothing of the sort had ever occurred to me.*

"Your mom's not so good at remembering things," he added. "Like last year when she left us at the zoo, and we had to call my mom? Don't you remember?"

*How could I forget?* This is your brain. This is your brain on drugs.

That night I lay awake listening to the sounds of Stan's radio program seeping up through the floor. Thurman had been scarce for several days, and the peaceful quiet was a refreshing change. Closing my eyes, I tried to imagine what Dave was doing at that very moment. I dressed him up in his favorite light blue button-down shirt, with his gray sports jacket and took him around to his favorite restaurants like a paper doll. For some reason that soothed me, so I had him take a seat and order a beer.

He leaned back in his chair, holding the tall, amber-colored glass in the air. "Here's looking at you, kiddo."

I created a paper-doll image of myself to sit across from him. I told him my coat didn't fit anymore, that my saddle oxfords were almost too small and there was no one to help me with my homework.

He leaned forward in his chair, all flimsy and imaginary in my mind, and said, "That's okay. I'll help you."

It made me cry. I didn't know where Dave spent his days. Still, in the morning, I lay there, staring at the trees outside my window and imagining him making coffee. Images of him ran through my mind all day. At the most unexpected times I saw him leaning against a wall, talking on a payphone, or noticed the way he always glanced up in the rearview mirror when he asked me a question. I took photographs of him to Kimball's Drug Store down the street. My grandmother helped me put them on the copy machine. She bought me magazines, glue, and some new ribbons for my hair. Then we walked home together, and I spent the rest of the afternoon cutting out the copied pictures of Dave. I looked at all of the magazines, page by page, ripping out photos I liked. Carefully I cut out men's clothes and glued them on the pictures of Dave until I had a real set of Paper Dave Dolls. I knew it was weird, but everything was so far away. I just wanted something to hold onto. I didn't care if I was weird.

Every morning I wondered whether the world was real or not. I went to bed imagining I lived somewhere else. In the back of my mind, I held onto the idea that if I was good enough, then eventually Dave would miss me enough to call. I'd meet him at the end of the driveway with my bags packed, and he'd tell me how much life sucked without having me around.

My guidance counselor, Zelda Green, thought I was different and strange but exceptionally smart. Since my mother showed no interest in helping me do anything, Zelda went to a lot of trouble to get me signed up in every conceivable program, camp, club, *whatever.* Not only did I learn a lot, but I didn't have to hang around at home hiding in my room.

Each morning I woke in the dark, eerie house. I'd go to the bathroom, dutifully brush my teeth, wash my face, comb my hair, go back to my room and choose my outfit according to the one I believed Dave would like best. I'd get dressed, get my lunch out of the refrigerator, and walk to the bus stop in the cool morning with dew darkening the tops of my tennis shoes.

At school I read about people who traveled the world like Marco Polo or the Wright Brothers or Alexander the Great. Thrust deep into my imagination there was always a part of me that prayed one day Dave would pull up out in front of my school. All the people in my class would turn and stare as he got out wearing his leather jacket. He'd walk through the big double doors into the office where the secretary, Mrs. Lions, would call me out of class. I'd be whisked away into the waiting car, then to a plane, then to Mexico City, where we'd buy a hacienda and live. Year after year, decade after decade, people at my school would talk about the day Cotton Alexander was whisked away in a limousine by the coolest man on earth.

The reality was every day at 2:30 PM the last bell rang. I'd quietly gather all of my books into my bag and walk to the corner where I waited for my bus. My mother had long since decided that picking me up from school was way too much trouble. I stared out the windows of the bus. Kelly's Diner rolled past. Then Cosby Freight, the RV lot with brightly colored flags that flapped on blue cord even on the stillest of days, and down to the highway that rode past one of Dave's favorite restaurants. I always looked to see if his car was there. If no one was sitting next to me I'd take out my Paper Dave Dolls and look at them until my heart pinched deep inside my chest.

My stop was second to the last, so I had a lot of time to think. It was quiet and the whooshing of the highway took me back to times we drove to Mexico or New York. I'd close my eyes and remember the way the car smelled like coffee and exhaust at the filling station when we stopped for gas on road trips. A deep breath moved up through my chest, settling in my lungs, and I held it there a moment, making promises to myself about how I'd get back to my life. The life I wanted to live. On good days, the Paper Dave Dolls conjured up the scent of expensive cologne or the smell of Dave's leather jacket. On off days I stared into the distance that whizzed by on the other side of the window and willed myself not to cry. Some days I did cry, sunk deep in my seat, tears streaming down the front of my shirt. Then the bus would come to a stop three blocks from our crappy house, and I'd haul my butt up and clomp down four steps to the ground. I always stood on the shoulder of the road watching the bus pass out of sight. That delayed my walk back to the house on the edge of nowhere. That's where we lived. *Nowhere, Mississippi.*

# CHAPTER TWENTY-SEVEN

*A Purse Full of Money*

On weekends I begged to stay at my grandmother's house. This plea wasn't met with much resistance. My mother didn't care what I did as long as I left her alone. With Thurman scarce, days seemed remarkably long and hinted at possibility. I resumed my normal snooping around the house all weekend. On Friday mornings I packed my suitcase and took it to school, where I left it behind my teacher's desk until the final bell. My grandmother took the bus all of the way across town, three transfers in all, to meet me out front. I was so excited to see her every time. I ran as fast as I could across the trampled grass, suitcase bumping against my thigh.

"Hey," I yelled. "It's Friday."

"It's Friday alright."

Breathless from my sprint, I blurted out, "How was the ride over?"

"Good." She took my suitcase. "I sat next to a man who worked for an alien testing facility in Arizona."

"Really?"

"Yeah. I believe he said he had a chip in his brain."

I stopped, looking up at her. "Did you ask him if he knows Dr. Jeever?"

She laughed, "No, but I bet Jeever knows him."

Back at the house Stan was all smiles when we walked through the door.

Late one night him and I prowled around to see if we could find a snack cake or fruit pie or a rogue Milky Way bar that fell from the 12-pack. I pulled out the pasta holder I'd made with my Trash to Treasure kit. Sure enough, inside lurked a cherry-filled fruit pie. I couldn't remember stashing it, so I checked it for mold. Stan plugged the percolator into the electrical outlet. I dug around in the freezer until I found the cold brick of peach ice cream jammed behind blocks of government cheese.

In the middle of our midnight snack attack, Stan broke the silence. "Do you think Thurman will come back?"

The butter knife in my hand sliced through cherry goo. I looked over at him, my brow furrowed, my eyes tight. "Why would you ask that?"

"I don't know." He poked at a hunk of frozen peach trapped in cream. "I guess it's just 'cause he's been gone for week now and he ain't got no money or food; and I reckon someday he's got to get hungry enough to come back here. Right?"

*I hope not.* "I thought he went out to get smokes."

"He did. Weeks ago. Mother thought he was staying at someone's house."

"Who's house?"

He shrugged.

"So, he's gone?"

"Well, he's not here," Stan said.

The conversation gave me the creeps. I really didn't care to imagine the thankless job of predicting Thurman's return. I hoped he never came back. I hoped he disappeared or got lost or fell off the edge of the earth or was eaten by angry man-eating trolls. I ignored the question altogether and turned my attention back to my half of the fruit pie.

"What do you suppose he eats?" Stan pressed.

"People," I said. "Drop it."

A stubborn determination crept into his voice. "No. Where does he get his money? He ain't got no money. It's all here."

"What are you talking about? Are you talking about Granny's money?"

"No. His."

I pushed his half of the fruit pie right in front of his hand. He looked down at the red gooey filling oozing onto the paper wrapping.

"His money," Stan whispered, leaning across the table. "He'll come back for it and what if he does something bad?"

"What *money?*"

"All of the money them lawyers gave him when Daddy died."

"That was a long time ago." I raised an eyebrow.

He nodded. "Yeah. I know."

Sweet pools of melted ice cream formed in my bowl. The percolator gurgled and chugged. Finally, I said, "Show me what you're talking about."

Stan heaved himself up from the table. The hall leading to the sunroom where my grandmother slept was full of quiet shadows. Stan opened the closet door, trying to keep the bottom from scraping the floor. Slowly, he extended his arm inside feeling around, making the coat hangers tinkle against one another.

"Shhhhhh," I whispered.

"I am," he whispered back, glancing down the hall.

He looked like some alien creature, standing there with his arms disappearing in and out of darkness. He took a step deeper into the closet then backed up. Extending his arm high, he felt around on the very top shelf where I'd never been able to reach, not even with a chair. Seconds later he pulled down an old purse that looked like it was a hanging plant holder. It was absolutely hideous. The strap was big and thick and frayed from wear. Stan backed into his room, motioning for me to follow, clutching the hideous purse to his chest. We crept to his room. In a sudden fit of paranoia, he walked around and closed the blinds.

From down the hall I heard the wheeze of my grandmother's snoring. Stan set the purse ceremoniously in the middle of the bed, then nodded in my direction as if to say, "See I told you."

Slowly he unzipped the top, holding his breath like a jack-in-the-box was going to pop out. I was not convinced Thurman had any money and watched only half-heartedly. My attention drifted back to my bowl of melting ice cream on the table. Once the top was open, Stan stepped back, waving his hand for me to look inside. I did. To my utter surprise there were twenties, fifties, and hundred-dollar bills. But there were also fives, tens, and one-dollar bills all wrapped up with rubber bands that had long since broken, with bills crammed down the sides all crinkled and bunched up.

"What?" I whispered, reaching for a wad of cash.

Stan held his hand over the top. "I saw him, all the time, when he thought I was sleeping. I used to watch. Like this." He squinted his eyes. "After a while I wanted to know why he came in here. So I looked."

I pulled several wads of money as big as my fist off of the top. There was more money underneath. A lot more. "How long have you known about this?"

Stan's eyes rolled heavenward. He thought awhile. A long while. The percolator gurgled in the other room. The entire house smelled like a warm cup of coffee. I peeled two -hundred-dollar bills from a roll.

Finally, he said, "Since 1973, I reckon."

"You reckon," I snorted loud enough to wonder if I'd blown our cover. We both listened, holding our breath. The wheezing snore of my grandmother traveled down the hall. I leaned forward and asked, "Have you counted it?"

He shook his head.

"Go get us cups of coffee. We're going to put our math skills to work."

"But—" he stuttered.

"No 'buts'. Go on. You can complain later."

Stan tiptoed into the kitchen. From behind he looked like an enormous bear sneaking through the forest. I found notebook paper on his dresser and a top drawer full of pens that didn't work. In my attempt to find one with ink I found a pencil with a dull lead on the floor. Good enough.

Minutes later he returned with big mugs of coffee, Vienna sausages, and a package of saltines. In a drum-rolling moment we lifted the purse, turned it over and dumped the contents onto the bed. Wads of money hit the mattress then rolled to the floor. Horrified, Stan ran after them, frantically grabbing each one and tossing them back on the bed like hot potatoes.

I organized my paper and pencil and money. I pushed a pile toward him with my forearm. "This is your section."

He pushed it back. "I don't want one."

"Doesn't matter. You get one."

"But—"

"You don't have to keep it, you 'fraidy cat. You just have to count it."

"Then we'll put it back?"

"Yes. Now, mark down what you count on the notebook paper and only put the counted money back in the purse. Got it?"

He stared at me.

I raised an eyebrow. "Got it?"

"Why are we counting this if we're not going to keep it?"

"Because it's treasure," I declared. "Pirates always count treasure."

"Oh." He reached for his pile. "Then we put it back?"

"Yes, Mr. Suspicious, we put it back."

Some of the rubber bands were so old they stuck to the bills like glue. I had to roll my fingers over the rubbery, wormlike pieces to get them to come loose.

A few seconds passed before Stan's paranoia rushed in. "He'll know we've been touching his money."

I rolled my eyes. "He hasn't been here in weeks."

"But he'll come back," Stan exclaimed, all grabby, trying to get the money back in the purse.

"Well, he won't be back before we're done counting."

"You don't know that" he whined.

"Just go get me some new rubber bands," I huffed.

The faded yellow stripes on his shirt left trails of light as he rushed to the kitchen. I started counting. Stan returned with six rubber bands of various sizes.

I was already up to $11,443.00.

Meticulously, he rolled up the bills I'd left lying on the bed. He wrapped a big wad of cash with a fresh rubber band and plopped it in the purse.

I pushed the notebook paper against his knee. "Get to counting."

An hour later, with morning birds singing in the trees and all of the loot returned to its proper place, we added up the figures on each piece of notebook paper. Then we calculated the total.

I couldn't believe my eyes.

$36,526.05

A lone nickel on the bottom was the only coin in the whole lot.

"That's a lot of money." I stared down at the paper, swallowing back a yawn.

"Uh-huh," he nodded, picking up an open can of Vienna sausages from his bedside table that looked a little dry around the edges.

"What do we do with it?"

"We leave it there," he said, "in case he comes back for it one day."

"Or night," I whispered.

Stan's eyes widened.

Ignoring his paranoia, I read from the paper. "$36,526.05. That could buy a lot of Vienna sausages."

Cramming one in his mouth, he said, "I already got these."

*Right.*

When I could no longer stand the persistent grumbling of my stomach, I raised myself from the bed and went to the kitchen. Ice cream didn't interest me anymore. I made a pot of cream of celery soup. Stan made grits.

The sun rose over the rooftops. In the confines of the kitchen we moved quietly and precisely, weaving in and out of each other's steps like people with a secret. I ate my half of the fruit pie. Stan ate his, too.

Halfway through my bowl of soup I was stricken with a case of the yawns so dastardly I had to climb up the stairs to my room to pass out. I positioned the fan to blow directly on my face and climbed into bed. In a moment of bliss, I drifted off to sleep, thinking about the getaway plan I could hatch with thirty-six thousand dollars. I could buy Dave a ticket. I could buy new clothes. I could do a lot of things. I had plenty of time. Downstairs Stan washed dishes, turning the water on and off, making the pipes jerk and rumble. Then, I heard him walking down the hall.

I could go live in Mexico City. I'd work out a good plan. The money was safe. Thurman was never coming back. I knew it—the way you know it's going to rain. And that purse was so ugly no one would ever think to steal it.

# CHAPTER TWENTY-EIGHT

*Thurman Disappears*

"Thurman is going to be on the side of a milk carton," I announced proudly as I walked into the kitchen.

Stan looked up from a bowl of gravy. "What for?"

I slid into a chair, leaning over a pile of biscuits and butter.

"Because I just heard Granny on the phone talking about a missing person's report."

Stan looked confused. "Why would anyone want to find him?"

"I dunno." I shrugged my shoulders. "I just hope he doesn't come back."

"When was the last time he came home?" Stan asked. His brow furrowed as he tried to remember.

"The last time I saw him was when he punched Dave in the back of the head."

"He was here after that. Your mom was melting down, so you didn't come over much."

I sneaked back into the hall for an update. When I returned, Stan was still staring up at the ceiling. "She's calling a private detective."

Later my grandmother sent us off to the zoo alone. I played on the rides all day.

We spent an hour sitting on a bench in the monkey house.

Stan watched the monkeys swinging around in front of us. "I wonder why monkeys don't cover their butts."

"Good observation, given the fact that everyone in our family has a long history of showing their asses."

Stan chuckled.

At five o'clock we climbed into Stan's rusted old car. As we pulled away from the curb zoo workers locked the huge gates behind us. I waved goodbye to the bears and the sea lions and the big cats.

At home my grandmother was sitting on the gossip bench exactly where we'd left her. Stan helped her off to bed, dragging the rotary phone as far as the cord would stretch so she could sleep with it at the end of her bed.

Stan stayed up all night, so I stayed up with him. Sitting in the middle of his bed, watching him rock and sway to an old Pretender's CD I brought him up to speed in my personal life.

"Where did Dave go?"

"I don't know," I said.

"You think he'll come back?"

I shook my head.

He tipped his head low and said, "He was right nice to you, Cotton."

I burst into tears.

Stan put his arm around my shoulder. "You think he went back to Colombia?"

I shook my head and thought about my pack of love cigarettes hidden in the back of the hall closet. I wanted to believe everything would work itself out.

It was a quiet morning a few weeks later when the phone rang at 4 AM. It was so loud it scared the bejesus out of me. Stan and I were in the kitchen about to snarf down sweet potato pies and tumblers full of hot chocolate. We'd already drunk one pot of coffee. Our second pot brewed.

The first ring sent chills up my spine. Stan's gaze shifted to the hall.

Another ring.

"Should we answer it?" I whispered.

"We ain't even supposed to be awake," Stan said.

Our question was answered soon enough when boards creaked beneath my grandmother's feet.

"Hello?" She spoke urgently as if she'd been waiting for the call.

Stan and I huddled together in the corner, eavesdropping, munching on pie crusts.

"Yes. Yes," she said. Then, a second later, she gasped, "Thurman, is that you? *Thurman?*"

Stan and I exchanged a look. Why was he calling?

There was silence, then my grandmother pleaded "Please, Officer, put him back on."

She listened, lowering her butt to the gossip bench.

"I don't understand. Why won't he—"

I noticed Stan holding his breath, so I nudged him with my elbow. A deep sigh passed out of him.

My grandmother shifted her gaze over to us, covering the receiver with her hand. "What are you two doing out of bed?"

*Busted.*

I shrugged my shoulders.

She turned her attention back to the phone. "Yes. Yes. What was that?"

There was a pause. I heard the garbled sounds of a voice on the other end of the line.

Her hand landed limply on the seat of the bench. "I don't understand."

*Neither did I.*

After a few seconds, she picked up a pen, wrote down a number, hung up and immediately dialed. "Yes, yes, my son just called me from there." She listened, a deep frown forming on her mouth. "What? But you picked him up and— What?" Her eyes swelled to the size of grapefruits, and she looked very, very old.

The phone fell away from her face, landing on the floor with a thud. Stan and I were close enough to hear a man's voice say, "I'm sorry, madam. There's nothing else we can do."

Then the voice thanked her politely and hung up.

"What's going on?" I walked closer, picking the phone off the floor.

Tears streamed down her cheeks. She looked at the phone as if it had answers.

The percolator filled the house with a rich scent.

"He's not coming back," I demanded, mad that he even called in the first place. The veins on my forehead popped out. "You're not sending him money, are you?"

Stan stepped up behind me and laid his hand on my shoulder.

Finally, she looked up at us, big tears caught in her eyelashes. "He can't stay out there, Cotton. He doesn't have his medicine."

"So? He left. He doesn't just get to come back whenever he wants and terrorize everyone. No one wants him to come back anyway."

"It doesn't matter if anyone wants him to come back. He has to have his medicine."

"But his medicine doesn't work."

Her eyes fixed on mine. "His medicine is what keeps him from getting worse."

It took me a minute but then a light bulb clicked on in my head. The words *keep him from getting worse* echoed in my head. I understood. Finally. The medicine was what kept him from hurting us all these years.

With a deep, resounding sigh she laid her palms flat against her thighs.

"Are you going to get him?" I demanded, unwilling to give up my position.

"I have to. I can't be responsible for what he might do out there."

I looked back at Stan to get him to tell her how much he didn't want Thurman to come back, but he was gone. No one was going to take a vote. Everyone was just going to let him come back home.

My grandmother reached for the phone book. The conversation was over. I walked into the kitchen. Stan hunkered down at the table, drinking heavy cream from the carton.

"Has he ever run away before?" I flopped down in a chair.

Stan chewed thoughtfully. "No. I'm thinking this is the only time he ever left."

I leaned back in my chair to eavesdrop. After my curiosity was satisfied, I whispered to Stan, "She's calling the bus station."

Stan talked with his mouth full, "I remember him before his medicine, Cotton. He ain't right without that medicine. He needs it."

"He ain't right with it. Besides, big deal. I'd send him his medicine every day if agreed to stay away from here."

"He won't take it," my grandmother said from the doorway.

"I don't want him to live here," I persisted.

"Don't no one else want him either," Stan said.

"Ain't that the damn truth."

"Cotton, stop saying 'damn' and go call your mother. You're going to have to go back home for a few days."

That night Stan drove me back to the house my mother rented. My grandmother's suitcase was in the trunk. I turned around so I could see her sitting in the dark backseat.

I didn't want Thurman to come back.

I really didn't want to stay with my mother.

I got out of the car without saying a word.

Stan pulled away from the curb. My mother was in the living room, flopped on the couch, stoned. She was wearing a short dress with no underwear. It was gross.

"I have a date later," she slurred.

I nodded and kept walking toward my room.

"Don't tell anyone I left you here," she yelled after me.

"Whatever you say."

A week later my grandmother returned empty-handed from Texas. She had a full bottle of pills and no Thurman. When she thought Stan and were sleeping, I heard her go to the basement. She opened the air ducts, tapping and thumping until she found every bag of weed.

The next morning, I got up early and looked everywhere for the bags of marijuana. They had disappeared. I went and sat on the end of my grandmother's bed. She woke up, staring at the ceiling, her eyes adjusting to the light.

Finally, she took a deep breath and asked, "What really happened when Thurman came to stay at your house?"

I told her the entire story. She laid on her back, listening.

When I finished, she said, "I just don't know what's wrong with him."

"I don't know what was ever right about him."

"He was a good boy. Sometimes." Then she leaned forward, patting my hand. "But I guess he was never sweet like you."

"What happened when you were in Texas?"

She thought about my question a minute. Then she shook her head and said, "Not much. I sat in a motel and talked to a private investigator. I tried to talk to anyone who'd seen Thurman. I read the newspapers."

"For what?"

"To make sure no one had been hurt."

*Oh.*

Stan shuffled around in his room. My grandmother drifted off to sleep.

Every night I laid in bed listening for the sound of Thurman's footsteps coming up the stairs. I listened for the sound of his car idling out front or the maniacal laugh that gave me goose bumps. But he didn't come back. At least, not then. For the first time in my life the Bogeyman had gone to live underneath someone else's bed.

# CHAPTER TWENTY-NINE

*It Runs in the Family*

The first day my mother disappeared I didn't notice because I'd made such a habit of hiding in my room. The house was really quiet when I got up for school.

Diggy was drinking water from the faucet.

"Is anyone here?" I asked.

He shrugged his furry shoulders.

Diggy walked with me in the dark to the bus stop.

That afternoon, I returned from school and knocked on the front door. No one answered. I fished around behind a stack of old cinderblocks for the key. A big puff of silence greeted me as I walked through the door. I knew something was wrong. Nothing in the kitchen had been moved. Nothing in the bathroom had been moved, including the roll of toilet paper on the floor next to the sink. My heart started to beat a little faster. I ran out into the hall, looking in both directions.

"Hello?" I yelled loudly.

No answer.

I ran to my mother's bedroom.

That's when I found the needles in the trash can. Well, next to the trash can. I stood there staring at wads of tissue paper stained with blood, syringes laying like bodies, dried-up vomit crusted to the floor. It was like an oracle divining the future. Suddenly, I remembered the hotel in New York and sat down and cried. I remembered how I couldn't come in her room. I remembered the way Dave took out his gun in New York when he saw the man walking out of our hotel room. Finally, I stood up and wiped my face because I didn't want to cry. I was just afraid of being alone. A big sigh sputtered in my stomach. I went to the kitchen to make a peanut butter and jelly sandwich for dinner. The silence was spooky. I did my homework, wondering where Diggy had gone and if he would come back by the time I fell asleep. I launched myself out of bed and made sure every window and door was locked. I dragged my blankets and pillow to the closet thinking that if someone broke in, they wouldn't find me. The dark confines of my new sleeping arrangement were nice, but I woke all night long to the sound of every squeaking, creaking, thumping, shuffling noise. I burrowed deeper into my blankets.

When I woke to the sound of my alarm on the bedside table, Diggy was sleeping next to me. After making my rounds to see if my mother had shown up in the middle of the night, I tried to pretend nothing was wrong.

Four days later, on Friday, my guidance counselor, Zelda, met me in the school hallway and asked me if I was okay.

"Yeah, sure," I chirped. "Why?"

She led me down the hall into her office. "Because you've missed school five times this month. We've been calling your mother to get written notes to excuse your absences. She hasn't called me back."

*The answering machine.* I'd completely forgotten to check it. My palms started sweating.

Desperate for a good answer, I blurted out, "I had to go out of town to be in beauty pageants."

It was not a good lie. The look on her face told me so. She leaned closer, laying her arms on her knees. "Cotton, I need you to tell me if everything is okay."

The sound of her voice was so sweet and sincere that I completely fell apart. Through my big, blubbering sobs, I croaked, "No. No, it's not okay." I told her my mother never came back.

"That's what I thought," she sighed, spinning around in her chair. She picked up a legal pad, flipped a bunch of pages back and asked, "Is there someplace you can stay?"

"With my grandmother."

Zelda held her pen poised over the yellow paper. "Where does she live?"

"Across town in the historical district."

After giving all of the information, I went to sit in the waiting room. I glanced around to make sure I was alone. I didn't want anyone to know what was happening. After a few minutes, Zelda came out wearing her coat.

"Come on." She took my hand. "I'll drive you over."

Out in the parking lot a gray sky stretched low over the city. I could smell rain. A shiver ran down my spine. Zelda opened the passenger door for me. Inside, the car was loaded with gadgets and smelled brand new. When she turned the key in the ignition classical music began playing. She listened to the same radio station as Stan.

I started crying.

She turned a knob on the panel and the music shut off. "Cotton, why are you crying?"

It took me a minute. Tears choked in my throat. Finally, I said, "I was scared."

Her lips tightened into a frown. "I know you were, honey." She patted my shoulder. "I know. It's my job to know."

Thunder rumbled over our heads.

My grandmother walked down from the front porch as Zelda pulled her car to the curb.

Zelda put the car in park and got out. "Are you Sara Alexander?" she asked.

I opened my door and got out.

My grandmother took my hand and said, "Yes, I'm Cotton's grandmother."

I huddled close, squeezing her hand. Her body was warm, and she smelled like doughnuts and coffee. I wanted her to be a kangaroo so I could climb into her pocket and hop away.

Zelda leaned against her car, fixing her gaze on us. "I'm going to have to press charges against her mother. You understand what that means, don't you?"

I looked up at my grandmother and saw her nod. I could hear Stan breathing behind us.

Zelda knelt down in front of me. "Will you be okay here?"

I nodded.

"All right," she touched my head and smiled. "I'll see you in school."

After Zelda drove away my grandmother turned to me. "Cotton, why didn't you call me or Stan and tell us you were alone?"

"I thought she would come back."

She sighed. "Oh, Cotton, I am so sorry she left you there. Let's go eat dinner," she steered me toward the front door.

Stan stared at us. "What's happened?"

"Connie never came back to get Cotton."

I stared at them through red-rimmed eyes.

Finally, Stan reached for my hand, "That's okay. Connie ain't never really been nice to anyone."

That night my grandmother let us bring the television down to Stan's room since I didn't have school the next day. Everything was so much nicer with Thurman gone. I could lie back and watch a movie without having to brace for the worst. We watched Cary Grant and ate fried Spam sandwiches with mustard and a two-liter of soda. Stan burped and giggled like a girl until he fell asleep.

The next morning, I woke to the sound of someone breathing. When I opened my eyes, I saw my grandmother standing over me.

She smiled and said, "Good. You're up. Let's go."

I rolled over, yawning. "Yeah. Where are we going?"

"We're going to have to take a taxi and go get your stuff."

I pushed myself up on my elbows, looking around. Stan was a big lump sleeping next to me. I rubbed my eyes. My grandmother extended her hand, and I took it. The floor was cold, but it felt good to be standing. It felt good to be holding someone's hand.

The landlord was surly and smelled like cigarette smoke. His skin was yellow, and his teeth looked like they'd never been brushed. He argued with my grandmother for a solid fifteen minutes before finally saying, "Alright. You can have the kid's stuff, but the rest is mine. That woman is two months behind on the rent."

*That woman* was my mother.

My grandmother and I walked to the porch.

The landlord extended his arm in front of the door. "Just the kid," he said.

My grandmother sighed in a way that told me she was annoyed. She squeezed my hand, then knelt down slowly so we were face to face. "Okay. This man is going to let you go inside. I want you to go get all of your stuff and bring it out here. Okay?"

The smelly landlord unlocked the door.

The inside of the house was quiet and still. Everything was just as I'd left it. My new Nancy Drew book on the sofa. My tinfoil sword on the floor. Diggy was standing in the hall. I glanced back over my shoulder to make sure no one was watching.

I whispered to Diggy, "Come on. Help me get all of my stuff."

Since my blanket was still in the closet, I pulled it out, spread it open and laid all of my clothes on top. Then I went to the hall closet to get a suitcase. I gave the door a good jerk because it always scraped the floor. I stood there staring into the dark hollow. It took me a minute to piece it together. Then I knew. The closet was empty. The suitcases were gone. My mother never intended to return. I was so mad I ran to her room. I flung open the closet door. The empty shelves and hanging rod left no room for doubt. All of her clothes were gone. Quickly I turned and scanned the room for inventory. The jewelry box that normally sat on the dresser was gone.

"Cotton?" My grandmother yelled from the front yard.

"I'm coming," I huffed.

"Come on," I said to Diggy. "Let's go get my stuff."

I filled every backpack, duffel bag, and plastic tote I could find with my shoes and socks and books. My little hatbox was still under my bed, my pink purse with my cash inside. I filled it with clothes and my pack of love smokes from South America.

The creepy dollhouse leered at me from the corner. Dirty clothes draped over the side. From where I was standing I could see the dark, empty rooms. It seemed so weird to finally be able to leave its perfect rooms behind.

I grabbed a glass from my beside table and raised it in a toast to Hank and Sadie.

"We'll always have Paris," I said, wistfully. I'd seen someone do that in a movie once.

Then I dragged all of my stuff to the front door. While my grandmother put my stuff in the taxi, I walked through the house one last time. At the back door I stopped, looking out across the dusty brown yard. In that moment I realized I'd never played out back, never even set foot out there. *I lived in a house where I never even played in the backyard.*

Diggy thumped his foot.

"We're on our own," I said.

He nodded.

"Are you okay with that?"

He nodded again.

# CHAPTER THIRTY

### *To Grandmother's House We Go*

Jeever heckled Stan for weeks. After he took his meds, I went and sat in the hall at the gossip bench and willed my mother to call. Granted, it never seemed like she wanted me around, but I was having a really hard time believing she just didn't care about what happened to me. Mostly I doodled on the notepad next to the phone and tried to use my Jedi mind power. When it didn't work, I hoisted myself up and went upstairs. Since Jeever had become a houseguest, I slept in Thurman's old room with the door locked. Just in case.

I moved all of Thurman's old junk out into the already-stuffed hall closet. The scales, the grow lights, the 8-tracks, the hydroponics dope-growing kit. It all went, one by one, as me and Diggy dragged them out, dusting our hands off when we were done. Because I was sure Thurman would never come back, I snuck downstairs and out into the alley with a garbage bag full of his old clothes. I dumped them in the neighbors' can and ran. Everything he owned had stains in the armpits and would surely be mistaken for trash.

Instead of running back to my house I ran down the alley to Preston Brown's. I found him sitting on the edge of the sandbox as I rounded the corner of his garage.

"Hey," I said, catching my breath. "Whacha doing?"

"Thinking about summer vacation."

I walked out into the cool grass and took a seat. It smelled wet and clean. "What about it?"

"It's almost here."

I stretched my legs out in front of me, thinking. "Yeah, you're right. It's just a month and a half away."

He carved pictures in the sand that I couldn't see from my angle. I just saw his arm moving and heard the *shhhh* of the sand. Finally, he sighed big and loud and said, "I have to go to church camp again."

"Maybe God could write you a note," I offered.

"Very funny."

"It's something to do. I mean, it can't be that bad."

"It is."

"Did you talk to God?"

"God isn't the problem. Ned Bender is the problem. He threatens to beat me up every year and is true to his word."

A cool chill moved across the yard as the sun fell below the rooftops. A lion roared at the zoo. I looked over at my friend sitting on the edge of the sandbox. His glasses held the last glimmer of evening sun. His brown hair tumbled down into his eyes.

I'd known him my entire life.

I pushed myself up from the grass and blurted out, "You're my best friend."

"Duh." He smiled.

"I mean it," I said, wedging myself down on the edge next to him. "Maybe if we start a business together then your father won't make you go away to camp and get beat up by God's followers."

"Very funny."

Suddenly, the sound of Stan screaming at Dr. Jeever filled up the backyard. My muscles tensed. I was beginning to despise the sound of anything screaming.

After a few seconds, Preston asked, "Why does he do that? I hear him all of the time at night when my windows are down."

I shrugged my shoulders. "I don't know. He says that Dr. Jeever shoots him in the head with laser beams."

"Do you believe him?"

I had to think about that a minute. "Kind of. I guess it's like having a really bad dream. It's real when you're having it and not real when you wake up, but you still remember it, which makes it kind of real. Right?"

"Has anyone ever seen Dr. Jeever?"

I shook my head.

Stan let out another wail to let us know the laser beam hit his brain.

"His window must be open," I said.

Preston sighed, weaving his fingers together like he was praying. "Has your mom called?"

I shook my head again.

"I'm sorry I brought it up then. It's just been a long time, and I thought she might have called by now."

"My grandmother doesn't think she's coming back to get me. We have to go to court and talk to a judge."

"Maybe that's okay," he said, looking on the bright side. "You never seemed to spend much time with her anyway. Besides, now I see you every day instead of just on weekends."

Mrs. Brown appeared at the back door. "Preston, it's time for evening prayer."

Preston looked up at his mother. "Okay." Then he turned to me, "I gotta go. Call me later if you're bored."

I pushed off from the sandbox. "Give my best to the Holy Ghost."

I saw him tuck his head into his chest and smile so his mother couldn't see.

I walked back home in the fading light. The rich smell of moist grass and fresh dirt rose up from every single yard I passed.

I passed by my grandmother's room and saw that she was napping. Tomorrow was Saturday. If it only rained through the night, then maybe we could go to the zoo tomorrow. Passing through the kitchen I caught sight of my reflection in the window. Next week was my birthday. I would be nine years old.

Maybe my mother had been out buying me presents and was going to surprise me on my birthday. I sighed. *Maybe.*

Upstairs I loafed around, digging through Grand Daddy's old closet to find things to decorate my room. Big raindrops splattered against the bedroom windows. Outside, the streetlamps clicked on. From where I was standing, I could see straight out the window at rain slanting down through the light like thousands of diamonds hurling toward earth. It was so quiet inside that the steady drumming on the roof made me feel less alone.

I dug through the closet, stopping to admire an old shaving kit or cuff links or tie clips. Grand Daddy had been dead almost my whole life, and his pajamas were still wrapped in plastic, unopened, on a shelf. No one ever talked about him.

Diggy walked in from the hall.

"Hey." I looked up.

He thumped his foot and the fur on his ears flopped down into his face.

"What are you doing?"

He shrugged his shoulders, holding out big, empty paws.

"Gosh," I said, stuffing everything back into the closet. "Grand Daddy still has so much stuff up here. Everything has his name or initials on it. I held up a monogrammed handkerchief. "Herbert Alexander" was sewn across the front in cursive letters.

"Herbert," I whispered. "What a fuddy-duddy name."

Diggy wanted ice cream, so we walked back downstairs. I dug chunks of frozen peaches out as we listened to the raindrops. For some reason all the peace and tranquility made me really hungry. I found the can opener and ate an entire can of ravioli, cold.

When Diggy went outside to snoop around on the back porch, I went upstairs to read my book. Halfway up the stairs I had an attack of the yawns so intense I was asleep before my head hit the pillow.

The next morning a cold gray light filled my room. Stan was perched directly over me like a vulture. He'd shaved and put on clean clothes. It was the first time I'd seen him smile in weeks.

"Hey," he said, "you wanna take the bus over to the zoo?"

I raised up, rubbing my eyes, seized again with yawns. "What about Jeever?"

Stan sat down on the end of the bed, facing the door. "I think he's going to leave me alone today."

"How do you know?"

"Because I didn't hear him none last night." It *had* been quiet. I studied him a minute. "You sure?"

He nodded.

"Because that time you took off all of your clothes and ran down the street naked sure did shut Jeever up."

That slow, wonderful smile crept across his face as he smoothed out the wrinkles in his pants. "I'm okay," he said.

Because it was still raining on and off all day, we were practically the only people at the zoo. If it started raining, we ducked inside the Monkey House or the Reptile House and hung out until it slowed to a drizzle. On the way home we got off the bus to get fried chicken boxes, then caught the next one.

The house was so quiet when we walked in that I immediately became suspicious. Quiet houses were beginning to bug me. I sat my chicken box with its greasy stain on the living room table and walked into the hall. From where I was standing, I could see into my grandmother's room perfectly. She was in the exact same position she'd been the night before.

"Stan?"

"Yeah," he said, digging into his box.

"Can you come here?"

I turned just in time to see the smile wash off of his face. "What's wrong?"

"Just come here."

One. Two. Three. Four. His footsteps echoed in the hall, and even though he only had to walk about thirteen steps it took a lifetime. He stopped next to me, looking into the room.

"She's napping," he said.

"For two days?"

He looked up at the ceiling. Then his eyes wandered, searching for an answer. "Has it been two days since she was up? *No.*"

"Yes." Tears filled my eyes. I could see now that she wasn't breathing. She was so quiet. I knew. I just knew. I walked into the room and laid my hand on her leg, "Granny, it's me, Cotton. We brought you a chicken box."

Her leg was cold against my hand. My knees started to give out, and I sort of tumbled forward, falling across the bed. Tears burned hot in my eyes. When I finally opened my eyes, I saw Stan was still standing in the hall, mouth open, eyes wide.

I bunched up her blankets in my hands and cried. "No, please don't leave us now. Please—someone help us." I started shaking.

Behind me I heard the chicken box hit the floor. Stan ran into the room. "Mother! Mother, wake up." When she didn't move or answer he shook her and raised his voice. "Mother. Mother, wake up and eat some dinner with me and Cotton." He tried to lift her into a sitting position. "Mother," he yelled. "*Wake up.*"

It was so horrible. Her arms were stiff. Her fingers didn't move. A big yellow stain of urine had dried on the sheets.

"Please wake up," I sputtered weakly.

Stan accidentally knocked me into the wall, trying to get close enough to pull her out of bed.

I hit my head hard and pushed off the wall, annoyed. "Stop," I yelled.

He kept pulling and yelled, "Mother, wake up."

"Stan," I grabbed him by the arm, forcing back bile in my throat. "Stan, please stop. She's gone."

"*She's right here,*" he screamed with such a frantic, high pitch voice it sent chills vibrating down my spine. "Mother."

Then he collapsed onto the floor. "Oh, God," he whispered.

My whole body began trembling. I had no idea what to do, so I reached for her hand. It felt like bones covered in paper. I wrapped both of my hands around hers, blowing on it with my warm breath. I noticed she had combed her hair before she went to bed.

The choked, gurgling of Stan crying filled the space around us.

That's when I saw it. All around the bed and on the bedside table and even the pillow next to her she'd arranged my Trash to Treasure gifts. The pasta holder and the vase covered in hearts, a jar I'd covered with papier mâché and paper flowers. An ornament I'd made at school with a picture of myself glued to a sparkly silver ball and the Christmas card I'd just made for her were on the pillow. Every other object I'd ever made for her was placed close by. She'd taken it all out and surrounded herself with it. Surrounded herself with my love.

Stan wailed so loud it scared me. I picked up a Christmas card I'd made for her a few years ago. It had a terrible drawing of Santa Claus on the front. I opened it up and on the inside, it read: *Merry Xmas Grandma. I love you so much (more than ice cream) Love, love love your Granddaughter, Cotton.*

I'd misspelled the word Granddaughter.

Stuff was everywhere. Laid out for the world to see. There was a notepad and pencil on the bedside table. I grabbed it.

"Okay," I said, real loud. "This is what we're going to do." I wrote down the days of the week on the notepad, barely able to see through my tears. "Alright, I'll take the bus to school during the week. Then on Tuesdays, no, I mean Mondays, we'll go to the store and buy food. On Tuesdays we'll clean up the house together. On Wednesdays we'll take the bus and get fried chicken."

"What are we going to do without Mother?" Stan interrupted, the front of his shirt wet with tears.

"We'll just have to do everything ourselves."

"I don't want to," he choked, burying his face into the side of the mattress.

"Fine," I said. "I'll do the schedule, but we've got to do some stuff. We've got to get someone to help us. She can't just stay here."

Stan didn't say anything. I stood up, watching his back tremble from crying. I walked out into the hall.

*Think. Think. Think. What can we do?*

Dave.

I ran up to my room and dug through my dresser until I found his old beeper number. I dragged the phone from the hall over to the stairs so I could sit down, and I dialed. *Beep beep.* Please leave the number you are calling from, a mechanical voice informed. I did.

My hands were shaking so bad, and I couldn't stop crying. I stared at the phone. *Please call back. Please call back.* I had no way of knowing how much time had passed and I didn't want to call Time and Temperature because what if he called back at that exact minute. I was so dizzy and sick to my stomach that I leaned over and laid my head on the floor.

The phone did not ring.

Finally, I heard Stan moving around downstairs. I didn't want him to be alone, so I walked back down. He was standing in the hall, next to the chicken box he'd dropped on the floor.

Tears streamed down his face. "Cotton," he said. "Mother's dead."

The word slapped me in the face. "Don't say that. We love her. That means something. Right?"

He nodded; more tears pushed their way down his cheeks.

"We're going to be okay," I said, not convinced I would ever be anything, much less okay.

"What are we going to do?" he whispered.

"I don't know," I said, biting my lip. "I called Dave. He'll know what to do. We've got money. We'll be okay."

"The *money.* You have to get all of the money in the house, Cotton. If people come to get Mother, they might take it." Stan looked almost lucid. "Go. Go and get it."

Still shaking so hard I could barely breathe, I kept glancing at the phone on the gossip bench, willing it to ring. "What about all of the money in the bank?"

"Forget about that right now. Go get the purse and whatever else you can find."

Happy to have a goal to focus on, I ran off to get the key to the closet. *Just get the valuables,* I kept telling myself. *Just get the valuables.* I found the key and took it to the closet. Stan's crying echoed down the hall. It was so terrible. My arm shook so bad I could barely get the key in the lock. Finally I did, and the lock clicked open. There I was, all alone in the hall, staring at a dark closet. I dug around for the purse and pulled it out. Everything smelled like mothballs. Finally, I decided to turn on the light and check to see if anything else had been left in there. My grandmother loved to hide things in coat pockets. It had been her secret. As I stood there I began to rummage through the pockets of Grand Daddy's old coats. The first three held nothing, but the fourth one had a fat paper envelope like they give you at the bank. I pulled the flap open.

It was stuffed with money.

I set the purse on the floor at my feet, along with the envelope, and began frantically digging through every pocket trying to find all of the valuables. I found a diamond ring I had never seen my entire life. I held it up to the light.

"That was her wedding ring," Stan said behind me.

My heart jumped out of my chest. "God, don't sneak up on me."

"I didn't. She took that ring off after Daddy died."

"What do I do with it?"

"Put it all together. Let's get everything and put it somewhere safe."

I turned back to the closet, stuffing my hand down into another coat pocket. Nothing. Then another. Nothing. I pulled at an old velvet coat, stuffing my hand into its deep pocket. The feeling of paper rubbed against my fingertips. I gripped all of it, pulling it out.

"I think she hid money everywhere." I stared at the wad of cash in my hand.

We moved from room to room, robots in search of anything we believed we should keep safe. Money, old jewelry, a pearl necklace no one knew was real or not, old coins. We ensured our survival by proving that we had money to buy food and keep the lights on, because neither one of us had a job. I purposely tried not to even glance in the direction of her room as I went up and down the hall searching every room. Still, once I didn't look away fast enough and caught sight of her feet at the end of her bed. I looked at her feet, right there, where I'd seen them a thousand times. I loved those feet. I wanted them to stand up and walk over and give me a hug. I felt my face pull tight and the hot tears. I picked up Stan's chicken box and went back to making sure we had everything.

Finally, when we had searched every conceivable place, I went and stood in front of the pile we'd collected on the sofa. "We need a suitcase."

"There's some in the garage," he said.

He was gone a long time. I sat on his bed wondering what to do in a house with a dead person. It was awful. After a while I heard him creak up the back porch steps.

Morning birds started to sing.

"It took me awhile to find one with a lock," he said.

It was old and poo-poo brown, with a pebbled plastic outside. In all of my years of snooping I'd never come across that suitcase. "Where did you get this?"

Stan fished the key out of an inside pocket. "It was Daddy's."

A deep, dark blue spilled across the sky outside the windows. I thought about what the minister had said about heaven. I thought about chariots and golden apples and the stories of angels. "Do you think Granny and Grand Daddy are together up there?"

He stood straight up. "I reckon. That still don't make it right."

Together we piled the valuables into the suitcase. I put my jade donkey on top and locked it tight. Stan gave me the key.

"What are we going to do with it?"

"We need to hide it."

"We could bury it like Dave used to bury money." My words trailed off when I remembered he'd never returned my beep.

"Nah, the rain and worms will ruin it. Just stick tight to it for now."

Too exhausted to argue, I sat down on the floor, leaning my back against the sofa. Stan handed me a blanket. It had been so long since I'd felt warm. My eyelids were heavy. My arms drooped at my sides. Stan laid down on the sofa behind me and put his hand on my shoulder. I fell asleep crying.

The sound of the mail lady opening the box on the front porch woke me up. Sunlight flooded the room. Suddenly I wanted to run outside and ask her what to do. I wanted to throw open the door and say, "Could you come here for a minute?"

But I didn't. Stan was a warm lump behind me. I listened for his breath. The suitcase was propped upright next to the end table. I was starving. I went outside to get the mail to avoid having to walk down the hall. Outside, the air was fresh, cool, but a thick metal taste lingered in my stomach. I grabbed the mail.

Across the street, the mail lady called out, "Good morning."

*Now's my chance,* I thought. *Tell her. Tell her what's happened, and she'll know what to do.*

Instead, I waved and ran back inside. Stan still wasn't awake. I stopped just inside the door and looked at the envelopes in my hand. *Sara Alexander* was written on the front. Somehow seeing her name meant she was real, and it gave me the courage to go to the kitchen and get something to eat. I was so hungry I ate a liverwurst sandwich and a pimento cheese spread sandwich and made extras for Stan. The warm, full feeling in my stomach made me sleepy, and I went to Stan's room and fell asleep again.

I woke sometime in the afternoon to the sound of the toilet being flushed. Stan walked out of the bathroom. Dark circles shadowed his face. He looked old and tired.

"Cotton," he said. "We got to do something."

I sighed. I knew what to do. I got up and went to the gossip bench and called information. Then, I called my guidance counselor Zelda and told her the entire story. Stan walked into the hall and sat on the floor next to me.

After I hung up, I turned to him and said, "Come on. We've got to take this suitcase to Preston Brown. He'll hide it for me."

I dragged the suitcase three doors down and knocked on the door.

Mrs. Brown answered. "Preston's still at school, Cotton. What are you doing at home?"

I pushed the suitcase in front of me. "I need him to keep this for me."

"What is it?"

"A lot of personal stuff to me."

Her brow furrowed. "Then why don't you keep it?"

"I can't."

Suspicion crept into her voice. "Why not?"

Tiny speckles of salvia flew out of my mouth as I blurted out the truth. "I think my grandmother died."

*There, I said it.*

"You *think* or you *know*?"

"I think—I mean, I'm pretty sure. She won't wake up."

Covering her mouth with her hand, she said, "Oh, no, Cotton. What's going to happen to you?"

"I don't know."

Mrs. Brown put my suitcase in the hall closet, promising to take care of it. Then she put her soft, sweet-smelling arm around me and led me to the sofa. I sat down feeling very conscious of the fact that I hadn't changed clothes in days.

"I have to go back down the street," I said.

"Why don't you sit here with me? I don't think you need to go back just yet."

She squeezed my hand and smiled so sweet I couldn't say no. I was so happy not to have to go back just yet. Happy to sit there with my stomach churning. From where we were sitting we saw the ambulance, then an emergency vehicle. A police car cruised down the street. Then another. I watched from the sofa, hoping everything was okay.

It was like watching television. Then they left one by one. Mrs. Brown asked if I wanted to spend the night.

I shook my head. "I don't want Stan to have to sleep there alone."

"Oh, Cotton," she said, unexpectedly hugging me tight.

I wrapped my arms around her and for the first time I realized I loved the way Mrs. Brown smelled. Her hair, her clothes, her perfume. She was like God's flower, every day bending in the sunshine of prayers and faith. No wonder Preston loved her so much.

She took a deep breath and let go. "Okay, you come here anytime. If you get scared just come down here and wake me up."

I nodded.

The walk home was simple. I passed houses with lights on. They were people I didn't know. From the sidewalk I could see the living room light on at our house. Everything was strangely quiet. I listened for animals at the zoo. Nothing. The concrete steps on our front porch seemed thicker, heavier, swallowing up the sound of my footsteps. I opened the door and listened. Silence in general bugged me. The living room was empty. My glance swept forward into the hall. It was so awful, but I had to see if she was still in there. I had to see if she'd woken up and was startled to find everyone standing around her bed. My feet carried me forward, but I could feel myself holding my breath. I rounded the corner, and for a second sheer joy sprang to my mind. I saw a figure sitting on the edge of her bed, shoulders slumped forward. Then I saw that it was Stan, hunched over with his face in his hands. There was no one else in the room. I stood in the doorway, watching his shoulders tremble.

Because I didn't know what to do, I said, "I left the suitcase with Mrs. Brown."

Minutes passed.

Finally, he turned and looked at me with his tear-burnt face and said, "They took Mother away."

# CHAPTER THIRTY-ONE

*Jeever*

After they took my grandmother away Stan sat on the end of her bed and cried for twelve hours. At first, I stayed with him, hoping to come up with some way to piece it all together. But then I had to go to the bathroom, and the smell was terrible in her room. On my way I called Time and Temperature. Then, as I sat slumped and exhausted on the toilet, my stomach growled so loud it scared me.

I needed a plan. My ears rang. I just wanted some food. A can of Vienna sausages, oyster crackers, tomato soup.

I dragged myself back down the hall to stand in the doorway. "Do you want something to eat?"

It took him a minute, but finally Stan shook his head. He moved just enough so that I could see his skin was splotchy and red. The front of his pants wet with tears. Snot glistened on his upper lip.

"Are you sure?"

He nodded.

"Okay," I sighed, walking back down the hall.

My grandmother always made me soup, especially when I didn't feel good. Suddenly soup seemed like a good idea. If I could just sit down and eat a warm bowl of soup, then I would know what to do.

The pantry had enough food for us to survive about a week. Then we'd go to the store and buy more. No one would have to know my grandmother died. Stan and I had been to the store by ourselves before, I reasoned. We could do it. We'd be fine.

The second shelf was dotted with a dozen cans of soup. Tomato. Bean and ham. Beef with barley. Chicken and pasta. Cream of celery. My stomach rumbled loud and caused my belly to quiver. I felt a little faint. Stan's favorite was cream of celery. Mine was tomato. I located the can opener in the dish drain, opened each can, poured the contents into two separate saucepans, then snarfed down three pieces of liverwurst. Once I felt strong enough to stand up again, I added milk to the soup and turned on the burners. My stomach grumbled for more food. Suddenly feeling very confident, I melted cheese on top of slices of bread. The smell of everything cooking filled me with hope. I stood at the oven, peering down at glowing hot burners, watching cheese melt and bubble.

When I was done, I put it all on an old TV tray with a rusted picture of a fruit bowl on the front and carried it all to the bedroom. From what I could tell Stan hadn't moved an inch. I tried to set the tray on the end of the bed, but it was too lumpy and uneven. The soup sloshed over the edges of the bowls. I walked around and put it on the floor in front of Stan. His face was so red and swollen it looked like someone slapped him.

"I made some dinner," I said, quietly.

His eyes drifted down to the tray, then back to his hands.

"It might make you feel better," I offered.

His eyes narrowed at the edges.

"Or not," I added uncomfortably.

I ate my toasted cheese sandwich. The sound of my chewing in the small, dark room was so loud. I thought eventually all of my lip-smacking goodness would bring back Stan's appetite, but it didn't. He just sat on the bed and stared down at his hands. Sometimes his face crinkled up, breath caught in his throat and tears rolled down his cheeks. The third time this happened, I laid my hand on his knee and cried too.

My nose filled with snot, and I had to stop eating.

Without warning the sound of the phone ringing ripped through the hall. It was so startling and loud my entire body went numb with fear. Then I realized, *someone is calling.* I jumped up and ran.

*Ring. Ring.*

I lunged for the gossip bench. *Praise Jesus. Hallelujah.*

I snatched the received with both hands and pulled it to my ear so fast that I clonked myself in the face. "Ouch," I said. Then, "Hello?"

It was Preston Brown. "Hello? Cotton?"

"Yeah?"

"Are you okay?"

"Kind of."

"I've got your suitcase. I put it in my closet."

"Thank you."

"Are you okay?"

I exhaled, glancing down the hallway. "I don't know."

"What happened?"

I sat there a minute and listened to the sound of our breathing over the phone. I didn't really know what to say. I sighed big and deep wondering where to start.

"You don't have to tell me," Preston offered finally.

"It's not that I don't want to."

"I know."

"I just thought she was sleeping."

Silence emanated from the other end of the line.

"She was in her room when we came home, and Stan had been bothered by Jeever. I just thought that she needed a nap. That's all. So, I just left her alone."

"How did you find out?"

"I thought she'd be hungry after sleeping so long, and I went into her room to give her some fried chicken."

"Did you touch her?"

"Yeah."

"What did it feel like?"

"Cold. Like tree branches on the ground when it's really cold outside."

There was a long pause, then Preston said, "My mom said you can sleep down here if you want."

"I know. She told me."

"I have to go pray now."

"Okay."

"You can call me any time," he said quickly.

"Even while you're praying?" I managed a small, tight smile.

"Yeah."

It was quiet for a second.

"Cotton?"

I started to speak, but my nose burned, and fluid rushed to my eyes. I choked, then swallowed. Finally, I managed to blurt out, "What if I could have helped her?"

I heard Preston's chin rub against the phone.

"I mean what if I'd gone in earlier and could have helped her or called someone," I blurted desperately, articulating my worst fears. "What if I could have given her mouth to mouth?"

"I don't know."

"What if I could have called an ambulance or someone to pick her up?"

"I don't know," he said, so softly I could barely hear him.

"Will you ask God why?"

"Yes," he said. "I will. Call me tomorrow or tonight if you need anything."

"Okay."

When I hung up the phone, the floodgate of emotion I'd dammed up cracked and broke. I looked up at the ceiling and screamed, *"Why? Go ahead and tell me why. Why would you take her away from us? She loved us. She loved me. Go ahead and tell me why."*

I stood upright. Tears flooded my cheeks, splashing down against my neck.

"Why?" I screamed. "Why would you do this?"

When the ceiling didn't part like the Red Sea and reveal the face of God, I wailed even louder, throwing my arms and fists against the wall. "Why?" I pleaded, angry. Sobs choked the rest of my words. My forearms hit the wall.

I felt Stan's big bear arms wrap around me and hold tight. I threw my head back as far as I could and screamed louder than I'd screamed my entire life. Stan just took a deep breath and held on. I shook my fist and raged against the ceiling. He squeezed tighter and I tried to pull away, but he wouldn't let go.

"We could have helped her," I wailed. "We could have given her mouth to mouth."

For the first time in hours, he spoke. "I don't think that would have done us no good."

"You don't know that" I insisted.

"No. I reckon I don't."

It didn't matter. We couldn't change it back. It was already done. I pulled away from Stan and went back to the bedroom to eat my cold soup. With every mouthful I wondered if there was something in my magic book that could help us.

I didn't even know where it was.

The next morning, I woke to a knock on the front door. I was just disoriented enough to scamper off of the sofa and run to the door thinking it might be my mother or Dave coming to get me.

It wasn't either one of them.

It was the minister.

His eyes glowed bright in the morning sun. He removed his hat, laying it against his chest, and asked, "Is your grandmother here?"

I shook my head.

"Well, she didn't join us on Sunday or call for the bus to pick her up. In fact, no one has talked to her all week. She usually calls a few times to pray over the phone. So, I thought I'd stop by to see if she's okay." His eyes drifted up to the ceiling.

"She's not okay," I said. "Or, well, maybe she is now. I don't know."

The minister knelt in front of me, looking me right in the eye. His skin smelled like Ivory soap. "Did something happen?"

"I thought she was sleeping," I said, trying not to cry again.

He raised an eyebrow. "And then?"

And then I burst into tears and told him the entire story. It was awful. I'd never wanted to stop crying so bad in all my life. He just stayed there in front of me the whole time, shifting his weight from leg to leg, but always looking me in the eye. His brow knotted up and stayed that way. His lips pinched together. I cried so hard I could barely speak. Patiently he laid his hand on top of my shoulder. After I finally managed to spit out my last, snot-filled sentence, he exhaled a long breath.

"How old are you?" he asked.

"Almost nine."

*My birthday. I'd forgotten about my birthday. What about my party? What about my presents?*

"Who's helping you with the arrangements?"

"For my birthday party?"

"No," he said. "Who is helping you with your grandmother's funeral?"

That stumped me. "The hospital, I guess."

"No," he shook his head. "They just send her body to the morgue."

"The what?"

"The morgue." He was about to explain when he stood up, knees cracking, and asked, "Can I come in?"

That sounded good. I needed some company. I pointed to the sofa then ran down the hall to Stan's room. He was in the bathroom peeing with the door open.

"Who's out there?" he inquired, looking back over his shoulder.

"The minister. Make us some appetizers and coffee. Snappy."

Stan groaned. "What's the Jesus Man doing here?"

I ran back to the living room and sat down on the edge of a chair. I pulled my knees in tight, trying to look grown up. "Coffee will be served in a moment," I announced.

The minister nodded.

Stan plodded down the hall to the kitchen.

"Did your grandmother have a policy?"

"A what?"

"A life insurance policy. Maybe we should wait for your uncle." He hesitated. Then, he sighed and said, "On second thought, let's continue. A policy would pay money to a beneficiary to cover her funeral expenses."

My face was blank.

"Okay," he exhaled again. "Did your grandmother have a special place that she kept important papers?"

That was easy. "Yeah."

The smell of coffee wafted down the hall. I walked into her room and looked under the bed until I found the three handbags that held all of her important papers. When I looked up Stan had sneaked down the hall and was standing in the doorway.

"What's the Jesus Man doing here?"

"He said he came by because she didn't go to church."

"Humph," he said, looking back over his shoulder. "Crook."

I rolled my eyes. "Go back and make something to eat if you don't have anything nice to say."

The patchwork-square purse and the green quilted one had handles. The macramé one only had a broken strap, so I carried it and slung the other two over each shoulder. They were kind of heavy. Halfway down the hall I put the macramé one on the floor and dragged it by its strap. The minister stood up from the sofa when he saw me and walked over to help. We took them to the table and set each one down, careful not to let the contents dump onto the floor.

He raised an eyebrow. "Do you know which one might have the policy?"

I shook my head.

"Okay," he reached for the quilted purse. "Let's start here."

"Sounds good to me."

He pulled out a huge hunk of envelopes and papers bound together with rubber bands. Without saying a word, he opened each one, eyes scanning pages, separating them into stacks.

Uncomfortable with the silence, I said, "Aren't you going to ask me where my mother is?"

He stopped, studying me a minute, then said, "Your grandmother talked to me a lot. We prayed together. I know about your mother."

I wanted to ask him what he knew, but the tone of his voice said it all. It was so matter of fact that it surprised me.

"Do you know about me?" I asked.

Laying a stack of papers to rest on his lap, he said, "I know your name is Cotton and that you are a blessed little girl and that your grandmother loved you very much."

"How?"

"Because every week she told me and Jesus and anyone else who would listen how much she loved you." He picked up a new stack of envelopes and flipped through each one.

*Oh.*

Stan brought the rusty TV tray with coffee, yogurt and cold Spam sandwiches and set it on the table. Then he rolled his eyes and left.

I devoured my Spam on white bread.

Patiently the minister sipped his coffee, flipping through each stack until he'd inspected all three purses. He held two envelopes up. "Cotton, did you know that your grandmother had two life insurance policies?"

I shook my head, digging white bread off the roof of my mouth with my tongue.

"Do you know what these policies mean?"

I shook my head again, still digging.

"Well," he sighed. "I'll help you work all of this out. But first I need to make arrangements for your grandmother to have a proper burial. Okay?"

He stood up and walked to the door, carrying both envelopes. "I'll need these polices. Sometimes I have to help my congregation with things like this. It's not my favorite part but it does come with the job."

*The Jesus Job.*

"Okay," I said, happy to have someone in the house who knew what they were doing.

Then he left.

Stan peeked around the corner with a surly look. "What did he take?"

"He said it was a policy."

"Thief."

"*What?*"

"All those people pretend to talk to Jesus so they can get everyone's money and buy new cars."

"Are you being serious?"

"He just went through all of Mother's stuff and stole from us."

"You are a piece of work, Stanley Johnson Alexander. If Jesus Man can buy a new car with those two pieces of paper, then let him. What are we supposed to do? Did you know we're supposed to take care of all of this stuff?"

Stan looked down at the floor, ignoring me.

"*Did you?*"

Finally, he shook his head.

"Yeah, well, neither did I. I mean, who did all of this crap when Grand Daddy died?"

He sighed, loud. "I guess Mother did."

"You guess." I frowned. "Well, someone's got to help us."

I noticed Stan wasn't really looking at me. He was sort of looking over me.

"Hey," I snapped my fingers.

"Yeah?"

"We need help."

"From who?"

"The Jesus Man."

Stan huffed and walked back down the hall. A second later I heard him pick up his car keys. I followed him and stood in his doorway watching. Then he walked right past me and out the front door.

"What are you doing?" I yelled.

With one hand on the door, he turned, that vacant look filling up his eyes and said, "I have to go to Jeever's house. I think he may be hiding Mother."

*What?* The nightmare was getting worse.

Stan walked down the front walk, and for the first time all day I noticed he was wearing a big flannel shirt, boxer shorts, and dress shoes. He clomped his way to the car.

*What happened to his pants?*

What felt like a scream mellowed into a sigh as I watched him fumble with his keys, trying to unlock the door.

"Wait," I said, grabbing my pink fuzzy purse, running after him.

I had to knock on the passenger's window to get him to unlock the door. He reached over, careful not to make eye contact, and pulled the knob up. I climbed in, a little breathless from the whole ordeal. I wanted to ask him if he was okay, but I knew the answer.

The car engine sounded like a wild beast waking up. Without giving it time to warm up, Stan threw it in gear and backed out.

As we passed by Preston Brown's house I turned to look. From where I was, I could see straight through their living room and into the dining room where Mrs. Brown was on her knees praying. *Sweet Jesus,* I thought. *Say one for me.*

Suddenly I couldn't remember if we'd unplugged the percolator. "Did you turn the coffee pot off?"

When he didn't answer I decided not to ask again. In fact, I didn't say much of anything until after he circled the block around Jeever's house for the ninth time.

"What are we doing?"

Stan's eyes darted furtively across sidewalks and front yards of neighboring houses. "I think Jeever may have taken Mother."

"Taken her where?"

"I don't know," he huffed. "If I knew then I'd just go get her."

I blinked, still wondering how much of a joke this was. "She's at the morgue, wherever that is."

"No," his hands came down hard on the steering wheel. "He just made it look like she's dead so he could bring her back here."

*Okay. He's not joking. Let's move to Plan B.*

Our car slowed to a stop at the curb outside of Jeever's house. Yellow flowers bloomed in flower beds under the windows. I watched Stan squeeze and release the steering wheel. Not a good sign.

"Hey," I said cheerfully. "Why don't we go and watch a movie at the movie theater?" My words faded as a quiver in my voice betrayed my insincerity.

It didn't matter. He wasn't listening. To my tremendous horror, he slammed the car in park and jumped out of the car. I turned just in time to see him running up the driveway in his boxer shorts, his inner thighs jiggling. Without thinking I rolled the window down as fast as I could.

"Stan," I whispered loudly. "What are you doing?"

He was my last hope in the world. If he went in that house and attacked Jeever then where would I go? The police would take him away. How would I ever be able to take care of myself all alone in that great big house. I leaned farther out the window. "Get back in the car," I yelled.

Stan disappeared behind the house. *Dang it.* I was climbing out of the car when I saw him run back to the driveway. Sweat-soaked strands of hair stuck to his neck and cheeks.

I ran toward him, screaming, "Stop. You're scaring me."

He didn't look up. Instead, he ran into the garage. A second later he ran out carrying a brick. All of a sudden, he turned abruptly and hauled his jiggling butt up the front walk. Without stopping he hurled the brick through the front window. I closed my eyes as tight as I could and screamed.

The sound of glass shattering confirmed my worst fear. I forced my eyes open. Now he ran for the car. His dress shoes pounded against the grass. I just knew the police were going to hunt us down by his footprints. I turned and ran for the car, breathless.

We both slammed our doors at the same time. Stan jerked the car into gear and burned rubber.

I couldn't stop my body from trembling. "What in the hell did you do that for?"

Eyes glued to the road, he sped down the residential streets. "That'll teach him," he said. "Now he knows I mean business."

My voice quivered. "Teach him *what?*"

For the first time during the whole ordeal, he looked me in the eye. "Now he'll know we're onto him and he'll have to bring Mother back."

# CHAPTER THIRTY-TWO

## *The Minister Cometh*

The minister was standing on our front porch when Stan screeched to a stop at the curb. Since I'd spent the entire car ride waiting on a stream of cop cars to pull us over, I was relieved to throw open my door and get out.

The minister walked down the front steps with an envelope in his hand. "I was going to leave this for you."

"What is it?"

"It's all of the arrangements. A car will be here to pick you up the day after tomorrow. Okay?"

I took the envelope and opened it. Inside there was a copy of her insurance, directions to the funeral home, business cards that read *Morgan Brothers Funeral Home.*

It was horrible.

I started crying all over again.

Off in the distance I heard sirens. Stan heard them too. I saw his head raise up from the steering wheel where it had been resting since I jumped out of the car.

The minister's voice interrupted my thought. "Did you hear me?"

"Huh? No."

"Do you have anyone you need to invite?"

I shook my head. Stan furtively glanced side to side like a jailbird in waiting.

"Well, she has some friends at church who will want to come. Is it okay if I invite them?"

The sirens grew louder. "Sure," I said, looking to see if they were near our street.

Stan started the car. The engine rumbled and growled. He gunned the accelerator, threw it in gear and burned rubber outta there.

The minister watched the car slam on the brakes at the end of the street, skid and then fishtail around the corner.

"Is he okay?"

"He's having a hard time."

"Looks like it. Well, it is to be expected. He was very close to his mother."

Sirens blasted their shrill call closer and closer.

"Do you know where you uncle is going?" he asked.

I shook my head. I had no idea.

The sirens passed.

The minister knelt down in front of me. "Do you have somewhere to go?"

I could walk down to Preston Brown's house, but I couldn't bear the thought of his mother feeling sorry for me, so I said, "No."

His eyes drifted across our yard. I followed with my own. My eyes scanned our unmowed grass, the rusted porch rail, the chipped paint on the steps, the faded colors on the front of the house, the old swing that creaked and sagged.

*Home sweet home.*

He took my hand, standing up. "Why don't you come back to my house. We'll leave a note for your uncle."

*Fine with me.* I was terrified Thurman would come back while I was alone in the house. I ran into the house, grabbed my pink fuzzy purse, and ran back out.

He looked at me, puzzled. "Don't you have any clothes?"

I hesitated. "They're all dirty." I hadn't wanted to mention it, but it was true. All of the clothes I'd brought with me were in the dirty clothes hamper.

"What are you going to wear to your grandmother's funeral?"

"I don't know," I shrugged my shoulders. "I guess what I have on."

His jaw tightened. "That won't do. Show me where your clothes are."

I couldn't imagine why anyone wanted to see my dirty clothes, but I opened the door and invited him in. As we walked through the living room, I noticed I hadn't kept to my schedule very well. It was even worse in the kitchen. Dirty dishes everywhere. I thought Stan washed up after every meal. The minister glanced down at a pile of crusty pots on the floor.

"Looks like my clothes aren't the only thing dirty around here." It sounded so funny in my mind, but he didn't laugh.

We climbed the stairs. My room wasn't so bad, except that it still had all of Thurman's old furniture, so it didn't really look like my room per se. I pointed to the hamper overflowing with dirty clothes. He picked it up, carried it downstairs, and put it in the trunk. I looked around to see if Stan had parked and was hiding. He wasn't. At least, not that I could see.

Once we were on the road the minister asked, "Have you eaten?"

I had to think about the question. "This morning."

"Would you like to eat?"

The answer washed over me like a warm sunny day. "I'll have some hot soup," I said.

As it turned out, the Jesus Man liked soup, too. His wife was nice and smelled like honeysuckle flowers. She made us tomato soup and grilled cheese for dinner. The Jesus Man was nice, and we all had blueberry pie for dessert. Their house was so nice and quiet. Every so often the air conditioner would click on. A cool burst of air blew out across my knees. The minister chewed thoughtfully, and every time he caught me staring at him he smiled. I wondered if he was thinking about God.

After dinner we all adjourned to the living room to listen to music. Soft melodies made my eyes roll back in my head. The temperature in the room was so cool and dry. My stomach was full of homemade soup and pie. People sang about the salvation of Jesus, and my entire body felt numb and limp.

I woke the next morning in the guest bedroom. It took me a minute to remember where I was. A calm silence filled up the space. Birds chirped in trees outside my window. A pile of freshly washed and folded clothes sat on the dresser. I sat up to throw my legs over the side of the bed, but the sheets were so soft. My toes brushed against the cool softness. The feather pillow pulled me back down and my head flopped into its dreamy fluff. In seconds I was asleep again.

The next time I woke the minister's wife was standing next to me holding a tray of food. Breakfast in bed. Hotel Jesus was turning out to be quite an experience.

"Cotton," she said softly. "It's time to wake up."

I pulled myself up on my elbows. "I need to call my uncle."

"I'll bring you the cordless phone."

She left the room and returned several seconds later, saying, "We'll be leaving in a few hours." Pointing at the bathroom, she added, "You'll find everything you need in there, but if there's something else, then give a holler."

Once she closed my door, I pressed the *on* button and dialed. *Ring. Ring. Ring.*

I exhaled, using my Jedi mind power to get him to pick up. I looked at the clock. It was 10:38 AM. Five minutes later I hung up.

The bathroom had scented soaps shaped like roses, and towels with letters sewn across the front. Next to the sink a neat pile with a fresh towel, toothbrush, toothpaste, little bottles of shampoo, conditioner, and lotions, and one washcloth had been left for me.

I looked in the mirror. My greasy, stringy hair hadn't been combed in days. I ran my fingers through it, hoping to fluff it up. It kind of worked, but not really. My eyes looked droopy and tired. Freckles stood out on my nose. I stretched my neck to catch a glimpse of my shoulder. I pulled my sleeve up to get a glimpse of the bruise on my shoulder from Stan accidentally knocking me into the wall. A yellow, purple, black blob on the top of my arm. I sighed. My teeth felt furry. I could see my reflection only from my shoulders up, so I climbed on the toilet seat. I took myself in from all angles and scowled. My thighs were still fat.

I brought the cordless phone into the bathroom and called Stan no less than ten times while getting ready. The shower was good. I felt better. I wrapped a big fluffy towel over my shoulders and went into my room to pick out some clothes. I chose my favorite orange pants and a purple long-sleeved shirt with butterflies all over it.

I sighed. It would be nice to be a butterfly. I could fly anywhere and hang out on flowers and live in trees. I wouldn't have to talk to people or live with anyone. I could just be a butterfly.

Someone knocked on my door.

"Yeah?"

"It's almost time to leave," the minister said.

"Okay."

I put on my clothes, snarfed down half the oatmeal on my tray, downed a glass of OJ, and left.

The orange juice didn't agree with me. My stomach burned and rumbled down the long, tree-lined country roads. Acid rose up in the back of my throat, and I kept having to swallow it back down. The sound of tires relaxed me. I closed my eyes and imagined Dave was driving us out to meet Pablo. Trees whooshed past. The only sound from the front of the car was that of the minister and his wife breathing. I opened my eyes. The sky was a cool blue. I closed my eyes and tried to remember fractions to keep my mind occupied.

After a while I felt the car slow down, then turn. I opened my eyes. We wound up a long road that curved around a perfectly still lake. Big stone tombstones sprouted from the earth. I swallowed. It was the first time in my life I'd ever been to a cemetery. Ever. No one had ever taken me to Grand Daddy's grave. In fact, no one had ever mentioned going to visit him. It was so weird, like he just disappeared and left all of his stuff behind.

The minister turned around in his seat. "Normally you'd have a viewing and then the funeral service, but since so much time has passed, I just arranged for the service."

I had absolutely no idea what he was talking about. "Okay."

As we approached the main building, I craned my neck to look out the window. I didn't see Stan's car anywhere. My eyes searched row after row of cars. Jeever had probably told Stan to go run naked down the street again. I couldn't believe him. How was I supposed to get through all of this by myself?

People I didn't know walked toward the building. I assumed that since I didn't know them, they wouldn't know me. Then I could be left alone. The minister's wife helped me out of the car and held my hand.

I don't know what I thought was going to happen, but the reality was awful. As soon as we walked inside, complete strangers started walking up to me telling me how sorry they were. After a few seconds, the minister asked me if I wanted to go see my grandmother. Of course I said yes. Except I meant I wanted to see my real grandmother, alive and well. Instead, I was ushered into a room where I saw the waxy profile of a woman in a coffin who only kind of looked like her. Laying perfectly still she didn't look like she was napping. She looked like an imposter.

Someone tapped me on the shoulder, but I just kept walking toward the coffin. It wasn't true. This wasn't happening. I wanted to go home. I wanted to go and eat soup and get a plan together for the rest of my life. I wanted to go to the library and the zoo and not have to cry anymore.

I felt a hand on my shoulder and looked up to see the minister. "It's okay if you're afraid. The Lord will stand by you."

"Where's my uncle?"

The minister glanced all around the room. "I don't know."

"I want to wait in the car."

"But—"

"I want to wait in the car," I said, louder.

After they buried the strange wax woman who looked nothing like my grandmother, I got to go home. Stan was sitting in his room eating a piece of fried chicken when I walked in carrying my clean clothes.

"You missed her funeral," I said.

"Yep."

"You didn't get to say goodbye."

"Nope."

"I can't believe you."

He shook his head. "Jeever's got Mother in the basement of his house."

"Oh, stop with all of that crap."

Stan chewed thoughtfully. "I bought you a chicken box. It's on the table."

Two days later a woman I'd never seen before knocked on our front door. Stan and I had been in the kitchen for half an hour trying to make lunch. I thought it might be my mom, so I walked to the door, but as I approached, I saw there were two women. Neither of whom I recognized.

"Yes?"

"Are you Cotton Alexander?"

I nodded, hesitant to reveal any information.

One woman was wearing a skirt with plump legs poking out at the bottom. The other woman had frosted hair and wore orange lipstick.

Plump Legs asked, "Is your mother home?"

I backed up a step, ready to close the door. "She's at the store."

Orange Lipstick laid her hand against the door. "We'd actually like to talk to you."

I shook my head. "I don't want to talk."

Plump Legs pushed her way in. "Then I'm afraid we'll have to wait and talk to your mother."

"Who are you?" Stan asked from the hallway behind me.

Orange Lipstick extended a hand. "Hi," she said brightly. "Are you Cotton's father? I'm Judy Dennis. We're from the Department of Social Services."

I sighed, stepping aside, wondering how I was ever going to get out of this. I directed Plump Legs and Orange Lipstick to the sofa. "I'll get some refreshments."

I pushed Stan down the hallway. In the kitchen I jerked open the freezer, trying to think of the best story to tell. "Get some soda," I said.

Back in the living room, Plump Legs sipped her fizzing soda, then said, "Cotton, the hospital workers called us and filed a report saying that your grandmother had passed away. Since she was listed as your temporary guardian, we know you must be here alone."

"I'm not alone. Stan is here."

He produced a weak smile.

Orange Lipstick said, "I thought your mother was coming back."

"Well, she is," I ventured. "But right this minute, Stan is here."

"Yes he is." Plump Legs sighed like she was tired.

Her sidekick jumped in. "Cotton, your grandmother has known for some time that she was going to pass away. She had a last will and testament in the front pocket of her housedress. The EMTs found it and turned it over."

"What do you mean?"

"She was diagnosed with cancer of the uterus eight months ago."

Stan and I exchanged looks. That's when the minister had started coming around and all of the open pleas to Jesus started.

Plump Legs went on, "She stated that you had not seen or heard from your mother in more than six months. She stipulated that if anything ever happened to her then you were to go and live with your father. Do you know where he is?"

"Do you have the Will?" I asked.

She pulled several folded sheets of paper out of her purse, handing them over. "I brought a copy."

My heart raced as I flipped through the pages. I'd never met my father in my life. Finally, I found the paragraph. My eyes scanned the words until I saw the name. My salvation.

"Do you know where he is?" Orange Lipstick asked.

"He's away on business," I offered up quickly.

"Is that the truth?"

"Sort of."

Plump Legs sighed. "Cotton, you're going to have to come with us until we find him."

# CHAPTER THIRTY-THREE

### *The Group Home*

It wasn't bad. It wasn't great, either.

I went to live in a big two-story house where a bunch of other kids who didn't have anywhere to go went to live. A girl my age named Tyra was waiting to go live with her grandmother in New York. The oldest girl was fifteen and climbed out on the roof to smoke cigarettes. The rest of us kept to ourselves and tried to blend in.

We made popcorn balls and watched movies. We went on an outing to the zoo. It was the first time I'd ever been without Stan. It made me sad to see the monkeys and the polar bears. I wanted to go home and make coffee and listen to radio programs. When we got back that night, I called Stan. He didn't answer. I called again. Still no answer. He'd never been good about answering the phone, but when he didn't pick up the third time, I called Preston Brown.

"I don't think he lives there anymore," Preston said.

"*What?*"

"Well, some people came by and took him and a lot of his stuff. Then they closed all of the curtains and locked up the place. I sat out on the sidewalk watching."

"Huh?"

"Yeah, weird. Hey, are you okay?"

"Yeah. It's not so bad here. It's really quiet."

"Cotton?"

"Yeah?"

I could hear him breathing. "It's not as much fun with you gone."

I sighed. "I know. I miss you, too. Hey. What do you do for all of those hours you're at church?"

"Talk to God, mostly."

"Do you think he listens for a full hour?"

"Why?"

"I don't know. I guess it just seems like a long time and how can he hear with everyone talking at once?"

"Mom says he hears all of our prayers."

"Maybe he records them and listens later."

"Yeah. Maybe."

"Listen, can you put in a good word for me with the Holy Ghost?"

"You got it."

I hung up the phone and stood up from the wooden chair in the hall. I hitched up my gumption and walked downstairs. The evening-shift person's name was Paul. I stood in the doorway and knocked on the wall.

He glanced my way and smiled. "Hey, kiddo. Come on in. What's on your mind?"

"My uncle didn't answer the phone. He doesn't really go anywhere by himself. I think I should go over and check on him."

Paul's brow twisted into a knot. "Cotton, come over here and sit down."

He gestured to a big stuffed chair, but I wasn't interested. "I'll stand. I really just want to go over and make sure he's okay."

"He's okay."

"How do you know?"

"Judy Dennis called today. There have been some changes to your uncle's case."

"He doesn't have a case."

"Yes, he does." Paul spun around in his chair and pulled open a file cabinet. "She faxed over some information for us to put in your file."

"My *file?*" I felt my knees weakening. My entire life had been reduced to a file.

He pulled out a file folder I could now see had my name on it. My hands began to shake.

Paul sighed, opening my folder. "All of the earth-shattering events seem to happen on my shift." He flipped through several pages, then stopped and looked up at me. "It seems they have taken your uncle to live at a home where he can be monitored."

"He has a home."

Yes, well, I'm sure he does. But now he has a new home."

"Where?"

Paul leaned forward, handing me a piece of paper with an address and telephone number on it.

"What is this place?"

"It's a group home. It's kind of like this place except he lives there permanently."

"What about my grandmother's house?"

"Judy said they are going to sell it and give the money to you and Stan for your care."

"But he doesn't want any money. He wants his house."

"I understand, but I don't think your uncle can live by himself."

I heard my hand hit the wall before I felt it. Tears swelled in my eyes. It made me so mad. "No," I screamed at him. "That's our house. That's where we live."

"Cotton," Paul said gently. "Your uncle hurt himself pretty badly and had to go to the emergency room."

My heart sunk to my knees.

He continued, "The doctor ordered an evaluation. Your uncle can't live by himself."

Tears streamed down my cheeks. "I want to see him."

"Sure you do," he nodded. "That's fine. I'll arrange for someone to take you over tomorrow."

I was too stunned to move. I just stood there.

"It's okay," he said, wheeling his chair over to lay a hand on my shoulder. "My shift doesn't end for another half hour. I'll call the group home right now and make arrangements."

I nodded silently, then turned and walked back upstairs.

*How could they just make us go somewhere else?*

I walked upstairs to my bed and sat down. My feet hurt. My shoes were too small, and I had to curl my toes under to make them fit. I looked down at the worn leather, creased and scuffed at the toes. They had been brown once and matched my brown and orange checked bell-bottoms and poncho. Now, they just looked old. It was the way I felt. I was afraid to take those shoes off. Dave had bought me those shoes. I untied the laces and pulled them off. My toes cramped and throbbed as I tried to stretch them out. I glanced around the room. I was all alone. Everyone must be downstairs watching a movie. All of the twin beds in the room were neatly made. Each bed had a small table or nightstand next to it. Two framed prints of purple flowers hung on the wall. The flowers were irises. I knew that because Iris and Lily of the Valley were my mother's favorite flowers. Underneath the prints a copy of the house rules was taped to the wall.

*Rule Number One—Smoking, drugs and alcohol are strictly prohibited on these premises. Anyone caught with these substances will immediately be reported to the Authorities.*

My mother wouldn't have lasted five minutes.

*Rule Number Two—Food and food items are allowed only in designated areas.*

I massaged my feet, wondering if Stan's new home had rules taped to the wall. Stan hated rules.

I pulled my legs up and slipped under the blankets. My mind was filled with questions. Who locked our house up? There must be some way for me and Stan to be able to go home and live. Maybe if we didn't turn the lights on at night no one would notice that we moved back in. We could keep the blinds closed. My eyelids felt heavy. We could make it work. Maybe we could live in the garage until the whole thing blew over. Tomorrow I was going to see Stan and we'd hatch a plan.

At six AM Aliene knocked on the door. "Good morning, ladies. Time to wake up."

Aliene was nice and bright in the mornings, and I liked the sound of her voice. At that time of day people moved pretty slow. I gathered up my pile of clean clothes and went to take a shower. The Fresh Mint soap and hot water spraying down on my face was nice and invigorating. I breathed in the crispy, moist air and said aloud, "Today is the first day of the rest of my life." It felt good. I washed my face and hair and stayed in the steamy cavern until someone knocked on the door.

I dried off and pulled my pants on. The button was already loose. I kept pulling and pulling, trying to get them buttoned, but they didn't fit. Finally, I sucked my stomach in as tight as it would go and pulled. *A-ha. I did it.* I leaned over to pick up my shirt off of the chair and the button popped off. I pulled my shirt down, stretching it to cover my missing button.

The company van that drove everyone to school was idling in the driveway. Four people were on staff at all times. One of them was named John Hester. He was young and wore geeky clothes, but he was nice. He walked out the back door of the house carrying a folder, spotted me and said, "Come on, Cotton. We're going in my car."

He unlocked my door and I climbed in. Once he'd logged his mileage and backed out of the parking space we were on our way. It was nice not having to ride in the van. Sometimes when I had to ride with all of those people it reminded me that I didn't have a place to call my own anymore. My stomach growled.

Mr. Hester looked over. "Do you want to stop for breakfast?"

"No. I just kind of want to get there. Maybe later."

"Okay. We'll eat on the way back."

At every traffic light or approaching street I wondered if we were going to turn. I'd never been to that part of town before. Finally, Mr. Hester pulled his car to a stop at the curb in front of a big, brown three-story house.

"This is it," he said. "102 Oakdale."

The lights were on inside the house. I could see people walking around. My eyes searched from window to window, but I didn't see Stan. I kind of thought he'd be sitting on the front porch with his suitcase packed. "Are you sure this is the right place?"

"Absolutely," he said cheerfully, getting out of the car. "Come on."

Tentatively, I put my hands on the door handle. I was afraid to get out. What if this was a trick? But why would it be? My stomach growled again.

Mr. Hester walked around and opened my door. I noticed a smiley-face sticker on his dashboard.

He leaned his head into the car. "Hey. What is it?"

I swallowed. "I don't know."

"Come on. I bet your uncle is waiting on you."

He obviously didn't know Stan. I bet Stan was upstairs coming up with a plan to bust out of the joint.

A woman in a plain white uniform answered the door. "Yes?"

Mr. Hester motioned toward me. "We're here to visit her uncle."

The woman's eyes stared at me. "Yes," she said. "He's outside."

We followed her through a large room with a television against the wall. Two men paced back and forth on a threadbare carpet, talking to themselves. Apparently, the Voices were pretty popular there. The three of us walked through a hall, a kitchen, a laundry room, and out a back door to a covered patio. Stan was sitting with his back to us, listening to a portable radio pressed to his ear.

My toes cramped.

"Mr. Alexander?" The woman said. A second later, when he didn't look up, she repeated, "Mr. Alexander. Your niece has come to see you."

I'd never heard anyone call Stan "Mr. Alexander" in my life.

I stepped forward. "Hey."

Now, he turned to look at us. "Hey." His fingers fumbled with the switch to turn his radio off.

Mr. Hester laid his hand on my shoulder. "I'll wait for you out front."

"Okay," I said, walking toward Stan's table.

The woman regarded Stan carefully. "I'll hold your radio if you like."

He clutched it to his chest. She looked like she wasn't in the mood to argue and left.

We were alone.

Inside the house someone let out a long, anguished wail. I was beginning to think Stan wasn't the only one Jeever bothered. I pulled an empty chair out and sat down quickly. We had a lot of work to do if we were going to come up with a plan.

"So, what happened after I left?"

Stan stared off across the backyard. It was pretty bare. "Well," he started, then stopped. "I was making a sandwich, and I couldn't stop crying. Then I guess I had an accident..." His words trailed off.

I noticed a bandage poking out from under his shirt sleeve.

"Jeever just kept tormenting me. He said he had Mother and if I cut my arm then he'd bring her back. I was all by myself. Nobody called to tell me where they'd taken you. I was so tired. I realized I couldn't get the bleeding to stop. Jeever was laughing at me."

"So, did you call an ambulance?"

"No. I called a taxi."

"Why did you call a taxi if you couldn't get your arm to stop bleeding?"

"I don't know," he said. "Mother always called taxis."

That didn't make a lot of sense, so I leaned forward and said, "So, let's get a plan and get outta this joint."

Stan shifted uncomfortably.

My toes ached. "So, what do you say?"

Purposely avoiding my question, he asked, "What's it like where you are? Do they treat you okay?"

I glanced around the yard, happy to be able to talk to someone I knew for a change. "It's kind of like this place, I guess. It's a house and they let us order pizza and watch movies on the VCR."

Lights of recognition flashed in his eyes. "We order pizza too. Did you like it?"

"The pizza? Yeah, it was okay. A little greasy."

"I picked all of the onions off, but I ate three pieces."

"Alright, enough about pizza. Do you think they'll let us go back and live at our house?"

Stan's eyes dropped to the table.

"Or we could get an apartment," I blabbered on. "Do you know how to rent an apartment?"

"The thing is, Cotton—"

"Or maybe we could just buy another house. Do you think someone would sell us a house?"

"Maybe, but—"

"Maybe what?" I interrupted. "You're not being very helpful."

Gray sky rumbled over the treetops. The shadowed light felt low and thick.

Stan cleared his throat and started again. "The thing is—well, I don't really want to leave here right now."

"What?'

"Maybe if I could just stay for a little while."

My mouth fell open. "Until when?"

Tears pressed against the back of my eyelids. What a crappy day. "What did I do?" I croaked.

"Oh, no. It's not you." He reached for my arm. "They gave me some pills and when I take them, I don't hear Jeever no more."

Tears trickled down my cheeks. "What kind of pills?"

He looked up into the sunless sky. "I don't reckon I know what they are. I just know what they do. The doctor made me take a lot of tests. Then I went to his office, and he talked to me and gave me some pills."

Someone inside the group home let out a terrible scream.

*I'll second that.*

Stan leaned forward. "I ain't never gone so long without Jeever tormenting me."

It was true. Stan had known Jeever his entire adult life. A cold chill seized me. Diggy had been pretty scarce lately. That worried me.

It must have been the medication because Stan was pretty chatty. "And then I can just sit and listen to my radio programs without him pestering me all day."

Two men walked out the back door. They looked like patients, but after they lit cigarettes and started making notes in a logbook, I revised my assumption. It didn't matter. They were only a distraction.

"So, what are you saying," I demanded.

"Well," he started hesitantly, "I'm not sure."

"Why can't we just leave," I pleaded in a breathy whisper.

"Because I need to stay here for a while and take this medicine and see if I can get rid of Jeever." Then he leaned forward conspiratorially and informed me, "He's not real, you know."

*Son of a gun.*

You could have knocked me over with a feather. I was too stunned to move. Lightning flashed in the sky. The two employees stubbed out their cigarettes and walked inside. Now my aching toes made my legs cramp. I didn't know what to say.

Stan took a deep breath. "Maybe they'll let you come live in my room," he offered.

"Yeah, maybe," I said, suddenly feeling exhausted and tired. My chest and face felt drawn to the table. If I could just lay my head down and take a nap, then all of this would go away.

Stan must have sensed my shift. He grabbed my hand and squeezed with convincing tightness. "I won't let anything happen to you."

I stood up to get the ache out of my legs. "I know."

He smiled anxiously. "Maybe you could go and live with Preston Brown for a little while."

A wave of dizziness passed over me. "Maybe." I backed away from the table.

"Does he still have your suitcase?"

I nodded without really even paying attention to the question.

Stan walked around the table and put his arm around me. "You'll be okay, Cotton."

"I don't believe you, and the very fact that you are standing around here blowing smoke up my butt makes me that much madder."

His entire face slackened. I pulled away and stomped off around the side of the house. A raindrop splattered against my forehead. The cold, tiny burst of water sent a shock wave through my body. That was it, I thought. The end of the line. I heard Stan running across the grass behind me.

"Cotton... wait up."

I did not stop. I stomped across the grass with my aching toes, picking up speed when I saw Mr. Hester leaning against his car, staring up into the sky.

Three more raindrops plummeted from the sky, landing on my face. I tripped and felt something on my arm. Disoriented, I turned far enough to see Stan. His eyes blurry and wet. His bottom lip trembled.

Holding onto my arm, he said, "It'll be okay, Cotton."

Tears flooded back into my eyes. "You don't know that" I screamed. "You're supposed to be my best friend."

Definitely. Not. Okay.

Suddenly I felt Mr. Hester's hand on my other shoulder, steering me toward his car. "I'm going to have to ask you to let go of her," Mr. Hester said firmly to Stan.

Big, wet drops rolled down my uncle's cheeks. I ran to the car and got in. When I turned and saw Stan running across the street after me, I locked my door. Mr. Hester jumped in on the driver's side as Stan clawed at my door handle.

"Cotton," Stan yelled through the glass.

Irritated, I rolled my window down just enough to yell back. "You're not my friend anymore." Then I rolled the window up tight.

It took Stan a second, but he burst into tears again.

Mr. Hester put the car in drive and pulled away from the curb. Stan stumbled into the street. I watched him in my side view mirror until we turned the corner at the end of the street. *Butt munch. Traitor. Defector. Turd.*

Once we'd turned onto the highway, Mr. Hester said, "That didn't go so well, did it?"

I shook my head.

"Is there anything I can do?"

It took me a minute, but finally I reached down with one hand and pulled my shoe off. "My shoes don't fit me anymore."

"Really?"

I sighed. "Yeah."

"Since when?"

"About a month ago."

"Are you serious?"

"Yeah. Maybe more."

When I looked over his brow was furrowed. Windshield wipers slapped against the rain. It was so dark outside it felt like the end of the day.

He looked at his watch and said, "We don't have to be back until lunchtime. Do you want to go shopping?"

I nodded but only because it was better than crying. Then I pried my other shoe off with my big toe. I was so afraid to throw away my shoes. What was I going to do without them?

In the parking lot to the outlet mall Mr. Hester said, "Since it's raining, I'll let you off at the front door and park."

I jumped out at the curb and ran barefooted to the big glass doors. The wet concrete was cold. Not many people were shopping so I stood outside the doors watching rain pour off the corner of the awning. Mr. Hester got out of his car with an umbrella and walked briskly across the parking lot. He reached for my hand, and we walked inside.

The mall was practically empty. Cool, dry air welcomed us. We walked to a shoe store, looked inside, and then walked to the nearest department store. Except for the salespeople there was barely anyone in the store. After I tried on seven pairs of shoes, he bought me two new pairs and twelve pairs of socks. I was grateful to walk to the register with my feet wrapped in warm, cushy socks and shoes that fit.

Before we checked out Mr. Hester asked, "Is there anything else you need?"

"Yeah. Somewhere to live."

The saleslady looked at me.

Mr. Hester laid his hand on my shoulder reassuringly. "I'll help you with that, too."

Once we were out in the middle of the mall, he asked me if I needed anything else. I remembered the button popped off my pants. A few of my shirts had holes in them where the hem had unraveled. I couldn't even find my pajamas. I'd been sleeping in a pair of sweatpants I hijacked from the lost and found.

"Did you tell anyone?"

I shook my head, sucking in a breath. "I just kept thinking I'd be able to go home and then someone would take me shopping. I just thought that someone would come get me and it wouldn't be a big deal."

Mr. Hester steered me over to a bench in the middle of the mall. He patted the seat, giving me a hand up.

After he set my bags on the floor, he knelt in front of me. "Cotton, I'm going to help you find somewhere to live. I promise. Because that's my job and because I like you. You are very likeable."

The fact that someone was being so nice to me caused tears to trickle down my cheeks. It was embarrassing. For weeks I hadn't been able to go anywhere without turning off the water works. A heavy, twisting feeling tugged at my heart. The smell of won tons and beef with broccoli wafted down from the food court. Thunder rumbled overhead.

"You promise?" I stole a glance down at my new shoes. They did feel good.

He stood up confidently, reaching for my hand. "I guarantee it."

Even in my relief I swallowed and asked, "You're not going to turn me out on the street?"

He laughed and crossed his heart with his hand. "That's not the way this works. Come on. Let's get you some clothes that fit."

As we walked through the mall I stared down at my new shoes. The idea that I was now on my own started to settle over me. At least I was marching into my new future in clean socks.

Back at the group home Mr. Hester helped me unload everything and get it up to my bed. Then he went down to finish his shift paperwork. The thing that really sucked about the group home was that no one had their own room. There was zero privacy except for the bathroom. I'd learned that if I spent too much time crying in the shower then it made my face red and puffy. When I came out everyone knew what I'd been hoarding the bathroom for. I wasn't the only one who cried in the bathroom, though. I think it must have been how all of us kept it together. We were never really given the space to fall apart. Today was a little different. The house was completely empty except for us. All of the residents and staff were on an outing. In the welcome silence I pulled all the tags off my new clothes and put them away in the drawers with my name on them.

For a few minutes I sat on my bed wondering where Diggy was. Maybe he didn't know I'd moved. Maybe he was trying to find me. How could I contact him? He didn't have a telephone or a mailing address. Normally he just showed up. Except he hadn't shown up in weeks. Tears swelled in my eyes. I wasn't sure why. I wasn't thinking about anything that would make me cry. But I did cry. I looked out the window. It was still raining outside. I liked having one moment to myself while no one was looking. My shoulders slumped forward. I felt like people had been watching me my entire life.

When my tear ducts finally dried, I gave in to the rumbling in my stomach. Downstairs Mr. Hester was standing in the doorway to the living room, drinking a cup of coffee, watching the midday news on television. A cool breeze blew through the screen door. The air swept across my face. It was good.

Mr. Hester smiled at me. "Did you get all of your stuff put away?"

I nodded. "Yeah. Thanks. I'm kind of excited about wearing my new pajamas tonight. They're really soft."

He sipped his coffee. "Good. I'm happy to have helped."

The coffee smelled good. I pointed to his cup. "Hey. Can I get a cup of that?"

"Help yourself." Then on second thought, he added, "Did you ever get anything to eat?"

I shook my head.

"That's what I thought. Listen, go sit down and I'll make us lunch."

That sounded like the best idea I'd heard in weeks. I flopped down on the sofa that was too soft in certain places, mindlessly staring at the news. A news anchor stood out in the middle of a field. Sirens blared behind her. Helicopters jostled the sky. Her hair was perfect. She clutched a microphone to her chest. Suddenly, footage of a village in Colombia filled up the screen. It looked really familiar. I grabbed the remote control and turned the volume up.

*Crash. Boom. Clank clank.* Mr. Hester dropped something in the kitchen, scaring the crap out of me. My toes curled in my new, cushy shoes.

Men in uniform filled up the television screen.

*What was going on?*

Police dogs walked behind the news anchor.

The anchor hoisted the microphone to her mouth and said, "The international community reported that authorities had been engaged in a standoff with the famous leader of the Gustavo Drug Cartel, Pablo Cruz Revilla, that has left many dead, including the leader himself. Colombian officials reported the death of Revilla from the national news source in Bogotá."

The unforgettable face of Pablo filled the screen. Then several photos flashed, one after another. In one he was smiling and wearing a bracelet. Instinctively I touched my wrist. *My bracelet.* When my fingers searched and found nothing but skin, I looked down and realized I wasn't wearing it. I heard a noise and turned around quickly. Diggy was standing in the doorway. I jumped up from the sofa, so happy to see him. As I moved closer, I saw that he was pointing to the television with tears in his eyes. I looked back at Pablo. Suddenly I realized my entire life was locked in a suitcase in someone else's closet.

Diggy stepped backwards into the hall and started to fade. I'd never seen him do that before, and my heartbeat fast. I raced after him but the grays in the room blurred together. The sound of the rain outside deepened. The face of Pablo flashed behind me, and I saw it reflected in a mirror on the wall. His face shrunk smaller and smaller until the entire room was a tiny gray dot. I felt the free-falling sensation of my body dropping to the floor. I saw the brown shag carpet about to greet my face. And then... I fainted completely.

After the day I'd had, it was a relief.

# CHAPTER THIRTY-FOUR

*Dave*

On the bathroom wall of the group home someone had taped a sign that read *In the end everything is okay. If it's not okay, then it's not the end.* I loved that sign. It was the perfect prayer to recite over and over.

After a while I fell into a rhythm at the home. I went to school, hung out in the common room reading books, went on weekend outings and talked to counselors and lawyers until I thought I'd turn blue. I had to go before a judge three times and talk a lot about what everyone referred to as my grandmother's estate. I'd always thought an estate was something rich people had. I learned that apparently my grandmother had been squirreling away money her entire life. She had a pile of it. So did Grand Daddy. From what I could tell that old fuddy-duddy saved every dime he'd made working at the post office. Rain, sleet, snow, or shine.

It went on like that for almost a year. Everyone trying to settle her estate before sending me off to live somewhere. I was very against a foster home, and so Orange Lipstick and Plump Legs arranged for me to go live in a boarding school run by nuns. A lot of kids came and went. Tape with their names written on it was pulled off and replaced on each drawer. I knew that soon I'd have a place to go, a safe place.

*If it's not okay, then it's not the end.*

Someday I'd get to pull the tape with my name on it off of the drawers.

One day, Mr. Hester turned the van into the parking lot, and I saw a sky-blue Buick Skylark parked in a space. I looked it over as I grabbed my backpack, climbing out. On closer inspection I saw it was used and closer still I saw my suitcase on the backseat. On the way up the front walk my legs slowed, eyes glued to the front window. Just inside the office stood Dave. He was talking to Paul. As the other kids barreled through the front door, Dave looked over. When he didn't see me, he glanced out the window. I couldn't get myself to move. Paul looked out at me and pointed. Then Dave walked through the front door and out onto the porch.

"Hi," I sputtered.

He smiled.

*Wow.*

A long time had passed since I'd seen that smile.

Paul stepped out behind him. "Hey, Cotton. You've got a visitor. Why don't you guys go around to the patio out back?"

"Sure," I said, trying to pull myself together.

Dave walked over, laying his hand on my shoulder. "Long time, no see."

"How did you find me?"

"Well, I went to your grandmother's house, but I guess you know that she doesn't live there anymore so I walked down to your friend's house. The little boy who prays all of the time and his mom told me."

"Yeah, I've been here almost a year."

"Really?" Dave glanced up at the house. "That's a long time."

I took a deep breath. "Yeah, it is. Come on, I'll take you around back."

The patio tables were sturdy and concrete. I sat down. Dave sat across from me.

"So how long do you have to stay here?"

"I guess until they settle my grandmother's estate. Then I go to live at the boarding school until I turn eighteen."

"What about your mother?"

I bit my lip, shifting a little. "Didn't Preston Brown tell you?"

Dave shook his head.

"She never came back for me."

He just sat there staring at me. It was so quiet I could hear him breathing. "What do you mean?"

I sighed. It had been a long time since I'd told the story. "I mean, she just took her stuff and never came home one day. Then my grandmother died, and it was terrible."

His head nodded up and down.

I shrugged. "And so DSS brought me here to get some people to help me get my life together."

Dave chewed on his thumbnail a minute, then said, "I'm sorry. I didn't know any of that."

"Yeah, it's kind of hard to know things when you don't call."

A big burst of silence hovered in between us.

Dave cleared his throat. "I'll take that."

"Didn't you get my pages?"

"Ummm, no, not exactly. I had some legal problems, and my beeper was confiscated."

"What does that mean?"

He looked away, then back, furrowing his brow. "It means I was arrested."

"Are you still arrested?"

He smiled. "No. I got out on bail and had to pay a lot of lawyers a lot of money to get me off."

"So, are you okay?"

"Sure. I've got a few things to work out but mostly I'm okay."

"They killed Pablo. I saw it on the news."

Dave sucked a sharp breath in. "Yep. They chased him down and killed him dead. Just like they said they would."

"Why?" The sound of my voice sounded so small. I glanced around the backyard. The bluest sky I'd ever seen stretched in all directions. A light breeze blew through the trees.

"Well, let's just say he had different priorities."

"Do you miss him?"

His eyes drifted up to the treetops, then he squinted into the sunlight. "Yeah. Yeah, I miss Pablo. He was the most ruthless son of a gun I've ever known."

Mr. Hester stepped out the back door. "Hey. Cotton. We're having dinner. Do you want me to bring a plate for you and your guest?"

I looked up at Dave. He nodded.

"Yes. Please."

A second later Dave reached across the table, touching my arm. "They seem nice here. How are you doing?"

"It's okay. It's quiet. There's no Thurman or Jeever. It's an okay place. When everything is settled, I'll go live with the nuns."

"Well, that sounds good." He shrugged his shoulders. "Right?"

I nodded. I'd never even met a nun before. Truthfully, they scared the bejesus out of me.

"I just came by before I moved to say goodbye."

The word *goodbye* exploded in my head like a gunshot. I swung my legs over the concrete bench, tripped on uneven ground, and walked off. "Save it," I yelled back over my shoulder.

I heard the scuffing of his shoes against the brick walk behind me. "Cotton? Wait. I didn't get to finish."

"Good." I stomped over, pointing to my suitcase in the backseat of his car. "Where did you get this?"

"Your friend told me to give it to you."

"Well, you have to take it back. I can't take it inside."

"Why not? It's your personal stuff."

"For one thing I don't have a safe place to keep it. For another, they check all bags coming in and they'll never let me have what's in that case."

Dave looked worried. "What's in there?"

I spun the numbers around until I remembered the combination. Then I popped the latch on each one. I lifted the top to reveal a window to my past. The donkey with its basket full of jade sat on top, just as I'd left it. Suddenly I was flooded with emotion. Preston Brown hadn't even opened it. He'd just kept it in the closet like he promised. The old, ugly purse was in there with money spilling out.

I looked over at Dave. "That's what's in there."

I closed it, spun the combination, and looked him in the eye. "So take it back and stop meddling in my life."

I stomped off across the parking lot, headed for the front door.

Dave ran after me, catching up. "Cotton, where did you get all of that money?"

I turned, shooting daggers from my eyes. "It's none of your business but it was all of the money in the house. Stan was afraid they'd take it from us, so I hid it."

"Who would take it?"

"The Jesus Man, Doctor Jeever, the DSS workers. Who knows? I hid it. But it's mine. So take it back and get Preston to keep it in his closet."

I pulled away from Dave, running up the front steps. "Now I know why you liked my mother," I yelled just to be mean. "You're just like her."

I slammed the door, running straight for the stairs. All of the residents were eating dinner, so no one saw me. I ran up to the room and threw myself on my bed. Man, people were so annoying. Raising up a bit I could see Dave perfectly, just standing there in the front yard staring at the house.

Moments later, Mr. Hester knocked on the door. "Cotton? Are you okay?"

I turned to face him. I was mad but I wasn't crying. "He didn't come back to get me. He just came to say goodbye." The last few words choked in my throat. I looked back out the window. Dave was walking to his car, head down.

I wanted to throw open the window and scream, "I can't stand you." But that wasn't really true. It was just the last encounter in a long line of disappointments that had left me feeling sorry for myself.

Mr. Hester interrupted my mental pity party. "I can bring your dinner up here so you can have some alone time, but you'll have to eat it in the hall."

I swallowed back my sadness, pushed myself up on my arms and said, "Okay." Tonight was spaghetti night. At least that was something to be happy about. "Can I have extra cheese?"

Mr. Hester regarded me a moment more, then said, "Absolutely."

I turned just in time to see my future drive away in a sky-blue Buick. The back taillight was busted and there was a dent in the trunk.

That night during free time I called Preston Brown.

"Did he bring my suitcase back to you?"

Preston sounded confused. "No."

*Dang it.* That low-life jailbird was going to steal my money. "Why did you give him my suitcase?"

"Because I thought he was coming to get you out of that place," Preston reasoned, his voice quivering.

"No," I heaved a big, fat sigh out of my chest. "He was just coming to say goodbye."

That night I lay in bed thinking about the Paper Dave Dolls in the shoebox underneath me. I could use them to wipe my butt. An involuntary snort cracked the silence. What a waste of time. What a *butthole.* We weren't allowed to swear in the home. It was against the rules. But I could think it. I should have just taken my suitcase and hid it down in the basement behind the cases of apple sauce no one ever ate.

For three days I called Preston Brown when I got out of school.

"I'm sorry, Cotton. He hasn't shown up."

I shook my head. "Yeah, he's not gonna, either."

"I feel so bad."

"Don't. You thought you were doing a good thing."

He was really quiet for a minute.

"Are you still there?"

"Yeah," he said. "I'm going to ask God for help."

"Sounds good to me."

On Saturday all of the residents went to the zoo. It was so weird. I tried to conjure up an image of Stan waiting in line at the concession stand, but it felt like the past was a dream. I could see him out in front of the monkey cage wearing his flannel shirt and yellow pants, but I couldn't get the feeling. I couldn't remember who I was back then.

On the ride to the group home, I made plans to walk straight upstairs and thrust my head under a pillow when I saw the sky-blue Buick parked out front. The van turned into the lot and Mr. Hester parked. Someone opened the side door, and everyone piled out. Except me. I waited and watched the Buick. After a few minutes Dave got out.

"What does he want?" I mumbled out loud, stepping down to the ground.

Dave stood on the sidewalk watching me huff over, swinging my arms to indicate that I didn't care about him or whatever he wanted to say.

"Hey," he said, shielding his eyes from the sun. "Can I talk to you?"

"You can talk about why you never took my suitcase back to Preston Brown."

Dave leaned against his car. "Yeah. I can explain that."

I put my hands on my hips, staring straight through him. "Go ahead."

He took a really deep breath. "After I left here the other day—"

"You went and spent all of my money."

"No," he shook his head. "You've got this all wrong. I went and talked to your case worker."

My muscles slackened. The frown I'd pulled so tight across my face let up a bit. "How do you know about my case worker?"

Dave pointed at the group home. "They told me. When I told them my name, they thought I was your dad."

I felt my shoulders slump forward. I needed to sit down. I walked over to the curb and plopped down. "My grandmother left a will and said I was supposed to go live with you. She wrote that you're my dad. I thought you were going to come get me. I guess I was really mad when you didn't."

Dave lowered himself to the ground next to me. "Yeah, that's what your case worker said. That kind of changes everything, doesn't it?"

I glanced over at him. The sun dropped low behind his head. "How?"

"Because if I leave you here then I'll always know I didn't do the right thing."

My nose burned as tears pushed against my eyelids.

"When I came the other day, I thought this was just a temporary thing and that someone was coming to get you. Then I talked to Judy Dennis, and she assured me that isn't the case."

I didn't know what to say. I'd spent days working myself up into a tizzy because I'd thought Dave stole my suitcase. I'd spent all of last night imagining myself ripping the heads off of my Paper Dave Dolls. Now I was so surprised I didn't know what to say.

"And so I drove back over here to find out what you want to do."

"What are my choices?"

"I guess your choices are to go with the nuns or go with me. Personally, nuns give me the creeps."

The sky opened up. Angels sang. I turned to look him in the eye. "You mean it?"

"Yeah, but Cotton, I'm not perfect. In fact, in a lot of ways I guess I've really screwed some things up. But I can't just leave you here. I mean, where do you go on holidays?"

"I stay here and eat with the staff."

"Who bought you Christmas presents?"

"Mr. Hester took me to the mall, and I bought my own Christmas presents."

Dave frowned. "See, I didn't know that."

"So, what do we have to do?"

Dave shrugged. "I guess I just need to call Ms. Dennis tomorrow and let her know."

Before I knew what I was doing I threw my arms around Dave and squeezed. I rocked and bobbed, holding on tight, thrilled to finally have something in my life to be excited about. "Yeaaaah!!" I stood up and danced a jig.

Dave laughed. "Alright," he said. "Let's do this thing."

The next day Judy Dennis faxed over a piece of paper giving me a pass to spend the weekend at Dave's apartment. I packed my bags and dragged them downstairs.

Mr. Hester was in the office filing paperwork.

"I don't think I've ever seen you so excited," he said.

"I've never had anywhere to go before."

I practically leapt into the front seat of the Buick. Dave put my bags in the trunk and then got in on the driver's side.

"Is this your car?"

"No," he said, checking the rearview mirror. "It's Tommy's. He owes me money."

Dave lived on the other side of town in an apartment complex. There was a big fountain at the entrance. I was so excited. I hadn't slept anywhere but the group home in over a year. We parked and walked down a winding concrete path. Dave unlocked the door and carried my bags inside. The apartment was bright and new. Perfect white walls and creamy beige carpet filled up the space. I walked room to room, fascinated. Except for some milk crates and lawn chairs in the living room and a mattress on the floor in the bedroom, there was no furniture.

Dave put my bags in the hall and walked into the kitchen. "Do you want something to drink?"

"Sure. What happened to your furniture?"

He peeked around the breakfast bar. "What do you mean?"

"I mean, where is it?"

"Oh, that. Yeah. This is kind of temporary until I work some things out."

"Like what?"

"Cranberry juice or instant tea?"

"Cranberry juice. Like what?"

Dave walked out of the kitchen carrying a plastic tumbler. He handed it to me.

"Come on. Let's get some Chinese food, and I'll tell you what I got going on."

The fragrance alone was divine. Moo goo gai pan. Egg rolls. Little round serving dishes with mounds of steamed rice. Beef with broccoli. Egg drop soup. The Pu Pu platter. Yummy, garlic sauce, deliciousness. I was in heaven. I snarfed down all kinds of tidbits while Dave leaned in close, whispering over his chicken skewer.

I realized he wasn't joking. "So, what are you saying?"

"Well, I'm saying that I couldn't go back when I was under surveillance. Then after I got out on bail, they tailed me everywhere. It was too risky, so I let it go. I didn't go back to the house, and I guess the landlord kept the stuff, but now someone else lives there."

"So, just wait for them to go to work."

Dave filled his cup with piping-hot jasmine tea. I held mine up for refill. He put the pot down and rolled his eyes. "I think they're retired."

"Why?"

"Because they never leave. It's a husband and wife. They putter around the yard all day, then start watching TV."

I leaned across the table. "Do you mean to tell me you left all of your money buried out behind the house?"

"Sure." He pulled a hunk of beef out of the sauce, popping it in his mouth. "What was I supposed to do with it?"

"So go out there at night."

"I tried that. The old man came out in his boxer shorts with a shot gun. I ran like hell."

"Oh." I picked at the crab puffs. Finally, I took a delicious bite of egg roll and asked, "What are you going to do?"

He shook his head. "I don't know. Every dime I have is out there."

I held a forkful of moo goo gai pan in the air, ready to devour its warm, fragrant goodness. "You need a plan."

"You're telling me." Dave raised his hand to a passing waiter and ordered a beer.

That night I slept in the bedroom on the mattress. The gentle sound of the air conditioner clicking on and off was nice. Moonlight streamed through the windows, reflecting off white walls. I had a soft, blue blanket to keep me warm. It had been a long time since I'd slept in a room by myself. In the middle of the night I woke to a noise. Disoriented, I glanced around. I heard Dave flush the toilet, then walk down the hall. When I looked over toward the empty closet, I saw Diggy.

"Hey," I whispered. "Where have you been?"

He thumped his foot, then pointed to a pile of junk mail on the floor.

I leaned over, trying to focus. I heard the lawn chair creak in the living room.

"What?"

Diggy thumped and pointed again.

"Okay. In the morning. Let's go to sleep."

Diggy curled his lips back in a big, furry grin and crawled up on the mattress next to me.

The next morning, I shuffled down the hall to find Dave sitting in a chair, feet propped on a milk crate, drinking coffee. "Hey, kiddo. How did you sleep?"

Diggy crowded around me, worrying me about the mail. "Can I go check the mail?" I asked.

"Sure. Just flip the box up that has an 11 on it."

Outside, I walked down the winding, shaded path the mailboxes at the entrance.

The keys jangled at my side. "You better have a good explanation for this."

I opened the box. Inside was a flyer that urged Dave to sign up to win a free vacation on a cruise ship. I held it up in the air. "This? You dragged me out of bed for this?"

Diggy ran over to the grass and started digging. I stared at him completely dumbfounded. After a few seconds, he smiled and pointed to the hole.

Huh?

He grabbed the flyer out of my hand and pointed to the hole.

"Oh, my gosh," I said aloud. "You're a genius." I ran all of the way back to the apartment.

Dave stared at me with big eyes as I burst through the door. "Are you okay?"

I waved the flyer in the air, wild with excitement. "You make them think they've won a cruise."

"Who?"

"The retired people in the house. Then they'll go away for a week, and you can dig up your money."

Dave didn't move and for a minute I thought he hated the plan. Then suddenly he jumped up, proclaiming, "Cotton, you're incredible. That's the best plan I've ever heard of."

We went to the stationery store. Then to buy a computer and printer. With dedicated precision we typed up a letter informing the occupants they had been selected as the Grand Prize Winner. We went to the travel agency in the mall, bought a cruise for two, inserted all of the travel info in with the letter, put it in a big envelope, crossed our fingers and mailed it.

That night we ate Chinese food leftovers Dave heated up in the only pan he owned. I told him about all the money my grandmother left.

"Where is it?"

"They say it's in a Trust. I think a Trust is just a bank account."

"Kind of. It protects your money. So, what are you going to do with it?"

"I don't know." I shrugged. "I've never even seen it."

"You wanna go into business with me?"

"Maybe."

"As soon as I get my money I'm going to get out of here and start a business. I'm gonna have a real job. Truthfully, that whole thing with Pablo scared me. I mean, they could have ambushed him that day in the woods. Something could have happened to you. They could have just gunned us all down. It's not worth it."

I chewed my piece of chicken thoughtfully. That had never occurred to me. I'd never given a single thought to the fact that all of us could have ended up like Pablo. I reached for a fortune cookie. After pulling the wrapper off, I cracked it open. Inside, the little slip of paper read *Your first choice will be the one to follow.* Stuck to the paper was a second fortune. That slip of paper read *Now is the time to try something new.*

I looked up at Dave, "What does yours say?"

He pulled his fortune cookie apart. A second later he smiled. "It says 'Commit to what you feel in your heart.'"

Then I saw it. Across the room, on the floor, behind a milk crate. I stood up and walked over. A cord wound up from the back where it was plugged into the wall. I pointed, "You have a phone."

"Yeah," he said, indifferent. "It doesn't ring though because I never give out the number."

"But you have a phone," I said, illustrating with a sweeping hand gesture.

"Yeah, well, you gotta start somewhere."

The next morning, we went to eat at a diner before Dave drove me back to the group home.

"Keep your fingers crossed," I said, getting out of the car.

He held up both hands, fingers crossed.

That night, during free time, I called Preston Brown. "Hey, did you talk to God about me?"

"Yeah. *A lot.* Why?"

"Because something happened."

"What?"

I told him everything.

"I knew it," he said loudly.

I hung up and called Dave. Four rings later he picked up. "Any word?"

"Not yet."

"Alright. See ya later, alligator."

"After a while, crocodile."

The next two days dragged on with intense anticipation. Finally, on Wednesday, Judy Dennis came to see me at school. I was called out of social studies class to talk to her in the empty science lab.

She wiggled herself onto a stool, pulling out a folder. "How are you?"

"Good."

She pulled out a stack of papers, laying her hand on top. "Cotton, I'm going to recommend that Dave Andrews be named your guardian, but I wanted to talk to you first. Okay?"

I nodded. Glass flasks and beakers sat in rows on top of the counters. My eyes followed them all of the way down to the Periodic Table.

"For starters, do you want to live with him?"

"I never wanted to not live with him, but my mom made me go with her."

Ms. Dennis made a notation on the stack of papers. "And do you consider him to be a good person?"

"Sure. Everyone likes him."

"Name one thing you like about him."

"He cares about me."

Ms. Dennis looked up from her papers with a faint smile. "That means a lot, doesn't it?"

"From where I'm sitting, yeah, it does."

She exhaled. "Well, then, that about does it. I've talked with him several times and he's filled out all of the paperwork. I'll file it."

She collected her papers and asked me to sign. Then she stuffed them back in her bag and stood up. "It's been nice working with you. I'm glad this is how it worked out. It was rough for you at first." She extended her hand to shake. I did.

She walked me back to class. I watched her walk all of the way down the hall to the big double doors at the end. She was wearing a pair of navy-blue pants, and with her high heels on she didn't have plump legs at all.

The sky-blue Buick was parked in front of the group home after school. I ran over, excited. "Judy Dennis came to talk to me today. She said she's recommending you to be my guardian."

Dave nodded. "That's not why I'm here."

My face fell a little. "What does that mean?"

"I got a phone call today."

That didn't sound so good. "From who?"

Dave leaned against the trunk of his car, looking serious. "From some dude calling to collect on his free vacation."

It took me a minute to grasp what he was saying but his smile gave it away.

"Oh my gosh. He called? It worked?"

"Like a charm." He put his arm around my shoulder. "That was a brilliant idea."

Two weeks later the married couple sailed away. Dave and I drove over after midnight with a trunk full of shovels, bags, flashlights, and a metal detector. There still weren't any neighbors so Dave parked out front. I looked around remembering what it was like to live there. I remembered playing with Inca and climbing trees. I remembered reading my library books and trying on new clothes.

I looked over at Dave. "What happened to the dog?"

"He's staying with Louise. My apartment complex doesn't allow pets."

We got out of the car and walked to the trunk.

"Here, help me carry some of this stuff."

I looked over at the window that used to be my bedroom. "Okay. How many of these things do we have to dig up?"

Dave stuffed the metal detector under one arm. "Fourteen, maybe fifteen."

"*What?*"

He shrugged. "Sorry. I never liked banks."

It took six hours to find all of them and dig each one up. Dave had a pretty good marking system of burying them east of a bush but then he'd run out of bushes and just buried them everywhere. Sunrise glowed purple on the horizon. I looked around the front yard. I remembered waking up early to eat cereal and watch cartoons.

"I'm hungry." I looked around the backyard at all of the filled-in holes. Hopefully the married people would think it was groundhogs.

"Me too," he said, closing the trunk.

He put all of the metal canisters into a trash bag and took them into the apartment to count. I unwrapped my egg-and-cheese biscuit and watched. He pulled stacks of money from each one. It was fairly impressive. Fourteen containers with roughly twenty thousand dollars in each. I glanced at my suitcase in the hall closet. That's when I knew it was going to be okay. We weren't millionaires, but we had enough to get somewhere and start a business and have a home. I would be okay. *We would be okay.*

Dave looked up at me, flashing that smile. "A free vacation. Geeze. Why didn't I think of that?"

"Actually, Diggy came up with it," I said, trying to be honest.

Dave poured two tumblers of cranberry juice. "A toast to a new life," he said.

The plastic cups clacked. "I'll drink to that."

And that was that. Ten days later I was released from the group home into Dave's custody. We drove away in the sky-blue Buick with Mr. Hester standing at the curb waving. I had all of my belongings in the backseat. Dave had half of his cash stuffed into a sleeping bag crammed in the trunk. I'd talked him into getting travelers checks for the other half. It was quite a milestone. Phones and traveler's checks. Who knew what other fancy stuff lay in our future?

We drove straight for the highway.

"So, what's the plan?" I asked.

Dave winked. "Ever been to Mexico?"

"You speak the worst Spanish I've ever heard."

A huge laugh rumbled up through Dave's lungs. "That's funny. That's what Pablo used to say."

The sun was setting as we headed west. I turned around in my seat, looking back at the city fading away. After everyone had left, I'd finally gotten my turn. A blue sky dipped low into the horizon, melting into a creamy apricot sunset. I wanted to remember my grandmother forever. Staring at the colors, I conjured up an image of her standing on the front porch, looking off into the distance. In the late afternoon, as we crossed the Mississippi River, I could still hear her say, "If wishes were horses, I'd ride away."

# CHAPTER THIRTY-FIVE

*Epilogue, or as we like to say in the business, the wrap up*

Later on, people asked me what happened to the family who figured so greatly in my life. For starters, I never saw my mother again. I always thought one day she might go back to my grandmother's house looking for me. She wasn't alone in the disappearing acts category. Thurman was never seen again, either. Two years after we moved to Mexico the police showed up at Stan's group home. The Texas State Highway Patrol found Thurman's car idling on the side of a two-lane highway in west Texas. The report said the driver's door was open, the radio was playing static, and no one was to be found anywhere.

It gave me the heebees.

Stan had the staff at the group home help him put an ad in the newspaper and sell Thurman's old car. He mails me a ten-dollar bill wrapped in notebook paper every week, because I've never been able to explain to him what a Trust is.

Preston Brown did not become a minister as his parents anticipated. He said that after all the time he'd spent praying for me he finally knew God listened. And that was enough for him. He moved to New York when he turned eighteen and became the lead singer of a famous punk rock band. He's still my best friend. I have all of his albums.

Stan settled in at the group home. At first, I was really jealous and kind of mad about the fact that he wanted to live there more than with me. But eventually, knowing he was in a safe place, with a comfortable routine, filled me with a sense of relief. I didn't go see him when I left for Mexico because I was so mad. Now Dave and I go see him once a year and take him presents. He loves to show me every new thing in his room. He loves that group home so much. His favorite night is Wednesday. Karaoke night. I'll leave that to the imagination. Stan clutching a microphone to his chest singing "Love me Tender" is a sight every human being should witness at least once.

And Dave Andrews. I see his bright smiling face every day when he knocks on my door announcing breakfast. A few months after we settled in, I was enrolled in the English-speaking school. For my entrance I was asked to write an essay describing my life. I titled mine: Skinny Dipping in a Dirty Pond.

That about summed it up for me. And here you have it. That dirty pond I call a family shaped me in ways I only now understand.

For years I worried Dave incessantly to find a girlfriend, but he just smiled and said, "I'm married to my work." His work is a beautiful little restaurant we bought and renovated in the middle of the town where we live. The people love Dave and every night the tables are filled with laughing, well-fed diners. In the evenings I go and sit and drink coffee. Candles sparkle and twinkle on the crisp, white tablecloths.

Dave pulls up a chair to take a break. "How ya doing?"

"Good."

He smiles. "Penny for your thoughts."

"Oh, I was just thinking about the opera. I've been studying La Bohème. Maybe we could drive to Mexico City next month and watch it on the stage."

"Sounds like a plan."

And that is how a lot of our days went. Dave cooked and washed dishes and made flower arrangements, all the while as content as he could be. It wasn't a fairy tale.

From what I can tell owning a restaurant isn't for the lazy. Plus, I had to learn Spanish along with everything else I had to learn in life. I didn't speak the language, and I was thousands of miles away from Stan and Preston Brown, but I had a Dad. For the first time in my life, I had a real Dad who tucked me in at night and made me pancakes for breakfast and said, "Good job," to every single little thing I did right. And it was wonderful.

Dave let me name the restaurant. I named it *Maria's*. I figured if he was going to be married to something it might as well be named Maria.

Diggy loves to lay out in the garden, sunning himself in the late afternoon light. His fur glistens and his whiskers twitch when he dreams. Sometimes when I'm out there with him and it's really quiet, I can hear my grandmother calling my name. It's like she's right there.

Most importantly, Jeever was never heard from again.

# Author's Note

The original drafts of this book were written in a creative autobiography class while I was living in Asheville. It was always my intention this book be a memoir.

The manuscript stayed nonfiction until, one day, my agent at the time called me and said, "Let's change the ending."

"Why?"

"Because the existing one is so depressing."

It's humbling to have a stranger tell you that your life is depressing. Standing in the parking lot of a coffee shop, talking on the phone, I agreed to fictionalize parts of this book. Later, I just liked the way it flowed and, if I'm being honest, I liked that Larry (Dave) and I escaped together. I liked the fictional ending better and so I kept it, but I end with the truth here to balance that out. The only parts of the ending that were changed were that I was not in the house when my grandmother died, though Troy (Stan) and I did gather as much as we could before my mother had a chance to get her hands on it. Larry was never a part of my future, though we did meet up when I was an adult. I did not stay in the house with my uncle Troy alone. My mother was there. He did believe Jeever was hiding his mother. And he did go to a group home, but that was years later. He did bust out a window, but it was the neighbor's. Though I toyed with the idea of making this book completely nonfiction, I finally decided to leave it as is, even though this book is, in fact, almost all true. It has a narrative flow. Taking it apart to make it something else seemed wrong. Perhaps I will compose a narrative that is darker, and clings more heavily to the horrors of the truth. A narrative that is a memoir. A narrative that takes on the madness. For the time being, this will suffice. It was a way to tell the story without so many messy complications.

I constantly remember things I could add. Moments, lines, words, expressions. It is the nature of recollection. But I have other things I want to write about. This novel begins when I meet Larry and ends two weeks after I turn eighteen, spanning fourteen years.

I changed some names and left this as a novel, even though it's anything but. Stan is my uncle Troy, Thurman my uncle Thurman, Dave is Larry. All very real people. They are all dead now.

My grandmother took my uncle Troy (Stan) to Europe in the late '60s to prove to him that World War II was over. After he came out of the mental hospital, he believed the Nazis were in power, and the war was ongoing. He was obsessed with Tsars, and believed he'd been a Russian Tsar in a past life. He talked about it constantly. He'd walk into the kitchen out of the blue and talk about how cold the winters were in Russia, and how hard everything was. It was part of how I came to Buddhism. I originally went to a temple to understand some past life my uncle Troy believed he lived. He thought he was tormented in this life by Jeever because of all the people he'd killed in a past life and said so often. Jeever never left him alone.

He was crazy, but I loved him. The truth is, in many ways he was less crazy than the rest of the world; in other ways he was totally nuts.

Truth is often stranger than fiction.

Supposedly, Troy had been sent to apprentice with an antique dealer when he was fourteen. It was pitched to my grandparents as an opportunity for him to learn a trade. Fascinated with history, Troy agreed. My grandmother wanted the opportunity to work out. She'd always wanted a career, her own money, her own life. My grandfather did not want him to go. Troy was his first-born child and, arguably, his absolute favorite.

It was not the opportunity of a lifetime for Troy. He was sexually abused and returned sullen, filled with rage, and prone to unpredictable outbursts. Declared to suffer from whatever diagnosis at the time is now known as bi-polar, he was sent to the state mental hospital at Bolivar. I know these details are true because I saw his paperwork from the hospital. I found it after my grandmother died. I know the story of the antique dealer is true because I heard variations of it from my uncle and my mother after Troy died. There was no way to verify it, but given the timeline and what happened, it makes sense. It's important to note that this novel was finished before I found that out. So, my childlike love for my uncle shines, and I do not have answers for why he is the way he is in this narrative.

What got left out is staggering. Mexico is reduced to a chapter. South America, though we were there for three months, is reduced to a few chapters. I wanted to tell this narrative from my perspective, beginning around age four. I have very detailed memories from that time, and to this day I remember how the streetlight slanted across the gravel drive the night I met Larry for the first time. Larry left when I was nine, and this narrative jumps forward at the end to when I ran away from home and was put in a group home, and then a rehab facility, because my mother told them I was a drug addict. After endless tests, they realized she lied. From there, they helped me get a plan to get away without going into foster care. I had a year and a half before I turned eighteen. Once I was eighteen, I could move in with my grandmother and take care of her. She died almost exactly a year before I turned eighteen. Everything in-between is left out, because honestly, it is a whole other book.

What also gets left out is the absolute madness, the madness that descends so far down, it is incomprehensible to most people. A lot of the happiness is left out as well. I saw and did some really cool things and had a lot of fun. It wasn't all bad with everyone, just my mother.

At eleven, I entered a Creative and Performing Arts school. My teachers pushed me to excel, encouraged me to apply myself and do my best. School saved me. It was my safe haven from my mother. I auditioned for the CAPA school when I was eleven. I still know my childhood friends. Once I was out of elementary school and in the CAPA school, a whole world opened up for me. A world that had nothing to do with my mother. School was perfect. I stayed in the Dramatic Arts program for six years and graduated. I was vice president of my sophomore class, an active member of the French Club, involved in all theatrical productions, an all-purpose geek girl, and very happy.

My uncle Thurman did, in fact, walk out of the house one day and never return. His truck was found idling on a remote Texas road, with the doors open and the headlights on, exactly as I described. His story is a lot more ominous than I detail here. Women's and children's clothing were found in the truck, but no evidence he'd been traveling with anyone, which made us pray those weren't the clothes of victims.

I strongly believe he buried a few people in the back yard. My mother found human bones out there. At a certain point, my grandmother stopped letting me play back by the garage. I'd watch my uncle from the upstairs bathroom window. He was out there night after night, burning something in an old grill. After my grandmother died, the body parts were found, and my mother refused to call the police. Instead, she called a friend who was a paleontologist. He confirmed the bones were human. The adults made themselves feel better by rationalizing. The house was built at the turn of the twentieth century. It could have been a burial from long ago, that was shallow due to topsoil erosion. It could have been a lot of things.

My mother threatened to lock me up in juvenile detention if I called the police. In fact, she threatened to lock me up any time I went against her, which was often.

My uncle Troy was forced to live with my mother, because she wanted his government checks for disability, as well as my grandmother's pension check. She obtained power of attorney over him when I was seventeen, and not yet legally old enough to take responsibility for him. He supposedly choked on a piece of broccoli that put him in a coma for nine days. Then, she turned off the life support. I never believed that story. She hid his death for three years, and when people came to the house, she said he was sleeping, or out on a walk. I will never believe he died of natural causes. He was alone with her in that house, and that was a dangerous place to be. He was her meal ticket and, though she hated all of us, she wasn't giving Troy up.

My mother was a classic, textbook psychotic, with a long history of drug abuse, child abuse, sexual abuse, and personal abuse. She was sexually molested in her teens and was just about the most broken person I'd ever seen. She, too, was toned down because her violence and anger, though prevalent and staggering in real life, became confusing in the narrative. She constantly screamed and raged and would hit me for something I said, or didn't say, did, or didn't do. None of it made sense. People questioned why a person would do such things. We all questioned why she did such things. I don't know that there will ever be any real answers though, so, in this narrative, she is greatly minimized.

It wasn't until years later, sitting in a forensic psychology class at Writers Police Academy, that a complete stranger made sense of my mother. Sitting in class that day, I was shocked to hear him describing my mother perfectly. All the violent, calculated, hysterical, manipulative behaviors that had always seemed so random actually fit a model. A model on a screen in front of me. The instructor at the front of the classroom was detailing the stages of psychosis. He had no idea he was describing my entire childhood. It was humbling. It was the first time in my life that I realized I was lucky to survive.

My mother hid within a system that justified drug use and propped up immoral behavior, and she thought she was cool. She hid well. I suspect she's not the only one.

I have another uncle who made it into the original drafts of this memoir, but he was removed. Donnie spent a lot of his adult life in California, and though my mother had contact with him, after he left, I only saw him two more times. Once, when he came to visit, and once when my grandmother died. Because he was so far away, it was hard to weave him into the overall narrative, though he did figure into events. I became closer to him when I found out my mother had been hiding Troy's death for three years. I was, in fact, the one who called him and told him Troy was dead.

The last years of his life I talked to him a lot, sometimes every day. I learned more about him, and other family members, in those years than I'd ever known. When he stopped returning my emails, I worried, and did an internet search. News stories abounded and, to my absolute horror, I discovered he'd been gunned down by police. There's a 911 call of him pleading desperately before he is shot. It's all online.

My grandmother was the most beloved person in my life. She died alone in the house with Troy, and he went to tell the neighbors. This is where this book diverged from truth. I was not in the house when she died, but immediately after. I spent a year living with Troy and my mother in my grandmother's house before leaving for college.

I never went back.

As I began to form this book, I realized that some timelines diverged and then intersected later. I realized I lived separate lives that never connected. The story of my life at school and with my friends is a completely separate story.

Larry, Troy, and my grandmother are the most complete. As I put this all together, I realized, in many ways, this is the story of my relationship with Troy, who I loved immensely. He was the one thread there when I was born, and there when I turned eighteen and left. Larry is a fully realized story within the larger story. My mother broke up with him before he sold a moving truck full of dope to an undercover officer in Florida. Because of the time period, and because the drug laws hadn't changed yet, his lawyer got him eighteen months up at the big house. It was a long eighteen months. Larry wasn't a career criminal. He was a shameless opportunist who had a high tolerance for risk. It's an important distinction to make.

His best friend and business partner, who figured a lot more into my life than he did these pages, got busted a few years later. By then, the laws had changed. He got twenty-five years.

I know all this because I looked Larry up as an adult. In a seedy little bar in Midtown, he bought me a beer, and told me the truth. He told me how my mother let my pony, Poncho Villa, and her horse Red, starve to death to get back at him for leaving. When I told him she said they were struck by lightning, his face darkened. "Both horses? Struck by lightning at the same time? That's funny. Seriously, I signed for the stables. I was the one who had to go pick up the bodies. It's the most gruesome thing I've ever had to do."

Larry knew the guy who owned my favorite restaurant, and we ate lunch there a lot. People filed past our table, high-fiving and saying hello. He had a way with people unlike anything I'd ever seen. A Zen-like ease. An ability to maneuver across a terrain of incredible risks. A guy who'd slide his arm over your shoulder, buy you a beer, and talk you down off the ledge.

People absolutely loved him.

Me, included.

That is not to say that, in this narrative, you should think I condone his choices. I do not. Those choices must have been hard to make, but they were his own. For all his faults, he was true to himself. That matters. It doesn't justify anything, but it matters.

For a long time, cocaine shipments arrived at our house in huge gift baskets and crates. Summer sausage and aged cheddar always conjure up images for me of half kilos of cocaine lining the inside of boxes. I especially liked the sweet and spicy mustard.

I saw and did some pretty amazing things as a kid. Taking a chartered plane across South America was awesome, but by middle school, I was already planning my own life. My #squadgoals did not include dope and insanity.

I had an imaginary friend for most of my childhood, named Diggy. He was part man, part dog. He knew things I could not possibly have known on my own and would alert me to danger. My mother despised him, and I'm pretty sure the feeling was mutual because, of all the people he told secrets about, she featured most prominently.

Later, my mother went to a psychic because she thought I was nuts. She asked the psychic if Diggy was me being crazy. The psychic told my mother Diggy was a Cherokee Indian spirit who guided and protected me. I found it written in a notebook in my teens.

There is a much larger story that doesn't fit in this narrative. Namely, my own. Which sounds odd, given that this story is about me, written by me. This is a telling of my family, and there are many branches that just simply didn't fit. They look like digressions on the page. My uncles were tormented their whole lives by things I can't even define. To call it mental health simply doesn't encapsulate the day-to-day horrors. It swallowed their lives. My story was a little different.

Once we moved to Mississippi when I was nine, I started carving a life for myself. Being able to go to the pool next door, or the lake, or the neighbor's house made a huge difference. I took advantage of that, and I took advantage of school. We abruptly left Mississippi because a guy named Ziggy, running with a bunch of bikers, turned out to be an undercover narc for the DEA. My mother found out because we were close to his girlfriend. She was a redhead like me, and I loved her. Sassy and smart, she figured out who he was and she told everyone. We moved almost instantly back to Tennessee. There, I went to a school nearby, with teachers who helped me excel, and from there I auditioned for the Creative and Performing Arts school. School was everything to me, and I had some truly awesome teachers. My drama teacher for three years in a row changed my life. She was hard on me and made me reach in the best possible ways. My high school English teacher, Ms. Tyler, was a blessing. My Etymology/Mythology teacher, Mr. Cox, was an incredible teacher who fostered my love for words and myth in ways that define me today. My high school years are a separate book altogether, and that became obvious as I put this together. With age came freedom, and with freedom came the ability to avoid my mother completely.

In 2009, I contacted my mother because I wanted Troy to come live with me. It was then I found out he'd been dead for more than three years, and she hadn't told anyone in an effort to continue living in the house. In a desperate attempt to justify what she'd done, she blurted out that my Uncle Donnie sexually abused her, and that Thurman had raped my grandmother, and that was the real reason he ran. By then, she'd lied to doctors, and on her paperwork, and to the hospital admin that she wasn't a drug user, in an effort to get a new liver. She knew she was lying. While awaiting her new organ, she blurted out a lot of things. By that time, Thurman had been missing for a quarter of a century, my grandmother dead for decades. I had no way to prove or disprove those statements. In her defense, they could have been true. On the other hand, she was knee deep in a pile of lies, and blaming her life falling apart on my uncles didn't carry the weight it would have if she'd been upfront about the rest of her life.

People always want to know what happened to my mother. I found out she'd forged my name on insurance policies to cash them in, hid my uncles death from everyone for three years, constantly threatened and harassed me whenever she managed to find out where I lived, took out a restraining order on my uncle so he couldn't take the house from her even though he was listed on the deed, absolutely destroyed the house my grandmother left to all of us in the will, and conned a hospital out of a new liver because she got hepatitis from a dirty needle. *Her words, not mine.* She constantly harassed and threatened to kill my uncle Donnie until he was, in fact, gunned down by police in 2013.

My mother died in a rented room. I hadn't seen her face to face in more than nineteen years. She died telling everyone my last name was Livingston. I learned this from her cousin. That tells you everything about my mother. She died not even knowing my name.

# About the Author

If you loved this novel follow

Lis Anna-Langston

on GOODREADS & AMAZON

for new releases, updates, and giveaways or subscribe at:

www.lisannalangston.com

LIS ANNA-LANGSTON was raised along the winding current of the Mississippi River on a steady diet of dog-eared books. She attended a Creative and Performing Arts School from middle school until graduation and went on to study Literature at Webster University. Her two novels, Gobbledy and Tupelo Honey have won the Parents' Choice Gold, Moonbeam Book Award, Independent Press Award and NYC Big Book Awards. Twice nominated for the Pushcart award, a Finalist in the Brighthorse Book Prize, William Faulkner Fiction Award & Thomas Wolfe Fiction Award, her work has been published in The Literary Review, The Merrimack Review, Emrys Journal, The MacGuffin, Sand Hill Review and dozens of other literary journals.

**You can find her in the wilds of South Carolina plucking stories out of thin air.**